I0594065

LOVERS OWN THE SILENCE

A NOVEL

MICHAEL WATT

Red Penguin BOOKS

Copyright © 2025 by Michael Watt

All rights reserved.

Library of Congress Control Number: 2025913641

ISBN

Digital 978-1-63777-743-5

Softcover 978-1-63777-744-2

Cover photo and book design, Renée Alborelli

No part of this book may be reproduced in any form or by any electronic or mechanical means, including information storage and retrieval systems, without written permission from the author, except for the use of brief quotations in a book review.

"Lovers Own The Silence" is a work of fiction. Names, characters, businesses, events, and incidents are the products of the author's imagination. Any resemblance to actual persons, living or dead, or actual events is purely coincidental.

The songs attributed to the fictional musical in "Lovers Own The Silence," "Black Maria," are real and were written by Todd Rundgren. They are "Izzat Love," "Love Is The Answer," "The Night the Carousel Burned Down," "Sweet," and "Shine." "Black Maria" is also the title of a Todd Rundgren song that originally appeared on his "Something/Anything?" album.

To my loving and ever-so-patient wife, Sharon Greaney, who deserved better from me, and sooner.

Contents

Part I

You'll have to ask Kamoosi

Chapter 1

Thank You, Baby Jesus

"Thank you, Baby Jesus, that's just what I'm looking for!"

The intruder, sporting black sneakers, pants, a long-sleeved T-shirt, and a woolen cap, tucked his flashlight under his chin, took the manila folder from the file cabinet drawer, and checked to make sure its contents matched the label. He closed the manila folder, slid it into the small of his back while keeping the lit flashlight tucked under his chin, and closed the file cabinet drawer. He turned slowly to his right, hoping to retrace his steps so he could exit the dark office as stealthily as he entered it, leaving no trace that he had been there so late at night. He had been in this office dozens–if not hundreds–of times prior to this, but always during the workday and never without permission. He took the flashlight from under his chin with his right hand and scanned the flashlight's beam against the wall to refresh his memory regarding the whereabouts of the door. As he stepped in that direction, however, he tripped over something on the floor, landing face-first on the carpet with a muffled thud.

"What the hell was that?" he whispered, still holding the

flashlight in his right hand. He took a mental inventory of his body to see if he'd suffered any damage and, realizing he was okay, turned so he could direct the flashlight to see what he tripped over. "I hope to God I didn't mess up any files," he thought out loud, realizing that if he had tripped over a stack of folders, he could never reassemble them exactly as they were.

The intruder's fears were unfounded as his concern quickly turned to disbelief. There, scattered about the office floor, were a dozen or so pornographic magazines.

Who the hell keeps dirty magazines in the office? the intruder thought. Then he remembered whose office it was and thought, *A better question is, why didn't I realize he'd keep a stack of smut on the floor?*

The intruder shined the flashlight along the floor and then gathered the magazines back into a stack. There were no other messed-up piles to reconstruct, so the intruder checked to make sure the manila folder he had come for was still tucked into his belt and quickly crawled along the carpet toward the door. Once he made his way out the door and into the hallway, he again stayed low to the ground while scurrying to leave the building through the warehouse. Once he made it outside, he stopped to collect his thoughts and do a mental scan to make sure he didn't hurt himself by stumbling over the magazines. His ribs hurt, but that was the extent of the damage.

The next stop was home. If the contents of the file folder were what he hoped they were, then he had a lot of planning to do. Every step along the way in his next course of action had to be conceived and executed perfectly because when you take a swing at the champ, you sure as hell better knock him out.

Chapter 2

Thank God He's Gay

Catherine Tebow twitched nervously in her chair across from Professor Zahler's desk in his cramped college campus office. She wore jeans and a white, long-sleeved T-shirt. She ran a brush through her hair before leaving her off-campus apartment but didn't bother with makeup or lipstick. She rarely did, partly out of a lack of interest but mostly because she didn't need it. Her green eyes made you want to wish every day was St. Patrick's Day, and her auburn hair was full and luscious, like a dish of Tiramisu in a steakhouse restaurant. Despite being five-eight, she did what she could to not stand out, perhaps because she reached that height in eighth grade, a time when being taller than the boys did not serve her well. Although she had what Polite Society would refer to as a "nice figure," she preferred not to draw attention to that, either. She wanted people to accept her for what was between her ears, not under her sweater. Besides, even if she had voluptuous breasts, they wouldn't help her here.

Professor Zahler sat at his desk and stared forlornly at his laptop screen. He pursed his lips and, out of habit, went to run his fingers through his hair but remembered that ship had sailed some time ago. He opted instead to rub the three days of mostly gray stubble on his chin. Catherine wasn't a fan of the unshaven look. She understood Professor Zahler was just trying to look somewhat grizzled so he could stay current with the fashion trends of the modern-day college campus, even though a rough day for him was getting a paper cut reading Saul Alinsky's *Rules for Radicals*.

Based on the body odor wafting in her direction and loitering overhead, locked in place by the four cinder block walls that constituted his office, he hadn't showered since she sat in his classroom two days ago. She had no intention of bringing this to his attention, however, as she was there to salvage her college career.

Thank God he's gay, she mused. *There's no point in even entertaining the thought of sucking his dick to get what I want. Not that I would, even if he were good-looking. At least I don't think I would. I'd like to think I wouldn't. I mean, standards and morals, right?*

Catherine had heard enough stories to know that carnal fraternizing among professor and pupil still existed, despite the current political climate and the aftereffects of the #MeToo movement. She knew, and knew of, fellow students who took the occasional classroom fantasy to the next level, or even willingly "did what they had to do" to "get what they needed." This shocked her, albeit mildly, because tenured professors today have so much more to lose should the dalliances become public. What saddened her, though, was realizing that many of her collegiate predecessors had been forced into similar-but-unwelcome situations and "did what they had to do," but not so willingly. *Those exploitative pricks should rot in hell,* Catherine thought, feeling her skin flush in anger.

Professor Zahler looked up from his laptop and at Catherine, making her involuntarily cringe that she even entertained such ideas.

"Tell me again why you're going to be late with your senior thesis?" he growled. "I seem to remember being quite explicit at the start of the semester that nobody–not even the editor of the school newspaper–would be allowed to submit his or her project after the deadline."

"Yes, sir. You made it quite clear," Catherine said, "and I had every intention of honoring that deadline. I just hit roadblock after roadblock with my original topic and eventually realized I was rowing against the tide, getting nowhere."

The truth was she was going to be late with her thesis because Catherine had gotten a late start. Like most journalists, she needed a looming deadline to be inspired and, like most writers, she embodied the famous quote, "I hate writing, but I love having written." But there was a modicum of truth in her statement–the part about hitting a roadblock.

"What was your original topic?" Professor Zahler asked.

"'Does the media exert undue influence in national elections?'" she replied.

"Do the media..." Professor Zahler responded.

"What?" Catherine asked, thrown off guard.

"Do the media. Not does the media. Media is a plural noun, requiring a plural form of the verb."

Oh crap, thought Catherine, *I've blown it all on a subject-verb agreement.*

"Well, regardless, the topic wasn't working," Catherine said.

"It seems like a meaty subject," he said. "What kind of roadblocks did you hit?"

Once again, Catherine found herself tiptoeing around the truth.

"Honestly, Professor Zahler, there's such a dichotomy in the coverage that it's impossible to determine where the truth lies. I'm sure it's somewhere in the middle, but my concern is my political prejudices will influence my research regarding who's exerting undue influence and who's calling balls and strikes."

Again, partly true. Catherine leaned to the right politically, making her something of a pariah on her college campus. She gave up arguing with Professor Zahler–a noted leftist–in class because it got her nowhere with him and alienated her left-leaning classmates. Her concern was if her research proved what she thought it would–and should–Professor Zahler would give her a poor grade, regardless of the quality of her research.

"So what do you suggest as a new topic?" Professor Zahler asked.

"The role ego plays in running a successful business operation, being a successful leader," Catherine replied, holding her breath in anticipation of his reaction.

"The ego?" Professor Zahler asked.

"The ego," Catherine replied. "Think about it. Business, media, politics, organized religion, and even academia have one thing in common–egotistical leaders. Christ, the whole public relations industry is predicated on egos. What was it you used to say in class, 'Nobody ever went broke appealing to a man's ego.' They're all driven by their egos–men and women. Some go too far or do terrible things or things they regret just to appease their egos. Others make it work for them. I'd like to explore the various facets of the ego's role in making or breaking people. High-profile people."

Professor Zahler sat back in his chair, pondered the matter for a few moments, and then pushed away from his desk.

Oh, good Lord, don't tell me he wants... Catherine thought for a split second. But then Professor Zahler stood up to stretch.

"I have to admit I'm intrigued," he said. "But I'm still pissed you're going to be late with this."

"I know and I'm sorry, Professor," Catherine lied.

He picked up his cell phone and started flipping through his contacts. "I'll tell you what. You know Professor Kamoosi, right?" Professor Zahler asked.

Catherine flinched. She never had him as a teacher, but his reputation preceded him. She had heard he could be tough on his students. Plus, he wasn't an academic like Professor Zahler. He had decades of experience working on a daily newspaper and often reminded his students that the errors his professorial colleagues tended to overlook in class could "prove fatal" in "the real world."

"I know of him, but I never took one of his classes," Catherine said.

"You should have, Catherine. His courses are more challenging than most, but you always struck me as someone who welcomed a good challenge. You certainly took on the school administration enough times with your editorials."

Catherine relaxed for the first time. It looked as if Professor Zahler was going to go along with her request and not flunk her for being late.

"Thank you, Professor. Don't forget you're the one who reminded us of that George Orwell quote. 'Journalism is printing what someone else does not want printed; everything else is public relations.'"

Professor Zahler smiled.

"So why did you ask if I know Kamoosi?" Catherine asked.

"Oh, yeah. Kamoosi," Professor Zahler replied. "Years ago, there was a guy on Long Island. A real colorful character with a HUGE ego in a region known more for its vanilla and not so much for its Tutti Frutti. I forget his name, but I do remember that something about it was goofy. Anyway, he created and ran a niche business that made millions. Donated to dozens of charities and had his name on buildings all over Long Island. Drop-dead gorgeous wife. Seemed like he was in the news every day for one philanthropic thing or another. Kamoosi wanted to do a deep-dive piece on the guy, but as much as the guy loved publicity, he wasn't too keen on any one person knowing too much about his business or personal life. Finally, Kamoosi got him to agree to sit down for a long interview, and guess what happened? The guy drops dead. Dead! Forty-nine years old. I know that sounds old to you, Catherine, but 49-year-old men are not supposed to drop dead. So Kamoosi did some digging around and discovered all kinds of financial and sexual shenanigans going on behind the scenes, but nothing he could put to print. He even considered writing a novel about the guy...geez, what the hell was his name...but after investing dozens of hours interviewing the people involved, he decided not to."

"So what happened?" Catherine asked, sitting up in her chair. "Why didn't he write the book? Did the story go public?"

"No. I don't remember exactly why. You'll have to ask Kamoosi," Professor Zahler said. "I'll text you his contact information. If you can get him to share what he learned about this man, you'll be handing in a hell of a thesis."

"Thank you, Professor. I really appreciate this," Catherine said, getting up to leave. "I don't know how to thank you."

"Well, I can think of one...nah. You're not my type," Zahler said, with a chuckle. "Just turn in an outstanding thesis. Good luck with Kamoosi. Keep me apprised."

Catherine was so relieved to have achieved her goal from the meeting that she ignored the inappropriate comment. Her phone buzzed as she walked down the hallway of the school building. As promised, Zahler sent Kamoosi's contact info. She figured she would wait until she got back to her apartment before she reached out to him. She wanted to word the request carefully to ensure he'd want to work with her.

It was the kind of October afternoon that made all the challenges of living on Long Island worth overcoming. The leaves were just starting to change colors, and the crisp air made walking a joy. As she turned the corner to head down the block where she shared a house with several classmates, she tried to anticipate what it would be like to work with Kamoosi on this project, assuming he went along with her request.

Catherine was in the fall semester of her senior year, her third semester as the editor of Mitchel College's weekly student newspaper. She fancied herself a Big Shot on campus, albeit a small campus in a liberal arts college. She had met Kamoosi briefly about a year ago at a student-faculty social event hosted by Mitchel College's communications department. When they were introduced to each other, Kamoosi said, "It must be quite a challenge to crank out a weekly newspaper with an all-volunteer staff and limited resources."

Catherine tried to decipher on the fly whether he meant that as a compliment or a sign he did not think highly of the newspaper's quality.

"We do what we can with what we have," she said, waiting to see his reaction.

"H'mmph," Professor Kamoosi grunted, and then turned to walk away.

Screw you, Catherine remembered thinking to herself at the time, making a mental note to stay out of his classroom.

As she put her key in the back door of her residence, she found herself regretting that course of action and wondering if perhaps her ego played a role in it.

Did I not take his class because of what he said, or because I was afraid I wouldn't ace his course? Catherine wondered. *The other professors in the communications department seemed impressed with me and the newspaper. Not Kamoosi, though. H'mmm. Maybe I should wear that V-neck sweater when I go see him,* she thought, and then laughed. *You're such a phony, Catherine.*

Chapter 3

Never Assume

His real name was Vasilios Evangelos Kamoosi, but everyone knew him as "Angelo." He might have had the nickname "Moose" if he were a Frat Boy or perhaps over six feet tall, but Angelo was five-nine in his stocking feet and never saw the attraction of joining a fraternity. "I don't need a bunch of friends to make me feel like a man," he once explained to a colleague when asked if he belonged to a particular fraternity as a college student.

Angelo looked down at his watch and frowned as Catherine opened the gate in the wooden fence and closed it behind her.

"You're late," he said as she navigated the narrow, weather-beaten wooden walkway leading up to the deck where he was sitting, sidestepping a puddle of rainwater left over from the night before. He stood up to shake her hand and gestured for her to sit in the chair not too far from him, next to the all-white plastic resin table. It was after Labor Day, so the beach umbrella, usually in the middle of the table, had been put away for the season.

"I know and I'm sorry, Dr. Kamoosi," Catherine said, taking her seat and adjusting her chair so she was directly facing him with the sun over her left shoulder. "The GPS had me driving in circles, and then I wasn't sure if this was the right place. I was looking for a driveway, and that looks more like a parking lot," she said, gesturing in the direction of the parking area on the other side of the wooden fence.

"Living next to the community center has its advantages," Angelo said. "I get to pretend their parking lot is my driveway and, well, I'm not sure how they benefit."

Catherine was also late because she couldn't decide how to dress for this interview. Although she never had Angelo as a professor, she was aware of his reputation as a curmudgeon and his Old School tendencies. She also knew it would take place at a beach house close to the water in October, so she had to find that happy medium between dressing respectfully, beach casual, and being warm enough. She cursed her lack of fashion sense, which she attributed to having only worn the uniforms that came with attending Catholic schools through high school and to the fact that she rarely, if ever, truly cared about her appearance.

"If I had a penis, I'd simply toss on a pair of khakis and a blue, button-down shirt," she muttered to herself as she rustled through what passed for a wardrobe, knowing the clock was ticking. "But no. I have to find just the right outfit, one that says 'take me seriously' while at the same time doesn't make me look like a candidate for a nunnery."

Catherine finally decided on a blue polo shirt, capris, and loafers with no socks. Angelo was sitting on the wooden deck in Oak Beach, overlooking the Great South Bay on the south shore of Long Island. One could see the westernmost point of Fire Island about a mile or two south, but he rarely, if ever, spent time there. He had quasi-retired from a long career as a reporter covering Long Island's business community for *Newsday*, the region's daily newspaper. Like most other print-based publications, *Newsday* was feeling the squeeze caused by the changing news consumption habits of the community it covered, but in its heyday, the paper's brain trust exercised tremendous influence in the region's collective decision-making processes.

Angelo's knowledge of the business community, its issues, and what drove Long Island's captains of industry made him a reluctant, bordering-on-unwilling Power Broker. A favorable story or profile by Angelo in the newspaper's business section could make or break a career, but Angelo rebuffed all efforts from parties outside *Newsday* to engage his services or insights. Recently, however, when he saw *Newsday* encouraging retirements and not replacing those who left, he secured a gig teaching journalism at Mitchel College on Long Island.

His classes were notoriously challenging. Angelo believed students should earn their high grades by doing more than showing up and receiving extra credit for being sober. He was leery of becoming the Crabby Old Man on Campus, though, so he embraced modern technology to ensure he could relate to the 21st Century college student, even though modern technology when Angelo was a college graduate with a communications degree in the late 1970s meant toiling on an electric typewriter.

Rather than jump right into the Fourth Estate as a reporter, however, Angelo thought it would be fun to own and operate a bar with a friend from the college he attended, not far from where he grew up in northeast Pennsylvania, in a town called Newfoundland, which is on the outskirts of the Poconos. Not just any bar, mind you. In this case, it was the bar that he and his buddies basically lived in during their junior and senior years when they weren't publishing the school's student newspaper.

The previous owner had had enough of the hassles that come with running a business predicated on breaking the law by catering to underage drinkers living nearby on a college campus. Angelo worked all sorts of hospitality-related jobs through high school and college and figured running a bar was simply the next natural step, especially since his friend-slash-partner was providing the financing, courtesy of his parents' largesse. It wasn't. The transition from bar customer to bar owner is like going from being an uncle to being a father. It's all fun and games when the newborn arrives, but sooner or later, it's time to change the diaper or rock the baby back to sleep at three in the morning.

That's how he learned that taking risks is just that—risky—and the entrepreneurs who take risks and succeed deserve to enjoy every piece of fruit they harvest. He also learned, quickly and painfully, how fickle young people can be. Most of the bar's regulars—his buddies—had graduated and moved on. The underclassmen behind them were not as interested in Angelo's establishment as a social outlet, opting instead for a newer, trendier place down the street, just as willing to overlook that "age" thing.

He also learned firsthand the pain caused when the entrepreneur fails to cover payroll. After about a year, Angelo ran out of excuses as to why he couldn't pay his bills, his buddy's parents said, *"no mas,"* and the bar closed. Shortly after that, Angelo got wind of a journalism opportunity at *Newsday*, on Long Island, just outside of New York City. He journeyed over the bridges, did some exploring when he wasn't sitting in traffic, and was pleasantly surprised by what he discovered. He was even more surprised when *Newsday* offered him a position in the newly created business section.

He had no way of knowing he was getting in at just the right time.

Long Island's like no other part of the country, especially when you consider it technically doesn't exist. It's an island, all right, although in 1985 the United States Supreme Court declared Long Island part of the mainland of New York and therefore a peninsula. Go figure. Perhaps that's why it suffers from an identity crisis bordering on an inferiority complex. It doesn't help that two of New York City's five boroughs–Brooklyn and Queens–are physically ON Long Island, but if you refer to anyone from those two communities as a Long Islander, they will stab you.

When most people speak of "Long Island," however, they're referring to the land mass under the jurisdiction of Nassau and Suffolk counties, which overlap 13 townships, 96 villages, and two cities. In other words, there's no Long Island government, but there's plenty OF government. Combined, the counties have a population of 2.7 million, fueled by a post-World War II migration that turned the potato fields of Island Trees into Levittown and hundreds of similarly laid-out housing developments. Knowing how all this bureaucracy works–or doesn't work, especially in conjunction with the myriad industries that flourish in the region–was Angelo's *raison d'être.* He was a fount of knowledge built painstakingly through one-on-one interviews, press conferences, old-fash-ioned, shoe-leather reporting, and meetings. So many meetings. County, town, village board meetings. School board meetings. Business association meetings. Corporate board meetings.

Angelo attended so many meetings that he started to notice how they all seemed to have the same cadence and rhythm, regardless of who was leading or participating. Every meeting chairman, for instance, turned into Captain Kirk at the helm of the Enterprise once the meeting began. They claimed they wanted to keep things moving, but the meetings always ended up being longer than necessary.

By enduring the endless meetings, however, he accumulated a unique and valuable insight into how Long Island functions. There's no doubt he could have set himself up nicely financially had he accepted any of the numerous offers to serve as a consultant to the many entities looking to tap into that fount of knowledge, wisdom, and experience. But Angelo wasn't interested.

"What I think should be done about anything in business or government is irrelevant," he explained to one CEO looking to pick his brain over coffee in a diner, where Long Island's most important conversations take place. "You can't be a reporter AND get involved in the decision-making process. It's like that fellow, what was his name...Lester Bangs...said in *Almost Famous*. 'You can't be friends with the rock stars. You must be honest and merciless. Once you start going to the parties, you become one of them, and once that happens, you're a part of it and therefore you can't report on it.'"

Although the sun was shining in all its Long Island autumnal afternoon glory, the cool breeze coming off the water was such that Angelo kept his windbreaker on over his long-sleeve polo shirt, khaki shorts, and deck shoes. His daily, hour-long walks helped him stay trim, and his full head of salt-and-pepper hair gave him the air of dignity enjoyed only by the male of the species. However, a random sampling of social media would indicate that the population of women embracing their silver status seems to be expanding.

Angelo and Catherine sat in silence for a moment, sizing each other up. Catherine also realized she needed to calm her breathing, as she was still anxious about being late and not getting things off on the right foot.

"Why did you refer to me as Doctor?" Angelo asked.

"Excuse me?" Catherine responded, still trying to collect herself.

"You said, 'I'm sorry, Dr. Kamoosi.' I'm not a medical doctor. I don't have a Ph D. Why did you call me 'Dr. Kamoosi'?"

"As I wrote in my text, Professor Zahler said I need to interview you for my thesis project," Catherine explained. "He's a doctor, so I suppose I assumed you were, too."

"First rule of journalism is never assume," Angelo snapped.

"I was taught that the first rule was 'tell the truth,'" Catherine countered.

"You can't get at the truth if you're busy making assumptions," Angelo harrumphed, not quite ready to concede his error, no matter how impressed he was that she knew this. "If you're going to be a journalist, you need to question everything you see and hear. Everything."

"I'm not going to be just a journalist," Catherine said, perhaps with more emphasis on the "just" and more defensively than she intended. "I'm also majoring in business administration. I want to understand what it takes to run a company so I can take business reporting to another level. I may also want to run my own business someday, but that's way down the road."

"What's your thesis topic?" Angelo asked.

"The Role of the Ego in Running a Successful Enterprise," Catherine replied.

"So why do you want to interview me?" Angelo asked. "I started a business and it closed within two years." After that, I was 'just a journalist,' as you so eloquently put it."

If Catherine noticed the dig, she ignored it. "Professor Zahler says no one knows more than you about Long Island, especially where all the bodies are buried and whose closets are best left unopened."

"I don't know about that," Angelo replied. "I've come to learn the more I know, the more I realize what I don't know, and that's humbling."

"So what do you know about egos and running a business? Do you need one to be successful?" Catherine asked, trying to get him to bring up the business owner Professor Zahler had mentioned. She hoped Angelo would be more inclined to discuss the man if he thought doing so was his idea.

"You need an ego to get out of bed in the morning," Angelo said. "It drives everything you do, the decisions you make. Everyone has an 'ego,' per se. Don't let anyone tell you otherwise. The trick is to make the ego work FOR you, not against you."

"What do you mean?" Catherine asked.

"Take me, for instance," Angelo said. "When I was your age—you should pardon the expression—I had it in my head I wanted to own a business, be the boss, the Big Shot standing in the corner. I let my heart make the decisions, and as a result, I had my head handed to me."

"What did you learn from the experience?" Catherine asked.

"Don't let your ego make your decisions for you! Take a step back, think things through. Listen to your heart but include your head in the discussion. And pray."

"Pray?" Catherine asked.

Angelo chuckled. "Would you feel better if I said meditate? Prayer is a form of meditation. The point is to strengthen your connection to your Higher Power so it can guide you."

"Your Higher Power? You mean God?"

"Lots of people refer to it in many different ways," Angelo explained. "God. Higher Power. Energy. Source. The bottom line is, we're all connected to it, and the people who know how and when to tap into and maintain that connection enjoy the greatest success. I'm talking about true, sustainable, meaningful success."

"What do you consider true success to be?" Catherine asked.

"Successful people are those who can honestly say they are who they want to be, as long as being who they want to be doesn't hurt others. Financial independence doesn't hurt, either."

"You mean F-U money?" Catherine asked, hoping to sound worldly.

"F-U money, yes," Angelo said. "Enough money in the bank so you can tell The Man to go scratch when he tells you to do something you don't think is right or worthwhile."

"So out of all the people you met and dealt with over the years, who would you consider the most successful?" Catherine prodded on, leaning forward a little, hoping to nudge him along. "And what role did the ego play in his or her success?"

Angelo thought for a few moments.

"I'll go you one better," he said. "I'll share with you a story–a true story, although you may doubt me at times–about three people whose lives and careers were so entangled it bordered on the incestuous, although not in a sexual way. Or maybe it did. That part got a little murky at times. I'll leave it to you to decide which one was 'quote-unquote' the most successful, but I can say for certain the ego was a driving force for all three."

Bingo! Catherine thought.

"That would be terrific," Catherine understated, relieved that she had her thesis subject nailed down. "Is this something you can share with me now...?" Her voice trailed off. As grateful as she was to move forward on this, she wasn't sure how much time would be involved and how much longer she would need to stay.

"No," Angelo said. "We'll need to clear a day to make sure

we do a thorough job. And I'll need to get some notes together. It's been a while since I've gone over any of the material."

Angelo looked down at his Smartphone and started tapping.

"How does this Sunday look? You can come out here for lunch, and we'll make an afternoon of it. Mrs. Kamoosi will be attending a baby shower, which means we can work uninterrupted for a few hours, followed by an influx of baby shower cookies and desserts when she returns. She always brings home something sweet from these things."

"Sunday it is," Catherine said, not even bothering to check her calendar. If she had a conflict, she would cancel whatever it was. Her journalism jones was kicking in, and her instincts were screaming she was on to a great story. She had no idea how great it was.

Chapter 4

Let the Dead Bury the Dead

"Right on time!" Angelo said with a laugh as Catherine walked through the gate in the fence between his property and the community parking lot at the pre-arranged time of 12:30 pm.

"Like anything else," Catherine replied, "it helps if you know where you're going."

"This may take a while," he told Catherine. "Are you hungry? I have some cold cuts and fresh bread inside if you're hungry. Fresh bread makes all the difference."

"I may take you up on that offer," Catherine said.

Angelo laughed. "When I was in college, my motto was, 'anything free is good,' especially when it came to meals. I tell you what. I'll go inside and get some lunch together. Feel free to stretch your legs and take a biology break if need be. This may take a couple of hours, but I assure you it's worth it."

Catherine chuckled at Angelo's euphemistic way of suggesting she go to the bathroom, but it was a good idea, so she followed him into the small beach house. He veered off to the kitchen on the right and gestured to Catherine that she would find the bathroom straight ahead. The house itself was simply furnished with an L-shaped sectional couch in the corner flanked by easy chairs. There was a fireplace in the west wall, no television set, and plenty of windows, no doubt to maximize opportunities to watch the sun set. A couple of bookshelves held various forms of artwork featuring dozens of lighthouses.

"I half expected to see shelves lined with books and newspapers strewn about the living room," Catherine said.

"We're a quarter century into the new millennium," Angelo said. "I listen to my books and read my newspapers online."

"What about the lighthouses?" Catherine asked.

"What about them?" Angelo asked back.

"You seem to be a fan."

"The collection is my wife's handiwork," Angelo said, resisting the temptation to make a joking reference to their phallic nature. "She's infatuated with them. I like them because they speak to the unpredictability, sensitivity, and sheer power of the ocean."

"How is Mrs. Kamoosi?" Catherine asked, conversationally more than anything else.

"My wife goes by her given name, Siobhan Molloy. She works in marketing."

"Siobhan?"

"It's Irish. It means 'God is gracious.' It fits her to a tee."

"I don't see any photos of her, or you, for that matter."

"We know what we look like," Angelo said, arranging turkey, roast beef, ham, Swiss cheese, and piles of freshly baked slices of bread on two platters. "Would you like some chips? Mustard? Mayo?"

"Sure. Mustard, please. No kids?"

"We found each other late in life," Angelo explained, reaching into the cupboard for a bag of potato chips and a jar of mustard. "Neither of us had–or wanted–kids. Parenting isn't for everyone."

"I didn't mean to pry," Catherine said, wondering if she struck a nerve.

"You're not prying," Angelo said. "You're asking questions. That's how you learn, by asking questions and then listening to the answers. Not enough people ask real questions or wait for answers. They just wait until it's their turn to talk. Or they don't even wait. They just jump in mid-sentence."

"I hate that," Catherine said.

"Me, too," Angelo said, picking up the plates. "Why don't you go do what you came in here to do, and I'll meet you back out on the deck?"

"Oh, yeah," Catherine said. "See you back on the deck."

She went about her business in the bathroom and came out feeling refreshed and ready to eat. Angelo called out from the deck. "Check to see what's inside the refrigerator if you want something to drink. There should be a soda or some beer. If there's some water, can you grab one for me?"

There was soda, beer, and bottles of water. Catherine grabbed two. She made her way back to the deck and resumed her position at the table. The breeze was gentle and soothing on an unusually warm October afternoon.

"Great day to tell a long story," Angelo noted, laughing.

"I'm all ears," Catherine said. "Let me get my notebook, though. I like to take notes while I record. I assume you're okay with me recording our conversation?"

"There you go assuming again," Angelo chided, but with a chuckle. "I'm fine with you recording. I should have recorded the countless hours interviewing some of the people involved."

"If you did the legwork, why didn't you write the novel?" Catherine asked.

Angelo sighed. "Life has a funny way of scooting by, especially as you get older," he said. "Deep down, I'm still not sure how I feel about what transpired, or whether I want to be associated with it. Another part of me wants to forget it ever happened. But I suppose it's worth revisiting."

"I certainly hope so," Catherine said. "Excuse me for a moment while I go get my notebook and phone."

Catherine quickly made her way back to the car, trying to remember how much battery power she had left on the phone. Angelo watched her walk away and involuntarily snorted. *I would have been all over that back in the day*, he thought, knowing full well it wasn't "back in the day" and, even if it were, his being older than 60 rendered him invisible to women younger than 50, not that he had any interest in being seen by them.

Catherine returned from her car with the tools she needed and got comfortable in her chair.

"What's so funny?" Catherine asked.

"What do you mean?" Angelo asked, not realizing she had heard him snort.

"You snorted when I got up to go to the car," Catherine said. "Did I say or do something funny?"

"No, it wasn't you," Angelo said, with a sigh. "I was thinking about the olden days, when it would be harder for a young woman to establish herself in the business world because of guys like me."

"What do you mean, 'guys like me'?"

Angelo sighed again and shifted in his seat. "I cringe anytime I think of how I conducted myself as a younger man," Angelo said. "I could be a real insensitive, insecure, immature jerk at times."

"Wow. Really? How so?"

"Let's just say it took me too long to realize that the thoughts I entertained were not necessarily entertaining, nor worth sharing. I'd just as soon not get into it, Catherine. Let the dead bury the dead. I wasn't the only one, but I'm the only one I'm responsible for, so over the past few years, I've been trying to make amends. You can't unring a bell, but you sure as hell make sure you never ring it again. And when you hear the story I'm about to share, you'll see that such behavior–men behaving badly–was much more commonplace. The so-called 'Me Too movement' was long overdue and still has a ways to go. Perhaps in your lifetime, we'll reach a point where everyone leaves his or her gender at the door and we can work together as individuals and equal peers. Something like that."

The subject hung in the air like a rain cloud blocking the sun while trying to decide if it was going to release a deluge or move on.

"I hope you're right, and I thank you for being so open with me," Catherine said after a few moments of not being sure what to make of Angelo's comments. "So, how do you want to do this?"

"It works best if I tell you what transpired chronologically, although I may have to provide some context on the cast of characters."

"Cast?" Catherine asked. "You said there were three people involved."

"There are three people–Billy Bate, Melinda Bate, and Grace Duffy–at the heart of the saga, but there were a handful of folks whose lives were also impacted. They all brought their own brand of crazy to the table over the course of several years in the 1990s, culminating in one crazy week in September 1997," Angelo said. "I will walk you through what transpired based on what I was told. Keep in mind, however, that 'the week that was' took place in the 1990s, when the Internet was in its nascent stage. Only a Chosen Few had cell phones, and there was no social media as we know it today. What transpired over the course of some 90 hours was remarkable enough. I cannot even imagine the level of shitshow it would have achieved with the all-knowing keyboard wizards of today chiming in online and in social media."

"So where do we start?" Catherine asked.

"As that noted philosopher Maria von Trapp once said, 'Let's start at the very beginning,'" Angelo said. "After it all went down, I interviewed most of those involved. Based on what I learned, I can now fill in the blanks. Believe it or not, it all started with a concert."

Part II

Who, or What, is a Homer's Drool?

Chapter 5

Homer's Drool

"I'm so excited!" Betty Bate exclaimed as she breezed into her father's office. That she did so without prior clearance from Martha, Billy's executive secretary, did not endear her to Martha. Betty was the only person to enjoy carte blanche office visitation-without-clearance privileges, but Martha still found Betty's habit of disregarding her disrespectful and off-putting. Martha was young and voluptuous, and her dark hair and dark eyes exuded exotic, but her professional demeanor was Old School Secretarial Soul, especially when it came to her gatekeeper status. Prison guards took their responsibilities less seriously than Martha when it came to ensuring nobody got to see Billy without Martha's blessing, which pleased Billy to no end.

"Why's that? Oh, and good morning."

"I'm sorry. Good morning, Pop," Betty said as she sauntered behind his desk–again, the only person allowed behind there– so she could plant a kiss on his cheek. "Look what I have for you!" she said, leaving a bag of fruit jelly slices on his desk as she did almost every time she stopped by. Then she took a seat on the leather couch against the wall, opposite Billy's desk.

Betty crossed her legs, smoothed her white pants, and tugged at her salmon-colored, short-sleeved surplice top tied at the waist. She always wanted to look professional when she visited her father at his office, but as a 20-something student studying for a doctorate in psychology, she wasn't quite yet ready for business suits. Her dyed-blonde hair framed her soft brown eyes, and her cute-as-a-button nose was a gift from her father–not his genes, but his checkbook. While she shared her father's disdain for all things athletic, she did exercise regularly, and it showed.

It was only 10:00 am, but Billy ripped into the bag of jelly slices like a little boy opening a present on Christmas morning. It wasn't so much that he had a sweet tooth, which he did, but because he saw the bag of candy as a sign of his daughter's love and her desire to bring him a little happiness.

"Is this why you're excited?" Billy asked, popping a slice into his mouth.

"Oh my, no," Betty said. "Jeff and I just scored tickets to see Homer's Drool at Radio City Music Hall in September." Jeff was her fiancé, Jeff Doomey. A slight man with dark, close-cropped hair, his nose and ears were bigger than they should have been. It gave him an air of goofiness that belied his sharp mental acuity but prevented Billy from taking him seriously.

As soon as she shared her excitement, though, she realized she should have kept this bit of news to herself.

"What's Homer's Pool?" he asked.

"Homer's *Drool*," Betty corrected, "It's the band Johnny Straphanger started after 'Rock Quarry' went under. They got the name from the sound Homer Simpson makes when he sees a doughnut. We like that song, 'Chisel Me.'"

"Sounds like fun. We'll make a night of it," Billy said.

"Seriously, Dad," Betty said. "Jeff and I just wanted to check them out, keep it simple."

"Nonsense," Billy said. "I'll have Martha make all the arrangements."

"Arrangements?" Betty asked, although she knew what was coming next.

"We'll get our usual front row seats..."

"Dad–the show's sold out. We were lucky to get the seats we got," Betty said, trying to discourage her father and maybe bring the horse back into the barn.

"There's no point in going to a show if you don't sit in the front row, especially at Radio City," Billy said. "Don't worry–I'll take care of it. We'll get some dinner at Clegg & Cleary's beforehand."

Betty sat back on the couch, sensing defeat but not quite ready to give up.

"Well, it's during the week. We don't want to be out to all hours," Betty cautioned.

"All hours? Are you 65 or 25? What's the point of going out if you're not open to enjoying yourself?" Billy said.

"I'm 24," Betty corrected. "Can you at least be civil to Jeff?" Betty asked.

"I just told you I'm springing for front row seats at Radio City and dinner at Clegg & Cleary's. How is that not being civil?" Billy asked.

"You know what I mean," Betty said. "Be nice to him. Need I remind you we're engaged to be married someday? He's going to be the father of your grandchildren. It would be nice if we all got along."

"The thought of him putting his hands on something I brought into this world makes me crazy. It haunts me," Billy said.

"Some *thing*?" For God's sake, Dad. We live together. He's committed to me, and he is all I ever wanted in a soul mate. Isn't that enough for you?"

Billy grunted and then called to Martha, whose desk was right outside his office.

"Martha! Am I available on–what day did you say, Betty?'

"I didn't," Betty said, entertaining for a moment the hope that a miracle might ensue, and her father would be committed to attend something else that night. "It's Tuesday, September 2. The day after Labor Day."

Martha stood in the office doorway, looking down at her notepad. Billy's office struck that happy medium between wanting to reward yourself with the latest bells and whistles associated with being a successful entrepreneur and sending a message to your subordinates that squandering funds on anything non-essential is verboten. The black leather couch and chairs for visitors matched his mahogany desk, and the cabinets behind him, when closed, hid a state-of-the-art music system and television set. The private bathroom on the other side of the wall behind the couch was all black. The sink, cabinets, counter, shower stall, and toilet. Even the towels. If you weren't careful, you could hurt yourself or–worse–miss the toilet.

"Believe it or not, you have nothing on the calendar," Martha said, purposefully avoiding Betty's gaze and the unspoken plea to say otherwise.

"Great," Billy said. "Get seven seats, front row, Radio City, for the Foaming Goo on September 2. Then book my usual table at Clegg's," Billy directed.

"Homer's Drool," Betty corrected, sighing.

She knew whatever plans she had for a fun night with her fiancé were history. She wondered if she could sell the two tickets she had already paid for. Then she wondered how she was going to tell her fiancé what transpired without him getting upset.

"Wait a minute," Betty said, sitting up. "Why seven?"

"Well," Billy said. "There's me, you, Jeff, Melinda–and James, of course–and Pete and Re-Pete."

"Really?" Betty asked, exasperated.

"Really," Billy said. "Melinda's been barking at me to spend more time with her, and if she's coming, then so is James."

"She's your WIFE, Dad, and you're never home. Are you sure Melinda doesn't mean she wants YOU to spend more time with HER, not just dragging her along to events?" Betty asked rhetorically. "And most likely it's a school night for James. Do you want him out late if he has to get up early the next morning?"

James–never Jim, Jimmy, or Jimbo–was Melinda's pre-teen son from her first marriage.

"If it's the week of Labor Day, then it's probably the first or second day of class, and you know nothing important gets done then," Billy said. "Besides, he's 12. He'll bounce back better than the rest of us. One of the things he loves about me being married to his mother is the different experiences he gets to enjoy that his classmates can only dream about."

"And why do Pete and Re-Pete have to be there?" Betty wondered aloud. Pete and Re-Pete were Billy's pet nicknames for Peter Snodgrass and Pete Santini, two executives in their late 30s who ran the day-to-day operations of Billy's company, Carpe Diem Construction Fantasy Camps. Santini came on board as a teenager, and Snodgrass started working for Billy right out of college, so for the most part, Billy was the only employer they knew. Santini made full use of Billy's standing offer to pay for the education of any full-time employee, earning bachelor's and master's degrees on Billy's dime while also working for him 40 to 50 hours a week.

It was never made clear which one was Pete and which one was Re-Pete, nor did either one enjoy being paired together in this way. But Billy found it amusing, and if it worked for Billy, then everybody in the organization went along with the gag.

"What makes you think Pete and Re-Pete want to see a Homer's Drool concert?" Betty asked when Billy ignored her earlier question.

"You know the drill," Billy said. "Our IRS overlords must be appeased at all times, as my good friend Mr. Shadler reminded me on a daily basis. Therefore, business must be discussed if it's going down as a business expense."

Billy was referring to Stanley Shadler, who, before his passing, was Billy's semi-retired CFO. In his salad days, Stanley mastered the art of thwarting Internal Revenue Service audits under the auspices of true captains of industry such as John Hay Whitney, the publisher of the *New York Herald*.

"Shouldn't they be home with their families?" Betty asked, hoping against hope she could dissuade her father from pursuing this course of action.

"Carpe Diem has taken good care of their families, Betty. If being away for an evening is the price they have to pay, so be it," Billy said. "Speaking of which, I'd like to get back to my work here, so if you don't mind..."

"All right, Dad. I'm going," Betty said, coming back around Billy's desk to give him a kiss goodbye. "Let me know when all the details are finalized."

Martha made the arrangements. On Tuesday, September 2, 1997, seven people found themselves riding in a limousine through midtown Manhattan on an unusually cool September evening, six of whom wished they could be just about anywhere else.

James, being 12, was happy to be out on a school night, knowing full well he could talk his mother into letting him sign in late the next morning even though it was, in fact, the first day of a new school year. Both Pete and Re-Pete were missing out on spending time with their kids as they prepared for their respective first days of kindergarten, but like Betty, they "knew the drill" and came along without question or qualm. Jeff and Betty were resigned to the mixed blessing of a free meal in a midtown Manhattan steakhouse followed by front row seats to a show by a musical group they liked, the pleasure of which was tamped down by the nagging notion that at any given moment Billy could turn sullen and/or he and Melinda could start arguing.

Even when they were happy with each other and getting along, being out with them presented unique challenges. They both chain-smoked like death-row inmates but never asked permission from the others in the limousine before lighting up. They just did because they could.

They almost always traveled by limousine, especially if the excursion involved a night in Manhattan. Billy did this so often as he built up his business that he purchased his own limousine and kept a part-time driver on the payroll, as it was more cost-efficient than renting. He bought a white one, fresh off the assembly line, as he read somewhere that white limos stand out in a crowd of their black brethren.

As was their wont, Billy and Melinda sat facing forward, with James situated in between to serve as a buffer. Jeff and Betty sat on the one bench seat that faced to the left of where the car was heading, and Pete & Re-Pete sat on the bench seat facing to the right. They tried not to make eye contact amongst themselves, lest they tip their hands as to their desire to not have to endure this, and they worked extra hard to not show their collective displeasure sitting in the transportation equivalent of the kids' table at Thanksgiving. All four had enough experience dealing with the constant smoking not to make an issue of it, but the Marlboro fog wafting about in the enclosed area scuttled any desire for any discussion beyond the smallest of small talk.

The limousine pulled right up to the entrance at Clegg & Cleary's on 49th Street between Fifth and Sixth Avenues, and its occupants piled out one by one. Billy instructed the limo driver to "wait for us here," even though they could have easily walked to Radio City Music Hall from the restaurant after the meal. Walking was not something Billy embraced, especially when a grand entrance in a stretch limo was a possibility. The Clegg & Cleary's maître'd greeted them like long-lost relatives. The servers treated them like royalty, and Billy ordered his usual dinner of "hamburger, no cheese, nothing green, French fries, and a chocolate milkshake." But nothing else about the night would be business as usual.

Chapter 6

Dinner @ Clegg & Cleary's

Neither Clegg nor Cleary was still involved in the running of the steakhouse bearing their names, nor alive, for that matter. They passed away years ago, and legend has it they despised each other after the restaurant partnership was formed in the mid-1950s. But they loved feeding their mostly-male patrons elaborate, red-meat-centric meals and supplying the best in hard liquor, most of it brown—all at a significant profit. There wasn't a blender to be found in the bar. To step into Clegg & Cleary's was to step back in time, to an era when people dressed for dinner, and professional waiters—mature men and women—wore black vests, black ties, pressed white shirts, and long white aprons with professional pride. They listened—no pad or pen—as the orders were given and then, when the meals came out, placed the dish in front of the person who ordered it without having to ask, "Who had the veal?"

The décor was thick with testosterone. Framed artwork adorned the paneled walls—more Harvard Club than suburban, 1970s den—and the deep carpet absorbed any extraneous noises, not that there was much to absorb. The Clegg & Cleary's clientele kept their voices down. They didn't want anyone to know their business, nor did they care about the business of the other diners. It was as if the restaurant was designed by librarians—albeit librarians with a lot of money.

Billy loved going to Clegg & Cleary's for three reasons. Location—right around the corner from the theater where his favorite play, *Black Maria*, was performed nightly since 1988. Treatment—the Clegg & Cleary's staff always made a big deal when Billy dined there, regardless of whether it was a party of two or 20. The Joke—whenever he dined out, Billy would only order a hamburger (never a cheeseburger), fries, and a milk-shake, regardless of where he was or who he was with. This could be more challenging at times than one might expect, but Billy insisted. It was never a problem at Clegg & Cleary's. They even fashioned a special plate for his meal and made sure his fellow diners were aware of his special status when serving his meal.

Because Billy was treated like a Big Shot when he dined at Clegg & Cleary's, he dined there anytime he had business to conduct in Manhattan over lunch or dinner. Any time. Every time. Often after dinner, he would treat his guests to a perfor-mance of *Black Maria*, and Billy always paid. Always.

The Clegg & Cleary's waitstaff was happy to see Billy and his entourage. It had been a slow Tuesday night, but Billy's legendary generosity meant at least one or two people were going home well-compensated. Drink orders were taken. Pete, Re-Pete, and Jeff ordered Heinekens. Betty had a glass of Chardonnay, and Melinda opted to go with a glass of Merlot. James had a Coke, and Billy ordered his customary cup of coffee. Having coffee with dinner—as opposed to simply after-ward—was a habit Billy picked up from his beloved mother. She was raised on a farm out on the East End of Long Island, and children living on farms learned to drink coffee at an early age and had it with their meals.

An unspoken tension engulfed the table as the waiter brought the drinks, so he tried to lighten the mood.

"Where are we headed tonight?" he asked. "Another performance of *Black Maria*? You've seen that over a hundred times, haven't you, Billy?"

"I stopped counting once I got to 100," Billy replied, perhaps more dourly than an innocent, ice-breaking inquiry warranted.

"We're going to see the Homer's Drool!" James blurted out. "Front row seats!"

"Oh! I love those guys," the waiter said. "'Everlong' is a great song."

Silence.

"Can we get some bread?" Pete Snodgrass asked.

Despair descended over the waiter's face. He looked in the direction of the maître 'd and made eye contact. The maître 'd scurried over.

"The bread man never showed up this morning," he said. "That's the first—and last—time that's ever happened. I'm so sorry," he said.

Again, silence.

The waiter said, "Let me go check on your dinner orders. I'll be right back."

Pete Santini asked James if he was looking forward to going back to school the next day.

James jabbered on about how nervous he was heading into middle school. Everyone at the table assured him he would do just fine, even though nobody had any particularly fond memories of their days as a pre-teen student.

The rest of the dinner was uneventful if not perfunctory.

As they headed toward the front door and the waiting limousine, Billy pulled Jeff aside.

"I'm exhausted," he said. "You got anything for me?"

This was not the first time Billy would make such a request of Jeff, so Jeff was ready. He reached into his jacket pocket, pulled out a small bag containing two tiny orange pills, and slipped them into Billy's jacket pocket. "This should help you," he whispered to Billy, resisting the urge to point out that Billy wouldn't be exhausted if he'd stay home to get a good night's sleep in his own bed–instead of glomming on to his daughter's social life.

Betty and Melinda had retreated to the ladies' room, figuring–rightly so–the accommodations there were far more pleasant than what their options would be around the corner. No matter how glamorous Radio City Music Hall was, when thousands of people use your facilities, they tend to get messy. Upon their return, Betty sidled up to Jeff and slid her hand into his.

"We're going to walk over," Betty announced over her shoulder in Billy's direction. "We have our tickets. I need to work off that meal and get some fresh air."

They were out the door before Billy could speak a word of protest. Melinda hooked her arm around his and whispered, "Don't worry, more room for us in the car."

Billy grunted. "I prefer to travel as a family when we're out together."

Now it was Melinda's turn to grunt.

"As a family, huh? You haven't said a civil word to anyone, especially Jeff, all night. Is that what traveling as a family means to you?"

Billy didn't answer. They walked through the front door at Clegg & Cleary's, as they could see the limousine coming down the street to get them. Melinda tugged on Billy's left arm and brought him in close, making sure he could feel her right breast pressed against him.

"You seem a little down," she whispered into his left ear, "so I slipped a little something into your jacket pocket that should pick you right up. Trust me, you're going to need it when we get home." She gently bit on his left earlobe and made a sound that was a mix between a growl and a purr, just in case he didn't catch on as to what she had in mind.

Billy didn't respond audibly to Melinda's come on, but that was nothing new. Staring straight ahead, he reached into the left pocket of his jacket and realized he now had two little baggies in his suit jacket, although he had no idea what was inside the baggies themselves.

The five of them piled into the stretch limousine and sat in stony silence as the driver pulled away from the curb and made the half-mile journey to the front doors of Radio City Music Hall. They passed Jeff and Betty as they walked, but did not acknowledge them. A crowd of Homer's Drool fans had gathered in front of the historic venue, and many of them speculated as to who just might be in the limousine as it pulled up to the curb. Billy loved that. What he did not enjoy was the inevitable, unexpressed disappointment that ensued when people realized it wasn't who they hoped it might be—a celebrity!

Again they piled out, and Billy told the driver to meet them back there in about three hours.

"Do you anticipate going out anywhere afterward?" the driver asked. "If so, I'll want to gas up."

Billy instinctively grabbed the outside of his jacket's left pocket and felt the two baggies. "No, we'll be heading straight home. It's a school night for James."

Melinda and James were already inside the lobby with Pete Santini, looking at the event posters. Peter Snodgrass held back and was waiting on the sidewalk for Billy, waiting for him to finish with the driver.

He walked up to Billy and gently took hold of his right arm.

"You okay?" Peter asked. "You look beat."

"I'm fine," Billy lied. "I hope this concert isn't too loud. I have a splitting headache."

Peter Snodgrass drew Billy in closer.

"I have just the thing for you," he said softly, as he dropped something into the pocket on Billy's right side. "I call them Magic Beans. You won't feel a thing, but you'll still have the time of your life."

"Thanks," Billy muttered, without letting on as to what transpired earlier or inquiring as to just what these Magic Beans entailed. "Let's go inside."

Once inside, they reconnected with Jeff and Betty and made their way to the stage. The ushers recognized Billy. While they did not gush over him and his family as they did at Clegg & Cleary's, they did everything they could to make them feel comfortable in anticipation of the $20 bill that was sure to change hands. It did.

It wasn't until the lights began to dim in anticipation of the show starting that Billy realized he should use the bathroom now lest he miss out on anything.

"I'm going to hit the head," Billy said. "I'll be right back."

He sauntered off while the rest of his party settled in. Because he knew his way around the hall, he knew which bathroom would be less crowded. While he was gone, Melinda and James thumbed through the program they picked up in the lobby. Jeff and Betty swapped opinions as to which song Homer's Drool might open with, and Pete and Re-Pete looked at their respective watches, wondering if they might be home in time to kiss their children good night.

Billy returned a few minutes later and sat down in his front row, center-aisle seat without saying a word to the others. The lights dimmed for good, and Homer's Drool came out to uproarious applause. They launched right into "Monkey Tool," and the crowd was on its feet, clapping, swaying, and singing along–all except for Billy. Billy stayed in his seat. He wasn't beat. He wasn't a little down. He wasn't exhausted. He was dead.

Chapter 7

Trouble in Paradise

"Uh oh, there must be trouble in paradise," Bernie the bartender said when he saw Grace Duffy walk through the front door. "Super Mom is out on a school night."

"Paradise is fine, you should come visit," Grace shot back as she sauntered over to her preferred seat by the bar's corner. Bernie prepared and placed a tumbler of Dewars and water in front of her without Grace having to ask.

Bernie was a bachelor in his early 30s. He tended bar in The Broken Oar, a small pub near the train station in downtown South Huntington, walking distance from where Grace lived with her older sister Grail's family. Bernie's eyes were so blue you could hear calypso music simply by looking into them, and they were as inviting as a backyard pool on a hot summer day. His black, curly hair framed his alabaster face, and his eyes twinkled when he told funny stories, which he enjoyed doing more often than not as a means to seduce women, which he enjoyed even more. His predilection for sexual conquests, combined with his contempt for commitment, prevented Grace from ever taking Bernie seriously as a love interest, much to his chagrin. He wasn't an imposing figure, as some bartenders can be, but his shoulders were square and his biceps were thick, with enough definition to send the message that he was not to be trifled with. Whenever Grace needed a laugh or to do some harmless flirting, she would visit him at the bar, and Grail was kind enough to look after her toddler son, Slade, when she did. Grace usually nursed a Dewars and water as she watched Bernie practice his craft and weave his storytelling magic.

Grace was also in her early 30s. She was taller than most women but not distractingly so. Her chestnut hair was cut short but showed plenty of life. She had a nice enough figure, one fully recovered from having given birth a little more than five years prior, but no one would ever describe her as striking.

Despite putting up a brave front as a single mom, Grace knew she wanted more out of life and a man to share it with. A real man, a soul mate to love her and serve as a masculine role model for Slade. Somebody who made her want to be a better person but who loved her for who she is right now. She was thriving in her position as public relations director for Gibbons College, a small, liberal-arts school on Long Island, with her hopes set on becoming a vice president for the school in the not-so-distant future. Her sharp tongue and quick wit, so useful when dealing with her parents' tragic deaths in her late teenage years, presented a challenge for her professionally, as naked honesty is rarely rewarded in academic circles, and Gibbons was no exception. And then there was the truth about Slade's father.

Grace told anyone who asked that Slade's father was killed serving the country in Iraq. She hated having to lie, but the fabrication made for shorter conversations, and a violent death serving the nation in a faraway country was more convenient–and honorable–than the truth. Only three people–besides Grace and the father–knew the truth: Grail, Bernie the bartender, who was her friend since childhood, and Grace's former employer, Billy Bate.

Grail was Grace's Guardian Angel on Earth, even before their parents' untimely demise. Their father was murdered in cold blood–a victim of being in the wrong place at the wrong time–and their mother never overcame the grief of her sudden, painful loss. She died a year to the day after her husband was shot. Grail was a year older than Grace but seemingly light years more settled and mature, Catherine Duke to Grace's Patty. She had chestnut hair that hung halfway between her ears and her shoulder, which she kept in a hairstyle that could best be described as perky and efficient. She had a trim figure, which she attributed to "disciplined eating habits" and always being "on the go!"

Bernie and Grace grew up on the same suburban block and attended grade school, middle school, and high school together. She said she considered him to be the brother she never had, but if you fed her truth serum (or multiple Dewars and water), you might get her to confess she had deeper feelings for him. Because of their friendship, she knew Bernie could be trusted with her secret. Because of Bernie's penchant for skirt chasing, however, she wasn't so sure about her heart, so she kept it off limits from him.

Billy Bate was a different story. As far as Grace knew, Billy hadn't shared her secret with anyone. But she knew he was capable of keeping it under his hat until he could extract maximum benefit by sharing it. He could have blabbed it when she left his company to work for Gibbons, where he was on the Board of Directors and where she had earned her MBA on Billy's dime, but that would have made him look petty. So, as glad as she was that Billy kept quiet, his knowing kept thumping inside her head like Poe's tell-tale heart. Grace understood why Billy was unhappy when she left his employ, but her understanding didn't mitigate the trepidation she felt when she thought about when or how he might exact his vengeance.

Grace lived with Slade in the apartment of the mother/daughter house she shared with Grail, Grail's husband, Ron Satori, and their three daughters. Grail "married well," as they say on Long Island, and could afford to be a stay-at-home mom for her children, as well as Slade. Grace spent the bulk of her non-working hours with her "Little Man," as Grace liked to call Slade, rejuvenated by the unconditional love she enjoyed with her son.

The living arrangements with Grail soothed Grace's angst about having to spend so much time away from Slade during the day, but parting company each day ripped open a fresh wound healed only by diving into her work, which she found fulfilling yet frustrating. Her male superiors' need to have their hands held in order to meet a challenge never ceased to amaze her, especially considering the well-compensated positions they held as they molded young minds.

"To what do I owe the honor of your presence?" Bernie asked as Grace settled onto her bar stool and stirred her drink.

"I have to schlep to Manhattan tomorrow morning because a Gibbons' vice president is being interviewed on live television, and he wants me there with him to hold his hand, I guess," Grace said.

"That's some mighty important work you're doing there, Grace," Bernie said. "Is there any end to the glory of your position as director of public relations for Gibbons College?" he asked, rhetorically. "Why is he being interviewed?"

"Because he's an expert on getting people to contribute money to charities," she said.

"I'm already bored," Bernie said.

"That's not the half of it," Grace said. "It's for a cable channel with zero ratings. It's a complete waste."

"They should interview me," Bernie said.

"Lord help me for asking," Grace said, sipping her Dewars and water. "But why would anyone want to interview you?"

"I can talk about the art of seduction."

"You told me it was a science."

"It's an art. It's a science. Hell, sometimes it's a sport," Bernie chuckled.

"And what exactly would you have to say?" Grace asked, half out of morbid curiosity and half to get past this part of the conversation.

Before Bernie could reply, the opening notes from "Love Is The Answer," one of the tunes made famous by the musical *Black Maria*, started emanating from the jukebox, even though Grace and Bernie were the only two people in the bar.

"Name your price, a ticket to paradise..." the singer, Mike Nobile, started.

"Jesus Christ, turn that off," Grace snapped. "Who turned it on? We're the only ones here."

"The jukebox is programmed to play a song at random when it hasn't been played in a while," Bernie explained. "The idea being that hearing music will inspire the patrons to select more music."

"I can't stay here anymore..."

"Seriously, Bernie. Please turn it off."

Bernie reached under the bar, pushed a button, and the bar was silent again.

"Thank you. I had to sit through that goddamn *Black Maria* so many times, working for Billy Bate," Grace said. "I hate musicals to begin with, but this was pure torture."

"I hate musicals, too," Bernie said. "But we were talking about me being interviewed about the art of seduction."

"Yes, we were," Grace sighed. "Do continue."

"I'd start with this," Bernie responded. "The story's written in her eyes. You just have to know how to read. And when I hear a woman say, 'I love it when a man has a great sense of humor,' she's giving me the combination to the safe."

"That's not true of all women," Grace countered.

"You're right," Bernie said. "Other women are turned on by wealth and power. They end up miserable and lonely because rich, powerful guys only care about keeping their money and their power. For them, the sex is secondary to conquest, and love is never a factor. Sooner or later, those women find themselves on the cheating side of town, looking for laughs and the bedroom eyes. That's where I come in. I'm only too happy to oblige those poor souls."

"You're the Patron Saint of Pulchritude, Bernie," Grace spat out, part grumble and part sneer.

"Mock me all you want, Grace, but I always leave them smiling," Bernie said. "Except maybe last week."

"What happened last week?"

"Well, you know I'm not one for discussing conquests. Real men keep it to themselves," he said, leaning in. "But this one's too good.

"I was out west, visiting friends," Bernie continued. "After enjoying a couple of cocktails at an Applebee's or Fridays–like it matters which one–I struck up a conversation with a young lady sitting next to me. The next thing I know, she's inviting me back to her place. 'Wait here while I freshen up, and you can follow me home,' she says. She hops down off the bar stool–hops being the operative word–and I realize she's, eh, height-challenged. I couldn't believe it. She was half my size!

"My first inclination was to leave," Bernie said. "Then I thought, *The only thing better than having sex with a stranger in a strange city is having strange sex with a stranger in a strange city.*

"So I followed her back to her place—an apartment over the garage outside her parents' house. Greatest. Sex. Ever. Turns out she was a coxswain on her college crew team and got off barking orders at men. She kept telling me what to do and where, and how to do it. At one point, I was on my back, holding a tiny foot in each hand, swinging her back and forth like an agitator in a washing machine. She leaned forward so her tits—perfectly-shaped, I might add—swung to and fro. I tried to catch a nipple in my mouth, but she kept them beyond my reach. Meanwhile, she's commanding me in a drumbeat rhythm to grind my hips. 'Thrust! Thrust! Thrust!' She loved it. I loved it. We may have invented a new position or two."

"For which the world owes you a tremendous debt, no doubt," Grace said. "What happened next?"

"I conked out and woke up a few hours later," he said. "I knew right away I had to get out. The downside to wild sex with a stranger is the morning after, especially if her parents enter the picture. It was still dark, but I made my way over to the window, opened it enough to straddle the sill, and jumped to the ground. I nailed the landing without hurting myself or waking the woman. No doubt she woke up sore the next morning, in more ways than one."

"Why would she be sore?" Grace asked.

"Because I left and, because, you know, when I'm done banging, it takes a while to walk right," Bernie said.

"Perhaps she was glad you left. Maybe she prefers to sleep alone, or she didn't want her parents to see you there. I'll bet she was glad to be sore because sometimes a gal needs to get pounded good and hard," Grace said.

"Really?" he asked, dumbfounded and slightly deflated.

"I hate to break it to you, pal," Grace said. "But a

woman's urges are similar, if not the same, as a man's. The only difference is women fuck who they want. Men fuck who they can. Plus, we have to play the game differently because if we sleep around, we get a quote-unquote reputation. And then there's the pregnancy and STD threats. But the bottom line is sometimes a woman fucks a man simply for the sake of getting laid. Doing it without knowing much about him, or knowing you'll never see him again, adds to the excitement. Face it, Bernie. You were a one-night stand. If it wasn't you, it was going to be the bartender. And as for your so-called 'art of seduction,' my good friend, know this: No man who ever set on a course to genuinely explore a woman's mind and protect her heart has ever had to chase what's between her thighs."

With that, Grace drained her drink, blew Bernie a kiss, and said, "Thanks for the chuckle. And the visual. See you at the next one." She then turned on her heels and headed home.

―――――

Sitting on the train the following morning, Grace smiled as she recalled the deflated expression on Bernie's face. As much as she enjoyed his tales, deep down she found his insatiable appetite for matters *amore* unsettling.

Bernie can tell all the stories he wants, Grace thought. *But he can't possibly be happy. At least not as happy as he could be if he were to settle down with the right woman, especially if that woman were me.* Allowing this thought to escape startled Grace, as it marked the closest she came to conceding she had a thing for her friend. She immediately worked to downplay the sentiment.

The last thing I need in my life right now is the aggravation that comes with trying to get a bartender to settle down. A bartender! What kind of role model would he be for my Little Man, Slade?

She looked around to see if any other passengers on the train were entertaining similar thoughts or stories in their heads. *Of course not. They're thinking about the workday ahead, which is what I should be doing.*

Then her pager buzzed.

"A pager?" Catherine interjected, interrupting Angelo's story. "What's that?"

Angelo winced.

"My apologies, young lady," Angelo said. "I forgot how young you are. Before we had cell phones, we had pagers. If someone needed to contact you, they would call a phone number assigned to your pager. The pager would then 'go off,' letting you know that the person associated with the phone number that showed up on the pager was trying to get in touch with you."

"That sounds complicated," Catherine said. "How would you know if you should respond to the alert?"

"You had to know the phone numbers of the people who mattered most in your life," Angelo said. "I think at some point you could program the pager to identify certain phone numbers."

"Still sounds like a lot of work," Catherine said.

"It was state-of-the-art at the time," Angelo said. "Obviously, the proliferation of cell phones made the pager obsolete."

"Thanks for explaining that," Catherine said. "Let's get back to the story."

"Okay!"

Grail's number flashed on the screen. Grace sighed. It was 6:45 am. No one ever needs you to call you at that hour so they can share good news. Grace looked out the window to see where she was in terms of her train ride into Manhattan and realized she could get off at the next stop–the Jamaica train station–and call Grail from a pay phone there.

"Um...what's a pay phone?" Catherine asked, this time with a little hesitancy.

Angelo rubbed his face with his right hand.

"Seriously?" he asked.

"Can I assume that's what you called the phones you used to have put coins into if you wanted to make a phone call?" Catherine asked. "Like you see in the old movies?"

"Yes," Angelo sighed. "Like you see in the old movies."

"So what did you do if you didn't have any coins or enough coins?" Catherine asked. "How would you make a call?"

"Well, that was often a challenge, especially at six in the morning. If you let me continue, I'll walk you through how Grace handled it," Angelo said.

"All right," Catherine said. "I'll keep quiet. Please continue."

Chapter 8

Grace Calls Melinda

Jamaica Station, a major hub for the Long Island Railroad, was jam-packed with commuters scurrying to get to their respective destinations. None of them seemed overly concerned that Grace didn't have the change she needed to call from a pay phone, nor did they seem inclined to quiet down once she got Grail on the other line.

"Screw it, I'll call collect," Grace said, dialing o and then Grail's phone number.

"Collect? Really?!?" Grail said, once she told the operator she'd "accept the charges."

"I'm sorry, Grail," Grace said. "I don't have any change, and I don't have a phone credit card. I figured it was urgent, so I went the collect route. What's up? Is Slade okay?"

"Slade's fine," Grail replied. "Billy's dead."

"Billy? Billy who?" She thought for a moment. "Oh my God! Billy Bate??" Grace asked.

"Yes, the one and only," Grail said. "Melinda called me this morning, thinking she was calling you. She said Billy is dead and she figured you'd want to know."

"Dead? Shit." She pondered the news for a moment and then looked around to see if anyone had heard her say Billy's name. "How? Was he alone? Does Melinda want me to call her? Does she need me or anything?"

"She might have said something to the effect of 'please have Grace call me.' I don't know. I was busy getting the kids ready for school."

"Did she say how he died?" Grace wondered.

"She didn't say. Maybe she smothered him to death with her big fake tits," Grail growled.

Grail did not like talking with or about Melinda even under the best circumstances. Once, Grail accompanied Grace to a black-tie event honoring Billy and Melinda. They arrived in Billy's limo, which meant Grace and Grail had to ride backward and take in the cigarette smoke Billy and Melinda produced as if they were the king and queen of Marlboro Country. Grace tried to explain that riding backward and being trapped in cigarette smoke "came with the territory," but it upset Grail. "They knew I was nauseous, and they kept puffing away," she railed at Grace after the ride. "Such self-absorbed creeps. I should have puked right there on the stupid limo's floor."

"You're better than that, Grail," Grace told her.

"And so are you!" she shot back. "There is so much more you could be doing with your life than placating those two. I don't understand why you tolerate their crap."

Conversations between Grace and Grail about Billy and Melinda always took the same tone. Grace did not want to deal with it right now, not while standing on the platform at Jamaica Station, a transportation hub built with concrete and glass covered in grime dating back to World War II and possessing the warmth and charm of a jailhouse colonoscopy. She told

Grail she would call as soon as she knew something and hung up.

So many questions swirled in Grace's head.

Did Melinda want help making funeral arrangements?

Was Billy with her when he died, or did Grace have a potentially scandalous situation on her hands, which would require her letting the Gibbons College president know right away, even at this hour, because Billy was on its board of directors? (The only thing College Presidents hate more than being woken up early in the morning by their PR directors is being woken up early by a reporter asking questions requiring embarrassing answers.)

What was going to happen to Billy's family? To the company?

Grace wondered if Billy ever shared her secret with Melinda, the secret she let out in a weak moment late one night in Billy's office. If so, could Melinda be trusted not to blab and therefore derail her drive to be named a Vice President at Gibbons College? Is Melinda capable of doing so, especially if losing the Gibbons gig most likely would force Grace to return to Billy's–make that Melinda's, now–employ?

And what kind of boss would Melinda be? She and Grace got along with each other primarily because Grace knew a happy Melinda meant a happy Billy, so Grace did everything she could to placate the Boss' Wife. Massaging Melinda's ego would no doubt be just as unfulfilling as handling Billy's, probably even more so since Melinda didn't have Billy's business acumen or experience.

That consideration reminded Grace that she left Billy's employ for Gibbons because she wanted a more meaningful career.

It's one thing to toady up to a successful entrepreneur, Grace thought. *It's a different game altogether when the boss's only claim to fame is a fantastic body, some of which is man-made.*

What was it Billy used to say? Grace tried to remember. *Oh yeah...'never argue with a woman who can lick her own nipples.' How the hell am I going to make this work?* Grace asked herself. Then she sighed.

A few months shy of his 50th birthday, Billy Bate had his hands in everything and on everyone–especially when it came to women. His six-foot-two frame carried the body of a man who grew up working construction but hadn't lifted anything heavy in a few years. He wore his salt-and-pepper hair straight back–Michael Douglas-stylish but simple to maintain. His square jaw and deep-set eyes conveyed an air of gravitas he made work for him on many occasions, particularly at the nego-tiation table. The money he made from the multi-million-dollar business he created enabled him to buy a restaurant and invest in local real estate. His Big Boy Toys included a DeLorean, a helicopter, a yacht, and a small plane he was licensed to fly, which he did whenever he could. He fancied himself a philan-thropist, but he did not part with a dime unless he expected to garner media attention for doing so. Grace worked for Billy as his "Director of Special Projects," but, in reality, she was his personal PR flack.

Faults and shortcomings aside, he was also the kind of man you could go to if you needed help, guidance, or bail money. His insights and financial resources guided Grace through several difficult situations.

Grace knew she had to call Melinda. What do you say to a woman who has lost her husband, especially when there was a strong possibility that Billy was with someone other than his wife when it happened?

It was bad enough that she had to have such a sensitive conversation from a pay phone in a busy train station, but she wasn't about to compound the situation by calling collect. Grace sauntered over to a newsstand, bought a newspaper, and hoped the change she received would be enough to place the call. It was.

She punched in Melinda's number and held her breath. It was still only a little after 7:00 am. As the phone rang, Grace worried. *What if she fell asleep? How do I ask a woman who lost her husband last night how he died and, oh–by the way– was he forsaking his marriage vows at the time?*

Normally, Grace would consider such details idle gossip, but because Billy was on the board of directors at Gibbons, she had to tell Gibbons College President Chuck Biscuit as soon as possible. Plus, Billy was also someone Grace cared about. Nobody could ever truthfully refer to Billy Bate as a friend because he would never let anyone get that close. In the time Grace worked with Billy, their conversations were mostly work-related, and he never, ever dropped his guard.

Melinda answered the call. She sounded craggy but awake and willing to talk.

"Hello, Melinda. It's Grace Duffy. I just heard. I am so sorry," she said. "How are you holding up?"

"It's been a long night," she said, in a tone you might expect from somebody who spent hours waiting for Triple A to come fix a flat, not from a woman who just lost her husband.

"I can only imagine," Grace said and then took a deep breath. She needed to know how Billy died, and whether she had a "situation" on her hands.

"Do you want to talk about it?" she asked. "Can you tell me what happened?"

"We were at a Homer's Drool concert," she said, "Radio City Music Hall. Front row seats. The show had just started, but we were already dancing up a storm. Billy came back from the bathroom, sat down, put his head back, and died. They stopped the show and carted him out."

"Who else was there?" Grace asked.

"It was Billy, me, Betty, Jeff, James, Pete, and Re-Pete. We were out having a good time for the first time in a long time, and now this."

"What can I do to help? What needs to be done?" Grace asked.

"I'm not sure," she said. "I'll be at the office later. We'll have to make funeral arrangements. We can figure out things from there."

"All right, Melinda," Grace said. "I have a few commitments to deal with, and then I'll check in with you. I am sorry for your loss."

"Thank you."

Grace ended the call. She still had to meet Gibbons' Vice President Murray Jules in Manhattan. Since there was no immediate scandal on the horizon, she figured she could wait until she got into Manhattan to tell Murray and let him break it to Biscuit. She checked the train schedule and realized she had a few minutes until the next train into Manhattan. She thought about Melinda. Nature had been kind, but fate was a bitch. Divorced from her son James' father at 28. Widowed at 40. Great cheekbones. Long, lean legs. Jet-black hair Pocahontas would have killed for. Eyes capable of igniting charcoal. What nature did not provide, Billy bought for her– namely, breasts so full and firm they could distract a bishop.

Grace then considered the shit storm Billy's checking out was going to cause, given his penchant for philanthropy and philandering. Grace knew she was going to be forever associated with Billy because she worked side-by-side with him for several years. Fair or unfair, how she handled things would impact her future, especially at Gibbons. She needed to ensure

Billy's send-off to eternity maintained some dignity—no easy feat considering the clown-car procession known as Billy's life outside the office. Plus, there were the delicate matters of Grace owing Billy $60,000 and the secret Grace shared with him in a weak moment. If Billy took her secret to the grave, she was in the clear in that regard and could deal with the disposition of the loan later. If he told anyone her secret, though—and no doubt the next few days would reveal whether he did—her career—if not her life—would be ruined.

Chapter 9

Melinda's Bobblehead

Grace stood in the wings of the TV studio in Manhattan as Gibbons Vice President Murray Jules discussed the ins and outs of building an endowment fund for a college. She watched and listened, but heard nothing. The frenetic energy of her mind made her think of that entertainer on *The Ed Sullivan Show*, who kept five plates spinning on sticks stacked on a table while the orchestra played music at an increasingly frantic pace.

She had decided it was best to wait until after the interview before telling Murray about Billy so as not to throw him off his game. Murray was Old School and wrote the book on establishing endowment funds. Grace was hired ostensibly to replace him when he retired–supposedly in a year or two. Grace had her misgivings about whether Murray would ever actually retire–he was too much of a workaholic–and in her quieter moments, she questioned whether she would be up to the task of replacing him. But she also knew if she wanted to create a better life for Slade, perhaps even a home of their own, she would have to raise her game on the professional level.

She made small talk with Murray as he was being mic'd up prior to the interview, but not being able to tell ANYONE was taking a toll on her. She fidgeted and went to put her hands in her pockets to calm down before remembering she had opted for a red wrap-around dress instead of her usual pants and blouse. "Why don't these stupid dresses come with pockets?" she grumbled to no one in particular.

At last, the interview was done, and Murray thanked the reporter while disengaging from the microphone.

"How'd I do?" he asked Grace.

"Terrific!" Grace exclaimed, despite not having a clue as to what he talked about and therefore having no idea whether the interview went well.

"Listen," she said. "I have to tell you something."

"You know, it's nice to see you wearing a dress for a change, Grace," Murray said, either not hearing her or not caring. "You have a nice figure. I don't understand why you don't show it off more. I guess it takes an opportunity to impress these Hot Shot TV Guys in New York City to bring out the woman in you."

"I dress professionally," Grace said, momentarily taken aback by the inappropriate non-sequitur and therefore sounding more defensive than intended. "Regardless, I don't see how this is..."

She stopped, realizing this was a discussion she did not want to have at this moment, in this location.

"Listen, Murray. I have some disturbing news. Billy Bate died last night."

The administrator let out a long, low whistle.

"How? Was it sudden? Was he sick? No, he wasn't sick. I saw him just last week at the Board meeting," Murray said, rubbing his chin. "What happened?"

"He was at a concert at Radio City Music Hall with his

family. Just sat down, put his head back, and died in his seat. They stopped the show and everything."

"Goddamn. Billy would have loved that. Did you tell Biscuit?" Murray asked.

"No," Grace said. "I thought it could wait until you told him since there wasn't a potential scandal or anything requiring Biscuit's immediate attention."

"I'll go back to the campus and talk to him. He never liked Billy, you know. That's why he poached you. Just to stick it to Billy."

Murray paused to think while Grace pondered how to process that bit of information.

"Billy pledged some big money. Do what you have to do to keep that pipeline open," he told Grace. "Do you have a relationship with the widow? Is she board material? What is her name again?"

Grace snickered. *Was she a smart, innovative, and polished businesswoman worthy of being on a board of directors?* she asked herself. *No. Would the male jackasses running the school at this point fall all over themselves trying to impress and engage a woman with Melinda Bate's looks and resources, now that Billy was gone? Undoubtedly.*

"I'll have to think about that," Grace replied. "Perhaps I can work with her over the next few days on the funeral and keep an eye on her with that in mind."

"Sounds like a plan," Murray said. "Do what you have to do. I'll take care of Biscuit."

Grace told Murray she would take the LIRR to Mockingbird Heights, where Carpe Diem was headquartered, and call him later. They parted, and Grace walked the 20 blocks to Penn Station so she could clear her head before catching a train back to Long Island. Thank God she opted for the low heels, choosing comfort and functionality over aesthetics. She thought about Murray insinuating she was trying to impress TV executives.

Do I really dress that poorly? she wondered as she walked up Sixth Avenue. Then she started thinking about the last time she had seen Billy. He did not look well, but in the six years-plus she had known him, she would never describe his health as robust. He regarded sleep as a necessary evil, not something to look forward to at the end of the day. He smoked like a Chevy Nova in Cuba, and when it came to food, if it was green and good for you, he wouldn't eat it.

Unless it was green Froot Loops.

When Billy entertained business guests at his restaurant–often with Grace at his side–he made a point to tell the waitress, "Don't put anything green on the plate." One day, the chef, as a joke, accompanied Billy's order with a side dish of green Froot Loops. Everybody at the table laughed. Afterward, Billy told the chef to bring the Froot Loops every time he ate there. For Grace, the joke got old fast, but the guests–and Billy–loved it.

Grace arrived at Penn Station and bought a ticket to Mockingbird Heights. She felt a need to be there, and while Melinda made it clear she welcomed Grace's help, Grace was not sure if her arrival would be welcomed by her former fellow employees, as it had been nearly a year since she left Billy's employ. With a few minutes to kill before her train departed, she decided to get some more change so she could use a pay phone to call Tom "Doc" Ronkee, the public relations consultant Billy had on retainer.

Ronkee was based in Manhattan and had little regard for his Long Island client. But that did not stop him from cashing Billy's checks. He did what he could to elevate Billy's sophistication, but as he said often, "You can take the man out of Massapequa, but you can't take Massapequa out of the man." One night, for instance, he accompanied them to a black-tie dinner at the Marriott Marquis. After dinner, Billy and Melinda offered to take Doc home to his Manhattan apartment in their limo. Once ensconced in the car, they immediately lit up cigarettes. Ronkee looked at Grace and rolled his eyes. As the limo inched through traffic, Doc spoke excitedly about this new thing called "the Internet," about how he found himself in a "chat room" with Roman Polanski discussing how to make a movie, even though Polanski was in France and Doc was in New York.

"I still can't believe I got to discuss filmmaking with Roman Polanski," Doc said.

Neither Billy nor Melinda knew a thing about the Internet, but agreed with Doc and even suggested it was the greatest thing ever. Then they each simultaneously lit up another cigarette, signifying the conversation was over. The car remained silent for the few minutes it took to get to Doc Ronkee's apartment building and, once there, Doc climbed out and said his goodbyes. As soon as he closed the door, Billy and Melinda turned to Grace and, in unison, said, "All right. Who the fuck is Roman Polanski?"

Putting up a false front came naturally to Billy, like the time he met with Father Macchiato and Sister Luke from the local parish. The priest and nun, both younger than you might expect but reserved in nature, sat on the couch in Billy's office. Billy parked himself behind his desk, and Grace took the same position to Billy's right that she took during meetings because that's where Billy wanted her, as if Grace were his Consigliere. The priest told Billy about a parish problem and how he was the only one who could help them.

Billy listened intently as Father Macchiato explained why they were there with their hands out. As the priest spoke, Grace looked over at Billy and, for the first time, noticed several pornographic magazines on the floor behind him. The juxtaposition was jarring. In front of Billy were a man and a woman of the cloth begging for money while representing everything good. Behind him, sordidness published by people who had plenty of money. That was Billy's life: compassion and virtue paired with depravity like a Black & White cookie.

Father Macchiato finished explaining his situation and asked if Billy could help. Billy smiled and picked up the phone, dialing controller Mitch Schoop's extension. "Bring me 10 for Saint James," Billy said, his way of telling Schoop to cut a $10,000 check. The four sat there, not saying anything, waiting for Schoop to show up with the money. Once he did, Father Macchiato and Sister Luke stood up to leave. Grace got the sense that they had noticed the magazines and wanted to get out as soon as they had what they came for.

"Thank you, Billy. Thank you for everything," Father Macchiato said, "Having you in our parish is like having a saint walk among us."

Billy laughed. "You're just saying that because you see me every Sunday right up front." Billy attended the 9:30 am Sunday Mass, but only when he got up early enough to ensure a front row seat for him and Melinda. Billy believed being seen near the altar was good for his image. Melinda accompanied him under protest.

"God is everywhere," Father Macchiato said. "He doesn't care where you sit. What matters most to Him is what you are thinking and doing with your life." They shook hands, and Grace led the priest and the nun out of the building with no further discussion.

Ronkee earned his nickname by referring to his PR specialty–the post-crisis public relations campaign–as "the healing process." Doc and Grace spoke regularly, even after she left Billy's employ, and the conversations always started with

Doc launching into a stream of snarky comments about Billy. Knowing this going in, Grace had to speak up right away. A quarter only goes so far on a pay phone.

"Doc, I need to talk to you," Grace said, trying to be heard over travelers moving about in the train station, none of whom knew or cared about Billy.

"Let me guess," he said. "Billy wants to create bobbleheads in his image. No wait, even better. He wants to create a Melinda bobblehead, but instead of her head bobbing up and down, her tits jiggle."

"Doc, listen. I need to tell you something," Grace tried again.

"Let me call you back in a few minutes," he said. "I have some coffee brewing. I'll get a cup and call you."

Grace had a train to catch, and she could feel the time allotted to her on the phone about to expire.

"Doc, Billy's dead. He had a heart attack last night. I'll call you when I get to the Heights and have some more details."

"Holy shit," Doc said.

"You said it. Gotta go. Speak to you later."

Grace hung up with Doc and walked briskly to catch her train. She wondered what she would have to do when she got to Mockingbird Heights. She also thought about Pete Santini and Pete Snodgrass. They ran Billy's business for him while he was out doing his side projects. "Billy things," they called them. How would they react to seeing Grace? How did they feel about Billy dying? He was the only boss they ever had, even though they were in their late thirties. Billy taught them everything they knew, but their respect for him waned when he lost interest in the company's day-to-day operations. Billy's thinking it was funny to refer to them as Pete and Re-Pete, which he did often, did not help matters.

Grace also considered the transition question. Who was in

Billy's will? Besides running his businesses, Billy was a certified public accountant and a certified financial planner. Grace did not doubt that Billy's succession plan was delineated down to the smallest detail regarding who got what. Grace wondered if Billy was going to "reward" his staffers for their loyalty to him.

Then Grace remembered she was a witness to Billy signing his will a few years prior, although he wouldn't let her read it. *Looks like I finally get to find out what is in it*, Grace thought, and smiled a little.

Chapter 10

Return to Carpe Diem

The train pulled into the Mockingbird Heights station. Grace got off and walked the half-mile to the building where Billy ran his company, Carpe Diem Construction Camps. He built the business from scratch and was successful enough to live extravagantly. Carpe Diem is a Latin term and means "seize the day," which Billy cited as his favorite expression and life philosophy. Billy worked hard as a young man to build the company and was determined to squeeze every bit of fun out of life to make up for lost time.

Carpe Diem Construction Camps was similar to the fantasy camps baseball teams make available to their fans. Rather than shagging flies with their childhood baseball heroes for a week, Carpe Diem customers spend a day using construction equipment. Billy conceived the idea when he was working for his father's tiny construction company. They were digging a sewer connection outside an office building when the company's owner came out to monitor their progress. The business owner said he expected them to be further along than they were.

"Why don't you try doing it?" Billy's father, Jack, suggested, and not in a nice way.

"I will," the owner shot back. He climbed into the Bobcat cab and started the engine. His eyes lit up as he worked the levers as if he had done it every day. They couldn't get him out. Even though the executive was wearing a tailored suit, he was thrilled to make the "big shovel thing" move. He looked like a little boy playing with his first Tonka toy on Christmas morning. They let him dig, and he did a decent job, according to Billy, who told the story so often his employees could recite it by heart.

Billy couldn't sleep that night. He kept thinking there had to be more men resigned to a life behind a desk, but deep down yearning to work with their hands doing manly things like construction work. Billy decided to create a business enabling these men to become one with the earth, even if only for a day. He bought some used construction equipment from his father for his campers, as his customers came to be known. Working on property lent to him by a friend, Billy set it up so the campers could dig a hole, load a dump truck with dirt, drive the dump truck to the lot's other side, dump the dirt, and then reverse the process so the property was left intact by day's end. The campers loved it. They dug, they drove, they dumped, and then they did it again. For lunch, Billy provided the campers with Italian heroes and cold beer. They ate by the "construction site" and talked about sports, girls, and cars.

Carpe Diem was a big hit, and soon, Billy was opening camps across the country. He franchised the concept and traveled everywhere to make sure the franchisees did everything according to his specifications. Over the course of nearly 20 years, he had everything set up so "Pete and Re-Pete" could handle day-to-day responsibilities themselves, freeing Billy to pursue his many side interests. At that point, Billy hired Grace to coordinate them.

Walking to the Carpe Diem office helped calm Grace's nerves, and she was glad she opted to wear comfortable shoes. *Women are so much smarter than men, except when it comes to wearing shoes*, Grace thought. *Most guys couldn't care less about how their shoes affect their appearance. They just want to be comfortable.*

As she walked through the front door at Carpe Diem headquarters, she saw Rosalita, the receptionist who started with Billy years earlier, at her usual post. Billy loved to tell people Rosalita's ability to "answer the phone with a smile" was the secret to his company's success, but the puffiness and dark circles around her eyes indicated Rosalita wasn't smiling much this morning. Rosalita hit the buzzer to let Grace in from the lobby, and once in, Grace headed down the hall to find Pete and Re-Pete.

Although Pete Santini was already working for Billy when Billy hired Pete Snodgrass, it wasn't clear who was Pete and who was Re-Pete. Santini joined the company when he was still in high school. Billy liked him immediately and paid his way through college and then for his MBA. Because he believed in education, Billy had a standing offer to pay for anyone who worked for him to attend college, even the construction equipment maintenance workers. Pete Santini and Grace were the only Carpe Diem Construction Camp employees to take advantage of this policy.

The other Pete, Pete Snodgrass, saw himself as special for a variety of reasons, not the least of which being that he was first cousins with the actress Carrie Snodgrass. His co-workers had a nickname for him behind his back: Snob Ass. His demeanor reminded Grace of a saying her grandfather used many times:

"He thinks his bathroom doesn't need a fan." Snodgrass started working for Billy right after graduating from college.

Pete and Re-Pete, despite sharing the same first name, had little in common other than their long-time service to their employer. Santini was raised in Queens, one of New York City's five boroughs, while Snodgrass was a born-and-raised suburbanite. Santini was stocky, with well-defined muscles and a shock of thick, dark hair that matched his dark, inset eyes. Snodgrass was more of a fair-haired boy. Blond, wispy locks that hung down over his forehead, which, combined with his light blue eyes, might give one the impression he was a surfer dude in a previous life. He wasn't. They worked in sync since neither wanted to blow the sweet deal they had: six-figure salaries, company car, out the door by 5:05. Grace knew they would be together in Snodgrass' office because that's where they went anytime they needed to circle the wagons. Grace walked in, and Pete Snodgrass looked up.

"Grace Duffy! What the hell are you doing here?"

Chapter 11

Grief Visits Carpe Diem

The whole time she worked at Carpe Diem, Grace sensed Snodgrass tolerated her because the time Billy spent on his side projects reduced his opportunities to look over Snodgrass' shoulder. The downside? Billy's adventures cost money. Sometimes lots of money, like the time he invested a quarter-million dollars in a fantasy camp for pilots who wanted to fly MiG fighter planes. The only problem was that they had to fly them in Ukraine. Arranging travel to such a far-away land was complicated and expensive, so only a few pilots had any interest in making the trip. Billy lost every cent he invested.

Snodgrass' office was a borderline Man Cave, with all the accouterments you'd expect an ambitious, young executive to have: a private bathroom, a television in a cabinet, a mini-refrigerator, and a leather couch. It was almost as nice as Billy's office, although Snodgrass' bathroom was smaller, out of necessity. The boss always has to have the nicest office in the building. It's just the law.

Grace reached over Pete Snodgrass' mahogany desk to shake his hand. Snodgrass seemed more rattled than grieving, but still had the presence of mind to sneak a peek down Grace's dress as she leaned forward. Pete Santini was sitting on the couch to the left, looking like somebody had punched him in the stomach without warning.

"What do you think?" Snodgrass asked. "Fucking Billy. We all saw it coming. But still. This is wild."

Snodgrass was never sentimental, so Grace wasn't expecting a boo-hoo from him. Santini, on the other hand, was red-eyed and quiet. He was the closest Billy had to a friend among his employees because his tenure with the company dated back to the days when Billy still worked with his father's construction company.

"I'm sorry for your loss. This has to be quite a shock," Grace said, "although based on how Billy lived his life, no one could have or should have been surprised."

"How did you hear?" Snodgrass asked. "What brings you to The Heights?"

"Melinda called my sister this morning, and then I called Melinda," Grace said. "I had some work to do in the city and figured I could be helpful if I came here afterward. Is there anything I can do?"

"We're all right," Snodgrass said. "But if that bitch thinks she's taking over the company, she's sadly mistaken. Pete and I have been covering Billy's ass long enough. He hasn't paid a Carpe Diem bill in months and spent whatever money we made faster than a congressman up for re-election. I'm not—we're not—going to put up with it anymore," Snodgrass said, gesturing over to the other Pete as he said it.

"Have you spoken to Melinda yet?" Grace asked.

"The first thing she did this morning was padlock Billy's office," Santini said. "A fucking padlock! Like none of us could be trusted. I can't imagine what she has in mind for this place.

If Billy put her in charge, then we have a problem. A problem with a capital P."

So much for the grieving process.

Pete and Re-Pete sat in their respective seats, contemplating what fate had brought them for breakfast. Grace told them she was going to see how the others were doing, but she wanted to leave because she did not want to say anything more until she had spoken directly with Melinda.

There was little need for management besides Pete and Re-Pete. Mitch Shoop was the company controller, but his primary function was to provide Billy with petty cash. Katie McCourt was in charge of personnel. She had started with the company as Snodgrass' secretary, earning her sympathy from her co-workers. No one knew for sure what Candee Coyne did, but she introduced Billy to Melinda, and he was so grateful, Candee's job was forever safe.

Candee hated her name. Her father, she said, had a warped sense of humor. On more than one occasion, Billy said he could empathize with Candee because he hated his name, too. "If you've heard one 'Master Bate' joke, you've heard them all," was how he put it. Candee was also a Billy favorite because she was a single mom like Grace and many of the women who worked for Billy. He felt a single mom made for a loyal employee because she was less likely to quit a secure situation.

Carpe Diem Construction Camps was housed in an office building considered spacious, even luxurious, by Mockingbird Heights' standards, but the original Carpe Diem building wasn't much to look at. A few years back, Billy jumped on the opportunity to buy the building next door so he could expand his empire. He spent a small fortune re-doing the office so it would, as he put it, "match my business brilliance." He wanted everything to be perfect, and the construction dragged on for weeks. At one point, when things were at their messiest, Grace witnessed a conversation between Billy and the contractor overseeing the project. Billy questioned why there were three poles in the hallway, which was created when the two buildings were joined.

The contractor explained they were necessary because they were load-bearing.

"Don't worry, they'll be covered," the contractor said. "They won't look so bad."

"I don't worry and I don't care," Billy said. "I'm not spending the rest of my life looking at those poles."

"If you want to move them, it's going to add six weeks to the project and cost another 75 grand," the contractor said.

The three of them stood amidst a construction mess, with blue tarps barely keeping out March's wet and cold. Most people would have listened to the contractor and compromised. Most people were not Billy. He did not want to look at those poles. He knew if he conceded and kept the poles, they would taunt him, telling him he let others impose their visions on his will. Like most successful entrepreneurs, selling his vision short was unacceptable.

"I don't care," Billy repeated, "Lose the poles."

The poles were gone within the week, and neither the delays nor the extra cost were as significant as the contractor predicted. After the construction was done, Grace remembered that conversation every time she walked down the hall, as well as the time Billy said this to her: "Most people accept what life offers without questioning or contemplating whether it can be better. That's why they aren't successful."

Billy's new office complex included a special room designed specifically to house his extensive library of "personal growth" books on CDs and cassette tapes. Billy attributed his success to what he learned from Wayne Dyer, Napoleon Hill, Zig Ziglar, Earl Nightingale, Brian Tracy, and others. He instructed and encouraged his employees to borrow the materials. In the six-plus years Grace worked for Billy, Grace was the only one who took advantage because she wanted to understand Billy better.

Piloting his own plane was another source of Billy's optimism. "Whenever things get too cloudy or gloomy," he said to Grace on one occasion, "all I have to do is get in my plane and fly over the clouds. Once you do, the sun is shining and everything is all right with the world." Grace believed Billy's optimism rubbed off on her, although there was the one occasion when Grace's tendency to see things in as bright a light as possible almost earned her a trip to the unemployment line.

Billy and Grace were attending a business dinner when Billy's cell phone buzzed. After listening for a bit, Billy ended the call, turned to Grace, and said, "They're taking Mrs. Peterson off her life support," referring to his sixth-grade teacher with whom he had only recently been reunited.

"That's great!" Grace thought this meant she was doing better. It did not occur to her that the only reason people are taken off life support is so they can die in peace. The expression on Billy's face made Grace realize her mistake.

Billy had often credited Mrs. Peterson with helping him turn his life around. Billy was not setting the world on fire academically in grade school, and one day, his lackadaisical work habits drove Mrs. Peterson over the edge. "Dammit, Billy, you can do this," she said as she threw a piece of chalk at him. "You're smart. You have to do the work."

This marked the first time in Billy's life he had heard positive reinforcement. His mother referred to Billy as her "thorn among the roses" because he was the middle child between an older and a younger sister. Any attempt on his part to impress his father was met with derisive comments such as, "Are you sure you're not adopted?" The elder Bate laughed heartily every time he said it. So the teacher's encouragement unleashed the mental prowess of a little boy used to mental beatdowns. He was smart. He did have something to offer.

As Billy came to appreciate the teacher's impact on his life, he tried to contact her so he could express his gratitude, but the elementary school he attended had been closed for years. The Internet was not fully developed at this point, so he hired a private detective. Still no trace. During Grace's first conversation with Billy, the subject of grade schools came up. Grace mentioned her neighbor was a retired grade school teacher who taught in the school Billy attended, and she reached out to him on Billy's behalf. Turns out Mrs. Peterson had remarried, changed her name, and moved, which was why Billy could not find her. With Grace's intervention, Billy and his sixth-grade teacher were reunited, and she was thrilled to learn she had had such a positive impact on him. Then Mrs. Peterson became ill. Grace felt good about her role in bringing them together before she died.

Grace took all this in as she walked around Billy's "Positive Attitude Library." She wondered what would happen to the hundreds of books and cassettes. Would the widow let Grace have them, knowing what they meant to her? She could have asked Melinda right there and then, because when Grace looked up, she noticed Mrs. Melinda Bate standing in the doorway.

Chapter 12

Melinda Dresses Down the Petes

Grace stepped back to measure how Melinda was holding up without being too obvious about it. Her porcelain skin encapsulated eyes that were dark and alluring, serving as a fortress for her soul. Only two men were able to get past those eyes. One was Rick Strutt, her first husband and James' father. He had the body–and brains–of a Greek statue. The other was Billy. Melinda's first marriage dissolved when she discovered Strutt in bed with another man. "I should have known he was gay when he didn't try to fuck me right away like the others," she said to Grace on the one occasion when his name came up.

When Billy and Melinda met, she was living with her son James in a one-bedroom apartment in Rum Junction, a town on Long Island's East End, where the workers who catered to The Hamptons glitterati resided. There were whispers that Melinda was friends with Candee because they both worked for an escort service to supplement their meager incomes, but Grace worked to avoid paying attention to office gossip. The idea that someone with the given name Candee would become an escort seemed too contrived.

"I'm so sorry for your loss, Melinda," Grace said, stepping forward to hug her. As she did so, it occurred to her that this was the first time their bodies ever came in contact. No hugs, no greeting kiss, not even a handshake. "Thou shalt not touch anybody that belonged to Billy," was the unwritten rule. You weren't allowed to touch the building's walls, either.

"Thank you. We've got a lot to do," she said and then turned on her heel to walk toward Billy's office. Grace took it upon herself to follow and, as she did, she better understood the power Melinda had over most men and, it turns out, some women. It was her job to stay in top shape and look great so Billy could show her off at black-tie dinners, and she did her job well. Grace wondered what Melinda would do when she got to Billy's office. Would she sit behind Billy's desk? Nobody sat in Billy's chair because entering Billy's office in his absence was verboten, the exception being his secretary, Martha. Soon, Grace would have a better understanding of why this was so, but for now, she was curious to see whether Melinda would sit where no one other than Billy had ever ventured before and, if she did, how awkward it would be.

It was awkward. For Grace, anyway.

Melinda walked into the office and sat in Billy's chair without the slightest hesitation. She picked up Billy's cell phone–he was one of the first on Long Island to have one–and started playing with it when Pete and Re-Pete came in. If Melinda squatted over a framed photo of Billy and left a big turd on Billy's face, the fellows could not have looked any more disgusted than they did seeing her sit in their former boss' chair.

"Listen, Melinda," Pete Snodgrass said. "I can't believe Billy's dead. I can't say I'm surprised by the way he smoked and worked all those hours. My cousin, Carrie Snodgrass, had a friend who..."

"I don't give a shit about your cousin," Melinda blurted.

"Do you have anything to report to me about Carpe Diem? Are there any problems I need to deal with right now?"

"Uh, no...No, not at all," Pete Snodgrass said.

"How 'bout you?" she barked at Pete Santini, whose face was frozen in astonishment. Billy never spoke to Pete Snodgrass like that. Snodgrass was Billy's golden boy. Pete Santini said nothing.

"My husband dropped dead on me last night, so you'll excuse me if I don't have time for pleasantries," Melinda said. "I need you both to make sure this business keeps taking in cash while I handle this funeral bullshit. Any questions?"

They both mumbled "no" and left Billy's office. Grace stifled a chortle, as it was the first time she had ever seen Snodgrass verbally undressed. Ironically, Snodgrass and Santini had been "making sure the cash kept coming" once Billy lost interest in the day-to-day operations a few years back. The cash was used to fund Billy's side projects, even though they did more to feed his ego than grow the business. As they left the office, they were too angry to hear Melinda mutter "assholes" under her breath. She turned to Grace and told her to sit.

"Pete and Re-Pete my ass," Melinda said. "Snodgrass hates me because I'm a woman and a Hispanic, and Santini was too busy doing whatever Billy told him to do to grow a pair. I have no use for either one." Melinda paused. "We–Betty and I–are heading over to the funeral home later. Can you join us?" she asked.

Grace said she would. Then Betty Bate came into the office. At some point, she had confessed to Grace that she decided to become a psychologist so she could better understand what made her father tick. Billy treated his daughter like a princess. She did nothing to discourage him from doing so, but she could never get Billy to accept her fiancé, Jeff Doomey, even though Jeff loved Betty and also treated her like a princess, which is challenging when you're not the king.

Melinda asked Grace to leave her and Betty alone for a moment. As Grace left the office, she told them she would reach out to the local media and start coordinating coverage of Billy's passing. She set off to find a desk, a phone, and, with any luck, something to eat. *This obituary should not be a big problem*, she thought. *The media loves it when rich, successful businessmen drop dead at such a young age.*

Grace figured this was a good time to call Doc Ronkee back and made the call. Doc bypassed hello and fired his first question: "Who, or what, is a Homer's Drool?"

Grace explained. "The Drool," as they were known amongst fans and those in the music industry, was Betty's favorite band, named after the salivating sound Homer Simpson makes when he's turned on—usually by doughnuts with pink frosting.

"Oh, for God's sake," Doc said. "Well, what do we know about Billy's life? How do we explain who Billy was? Is it possible to tell his life story without mentioning the calendar?"

Grace winced. One reason Grace knew she had to leave Billy's employ stemmed from Billy creating a calendar from pictures Billy took of Melinda in various poses while wearing skimpy bikinis, including one where Melinda was spread-eagled across the hood of the Corvette he bought her. The picture was taken on the Brooklyn Promenade with the Manhattan skyline in the background. He then sent the calendar to every prominent Long Islander he had met and many more who never heard of him or Melinda. Grace coordinated the mailing and wrote the letter that accompanied it. It was not her proudest moment professionally.

Grace let out a long exhale and said, "Let me tell you everything I know about Billy. Maybe you can make some sense out of his life. I sure as hell couldn't, despite the many hours spent riding in Billy's limo with Billy and Melinda, coming back from the various black-tie dinners Billy loved to attend. Also, unbeknownst to Mr. Bate, I got to know his widow and his ex-wife well."

"Really?"

"Billy trusted me around Melinda, and you learn a lot from a woman when you are willing to listen and can be trusted to keep everything you hear locked in the vault. Melinda told me more than once that her ability to confide in me meant the world to her."

"What about the ex-wife? I think her name was Marietta," Doc said.

Grace chuckled. "He used to send me to his Marietta's house to 'drop things off.' Her payroll check and whatever. I had to go there at least once a week. Billy told me to take my time whenever I visited. He wanted me to look for signs his wife was dating or had a man in her life."

"You mean ex-wife?" Ronkee asked.

"Wife. Billy didn't officially divorce Marietta until days before he married Melinda."

"Wasn't he screwing around on Marietta?" Doc asked.

"Religiously," Grace replied. "But in Billy's world, what was good for the gander was not necessarily good for the goose. The only evidence of a male in her life was her cat, Frank."

"Did you resent being used as a messenger and a spy?" Doc asked.

"I did at first," Grace said. "But as I got to know Marietta, I found myself looking forward to our visits. She felt comfortable with me and shared some personal information. I'm not sure if she did it because she needed to unburden herself or tease me. There was some juicy information in there. To a certain extent, I knew what it was to be a Catholic priest and have somebody share their innermost secrets with you, but you can't tell a soul. It was a burden to honor my commitment to her."

Grace had no problem keeping Marietta's secrets because she had one of her own. She ached to share it with Doc as she needed his guidance, but she dared not bring it up because after she brought it up with Billy, she regretted doing so immediately.

Chapter 13

Everyone Has AN EGO

"Seems to me everyone mentioned so far has an ego," Catherine said to Angelo.

"Don't kid yourself," Angelo said. "We all have one. But it's like Tesla says, 'We are all one. Only egos, beliefs, and fears separate us.'"

"Tesla? The car guy?" Catherine asked.

"Sort of," Angelo replied. "Elon Musk owns the car company that makes the Tesla electric cars. He named them after Nikola Tesla, a brilliant scientist who pioneered the use of alternating current electricity. He also got screwed over by Westinghouse and Edison, to name a few. Talk about egos!"

"I meant the kind of ego that drives you to succeed in business," Catherine replied. "The kind I hope to discuss in my thesis."

"Oh, yes, the thesis," Angelo said. "What exactly is the topic again?"

"The role ego plays in leading a successful enterprise," Catherine answered.

"Ah. Well, Edison would be an excellent case study here, as

well, but I suppose you want to focus on something a little more contemporary."

They sat in silence for a few moments on the deck overlooking the bay. There were remnants of sandwiches and chips on the plates on the white deck table made from polyurethane. The gentle rippling of the Great South Bay lapping at the shoreline could be heard in the background, and the occasional, unidentified bird circled about, looking for God knows what. Catherine hoped her reminding Angelo about her thesis topic might spur some further comment from Angelo or even perhaps–dare she dream–a positive remark regarding the unique nature of her topic.

"What made you choose that for a topic?" Angelo asked.

"I'm always trying to figure out why some people succeed while others–most people, in fact–fail, or at least come up short in life," Catherine said. "We read about the success enjoyed by famous celebrities or captains of industry, and almost always at some point it's noted that he or she–mostly he, though–has a quote-unquote big ego. Why is that? And, if that is indeed the case, is a big ego necessary to succeed in life? Are humble people dooming themselves to a life of misery just because they're humble?"

"I suppose that depends on your definition of success, and misery, for that matter," Angelo said. "Not everybody wants to be rich and famous. Some people are perfectly content leading rather ordinary lives, lives that may appear miserable to you, quite frankly."

"Let me tell you a story about a business owner," Angelo said. "Not our friend Billy. We'll get back to him. A different man. He made paper goods, like paper party plates and the like, on Long Island, an expensive place to manufacture such items. He was offered $4 million, cash on the barrelhead, by a state government down south to move his business there, Georgia, I think it was.

"Now, the business owner was Jewish. An Iranian Jew, in fact. He said to me, 'What the hell is an Iranian Jew going to do with himself in Georgia?' He also expressed concern about the available workforce there. Say what you want about Long Islanders, but we work harder, smarter, and faster than anywhere.

"So the business owner flies down to Georgia to meet with potential workers. He tells me, 'I'm interviewing one fellow. I ask him about working overtime. He said he doesn't work overtime. I ask, "Why not?" He says, 'Why bother? The government is going to take it all away.' I say, "Not all of it." He said, 'Enough that it's not worth the effort.' I say, "Sure, it is." He says, 'No, it's not.'

"We go back and forth like this for a few minutes. Finally, the fellow puts his hands up, as if to signal 'enough.' "I tell you what," the man says. "I work eight hours a day. I buy a six-pack of beer on my way home and drink it while watching TV in my double-wide trailer. I'm a very happy man."

After telling me this, the business owner turns to me and says. "I own and operate my own business. I have access to helicopters, limousines, and dine at the finest restaurants. But I also work 20 hours a day, seven days a week, and am under constant stress. So who's the schmuck here?"

Catherine waited to make sure that was the whole story. After a moment, she said, "I'm not sure I get your point."

"The point is," Angelo said, "The business owner was a success, as you put it, but the worker in the double-wide was happy while the quote-unquote rich man, not so much."

"Seems to me nobody's all that happy at Carpe Diem, either," Catherine said. "I mean, I realize the man died, but even before that, nobody seemed too thrilled with life."

"I noticed that, too, as I got to know the players involved," Angelo said. "Rather ironic, when you consider that Billy, by most measurements, had truly 'won' at the game of life. And he had all those personal development tapes, all that information regarding the power of positive thinking. Sadly, he also had his peccadillos and demons."

"Like what? Anything juicy?" Catherine asked, sitting up straighter and then leaning forward.

"Now you're thinking like a real journalist," Angelo said. "Let me walk you through some of the back stories passed on to me by Grace and some of the folks involved, so you have a better understanding of what's going on and what makes the players involved tick."

Part III

The Back Stories

Chapter 14

The Monkeys Scream

Dealing with sudden loss was nothing new for Grace or Grail. Grace was in the throes of her senior year of high school, in Massapequa, on New York's Long Island. Between planning her prom, playing field hockey and lacrosse, she waited for word from the six colleges she had applied to, ranging from the reach of Brown University to the safety of Gibbons College. She was no different than most girls in her situation. Grail was already attending Gibbons, studying to be a teacher.

One spring day, their attorney father, Dan Duffy, was in the county courthouse, working *pro bono* to protect an elderly neighbor from losing her house due to a tax bill languishing unnoticed and unpaid because it came due the same week her husband died. Doing so served as a nice break from the work he normally did—processing paragraphs on paper to ensure face-less corporations got the best deal possible.

Walking through the courthouse lobby, he crossed paths with a corrections officer named Vinny. Vinny was in the midst of a difficult divorce from a spiteful woman determined to poison his relationship with their four children. After completing an overnight shift, dealing with society's worst human dregs, he headed directly to the courthouse for another round of custody battles with the court personnel he believed did nothing more than serve as pawns in his soon-to-be ex-wife's game.

Weeks prior, Vinny had fired his attorney. "Why should I pay somebody $250 an hour to tell me, 'What are you going to do?' That's the way it is," he said to anyone who would listen, and more often than not, that included co-workers who could not get away from him. "Everything is designed to come down in the woman's favor. The process is twisted and manipulated on purpose, so you have to have an attorney...guaranteeing work for those bastards. Screw it. I'm not playing along."

So he didn't. He represented himself and lost at every turn. Every ruling against him spawned another chattering monkey in his brain. Soon, the monkeys told him it was time to do something. "The system will crush you if you don't push back," the monkeys said, over and over, loud and intense like a late-night television commercial, as Vinny walked through the courthouse lobby.

"There's an attorney! Probably on his way to screw over a divorced dad somewhere in the building," the monkeys screeched in unison upon seeing Dan Duffy. Vinny remembered his service revolver strapped to his ankle, which he had with him because he was able to bypass the metal detectors at the courthouse entrance simply by showing his correctional officer's badge. "Take him out! Take him out! Take him out!" the monkeys screeched. "Show him who's the boss. Show him Vinny won't be fucked with. Teach the son-of-a-bitch a lesson!"

Vinny reached for his service revolver, dropped to one knee, and took aim. Pop! One bullet, right between the eyes. Dan Duffy spun and was dead before he hit the marble floor.

Blood flowed out of his nose as everyone else in the lobby scrambled for cover. Soon, the screaming started. Not the monkeys, though. They were happy and quite impressed with Vinny's marksmanship. The screaming came from the woman who ran the coffee kiosk in the courthouse lobby. It also jarred Vinny back to this reality, and in a flash, he realized what he had done. He didn't push back against the system. There is no pushing back against the system. The system rolls on without end. No, Vinny had killed a total stranger who loved his wife and kids. Vinny had no way of knowing this, and the monkeys couldn't care less, but he understood he had crossed a line. He also knew what to do next. He pointed the gun at his temple and pulled the trigger, saving the system time and money. Grace and her family, on the other hand, paid dearly for Vinny's actions.

Chapter 15

Making Slade

Dan Duffy had no life insurance and made no provisions for ensuring a steady income for his wife and daughters should he no longer be able to provide for them. No college fund, no IRA nest egg, no cash stashed under a floorboard in the den. Dan Duffy spent so much time helping others, like his elderly neighbor widow, that he neglected the home fires. The "system" wasn't much help, either. Vinny's "estate" didn't amount to much, but whatever was there was not going to be had without a prolonged legal battle with the woman who quickly discovered a "grieving widow" bore more financial benefits than "soon-to-be ex-wife." And legal action against "the system" for letting a corrections officer past security with a loaded pistol would be pointless and protracted, because "the system" protects those in it first and foremost.

Grace and Grail's mother drifted off to sleep on the first anniversary of her husband's murder and never woke up. The house was sold to clear the family's financial obligations. Grail and Grace were barely out of high school but on their own. Both were athletic and competitive, and they parlayed those skill sets and their good grades into scholarships at Gibbons. Grail got her degree in education, secured a teacher's position as soon as she graduated, and married Ron Satori, another teacher who subsequently made a nice living developing learning centers for challenged students. The babies came soon after.

Grace sought adventure after securing a communications degree. Neither provided much value, but her desire to live her life fully attracted her to Drex. They talked often about traveling the world together, but their conversations went no further than the bedroom, where wanderlust gave way to plain lust. Drex's piercing blue eyes, seemingly permanent facial stubble and a butt so tight you could use it to play bongos took Grace to places she never knew existed with any other beau.

Grail warned Grace about Drex, to no avail. The last time Grail brought up the topic, Grace ended the discussion with, "You want safe, and that's fine. I don't want to know I'm going to get laid because it's Saturday," Grace said. "I like thinking that at any given moment, my man is going to yank off my panties and take me right there and then. On the countertop. Against the filing cabinet. Whenever. Whatever."

"Suit yourself," Grail said. "It's your life."

One such spontaneous episode took place on a kitchen table, in lieu of breakfast. Grace, dressed for work in a silky blouse and long, loose skirt, couldn't take her eyes off Drex as he made a pot of coffee wearing a well-worn pair of jeans and nothing else. He picked up on her vibe, and the next thing Grace knew, her heels were in the air as Drex's jeans dropped to his ankles. With her butt on the edge of the table, hands around his neck and legs wrapped around his tight cheeks he took her hard, deep and fast. There was a flash, and she could feel his manhood explode inside her, bringing her to an orgasm that left her breathless and quivering.

It was over as quickly as it started, but it still put Grace behind schedule. She rearranged her disheveled skirt and blouse but left her panties on the floor–the sexual equivalent of a mic drop. The effect of which was somewhat diminished by the realization that she would be the one to pick them up off the floor later because Drex couldn't be bothered. Once in the car, Grace's legs were so shaky she could hardly drive. Not that it mattered. The warm, happy throbbing between her thighs rendered her oblivious to her surroundings and caused her to grin uncontrollably. Several weeks later, however, the pee-stick read pink and positive, and the grin was replaced with sobs. Subsequent discussions regarding marriage were lost on Drex. He had no interest in settling down.

Grail wanted to say, "I told you so," but she held her tongue lest she drive a wedge between her and her younger sister. She wanted to be there for Grace, especially when her older-sister radar told her the man involved could not be trusted. And if Grail's radar was pinging during the courtship, it nearly gonged when Grace's child decided to join the Human Race.

Slade's transition started on a quiet Sunday morning. Grace was reading the newspapers and savoring a mug filled with decaffeinated green tea. Then the contractions started, startling Grace because she wasn't due for a month. Drex was supposedly working as a taxi driver to earn some money, but when Grace called the dispatcher's office, they said he hadn't come in that day. Grace then called Grail, who came over immediately, packed Grace's overnight bag, and swept her off to the hospital, leaving the green tea to cool on the kitchen table where the baby was conceived.

As morning turned into afternoon in the maternity ward, it looked as if Slade's arrival would be imminent and Drex-less. Grail guided Grace through the process, and just as the medical crew started entertaining lunch suggestions, Slade made his debut. A beautiful, healthy boy with a full head of his father's hair. Grail cried. Grace cried.

"I wish Mom & Dad were here," Grace said.

"They are, dear," Grail replied. "In spirit, anyway. Too bad the same can't be said for the boy's father."

Grace wanted to be mad at Grail, but she couldn't. Grail was right. Drex should have been there. Grace was torn between being angry at his absence and worried about his well-being. The questions kept dancing around in her head as she fell off to sleep for the first time as a mother: *Where could he be? Why hasn't he called? How could he miss out on the birth of his child?*

Chapter 16

Edging God Out

"So what do you think so far?" Angelo asked.

Catherine muttered something along the lines of "hmmph" and stopped recording. "Seems to me Grace took a trip to the wild side after what happened to her parents, and then maybe recognized the need for a stable environment once the baby came. But Billy sounds like a control freak. Perhaps she over-compensated."

Catherine stood up to stretch, extending her arms to the blue sky while taking a deep breath. Angelo tried not to look, but he couldn't help but notice her full-bodied vitality.

Ah, youth, he mused, and then reminded himself that he was married and even if he wasn't, she was young enough to be his daughter and therefore off-limits.

Catherine returned to her seat on the deck and looked out on the Great South Bay.

"Many entrepreneurs are control freaks," Angelo replied. "When you build something from scratch, there's very little margin for error. One wrong decision, bad investment, or counter-productive hire can bring everything tumbling down. It's like playing Jenga, but in the business world version: if you pull the wrong piece, you lose your money and have nothing to show for your time and effort but a pile of debt and a bunch of pissed off people."

"It's like that quote from Ayn Rand," Catherine offered. "If a businessman makes a mistake, he suffers the consequences. If he fails, he takes the loss. If a bureaucrat makes a mistake, you suffer the consequences. If he fails, he passes the losses on to you."

Angelo was taken aback. He tried to remember the last time he heard someone quote Ayn Rand. He knew whoever it was, he or she wasn't born in the 21st century as Catherine was.

"How do you know about Ayn Rand?" Angelo asked. "I'm fairly certain it wasn't at Mitchel College."

"Well, it was, sort of," Catherine said, happy she had impressed Angelo. "Last semester Doc Zahler had made a derogatory reference to *Atlas Shrugged*, so over the summer I read it just to find out why it pissed him off so much. A lot of my professors have no idea what it takes to run a business, and it shows."

"Tell me about it," Angelo said, relieved to hear such sentiment from a student. Perhaps the Left and its Marxist-leaning professors hadn't completely corrupted the next generation. Perhaps there was hope.

"So how did it get to the point where Billy takes a bunch of people by limo to a Manhattan steakhouse, followed by a great concert at Radio City Music Hall–all on his dime–and yet nobody wanted to be there?" Catherine asked. "And what was in those baggies? Is it possible somebody wanted to expedite his demise? What did the cops have to say? Did anything nefarious show up in the autopsy?"

"Once again, you're thinking like a reporter! Congratulations!" Angelo replied.

"Somehow, during the chaos that ensued between the moment Billy sat back in his seat and when they carted his body out of Radio City, Billy's jacket was removed and then disappeared. Nobody knows–or at least nobody is willing to admit they know–who took the jacket off or what happened to it afterward."

"It just got sucked into the ether?" Catherine asked, with a tinge of incredulity. "That's strange. How about the autopsy? What did that reveal?"

"There was no autopsy."

"Really? I thought that was required?"

"You'd think, right? When I first heard there was no autopsy, I did a little research. Hang on, let me check in with Google." Angelo took out his Smartphone.

"Here it is: The law requires that the chief medical examiner investigate deaths of persons dying from criminal violence, by accident, by suicide, suddenly when in apparent health, when unattended by a physician, in a correctional facility, or any suspicious or unusual manner. The medical examiner is responsible for determining the cause and manner of death."

"Well, Billy's death certainly qualifies," Catherine said. "Did the family object to the autopsy being performed?"

"I wondered the same thing," Angelo said. "But here's what it says on the CME's website: 'Objections to autopsy which are not based on religious beliefs have no standing in the law.'"

"So somebody said something to somebody, or pulled a string somehow, but who?" Catherine pondered. "More importantly, why? Did they NOT want the medical examiner to find something? If my husband or father dropped dead in the prime of his life, I'd sure as hell want to know why."

"Again, great questions, Catherine. I wish I had some great

answers. I wasn't there when all this was going down, but that question kept nagging at me as the players walked me through what they learned and experienced during those three or four days. Just like nobody knows what happened to the jacket, nobody seems to know—or, again, wants to claim to know—how it came to be that a 49-year-old man dropped dead in New York City and no autopsy was performed."

"Doc Zahler said you interviewed a lot of the people involved in all this. Did you ever sit with Melinda?" Catherine asked.

"Unfortunately, no," Angelo replied. "Even if I did, I don't know how I would go down that road without seeming as if I was accusing her of trying to cover up a crime."

"What do you mean?" Catherine asked.

"Let's say she orchestrated the non-autopsy. She either did it because she didn't want the man she loved to be carved up and probed, or she was trying to hide something. If it was the former, then asking about it could be considered hurtful and intrusive, or maybe simply questioning her judgment. If it's the latter, then at best you're accusing her of trying to cover up a homicide."

Now it was Angelo's turn to get up and stretch. As he did, he walked over to the edge of the deck, staring out at the great, watery expanse of Great South Bay as the autumn sun shimmered across the water. Catherine looked on, curious as to what he was going to do or say next, like a student watching the professor walk across the front of the classroom toward the window.

"The whole thing threw me for a loop, Catherine," Angelo said after a few moments of reflection. "There was a time when nobody knew who this guy was. Then Grace goes to work for him and bam! He's a Big Shot. He's on the board of Gibbons

College and a few other prestigious organizations. Charities are honoring him. Reporters call him looking for his insights on Long Island's economy. He even had his picture taken with Jackson Ouellette!"

"Jackson Ouellette! Really? Wow! Why? How?" Catherine asked, genuinely impressed and curious as to how a small Long Island businessman would come to rub elbows with a normally reclusive billionaire.

Angelo chuckled as he sat back down at the table with Catherine.

"Grace gave me the backstory on that," Angelo said. "In the early 1990s, Billy and his entourage were walking through a hotel lobby in New York City, heading to the white limousine. Grace saw Ouellette up ahead of them. She turned to Billy and said, Billy! Don't look now, but Jackson Ouellette's standing over there on the other side of the lobby. Stay here and give me a 10-second head start. I'll head over that way to get in position to take a cool picture, and then you and Melinda go over to introduce yourselves. That'll be a great shot.'"

"Why would Grace have a camera with her?" Catherine interjected.

"Billy insisted Grace have a camera with her at all times, 'just in case.' And what happened in this case justified that seeming extravagance. Billy sauntered over toward Ouellette and introduced himself. Ouellette received him politely and even stuck out his hand for a handshake. Just at that moment, however, Billy pulled back just enough so that the photograph Grace took made it seem as if Ouellette was introducing himself to Billy. It was PR genius, really."

"How did Ouellette react?"

"It didn't matter because what Billy did next was just as curious. Grace disclosed that Billy said–to one of the world's richest men, mind you–'It's too bad your mother named you Jackson. If she had named you Franklin, you'd be five times richer than you are now.'"

"What the hell does that mean?" Catherine asked.

According to Grace, that's the question Ouellette's expression asked.

"Your last name rhymes with wallet, right?" Billy pointed out. 'It's like you were destined to make money. Well, Andrew Jackson is on the twenty-dollar bill. Benjamin Franklin is on the hundred-dollar bill. Since making money was in your destiny, if your mother named you Benjamin or Franklin instead of Jackson, you'd be five times richer.'

"Grace said Ouellette looked at Billy with a blank expression, as if he didn't know how to process what he just heard. Then Ouellette said, 'Well, it was certainly nice to meet you both,' he said, nodding at Melinda and then looking her up and down. Billy had neglected to introduce her. 'My car is waiting for me out front. I have to go.'"

"With that, Grace said, Ouellette brushed past Billy and made a beeline for the front entrance," Angelo said.

"What do you make of all that?" Catherine asked.

Make of what?" Angelo asked in reply.

"The whole thing. Billy ambushing one of the world's richest men? His comment about destiny."

"Billy was once described in print–not by me, mind you–as 'Long Island's answer to Ouellette,'" Angelo said. "So I suppose it was inevitable their paths would cross."

"What about his remark regarding destiny?" Catherine asked. "Do you believe in destiny? Is there some sort of supernatural force that pre-determines whether an entrepreneur is going to quote-unquote make it or not?"

Angelo rubbed his face with his right hand. "Well, clearly

destiny didn't want me owning a bar, at least for too long," he said.

"So you believe in destiny?" Catherine asked.

"Not necessarily," Angelo replied. "At least not in the sense of one's success being predetermined, regardless of what course of action you take."

"What does it take, then?" Catherine pressed further. "How do you know if you're on the right path? Is there a point where the ego kicks in and inspires you to forge ahead despite great odds?"

"The ego serves more like a catalyst," Angelo said. "It motivates you to want to achieve more than keeping a seat warm for 30 years with the hope that whatever you accumulate during that time is enough to sustain you through your remaining years."

"Catalysts send things into motion," Catherine said. "What keeps things in motion? What does an entrepreneur draw upon to keep going, especially during the tough, early times that seem almost like a requirement to go through? Is it inner strength, and if so, how does one go about developing said strength?"

"Inner strength is an absolute necessity to run a successful business or operation," Angelo said. "The most sustainable inner strength comes from faith."

"Faith in what? Yourself? God?"

"Both," Angelo said. "As Neville Goddard once said, 'Your level of self-confidence reflects the extent of your faith in God.' In other words, once you truly believe you are one with God, then you'll understand and embrace that God wants you to succeed and is all-powerful. When that happens, you'll have all the tools you need to navigate the rough seas of running a business. And have a great life, for that matter."

"So you have to be religious to run a business?" Catherine asked, confused and somewhat taken aback at the turn this conversation had taken.

Angelo laughed.

"Quite the contrary," he said. "You can be religious, but that's not going to make or break you. It's more like that passage from Proverbs: 'Trust in the Lord with all your heart and lean not on your understanding. In all your ways acknowledge him, and he shall direct your paths.'"

Catherine pondered the proverb. "That sounds a lot like, 'Let go and let God.'"

"What do you know about let go and let God?" Angelo snorted, a little dubious.

"I took a class in sociology and learned they espouse this course of action in AA," Catherine replied. "They also say, ego stands for 'Edging God Out.'"

"Right," Angelo said. "But you don't have to be a drunk to aspire to live your life by that credo."

"I thought Billy was all about his ego. Do you think Billy let go and let God?"

"That's what I was hoping to find out, Catherine. Like I said, he came out of nowhere, and my hope-slash-intention was to find out how he became such a success. But every time I interviewed him, all he wanted to talk about was his business ventures and philanthropic endeavors. I could not get past that veneer or crack that code to determine what made him tick. After he died, I eventually met with most of his so-called inner circle to see if I could put the pieces together posthumously. What I learned, unfortunately, was so convoluted, so crazy, I just had to walk away, more befuddled than ever. At some point, I decided I really just didn't want to have anything to do with the whole sordid affair.

"I can tell you," Angelo continued, "the stories and experiences shared with me created such a mixed bag of crazy, it's a wonder Billy lasted as long as he did. I'll share some of them with you and then walk you through the rest of the week, leading up to his burial at St. Charles Cemetery. Here it is more than 25 years later, and I still find myself shaking my head."

Chapter 17

'Pequa Pride

"I'll start with Billy," Angelo said. "Like I said earlier, I couldn't get anything out of him about his personal life, but Grace filled in a lot of blanks.

"Billy didn't talk much about it, but over time I learned a few things," Grace told me over coffee one day. "He grew up in Massapequa, which at the time was predominantly blue-collar. Now it caters mostly to the professionals...doctors, lawyers, and bankers."

"Wasn't Seinfeld from Massapequa?" Catherine asked.

"Yeah," Angelo replied. "Seinfeld. So is Alec Baldwin and, for better or worse, Joey Buttafuoco."

"I've heard of Alec Baldwin. He's that old guy actor who shot his movie director on set. Who's Joey Buttafuoco?" Catherine asked, afraid that this was somebody she "should know," like the vice president of the United States or a Supreme Court justice.

"Seriously?" Angelo asked.

Catherine winced, thinking, *I should have pretended to recognize the name.*

Angelo paused. "Now that I think about it, there's no reason you would know who Buttafuoco is. That was well before your time. What a prince."

"Why was he famous?" Catherine asked, curious but not wanting to go too far off topic.

"Explaining that whole mishegoss affair would require a separate meeting," Angelo said, laughing. "Let's just say you're better off not knowing and leave it at that. Ironically, Grace was also from Massapequa.

"Grace said Billy's childhood was defined by two factors: his father's twisted personality and his mother's inability to be happy with anything Billy did. I asked her if he talked much about his parents. She said, 'He once told me about an incident when he was eight that impacted his life. He was pedaling his bicycle back from serving morning Mass...'"

"Serving Mass?" Catherine interjected.

"Yes. Serving Mass. That's what Catholic altar boys do, and Billy was an altar boy, believe it or not."

"I know what 'serving Mass' means. I just can't believe Billy was an Altar boy," Catherine said. "At what point did he stop being a Catholic?"

"Technically, he never did," Angelo said. "Let's just say the lessons never really took. He probably resented the notion that there is room for only one Master of the Universe in the Church," Angelo replied.

"What's that supposed to mean?" Catherine asked, confused.

"Ah, never mind," Angelo said. "According to Grace's retelling of the story, on the way home from Mass, his bike hit a bump. There were no bolts on the front wheel, and it came loose from the frame. The tire rolled up ahead while the bike's front pitched forward and sent Billy flying. He hit the ground hard, landing on his chest with the full weight of his body, maximizing the impact, which knocked the air from his lungs. He lay there on the street for a few minutes, gasping for air, wondering if he had broken anything. He then crawled over to the curb and sat there for a while longer, trying to catch his breath. He calmed down to the point where he realized his bike frame was still in the street. The front tire was about 100 feet down the block.

"Billy managed to collect everything and drag himself home, about two blocks. His ribs hurt like hell, and his bicycle frame was bent beyond repair, but what bothered him most was the verbal beating he anticipated receiving from his father. As Billy trudged up the driveway with his bike frame and tire in hand, he heard laughter coming from the house. He looked up and realized his father was watching from the kitchen, finding amusement in Billy's predicament.

'If I told you once, I told you a thousand times, check your equipment before you use it,' the elder Bate told Billy as he came through the house's back door.

"Grace said that while Billy couldn't prove it, he always felt his father deliberately sabotaged his bike to make a point. Billy also told her he believed the experience prevented him from breathing deeply, and that any time Billy found himself in a difficult situation, he would need to take a moment to catch his breath before he could do anything."

"He said the experience taught him a valuable lesson," Grace went on. "Thereafter, he was forever 'checking his equipment.' The habit served him well as a pilot but could drive everybody who lived or worked with him nuts. He would say, 'I don't go by what others tell me. I proceed only when I am satisfied with my own two eyes that everything is as it should be. Assume nothing. Verify everything.'"

"If that's the case, his reluctance to trust others is under-standable," Catherine said.

"According to Grace, Billy's teen years were not much kinder," Angelo said. "His face broke out in pimples, but he shot up height-wise between ninth and tenth grade, enabling him to tower over his 5-foot-9 father. This development mitigated the physical intimidation, but the mental torture continued."

"Mental torture?" Catherine asked.

"From what Grace and one of the Petes shared with me, the father could be a real prick," Angelo said. "On a construction site one summer, for instance, Billy was taking some good-natured grief from his older coworkers about his acne. Jack cut through the conversation with an unkind, 'All the boy needs is to get laid. But that would take a miracle.'

Grace said Billy told her even the other construction workers saw this as unduly harsh and walked away. It was not the first time Jack Bate broke up a bull session. If somebody told a story, Jack would try to top it. It bothered him when his workers talked about their sons' successful athletic endeavors because he had nothing to share about Billy, so Jack started talking about Billy's cousin, Brian. A star high school athlete, Brian scored on the field and off. He was everything Billy was not, and as a result, Billy despised anyone who succeeded at sports."

"What about Billy's high school days?" Catherine asked.

"Billy worked after school and on weekends, usually cleaning up at his father's construction sites. During the summers, he worked full-time," Grace told me.

"College?" Catherine wondered, taking notes.

"The father assured Billy that everything he needed to know about life he could learn at the controls of an Earth Mover," Grace said Billy told her.

"And Billy's mom?" Catherine asked, writing faster.

"Apparently, Billy's mother got sick soon after Billy graduated from high school, and she never recovered," Grace told me. "She became frailer with each passing year, and by the time Grace started working for Billy, she was an invalid."

"How did she treat Billy? Did she ever tell Jack to knock it off?" Catherine inquired.

"I asked Grace the same thing, but she had responded in the negative," Angelo said. "Billy told her when he was a kid growing up, she was this big, powerful force in his life, and it hurt him to see her deteriorate."

"Did he ever reconcile with his mother?" Catherine asked.

"He didn't blame her for the way Jack treated him, if that's what you mean, at least according to Grace. Billy doted on his mother. She also pointed out that the Carpe Diem employees had a great health insurance plan because the mother was on the payroll, and Billy needed to make sure she was taken care of.

"Grace said Billy's mom died a few months after she started working for him. Oh, and Grace also mentioned that Billy's mom used to make him fried banana and peanut butter sandwiches, the kind Elvis used to like. He LOVED it," Angelo said.

"Those sandwiches killed Elvis," Catherine noted. Angelo laughed, partly impressed that Catherine knew this about the King and partly relieved she knew who he was.

"Sure, we know it now," Angelo said. "But who knew back then? If it was good enough for The King, it was good enough for Billy, which may explain why we are talking about him today in the past tense. I'm sure she meant well."

They sat in silence for a moment, contemplating the fried banana sandwiches.

"Wait!" Angelo perked up. "There was one other funny story Grace shared with me about Billy and his mother.

"Grace told me she attended the mother's wake, primarily

to pay her respects but also to figure out what his family was like."

"How was it?" Catherine asked.

"Let's put it this way," Angelo said. "Grace told me there was this horseshoe-shaped wreath from Jack with a sash across the middle reading, "See you later Sugar!" It seems Jack liked to hit the racetrack and bet on the ponies. Apparently, he saw this as an appropriate send-off for his wife and the mother of his children."

"See you later, Sugar?!?" Catherine gasped.

The two laughed and then paused to catch their breath. Then Catherine asked, "Did Billy enjoy anything? Did Grace tell you what Billy liked to do?"

"According to Grace, Billy liked handling machinery," Angelo said. "The rumbling of the construction equipment. The movement of the tools at his behest. It was probably the first thing in his life he could control. Move this lever or touch this button, and the crane will do exactly what you want it to do. Nothing could stop you when you were controlling a Concrete Crusher. That was the good thing about construction work. The control you had over things. You do it right and follow the plan, and everything works. Billy said it all the time. He also said the verbal abuse his father dished out at the construction site planted the seed of desire, which led to Carpe Diem Construction Camps' success. He was driven to prove his father wrong and because he hated being a slave to other people's projects."

Angelo thought for a minute. "I remember she quoted Billy as saying, 'I wanted to create a situation where I could control the work I had to do.' So while he toiled for Jack during the day, he laid out his plans for Carpe Diem at night. He took courses at Gibbons College so he could learn how to deal with specific problems, like payroll processing. Without realizing it, it turns out that he accumulated enough credits to merit a diploma. Gibbons even applied his credits to a post-graduate degree. In all, Billy ended up with a master's degree in business and passed the CPA exam. So, in addition to getting Carpe Diem Construction Camps started, Billy also became a CPA and a certified financial planner. He was good at squirreling away money made from the construction jobs he handled as a teen. Now he was learning how to make real money, investing here and there and learning the golden secret: It takes money to make money, and you can't get ahead working for somebody else."

"Now we're getting somewhere," Catherine cracked, "but it's still not very sexy and doesn't answer the question about needing an ego to succeed in business. What can you tell me about his love life? Surely, he must have had a girlfriend in high school or afterward."

"From what Grace told me, well, let's just say he started out slow and then made up for lost time. His first girlfriend quickly became his first wife, and by all accounts, she was a piece of work."

Chapter 18

Billy Meets Marietta

"Her name is Marietta Bernadette Maccarone, and I'll explain it to you the way she explained it to me when I interviewed her," Angelo said. "But I have to warn you, it gets a little graphic and racy. Perhaps I should have you sign a consent form of some kind before I go any further."

"Don't be silly," Catherine scoffed. "I'm a big girl. No doubt I've heard ten times worse on social media."

"No doubt you have," Angelo said, "But you can't be too careful these days. Things have a way of looking sinister when they're presented in black and white, out of context. When it comes to such matters, I have a credo that has served me well: 'Sing like no one's listening. Dance like no one's watching. Write like it's going to be read in a deposition."

"I'll sign something if it will make you feel better, or even just acknowledge my consent into my recorder," Catherine said. "But I assure you, you have nothing to worry about."

There was a long, pregnant pause. Angelo and Catherine looked at each other, wondering how it came to be that two adults would have to exert such caution when attempting to have an adult conversation. Then Angelo looked out at the Great South Bay for a few moments and said, "Nah. Let's go."

"Here's what Marietta told me. I have to admit I was a little taken aback, not only by her actions but by her willingness to share her thoughts about them with me.

"They met around the time Carpe Diem Construction Camps started to take shape. She was wholesome, taller than most women with shoulder-length, chestnut-color hair and brown eyes that could go from playful to steely in the time it took to say the wrong thing to her. That part I got from Grace. She said Marietta's smile made you want to be her friend, so much so you sometimes wondered if she was ever in a bad mood–until someone crossed her. Then you found out quickly she could be in a bad mood and make sure everybody around her was in a bad mood, too.

"Anyway, right after high school, she worked as a waitress at the Nautilus Diner near Gibbons College. Billy was not much older and preferred to go there after classes to have coffee and pore over his notes rather than go home to his father's verbal abuse. She was impressed by his disciplined work habits. It seemed to Marietta that the young men who came into the diner on her shift were more concerned about getting head than getting ahead. This turned her off, which was odd because Marietta loved fellatio and took great pride in her ability to perform it."

"Wait–she told you that?!?!" Catherine blurted, half-exclaiming and half-questioning.

"She did, indeed," Angelo said.

"Did you get the sense she was coming on to you?" Catherine asked, trying to comprehend how a woman could be so open about such a personal thing, especially to a man she hardly knew.

"Not at all," Angelo said. "She said it rather matter-offactly, like some people might say they're good at gardening or like to play pickleball. She liked giving head, to use her expression.

"Billy had no way of knowing this about Marietta," Angelo said, "but the true irony here is that it didn't matter because he had no clue about seduction."

"Sounds like a match made in heaven," Catherine interjected sarcastically.

"Oh, like I said, Marietta was a piece of work," Angelo replied. "I found her to be a fascinating woman with a unique perspective on sexual intercourse and gratification, not that I'm any kind of expert," he added, shifting uncomfortably at even the mere hint of interjecting himself into the discussion.

"She did elaborate and with surprising detachment," Angelo went on. "Marietta said she considered oral sex as a means to counterbalance the subservience she experienced as a waitress and as a woman. For every guy telling her what to bring to the table and for every loser who made degrading attempts to hit on her, there was a seduced lover in the front seat of a car who surrendered himself to her. She had a few unwritten rules about who she did this with and when. She had to be attracted to him, and she sized up a candidate in ten seconds, based on what she saw in his eyes. If she looked at a man and he looked away, he was summarily rejected. She also would have nothing to do with any man with bloodshot eyes. Marietta had suffered enough battles with the bottle as a kid growing up in a house where Anheuser-Busch was the King of Beers and the reason why her mother woke up every morning already defeated. Her father was long gone, disappearing soon after Marietta was born.

"Her temporary paramour also had to be somebody new to her, as Marietta was not interested in relationships. If she saw something she liked or sensed an adventure, then she had a candidate. It turned her on all the more if her lover remained anonymous. Sometimes Marietta would flirt with the fellow, and once he caught on, it was a matter of how soon she would be in his car, taking complete control. Even if the man initiated the conversation, Marietta let the guy think he was driving the bus, if only because his deluded empowerment fueled her pleasure. What particularly intrigued her was how long the guy would wait for her. Having to finish her shift sometimes meant the guy had to wait around, perhaps for multiple hours. When she wanted a real challenge, she would initiate the process with a guy who was on a date that wasn't going well and then smile to herself as he hurriedly dropped off the unsuspecting woman and came back. No married guys, though. Well, except for the one time, but Marietta swore never again. The guy came almost as soon as she got his dick out. "Who needs such disappointment?" she told me.

"Geez, you really get people to open up when you interview them," Catherine commented, bemused and bewildered. "Is there a trick to that?"

"I'd be lying if I said I wasn't taken aback by what she shared with me," Angelo said. "I've interviewed hundreds, if not thousands of people over the decades, and nobody–nobody! was freer or open than Marietta. Believe it or not, she got even more personal during our conversation."

"Really? Is that possible?" Catherine asked.

"Oh yes. She said later, by herself in her own bed, naked under the cool sheets, she would take care of herself while savoring the pleasure derived from controlling her lover. She said the sounds her conquest made while coming fed her sensations. Then she came, enjoying 'epileptic orgasms'–again, her words– she never experienced with a man."

"Yikes!" Catherine exclaimed. This time it was her turn to

squirm in her seat. She found herself mentally checking off the handful of sexual experiences she had under her belt.

"Did she have any kind of extended relationships with these fellas, or were they all one-night stands?"

"She said inevitably the diner lovers would track her down in the days following their trysts. Rarely did she entertain their awkward entreaties for a second go-round. Marietta paid no mind to her lovers once she was done with them. She didn't want to know their names or for them to call, although she happily kept the embarrassingly generous tips they left.

"So what happened with Billy?" Catherine asked.

"Billy was different, she said. Marietta wanted him, but not anonymously. She said she wanted to know his name and to sleep with him a second and third time and forever. Marietta wanted to have his children, and she came to this conclusion with quickness and certainty that scared her a little.

"And Billy?" Catherine asked.

"Billy didn't have a clue, according to Marietta. He was wrapped up in his books, business, and dad-bully. After a while, it occurred to him that this waitress with the quick laugh and natural smile was paying attention to him. Despite what his father repeatedly said could not happen, an attractive woman was interested in Billy Bate. He overcame his nervousness and suggested they go on a date.

"'I was thinking about seeing a movie this weekend and hoped you might want to come with me,'" Billy said one night.

"I'd like that," Marietta replied, to Billy's surprise.

They watched the movie *Taxi Driver*.

"*Taxi Driver*? Was it a documentary?" Catherine asked.

Angelo winced at being reminded once again that Catherine was young and he was not.

"No–*Taxi Driver* was one of Robert DeNiro's and Martin

Scorsese's first movies together. You've heard of those guys, right?"

"Of course I have," Catherine responded, rather defensively. "I took a History of Cinema class last semester."

Angelo winced again.

"It came out in 1976. And no, it was not exactly a feel-good, romantic comedy. Marietta said Billy liked DeNiro movies. 'Other actors, like Jack Nicholson, play themselves playing different characters,' Billy said to her after the movie. 'DeNiro can do anything. He can be funny, scary, tough, and touching. That's real acting.'

"Marietta didn't care. She liked being with Billy and away from her mother and the diner. Afterward, they got something to eat at a beer and cheeseburger place."

"How'd that go?" Catherine asked.

"It was as awkward as you might expect," Angelo replied. "Marietta said she ordered a grilled cheese sandwich, and Billy kidded her about it. He said he found it 'odd' that a woman would order a grilled cheese on a date. 'It was his first date. What the hell would he know about what a woman's supposed to order?' Marietta said to me, half-laughing, half-mocking. 'I like grilled cheese. So sue me.'"

"Did Marietta say what happened next?" Catherine asked.

"She said Billy smiled and said, 'I don't like cheese. I order a hamburger wherever I go. No cheese.' So Marietta jokingly said, 'They can put the cheese from your burger on my grilled cheese instead.' To which Billy replied, 'Sounds like a lot of cheese,' clearly not getting the joke."

"Wow! Talk about romance!" Catherine said, dripping with sarcasm. So did they have sex that night?" Catherine asked, right before wondering if she really wanted to know.

"No, according to Marietta. She said there were many other 'nights out' after that, but that you wouldn't call them dates, especially when you consider Billy rarely wore anything more elaborate than his jeans and a colored t-shirt, the extent of his fashion sense. They sat at other diners for hours. She listened as Billy walked her through every detail about Carpe Diem Construction Camps. She convinced him to go clothes shopping with her so she could pick out a few outfits he could wear. Billy started to look like a new man, and Marietta started to believe she had stumbled onto something special. She stopped having sex with strangers and focused her amorous energies on Billy. He did what many guys do when they first get access to the Promised Land: fell in love and proposed marriage. Marietta accepted. They set up shop as man and wife. Marietta said that at that point, Billy was emerging from Jack's shadow.

"She told me, 'Even though Billy's sexual inexperience precluded him from realizing how good he was getting it, having sex on a regular basis changed him for the better.' I guess Marietta had learned enough for the two of them and took immense pleasure knowing her man was benefiting from her escapades, even though she knew he knew nothing about her past. It did not matter. He was happy. She was happy. They married in a simple ceremony conducted in the local Village Hall by the Justice of the Peace.

"Her 'diner love affairs and waitressing days were history,' she told me. It was time to 'don the mask of a happy homemaker,' married to a man who was just now starting to feel the need for a mask of his own, lest Marietta—or anyone else—get too close."

Chapter 19

A Bigger Pie

"Sounds rather idyllic," Catherine said. "Two young people in love, or at least desperately grateful to have found each other."

"Well, it seemed that way, at first," Angelo said. "According to Marietta, they settled into a little apartment over Angelina's luncheonette on Broadway in Massapequa."

"What's a luncheonette?" Catherine asked.

"Seriously?" Angelo countered.

"Seriously," Catherine replied, a little annoyed.

"Don't mind me," Angelo said, picking up on her annoyance. "It's a combination of me forgetting how young you are, how old I am, and how much things have changed in such a short time." I'm realizing now, as we speak, that you don't really see luncheonettes around much anymore. But they used to abound on Long Island."

"Like diners?" Catherine asked, trying to be helpful.

"Ehhh, not quite. They had booths like diners, most of them, but the focus was primarily on the counter. You'd sit on a stool that could spin around and order your lunch from the guy who would prepare it for you, right there as you watched."

"What kind of lunch? Anything special?"

"No, just the opposite. You had your basic burgers, fries, coffee, sandwiches, potato chips, soups, and sodas straight from the fountain," Angelo said, waxing as poetically as one could about burgers and fries. "And your meal was served to you on a plate with genuine silverware."

"What do you mean when you say, 'sodas straight from the fountain?" Catherine asked, intrigued.

Angelo laughed. He was starting to enjoy this trip down memory lane.

"When you ordered a soda, a Coke, let's say, he would put a glass–a real glass–under a spigot. Then he would pull on the spigot, and as the soda water filled the glass, he would pump Coke syrup into it. Once it was filled, he would stir the concoction. Voila! Coca-Cola!"

"Coke syrup?" Catherine asked again, truly bewildered.

"Yeah, Coke syrup. He would mix it for you right there. And real syrup, too. Not this poison posing as high fructose corn syrup you kids consume today. There was nothing better!"

"Was it really that much better?" Catherine asked.

A Coke back then was a real treat," Angelo said, "but now that I think about it, there was something better. An egg cream."

"That sounds gross," Catherine said. "Who the hell wants to drink an egg mixed in with cream?"

Angelo laughed again.

"That's the fun part. There were no eggs or cream in the egg cream. Just syrup, milk, and soda water. Like chocolate milk, but with fizz."

"Yuck!" Catherine said.

"You're going to have to trust me on this one, Catherine," Angelo said.

"So if luncheonettes and egg creams were so great, how come you don't see them around anymore?" Catherine asked.

Angelo thought for a moment and shrugged.

"Running a luncheonette was a lot of work, hard work," Angelo said, "and nobody ever got rich running one. They were starting to die out, and then your Starbucks came along, and that was the final nail in the coffin. You see the same thing happening to diners. Young people don't like going to them so they're disappearing, which is a shame because once they're gone, they ain't coming back. Your generation just doesn't want to work that hard."

"Are you saying we're lazy? I don't think we're lazy. I think we're smart. Why the hell should someone break their ass seven days a week running a diner when they can make a small fortune being a social media influencer?"

"I suppose that's a discussion for another day," Angelo countered. "Let's get back to the tale at hand. Now that you know a little about luncheonettes, you'll understand that living over a hamburger joint would be less than ideal for most people, but Billy loved luncheonettes, according to Marietta. She said the apartment had a tiny kitchen where two people could eat together, but only if they walked single file past the refrigerator. The living area had room for a loveseat, coffee table, and an entertainment center, and not much else. The bedroom was really just a room with a bed in it, with two dressers wedged into the corners for their clothes. What the apartment lacked in size, it made up for with warmth and charm, Marietta said. She told me she learned everything she knew about interior design to create a loving environment from the books she borrowed from the local library."

"Sounds like they were making the best of things," Catherine said.

"Marietta said initially, Billy did not dread coming home at day's end, as he had as a young boy and man living with his parents. She was there, waiting for him with dinner on the stove or in the oven, which was greatly appreciated after a hard day's work on a construction site. They would eat, and during the warmer months ,go out for a walk after dinner. Billy would talk about his dreams for Carpe Diem, and Marietta would listen attentively and sometimes offer advice, but not often. On the surface, it seemed like an idyllic start to a marriage, but something started to gnaw at Billy, Marietta said. By her own admission, she was trying to tear down the mental walls he spent years building to keep out his father's ugly treatment, but Billy wasn't ready to let anyone in, no matter how good she cooked or how great the sex was."

"Did they get along?" Catherine asked.

"Marietta said everything was fine, initially, but then Billy started working late some nights, and then it was every night. At first, she did not mind. Billy wasn't big on non-Carpe Diem-related conversation when he was home, but he never drank, not even on the construction site with the other fellows during lunch or after a shift. She relished the absence of tensions, ever-present growing up with an alcoholic mother. No screaming or yelling or 'midnight runs for cigarettes' inevitably resulting in the 4:00 a.m. phone call from her mother in a bad situation. Eventually, Billy's late nights away from home started to bother her, though. She toyed with reverting to her diner days to break up the monotony but rejected going there because she was committed to making their marriage work. Marietta said she knew Billy was also committed to the marriage, but that his idea of 'commitment' differed from hers. She said Billy operated under the impression that paying the bills, not being abusive, and not drinking was good enough. In fact, she said, he felt he had created an 'ideal life' for his young wife."

"So what did she do?" Catherine asked.

"Well, one night Billy, was getting ready for bed. Marietta was already under the covers. 'Billy,' she said softly. 'We should think about having a baby. I know I'm ready.'"

"What did he say to THAT?" Catherine asked, genuinely curious.

"Billy grunted, Marietta told me. He said he was close to launching his plans for Carpe Diem Construction Camps, and the last thing he wanted was to bring more responsibility into his life. Then, after a few moments of consideration, he said, 'Giving you something to do might keep you occupied and allow me to focus on my plans. Yeah, a baby might work. Let's do it!'"

"He said that?" Catherine asked, incredulous.

"Marietta narrated what Billy had said that night: 'We could have a baby and bring it up in an atmosphere neither of us ever got to enjoy,' and then he slid under the covers with her. She thought Billy might actually hug her, but he didn't. She wasn't even sure he knew how to hug. But she knew she loved him more than ever at that moment. They didn't hug, but they made a baby. Nine months later and right on time, Billy and Marietta became the beaming parents of a baby girl. They named her Elisabeth—with an 's', not a 'z', just to be different— and decided to call her Betty, taking the B from Billy and the "ett" from Marietta. Betty Bate. The night she was born, Billy came to visit Marietta in the hospital carrying an armful of flowers, stuffed animals, and candy for mom and daughter."

"That sounds nice," Catherine said.

"Well ...," Angelo said.

"What?" Catherine asked.

"Marietta said she said, 'Wow—did you leave anything in the store for the others?' This is way too much.'"

'There's no such thing as too much for the women in my life,' Billy said.

'I feel so lonely in bed by myself. Why don't you sit here for a spell?' Marietta suggested, patting the mattress.

'I have work to do,' Billy said, as if he were turning down an invite to grab a beer with a buddy. 'They don't just hand you success. You must earn it.'

'Who's they?' Marietta asked, clearly hurt.

'Society. The World. The Universe. The Hand of Fate. Whatever that Guiding Force is that picks winners and losers,' Billy replied, according to Marietta."

"Wow," Catherine said. "How'd that go over?"

"Oh, Marietta's nothing if not feisty," Angelo said. "She shot back, 'I happen to think true success is being the person God wants you to be.'

'Well, I happen to think God wants me to be a successful businessman,' Billy said.

'Of course he does,' Marietta said. 'He wants what's best for all of us, as long as our best benefits others, as well.'

'What are you talking about?' Billy countered.

'Think of the world as a pizza," Marietta said. "The size of your slice doesn't necessarily diminish the size of the other slices, or at least it shouldn't. The trick is to work hard and make a big enough pizza for everyone to enjoy. If the size of your slice comes at the expense of somebody else's slice, then you're not doing it right. What you have is a lousy pizza. Nobody's happy.'"

'All that aside, I have to go. I have work to do," Billy said.

'Like what?' Marietta asked, clearly hurt.

'Stuff for school. Stuff for Carpe Diem. You know the drill,' Billy replied. He kissed her forehead and left. Not once did he inquire about Betty or even ask to see her. If Marietta did not know the drill, she quickly learned it. She was second in line to Billy's business. The same discipline that enabled Billy to pore over his books in the diner and inspired Marietta to open her heart was now keeping her from getting too close to him."

"That sounds so sad and lonely," Catherine said.

"Marietta told me she made the best of it," Angelo said. "She committed herself to raising Betty in as loving an environment as one can muster for a child when the mother and father are more roommates than life partners. As much as Billy wanted the world to think he was part of one big happy family, eventually, the energy and effort required to maintain such a façade wore him down, and he moved out. To his credit, he made sure Marietta and Betty had everything they needed in terms of shelter, food, clothing, and creature comforts, and he attended whatever recitals and the like he could as Betty transitioned from little girl to young woman."

"Why do you think he did that?" Catherine asked.

"I got the impression from Marietta and the others I spoke with that there was a feeling that gnawed away at Billy, a feeling that there was always something better going on 'out there' while he was stuck wherever he was. As a little boy, he'd heard his classmates talk about their home life and experiences, and they all sounded so much more glorious than the verbal abuse he endured in his cold and callous home. As a pimply faced, underweight teenager, he sat in stony silence as his male peers bragged about their sexual conquests, no doubt exaggerating or even fabricating their stories, but Billy had no way of knowing this. As far as he was concerned, he was the only male in his high school who had not gotten laid by the end of his senior year."

"So as much as Marietta tried to do for him, it wasn't enough?" Catherine asked.

"It's never enough when you look to outside sources for inner contentment, to be happy," Angelo said. "But Billy didn't understand that then, and by every indication, he never realized it as an adult. As much as Billy appreciated Marietta, he was not about to 'settle down' and 'lose out' on everything else life supposedly has to offer. That's not what the carpe diem spirit is all about. It's about grabbing life by the balls, pushing the limits of your endurance, and experiencing every visceral pleasure the Universe has to offer."

"Sounds like his ego was driving him at this point," Catherine said. "Sounds like he was okay baking a bigger pizza as long as he got the first slice, the biggest slice, and decided how big everyone else's slice would be."

Angelo smiled.

"You're picking up on this nicely," he said. "But you might be giving him too much credit for being benevolent."

"What do you mean?" Catherine asked.

"Well," Angelo said, "at first he was focused on growing his business, a bigger pizza if you will. But then he met his first 'Power Puff.'"

"Power Puff?" Catherine asked, mystified.

Angelo sighed. "You're not going to like this," he said.

"Try me," she shot back.

"Ooookaaaay," Angelo said, "but let me walk you through it without interruption. It's a sordid affair, but it may help explain what drives people–men, anyway–to succeed. Bear with me," Angelo said, "and remember not to shoot the messenger."

Chapter 20

Billy & the Power Puffs

With the new addition, Marietta had to make the apartment work for three, so she busied herself with redecorating to accommodate "Betty Bate, Her Bouncing Baby Bundle of Beauty," as she lovingly referred to her daughter. Billy moved out and on with Carpe Diem Construction Camps. The camp's premise was to let men be the men they wanted to be, even if for only a day, and it worked. Men of all stripes–Captains of Industry, powerful professionals, and community leaders–relished the opportunity to dig a hole and fill it back up so they could do "manly things" with their hands. Many were repeat customers.

"These so-called rich and powerful men appear to live a life I'm supposed to envy. The fact is they hate what they do," Billy said to Marietta one morning. "Every successful person I have ever met loves what he does for a living. Waking up every day to do something you don't like doing, or contributing to the realization of someone else' dream, isn't living. It's existing. I've never worked a day in my life because I love what I do."

He shared this with Marietta after she again challenged him on how little time he spent with his family. He saw it as a justification for where and why he was focusing so much of his energy. She heard it as a rationalization for why his business meant more to him than his family.

As the business grew, it presented new challenges demanding more of Billy's time. After he moved to his own apartment, he took classes to learn how to better manage his money. As his business and bank account grew, his father's presence in his life diminished. Billy was no longer the easily bullied adolescent, and, like all bullies, Jack backed off once he realized he could no longer intimidate his prey. This led Billy to conclude his life was going great. Marietta thought otherwise. As much as she adored her little girl, she did not like being left alone. Her constant urging of Billy to spend more time with them, even though he had moved out, had the opposite effect. He looked for reasons to stay away, and in doing so, Billy made two discoveries.

The first was the business dinner in a male-dominated corporate world. Billy figured out the best way for him to convince corporation honchos to set up "retreats" for their top management at a construction fantasy camp was to wine and dine them in nearby New York City. The second was realizing that some of the corporate bigwigs he entertained enjoyed the company of women other than their wives. "Power Puffs," Billy called them. Young, cute, playful, energetic women who were eager to please and often would seemingly "disappear" without a trace once they reached their "use by" date. They were attracted to power and wealth like ants to a sugar pile. It had to be the power and wealth, Billy thought, since none of the Captains of Industry he dealt with could ever be confused with George Clooney.

Billy marveled at how the Power Puffs laughed at their companion's unfunny jokes and seemed amenable to any and all suggestions. Their actions fueled his frustration with having to deal with a wife and child, and the juxtaposition between one night of business entertaining and the next night as a husband and father could be jarring. Billy would experience an evening at a nice restaurant, eating food expertly prepared by gourmet chefs and served by tuxedoed professionals. The women in attendance spoke only when spoken to, laughing at the appropriate times and leaning against their gentleman friends once dinner was over as a way to remind them that dessert was nothing compared to the body buffet awaiting them in the hotel room. The next night, Billy would visit with Marietta in her cramped apartment, discussing mundane realities while the baby demanded so much attention. Billy loved his wife and daughter, but he craved his exciting and glamorous nights on the town. The dinners in the City became increasingly frequent because they resulted in more business for Carpe Diem and gave Billy a reason to be out.

He was also still taking business classes at Gibbons. Toward the end of one semester, Billy was dropping off his final assignments at the dean's office when he noticed Naomi. She had been working there for months and watched Billy every time he stopped by, but this was the first time she caught his attention. Perhaps it was the sweater she was wearing, or the curvaceous body packed into the tight pants. He handed the papers to Naomi, and as he did, he looked her over.

"I'll make sure the dean gets these," she told Billy, smiling. "By the way, your jacket looks nice."

"Thanks," he replied. "Your sweater is nice, too."

Then he remembered the dinner planned for the next night. In a rare spontaneous moment, Billy invited Naomi to join him and his business cohorts. She accepted and told him to call her tomorrow with the details. He drove home, his head spinning with the fun he could have with a Power Puff to call his own.

Chapter 21

Billy Gets His Power Puff

Naomi's head was also spinning with possibilities. She longed to experience lust and power and the fabulousness associated with both. Billy's being married did not matter. He was her ticket to the world beyond her workaday existence.

Billy called her the next morning.

"Be ready at 5:30," he said. "Dress to impress."

That was the extent of the conversation. She did as she was told, wearing a little black cocktail dress with spaghetti straps and stiletto heels. She took the afternoon off for a complete makeover, and by 5:00 p.m., she was ready to walk the red carpet at a Hollywood movie premiere.

Corporate honchos taught Billy about the limousine's magical powers. Power Puffs loved them almost as much as power and money, so he used one whenever possible. He did not mention the limo to Naomi because he wanted to keep her off guard. He timed his arrival so it would still be light when the car pulled up to Naomi's home. She lived with her parents in Lynbrook, a working-class town near Mockingbird Heights where limousines only rolled down its streets for weddings, proms, or a funeral, so Billy's sleek white chariot had the desired effect. Her neighbors came out to see what the special occasion was and walked around the car like it was a vehicle from another planet.

Naomi took a deep breath to maintain her composure and walked the short distance from the front door to the car like a movie star, putting on a show for her parents and the neighbors watching by pretending that heading to the city for dinner and a Broadway play was old hat. Billy never got out. He smiled as he watched the commotion, and noted Naomi was "I Moan" backwards. *I'll bet she moans*, he thought with a chuckle, making a mental note to find out as soon as possible.

Naomi settled into her seat, and the car pulled away from the curb with everyone waving goodbye. Even though he lived on his own, Billy was still married, and his marriage status was no secret. Nonetheless, he did not mention Marietta, nor did Naomi bring her up. She knew Marietta would not be joining them. Naomi also knew she was invited not because she loved Broadway or appreciated the Fine Arts, but because there was a spark between them when he finally noticed her.

Billy handed her a glass of champagne as the car eased into the city-bound traffic. The alcohol and the bubbles sent a flash of warmth and excitement throughout her body and down to her toes. She instinctively crossed her legs. She and Billy made small talk on the way to the Marriott Marquis Hotel in Times Square, where they picked up their guests. The plan was to take the client and his date to dinner at Clegg & Cleary's and then to see *Black Maria*, the dark comedy Broadway musical about lust and life in small-town America.

Billy loved the show, and as he became better known on Long Island, his devotion to the play gained legendary status. People would introduce him as "the guy who's seen *Black Maria* over a hundred times." He swore every time he saw a performance, he picked up on a different nuance or wordplay he hadn't noticed before. In truth, he liked routine, not surprises. He needed to know what was coming next during the play, and he dined at Clegg & Cleary's as often as he saw *Black Maria* because he wanted the prestige associated with being recognized by the staff at a top-notch restaurant.

They met up with their dinner companions–a CEO looking to book team-building events at Carpe Diem and his Power Puff. Everybody but Billy dined on surf and turf while he ordered his hamburger and reveled in the attention doing so garnered. Naomi found this charming, and the others kidded him about it, but Billy did not care. Hamburger it was.

The four laughed and ate, and talked a little business. Billy already had the client's loyalty but was wining and dining him anyway, lest somebody else get his attention and take his business away. The client and his date ordered drinks during dinner and then after-dinner cordials. Billy pretended to keep up with them, but as was his practice, he had instructed the wait staff to simply serve him iced tea, looking like Scotch and water. Naomi nursed a white wine, not because she didn't want to party but because she preferred to take in every moment with great clarity.

After dinner, the limousine was waiting for them out front for the short ride to the theater. They were immediately ushered to their seats, and the four settled down for the night's entertainment. As soon as the curtain rose, Billy's hand slid toward Naomi's inner thigh, and she did nothing to discourage it. She remembered little from the play. All she could hear was her heart pounding. After the show, they dropped the other couple off at their hotel, and the car no sooner merged into Fifth Avenue traffic when Naomi raised herself from her seat and kneeled down in front of Billy. She slid her dress straps off her shoulders and exposed her breasts. Then, leaning forward and without saying a word, she unzipped his fly, took out his hardening manhood, and put her lips to its tip. The car hit a bump, and Billy unexpectedly slid into her mouth, almost choking her. She adjusted to the sudden intrusion without missing a beat as they proceeded past St. Patrick's Cathedral and down Fifth Avenue. She worked her magic, and Billy responded in kind as the limo turned to enter the Midtown Tunnel. She looked up at her lover. He gave her a quick smile, zipped up, and then turned on the limo's television. She had no way of knowing Billy was used to getting great head, even though it had been a while for him. He said he needed to watch the news, but in truth, he wanted to keep the conversation to a minimum.

Billy dropped Naomi off at her parents' house, again neglecting to leave the limousine. She got out and then leaned back to kiss him good night on the lips. He turned slightly, and she grazed his cheek with a kiss more affectionate than you would give a relative, but not by much.

"Thank you for a wonderful evening," she said. "I hope we can do this again sometime."

"You can count on it," Billy replied.

As Billy brought Naomi along for more dinners in the city, he learned she had a knack for bookkeeping that matched her passion for limo rides. Soon, she was doing both full-time for Carpe Diem. Billy loved a quickie and made sure the desk she worked at was sturdier than might normally be necessary. Sometimes he just wanted to play with Naomi's breasts. He liked walking up behind her while she was busy and cupping them with his big construction worker hands. She loved the spontaneity and the sex itself, especially during the workday. When she was doing actual bookkeeping, she could see how quickly the money was coming in. Considering Billy's nebulous home life situation, Naomi believed she had a winner on her hands. "So it will take me a little time to get him divorced and remarried," she told friends at the time. "It will be well worth it."

She became more comfortable with the nights in the city, so much so that the business dinner guests often assumed Billy and Naomi were man and wife. Then Naomi noticed Billy was going into the city, and she had not been invited. Billy had found himself a new Power Puff, and Naomi was done. He kept her on as a bookkeeper because she was so good at it, and Billy appreciated good workers. Billy saw no reason to explain why he stopped inviting her to accompany him on these sojourns, but as the Power Puffs arrived and disappeared over the years, Naomi realized it was him, not her. He was a generous boss, and every now and then, they would share a laugh about a dinner experience from the past. She eventually married, and not only did Billy attend the wedding, but he also gave the newlyweds beautiful Waterford Crystal. Naomi moved on to a new job without ratting out Billy. It was not her way, and she loved how she felt the first night in the limo.

Marietta, on the other hand, was not so accommodating.

Chapter 22

Billy's a Diver

Billy's success fueled his self-indulgence. Pornography, which helped him relieve the pressure associated with being alone through puberty, evolved into an obsession. He amassed enough dirty magazines to keep Larry Flynt in cigars and Scotch for years. *Jugs, Oui, Cheri, Biker Chicks* ... if it was in print and featured naked girls, it found its way into his collection. When X-rated videos became available to consumers, Billy bought an elaborate home theater system ... for his office. Simulated sex in surround sound. Marietta wanted no part, and this drove them further apart.

"What's with all the girlie magazines?" she said one day during a rare trip to his office. "Why would you want to look when you could have had the real thing with me?"

Billy chuckled. He was getting the "real thing" in hotels and limos. The sex hadn't turned him on–it was the acquiescence. Girls in magazines were seen but not heard, and the girls in the videos only said and did what the guys wanted to hear and have done.

"I like looking," he replied. "It relaxes me."

Marietta had been enjoying her visit. Then her eyes showed an ice-cold rage, like the ocean in January.

"Relaxes you? Relaxes YOU?!?" Marietta said in a voice bordering on a screech. "What about me?!? When do I get to relax? Where do I go when I want to get away from the world for a while?"

Billy tensed. "Why would you want to get away from anything?" he shot back. "I take care of your needs. I feed you. I put clothes on your back and keep a roof over your head. Give you the newest things. What more could you possibly want?"

That was the end of her visit and any pretense that they were still husband and wife.

Billy tried to portray himself as a family man, but spending time with his wife and daughter to be seen as a loving husband and father became too onerous. His predilection for porn and Power Puffs took over. If he had any doubts about moving out, they completely dissipated in a sea of nubility.

He made sure Marietta and Betty had every material thing they needed, and for the next five years, Billy was traveling more and making more money. The Power Puffs got younger and prettier. Besides having dinner and seeing a show in the city, they would spend the night in a hotel. He started taking pictures of them in various poses, none of which would make their fathers proud. Meanwhile, more business meant more employees and franchises nationwide. Pete and Re-Pete surfaced as Pete Snodgrass started working with Pete Santini. Together, they handled the day-to-day details needed to keep the business profitable while Billy focused on drumming up new business.

As the business grew and became more complicated, Billy realized he needed to bring in a money man. He hired Stan Shadler, an old-school soul, to serve as a controller. Shadler was pushing 70 and worked when he wanted to. He was the only

Carpe Diem employee who made his own hours, primarily because he was the only one who knew how to keep the IRS at bay, which was crucial considering Billy's entertainment expenses. During one audit, he convinced the IRS agent that the files the agent was looking for were destroyed in a flood.

In his prime, Shadler worked for men who could buy and sell Billy ten times over, so Shadler was never afraid to get in Billy's face and tell him when his antics were costing the company more than money. Shadler understood Billy, and as a result, Billy listened because he respected him like a son would respect a father. Shadler also understood how a person's ego and drive are keys to running a successful business.

"You can judge a man's approach to life by how he conducts himself at the ocean's shore," Shadler said to Grace once. "Some people jump in and frolic without fear. Others wade in and get acclimated bit by bit before they can enjoy themselves. Still others are happy to get their feet and ankles wet, without experiencing the pure joy of riding with the waves. Billy was a wader as he grew up, but eventually turned into a diver who jumps in and makes the most of the experience, regardless of how choppy or rough the waters are. There's a lot to be said for that."

He did not appreciate nor approve of Billy's skirt-chasing, though he recognized that sometimes it comes with the wave riding. Shadler's experiences taught him there are few Boy Scouts–or Girl Scouts–in the business world. Shadler also knew boundaries and consequences applied to misbehaving executives as well as anyone else.

In addition to knowing how to move money around to hide it from the federal government's prying eyes, Shadler knew how to set up an organization so it could handle rapid growth. With Carpe Diem bursting at the seams, Shadler encouraged Billy to delegate more responsibilities and add more staff, including Candee Coyne. She played den mother to the female staffers once they were hired by Santini, with Billy giving final approval. Billy almost always hired single mothers because he knew they would be less likely to switch jobs as long as their primary needs–decent salary, regular hours with flexibility in case the kids were home sick from school, and good healthcare–were met.

Initially, some of the single-mother staffers did double duty as Power Puffs, but Shadler quickly stopped the practice. "You don't eat where you crap, and you don't crap where you eat," he cautioned Billy. "One disgruntled gal screaming sexual harassment, and you will have attorneys and the government all over you, and you'll lose your company."

One day, Billy needed a Power Puff to accompany him to a last-minute business dinner at Clegg & Cleary's and a *Black Maria* performance. He told Candee Coyne to find one. Normally, Candee did not like to mix her personal life with her professional world, but pressed for time, she reached out to her friend Melinda Strutt. The hastily-made arrangements meant there was no time to have a limo pick up Melinda at her house, so the plan was for her to meet Billy at the restaurant. Billy was standing in Clegg & Cleary's lobby when he saw a woman come through the front door. She was wearing a cream-colored silk blouse, with buttons down the front opened enough to draw your attention, and a long black skirt matching her hair. The slit in the skirt accentuated her long legs and inspired desire. Her black curly hair framed and accentuated her skin's flawlessness as the bright red lipstick showed off her pearly white and perfect teeth.

He thought, *Please, dear God, let her be Melinda.*

It was, but even if it wasn't, Billy was not leaving there without at least introducing himself.

This is the woman I was meant to spend the rest of my life with, Billy thought.

Even though he dove right into the situation, gliding across the lobby and positioning himself so she would notice him, for the first time in years, he was nervous around a woman, and his palms were sweating like a seventh grader at his first boy-girl dance.

"Hello. My name is Billy Bate, and I hope you are Candee's friend Melinda," he said.

"I am Melinda, Melinda Strutt," she replied. She hated the name from the minute she met the man–her first husband–who gave it to her. She hated it even more when she divorced him and wished she could go back to the name she was born with–Melinda Matias. She kept it, however, because she wanted to have the same last name as her son.

"It's a pleasure to meet you," Billy said. "Candee has told me so much about you. She neglected to mention you're prettier than a brand new John Deere earth mover." He winced when he said it, and she pretended it wasn't the dumbest thing a man had ever said to her while sober. He took her by the hand and led her to the maître'd, who greeted them warmly and whisked the couple to Billy's usual table. Soon they were joined by their guests for the evening, a potential client along with his Power Puff.

The dinner and show bore no surprises, making it a success in Billy's mind. At evening's end, the client said he would get back to Billy about using Carpe Diem, but Billy was only half listening. The new business meant nothing to him at the moment. All he cared about was this beauty sitting next to him.

The feeling was mutual. Billy and Melinda were genuinely impressed with each other. Some might say smitten. There was no sex in the limousine on the way home and no television set. Billy wanted to get to know Melinda, and Melinda wanted to soak in all she could about Billy. They chatted like teenagers from Manhattan to Melinda's apartment in Rum Junction, a 90-minute ride with no traffic.

The limousine pulled up to the house where she had an apartment, and Billy walked her to the side door. They stood there under the porch light, looking at each other and smiling for several minutes. Finally, Billy said, "Well, I guess I should be going."

Melinda replied, "Yes. I suppose so. I had a wonderful time tonight. I hope we get to do it again soon."

"You can count on it," Billy said. They hugged, and Melinda planted a kiss on his cheek–and then giggled as she touched his face to wipe off the lipstick.

If nobody was looking, Billy would have skipped as he returned to the limo, but he had to stay cool in front of the driver. He made sure two dozen black roses were waiting for her on her doorstep the next morning. Two dozen–not the usual one–because nothing was over the top for Billy when it came to impressing women, and black for *Black Maria*. When she saw the roses, her initial reaction was that Billy was sending her a message that the date had not gone well. *Whatever,* she thought. *The last thing I want right now is a relationship. The only reason I need a man in my life is to have somebody around to take out the garbage.*

Billy was giddy. As much as he wanted for them to be lovers, he also hoped this relationship would blossom into much more and was committed to doing everything he could to keep this special. He knew Melinda could be a living doll for his right arm, something Marietta had no desire to be. With the company growing and the management structure in place, Billy had ideas about becoming an important presence on Long Island. He was tired of explaining who he was and what he did. Every Long Islander should know his name, Billy opined, and he should be able to walk through the corridors of power not as an ordinary citizen but as the "go-to-guy" elected officials consulted when trying to solve problems.

He needed to be a Somebody, and, in his world, having a bevy of Power Puffs or even a trophy wife was a prerequisite to acquire such status. Billy faced an additional challenge to his becoming a player in political circles on Long Island: You have to know who the players are and how to play the game. Billy understood strategy in the business world, but by his own admission, he did not have a clue about politics.

Then Grace Duffy came into the picture.

Chapter 23

What a Mess

"Wait, wait, wait," Catherine said, interrupting Angelo. "Let me make sure I'm up to speed here. Billy Bate was this shy, pimply-face, mentally-abused-yet-hardworking teenager who comes out of his shell after meeting a kind-hearted woman from an equally 'broken' home life with–how shall I put this–quirky ideas about sexual gratification."

"Correct," Angelo said, nodding.

"Okay. He marries this woman, his business is booming, and they have a daughter. Rather than relishing these positive developments, however, he starts gallivanting around with females who, for some inexplicable reason, are turned on by patriarchal power. There's no other explanation for how or why they are involved. He leaves his wife basically alone to raise their daughter, but alleviates any potential guilt for doing so by providing for all their material needs, as if that solves every-thing. Meanwhile, he's also keeping several pornography publishers in business while creating a small pornography cottage industry of his own. Am I right so far?"

"Now you're starting to see why I walked away from this

project," Angelo said. "The deeper I dug, the more sordid it seemed."

"And yet he's charitable. Meeting with priests and nuns. Serving on various community boards. Showing up for Mass and sitting in the front row."

"He was an enigma, to say the least," Angelo said.

The two had finished their sandwiches and chips, leaving the empty bags on the plates next to the glasses of water. It was a little past two in the afternoon, so Angelo suggested they shift their chairs so they could enjoy the autumnal warmth of the sun and see each other without either one having to shield their eyes.

"So, how did Grace fit into all this?" Catherine asked. "Did she not know about Billy's shenanigans, or did she know and not care?"

"Welllll," Angelo dragged out. "You know how necessity is the mother of invention? Along those lines, it can also be postulated that motherhood is the necessity of job security."

"Huh?" Catherine asked, stumped.

"Let me backtrack a little here," Angelo said, shifting in his seat. "Grace had entrepreneurial aspirations and an adventurous spirit, which led her to start a public relations firm with a partner, Bruce Wright. She was going to handle the creative end of things while Bruce developed the business and roped in the clients. At least that was the plan."

"So what happened?" Catherine asked.

"Welllll," Angelo trailed.

"Again with the welllll," Catherine said, laughing. "Let me guess. There's an ego involved here, too."

"Sort of," Angelo said. "I suppose the only thing worse than an egomaniac is an egomaniac without portfolio."

"What does that mean?" Catherine asked.

"Bruce Wright had an ego, but he didn't have the track

record of success to back it up. He wanted all the trappings of success without actually having to put in the effort to achieve success. There are no shortcuts in the business world. Not enough people realize you have to put in the time and effort AND achieve success before you can take your dick out and swing it around."

"Oh my, now there's a visual I wasn't expecting," Catherine said, blushing and laughing at the same time.

"Oh Christ, I'm sorry," a clearly flustered Angelo said. "I forgot my audience. That was uncalled for."

"Relax," Catherine said. "I've heard much worse, and from fellas who wouldn't know how to swing a dick even if they had one worth swinging."

"Anyway," Angelo said, anxious to change the tone and direction of the conversation. "Grace and Wright started this business and soon found themselves in a financial hole and in trouble with the IRS due to some aggressive business moves and careless practices on Wright's part. The plan was to have Wright drum up business while Grace handled the creative end until they could afford to hire more staff," Angelo said.

"That was Grace's plan, anyway. The first monkey wrench was Grace getting pregnant and Drex disappearing the day the baby was born. The second was Wright's reckless spending. He wanted to run the biggest PR firm on Long Island right away. He hired account executives, knowing the firm did not have the resources to cover the payroll increases. Wright persuaded Grace to sign up for multiple credit cards to purchase state-of-the-art computers and office equipment. He also used the credit cards to pick up the check at lunch or dinner, no matter who was at the table. Their biggest client was a local Lexus dealer, but rather than receiving much-needed cash in exchange for their services, Wright arranged to lease a luxury automobile for himself."

"Wasn't there anything Grace could do about this?" Catherine asked. "Couldn't she speak up for herself?"

"She could have, but she didn't," Angelo said. "She told me later on that she, quote, 'trusted Wright implicitly,' but after a little prodding, she finally admitted the truth. She let herself be intimidated by him. She acquiesced on all business decisions, figuring he knew best. The PR firm had other, small clients, but not enough to pay the bills, as the Long Island economy at the time was tanking. Wright's pushing the firm to expand forced the partners to cut corners elsewhere, like not paying rent or withholding taxes due to the IRS. Soon, it became apparent the firm was not going to achieve financial stability anytime soon. Even Wright knew they needed help, so he contacted Shadler, who was friends with Wright's father. Shadler, in turn, introduced them to Billy, thinking they could help Billy become a player and Billy could help them with their business."

"That seems like a reasonable solution, the proper course of action, no?" Catherine asked.

"It was, at least initially," Angelo said. "Shadler arranged for Carpe Diem to use the firm for public relations and marketing, and in exchange for those services, he managed the firm's day-to-day finances. This arrangement worked for a few weeks, and Billy had no qualms about advancing money to cover payroll and other expenses. The more money Billy contributed, the more he wanted to know about the day-to-day operations, just like any investor would. Wright chafed with each escalation of interference and then deliberately disobeyed a directive from Billy. When Billy got wind of Wright's move, he cut off all funding and severed ties with the firm."

"Just like that? Catherine asked.

"Just like that," Angelo said. "Every successful entrepreneur embraces the concept of not throwing good money after bad, and the money spent on Wright was bad, especially in light of his attitude."

"What did Wright do?" Catherine asked.

"He told Grace that he did not care about the pending financial peril and remained obstinate in his opposition to Billy's involvement. 'I'd rather be the king of nothing than deal with that prick,' she said he told her when confronted about sabotaging the business relationship."

"So, how did Grace react to that?" Catherine asked.

"Grace said she recognized the need to cede control to somebody like Billy, if not Billy himself. It became a contentious point between Grace and Wright that blew up one hot summer night when Grace attempted reconciliation by scheduling a meeting in Carpe Diem's conference room with her, Wright, Billy, and Shadler. Billy sat there, silent, waiting for Wright to apologize for his insurrection and, in doing so, hand over the firm, his manhood, and his soul to Billy."

"That must have been fun," Catherine deadpanned.

"Oh yeah," Angelo said. "Grace told me she tried to initiate a positive conversation, talking about potential clients and the successes the firm had getting publicity for charity organizations it represented *pro bono*. This was not what Billy wanted to hear. He looked over at Shadler, who quickly spoke up.

'We're not happy with the way you pursue business,' Shadler said. 'You spend too much time on the *pro bono* stuff. Exposure for the firm is great, but unless you have clients paying the bills, you're not going to be in business for long.' Shadler spoke in a stern but almost grandfatherly tone, but it did not matter. Wright wanted no part.

'We've done all right to this point, and we're going to stick to our plan,' he said.

'Done all right?' Billy spat out. 'Done all right? You owe the IRS more than 50 grand, and you're into Carpe Diem

Construction for another hundred thousand. How in the world do you see that as 'doing all right?'"

"Yikes," Catherine interjected. "I have to side with Billy on this one. Wright seems ungrateful, bordering on unjustifiably belligerent."

"Yeah, well, Grace said Wright did not have an answer. He told Billy the firm was not about to change how it did business. Billy grunted. 'Then we have nothing further to talk about,' he said. At that point, Billy got up and left. Wright glared at Grace, and then he left. Shadler and Grace looked at each other in exasperation. Shadler sighed. Grace had gone months without a paycheck, and with a newborn to take care of, she was ready to have Hitler take over the company if it meant some money coming in. Eventually, they left, too. Shadler headed to Billy's office, and Grace stepped outside. Wright was waiting for her," Angelo said.

"Uh oh," Catherine said.

"Exactly," Angelo said. "Grace said he got right into her face. 'What's with you and Bate?' Wright said. 'How come you didn't defend me in there?'

'I'm trying to make this work,' Grace replied.

'Fuck you,' Wright shot back. 'Fuck Shadler. Fuck Bate.'"

"Fuck Bate?" Catherine interjected, stifling a giggle. "That sounds immoral, like something you would call a young stripper."

"Grace told me the same thing," Angelo said. "She said when Wright said, 'Fuck Bate,' she giggled involuntarily. It sounded funny, but the giggling pissed off Wright even more."

'You better make up your fucking mind,' Grace said Wright told her. 'If you want to make this work you show your loyalty to me, not to some dick wad. This is bullshit. I'm out of here.'"

"So Wright's ego wouldn't allow him to work with or, more accurately, for Billy, even though he was in deep financial straits," Catherine surmised. "That's a pretty good example of the ego being counterproductive."

"There's a world of difference in the prepositions 'for' and 'with' when it comes to employment situations," Angelo said. "At least Wright knew himself well enough to realize that he couldn't co-exist with Billy, no matter how much sense it made."

"Well, bully for him," Catherine said. "What happened next?"

"Grace said she decided right after that meeting to distance herself from Wright and to figure out a way to go work for Billy, even though they still had a firm to run."

"She still had to work with Wright?" Catherine asked. "That must have been awful."

"Yes, it was," she told me. "The work environment got progressively worse. The staff stopped showing up for work once the paychecks started to bounce. Grace's personal financial situation grew more precarious. She and Slade moved in with Grail and her husband to ease the pressure temporarily," Angelo said.

"How'd that work out?" Catherine asked.

"After a few weeks, Grail told Grace she could stay with her, but only if she landed a good job. 'If you're going to stick with the pretense of running a public relations firm, then you can find your own place to live,' was the ultimatum Grail dropped on Grace," Angelo said. "Grace knew she had to keep a roof over her head and Slade's, so she told Wright the day after Thanksgiving she was moving on."

"That must have been an ugly scene," Catherine said.

"Not really," Angelo said. "Grace said by that point it was a fait accompli. She did explain that her departure meant the firm would have to relocate since Grace's father's friend was the landlord. Wright tried to operate out of a makeshift office in his house, but by Christmas, the firm was done, and Wright was never heard from again. Grace thought it only fair that she spruce up the office they vacated so the family friend could rent it again, presumably to tenants who would pay rent. The process included scraping the firm's painted logo–a big PR and LI intertwined–from the front window.

"It's the least she could do," Catherine interjected.

"Right," Angelo agreed. "But she told me about something that happened when she did it that's fascinated me ever since.

"Grace knew it would take a few hours, but it was something she had to do, a catharsis. On a cold, gray afternoon, days before Christmas and with Slade safely ensconced with Grail, Grace painstakingly scraped the front window using a straight-edge razor. As she scraped, she noticed a young man wearing a monk's robe and sandals, despite the December cold, walking up the pathway to the office front door. When the monk knocked, Grace thought, *Brother, if you're looking for money, you're rattling the wrong cage.*

"She invited the monk in and asked how she could help, even though she did not think she could. The monk looked around the abandoned office and then at Grace with the razor in her hand, and asked what was going on.

'It's a long story,' Grace said.

'I like long stories,' he replied softly.

'Swell,' Grace said. 'But I've got things to do.'

'Can I tell you about the work I'm doing?' he asked.

'You can tell me,' Grace replied, 'But it's not going to do you a lick of good. As you can see, my business has folded, and I'm cleaning up the mess. I'm broke. I don't have a dime to my name.'

'Nothing?' he asked. 'Are you sure? The men and women I work with face real poverty every day. Anything you can give would be a blessing.'

Grace remembered the change she had in her pocket. A dollar fifty-two was exactly what it would take at the time to purchase a coffee from 7-Eleven, and Grace figured the coffee would be her reward for completing her scraping penance.

'I have a buck-fifty-two in my pocket,' Grace told the monk. 'If you think that's going to help somebody, it's all yours.'

The monk extended his hand, accepting the offer. Grace cringed because she was really looking forward to the coffee. She reached into her jeans, pulled out the coins, and poured them into the monk's hand.

'God bless you,' the monk said. Then he turned to head out the door and into the steely-gray December afternoon.

'God bless me,' Grace said under her breath. 'God bless me. I had a buck fifty-two to my name, and he took it.' Grace neglected to learn the monk's organization's name. For all she knew, the young man was a con artist working a scam. Regardless, Grace said later she realized the universe was reminding her there's always somebody else worse off. She finished at the office and headed to Grail's house for dinner without stopping for coffee. It was no longer necessary, as Grace said she got the boost she wanted."

"That's so random and weird," Catherine said.

"To her credit, she made the most of it," Angelo said. "But a monk, of all people, coming out of nowhere. Really makes you wonder about signs from the Universe."

"Okay, so now what? Does Grace go and work for Billy?" Catherine asked.

"Not yet. With the PR firm done, Grace needed to find something to do to bring in cash while looking to write the next chapter in her career. She couldn't file for unemployment, as the firm never paid its unemployment insurance fees to New York State, and Grace was afraid if she filed, the State would have her arrested. She made it through the holidays by sorting and delivering mail as a temporary worker for the Post Office and kept phoning Billy and Shadler.

By the end of January, something materialized. The local hospital was hosting its annual fundraising gala and asked Billy to chair the Event Journal committee. Billy figured Grace could help him with this project, and if it worked out, they could make more permanent arrangements.

Grace was truly up against it. She needed some security. Quite frankly, if it weren't for Grail's ability to let them live with her and her family, Grace would have been homeless with a child. Going to work for Billy at Carpe Diem was truly a godsend.

Chapter 24

Shadler's Chocolates

"The event and the journal raised more money than ever before, and Grace became a full-time employee, but she was not welcomed with open arms," Angelo said.

Grace's arrival at Carpe Diem coincided with Melinda's moving in with Billy. Both developments marked professional and personal turning points for the Carpe Diem owner, who wanted something more than working day and night to figure out how to squeeze more nickels and dimes from his business. He was also ready for romance with one woman.

Billy delegated Carpe Diem's day-to-day operations to Pete and Re-Pete and made sure Shadler kept a watchful eye on both. This created tension between the Petes and Shadler, which Billy welcomed because he believed executives who know they are being watched tend to be more productive. It did not take much to get his administrative assistants to be his eyes and ears around the office, either. He surreptitiously rewarded underlings ratting out superiors with floral bouquets sent to their homes.

Shadler had his own methods. He kept a jar filled with

miniature chocolate bars on his desk and encouraged everyone to "help themselves." Throughout the day, Carpe Diem staffers would stop in for a "sugar fix" and inevitably share the latest office gossip when they did. Shadler would funnel the information to Billy, who filed it in his head to be used as needed. Everyone was so willing to get in good with the boss at their co-workers' expense, creating a toxic atmosphere, which did nothing for morale but kept everyone on their toes.

It did not take long for Grace to realize she had walked into a den of distrust. Santini kept his distance while Snodgrass made no effort to camouflage his concern that the new gal posed a threat since Grace had direct access to Billy. The clincher came one morning when Billy had peppered Grace with several phone calls in a matter of minutes, so when the phone rang yet again, Grace said out loud but to nobody in particular: "What the hell does he want now?"

Within minutes, Billy's secretary was standing outside Grace's office. "Billy wants to see you," she said in a tone reminding Grace of being sent to the principal's office in grammar school. Grace made her way down the long hallway to Billy's office and stuck her head in the door.

"You wanted to see me, Billy?" Grace asked.

Billy barely looked up from his desk. "Do you have a problem with me calling you?"

"No. No, I don't," Grace stammered.

"Remember who signs the paychecks around here," Billy said. "I'll call you as many times as I want, and you'll answer each call with a smile in your voice. Understood?"

"Not a problem," Grace said.

"Good. Get back to work," Billy said. Grace scampered back to her desk and looked around once she sat down. Billy was too far away from him to have heard Grace directly. Somebody must have been walking by when Grace said what she said, or maybe Shadler, whose office was directly across the hall. Regardless, it was clear to Grace that somebody ratted her out, and in record time.

Melinda's reception by the Carpe Diem staff was different, but not by much. She felt comfortable with Grace. What sealed the deal was a last-minute trip they shared into the city. Billy was already in Manhattan attending a conference when he invited a business colleague to dinner. He called Melinda around 3:00 p.m. and told her to meet him at Clegg & Cleary's by 6:00. She protested that three hours was not enough time to get ready and find a sitter for James. Nor was she thrilled about going into Manhattan alone.

He shot back, "You have two hours, not three. I'll have Grace pick you up at the house at five, and she can drive."

"Fine," she said, and hung up the phone. Then she looked at her watch. "Crap–now I have one hour and 55 minutes." Billy called Grace, told her to pick up Melinda, and gave her the same deadline. "No problem, boss," she said, even though Grail would not be happy with her prolonging the amount of time Slade had to stay with her at the last minute.

She was not thrilled with his assignment, but did pick up Melinda on time. Grace lightened up as soon as Melinda got into the car, realizing Melinda was miserable and in no mood to hear her bitch. Melinda wore a slinky black dress, and every time she moved in her seat, her skirt slit hiked up to show off the sexiest black mesh stockings Grace had ever seen: silky, sleek, and designed to tease with a hint of a floral pattern right where the stockings met the dress on two long, well-toned legs. Somehow, it didn't seem right to complain to someone who made such an effort to look so good.

Grace drove west toward Manhattan, and as she did, Melinda unleashed a fury of vitriolic frustration. Ever since she and James had moved in with Billy, he had virtually cut her off from all her friends and family, she said, because he wanted her to focus on him. "Don't get me wrong," she said. "I love living in such a beautiful home. But why live somewhere nice if I can't bring my friends over? And then he calls, and I'm supposed to drop everything–including my child–and cater to his whims. It's not right."

Grace said nothing, not even to acknowledge she, too, had to "drop her child." She simply nodded and kept one eye on the traffic ahead, trying to gauge if she was going to meet her deadline successfully. The other eye kept checking out the stockings and the legs inside. *Good God, that is a sexy woman,* she thought while nodding in agreement to whatever it was Melinda was saying. The Traffic Gods enabled Grace to get to Clegg & Cleary's with a few minutes to spare. The Parking Spot Gods were even more benevolent–Grace found one in front of the restaurant and did a masterful job parallel parking, no small feat in New York City, where truck drivers and cab drivers regard passenger cars as their mortal enemy. Grace slid the transmission gear into park, and they sat there for a moment, saying nothing. Then Melinda turned to Grace.

"I can't believe I did all the talking," she said. "Thank you for listening. I feel so much better now. I hope I can trust you to keep what was said between us."

"No worries," Grace replied, looking straight ahead for fear she might get caught checking out those legs one last time if she even glanced in Melinda's direction. "I hope you have a good time."

"I'm already having a good time, thanks to you," Melinda said, causing Grace to entertain the idea that Melinda was hitting on her. She let the comment simmer for a moment as Melinda thanked her again, got out, and glided into Clegg & Cleary's. Grace watched to make sure Melina made it inside safely and to study those legs a little longer. Then she turned to her left and steered the car back into midtown traffic.

Grace had no qualms about admiring other women, but it had never gone any further than that. Her experiences dealing with Slade's father had numbed her inside to the point where her sexual drive was nil. Even if she wanted to get laid, it's not like there was a line of lovers waiting for the opportunity to bed her.

Aphrodite herself couldn't land a man raising a kid on her own, Grace thought, and then chuckled. "Unless, of course, you have legs like Melinda."

She again pictured Melinda's stocking-clad thighs and wondered what Bernie would make of her doing so. Would he chide her for wanting to "play for the other team," suggest they enjoy a threesome, or compliment her on her good taste in women?

"Oh, Bernie," she sighed. "He always makes me laugh. And those eyes." Another sigh. Then she heard the voice in her head. *A bartender, Grace? Really? After your Drex experience, you're going to let a bartender be the role model for your son? Is bragging about a one-night stand with a little person what you want for Slade?*

Grace was no stranger to lesbianism, and as she drove, she thought about the stories regarding the late-night, clandestine "experimentation" in the girls' dormitories she had heard from her female friends who had gone away to school. *I suppose if I were to play for the other team, Melinda would be a good place to start,* Grace thought, and then giggled at the notion of sleeping with the boss' girlfriend. *It would serve him right for dragging us both into the city like this.*

The eyeful Grace enjoyed watching Melinda walk across the sidewalk, however, had nothing on what Billy's next project had in store.

Chapter 25

Oh! That Calendar

Billy loved showing off Melinda more than anything else, which worked out fine because Melinda loved being shown off. Her teenage dreams of being a fashion model gave way to marriage and motherhood. By the time she found Billy to bankroll her career, she was too old for the modeling she wanted to do, but was perfect for one magazine: *American Beauty and Bathing Suits.*

Each month, the publication features women modeling swimsuits and related apparel. What sets it apart from traditional media was that the models pay the publisher to be in each issue. These aspiring models would then use the published photos to develop a portfolio. Occasionally, this would lead to real modeling work. In reality, however, if the women who appeared in *American Beauty and Bathing Suits* had what it took to be models, then they would get modeling work without having to pay for it. Thousands from all over the country bought into the concept, and the one thing they had in common was the flaws that kept them on the outside looking in. Pete and Re-Pete tried to tell Billy it was all a scam, playing on the desires of impressionable women. Shadler thought it was wasteful but relatively harmless.

Billy spent thousands on the magazine, resulting in several "spreads" for Melinda but never the cover. Why Melinda wasn't chosen mystified Billy, so he called the publisher, Joey Cutillo.

"Joey, what's the deal with keeping Melinda off your cover?" Billy asked. "She's much better looking than the girls you've used."

Cutillo replied, "Melinda's gorgeous, Billy. A delightful girl. You're a lucky man."

"So why no cover?"

Cutillo paused for a second.

"Guys buy my magazine because they want to see something special and perky tits like Melinda's aren't special. Don't get me wrong—they're nice—but they don't sell magazines."

"Why would a guy buy your magazine?" Billy asked.

"For the same reason they pay you to dig holes for no reason," Cutillo said. "Reality doesn't hold a candle to what the imagination can do for them, and nothing kickstarts a guy's libido faster than a chick with big tits in a bikini."

The following morning, Billy and Melinda spread out Billy's girlie magazines on their bed. Melinda was not repulsed by pornography like Marietta but rather reveled in it. She enjoyed measuring herself up against what the women had to offer, and more often than not, she came out on the favorable end of the comparison—except when it came to her breasts. *Cutillo is right*, Melinda thought. *They were perky, but they did not turn heads—or sell magazines.* Melinda needed cleavage to ensure she and Billy would be the talk of any room they entered, so she had to have the best tits money could buy. So did Billy.

The two sprawled out on the bed, looking through the

magazines, trying to decide what breasts Melinda should get, like a couple picking out kitchen countertops.

"There–this is the set I want for you," Billy said, pointing to a young woman in a *Jugs* magazine who was squeezing together what looked like grapefruits. Melinda pursed her lips. "They're awfully big," she said. "Are you sure I can pull this off?"

"Trust me," Billy replied. "Nobody will be able to take their eyes off you."

His words sent an electric shock through Melinda's body, and she playfully pushed Billy on his back and straddled his waist. She leaned forward and gave him a long, wet, passionate kiss while her curly black hair cascaded over his face. She rubbed against his crotch, and in seconds, he was hard. They made love right there on top of the pornography like a couple on prom night. Within a few weeks, Melinda had her breasts and the *American Beauty and Bathing Suits* cover. Billy had his tata tiara for his arm candy.

A magazine cover seen by so few people was not good enough for Billy. "Nobody keeps his Oscar in a closet," Billy said to Grace as he explained what he had in mind: A calendar featuring Melinda posing in various string bikinis. The calendar also gave Billy something the magazine couldn't: creative control.

He wanted Long Island to know that the guy whose ears still singed every time he thought of his father's taunting at the construction camps about how no woman would ever want him, who grew up listening to "Master Bate" jokes and who married the first woman who would sleep with him was keeping company with a hot babe.

Melinda liked to model swimwear, and with her long legs and spectacular, man-made breasts, she did look stunning in a swimsuit. She might have been too old for *Sports Illustrated*, but for Mockingbird Heights and Long Island, this was, well, titillating. Each calendar month featured Melinda in a different bikini and pose. Billy snapped the photos himself.

One calendar page had Melinda sprawled across a white Corvette parked on the Promenade in Brooklyn, with the Brooklyn Bridge and Manhattan as a backdrop. In recognition of their first date, the December photo featured Melinda wearing nothing more than a satin jacket from *Black Maria*. In the picture, she is sitting on the hood facing right with her left leg bent, her right leg straight, and her back arched with her jacket opened enough to expose her left nipple (if you looked close enough–and most people did). Billy believed everybody who was anybody on Long Island would share his enthusiasm for this calendar. The mailing list Grace assembled included hundreds of elected officials as well as college presidents and leaders of business associations and chambers of commerce. He added the newspaper publishers and editors, as well as those included on the Long Island Business News' "Long Island's Top 100 Leaders." More than 2,000 calendar copies were delivered via Federal Express with a letter written by Grace but signed by Billy to explain why the recipient was receiving it. The letter related how Billy thought Long Island was a beautiful place to live for many reasons, one being his girlfriend, Melinda. Billy felt as if he were King of the World.

Billy and Melinda made an impression, all right. They were the talk of the Long Island business community and what passes for a social circle in the region. If social media had been around then, it would have blown up the Internet. The recipients who didn't know Billy and Melinda when they received it–and many did not–knew who they were now.

One particular recipient of note was duly impressed and decided it was time he met both of them.

Chapter 26

Wear a Tie for Wojo

One calendar landed on the desk of New York's junior Senator, Stan "Wojo" Wojciehowicz. Short, stocky, crass, and abusive, Wojciehowicz stuck out amongst his millionaire senator colleagues like a guy wearing a tank top to a country club picnic, not that he cared. He had little use for "those Senate putzes," and he considered the day a total loss if he did not cause someone to cringe at something he said or did. Senator Wojo, as he was referred to by friends and enemies alike, had a voice that reminded those who heard it of a shopping cart missing two wheels being dragged across a sidewalk. He thrived as a politician because he knew how to deliver the goods to his constituents, raise campaign cash, and manipulate the media better than any senator not named Kennedy.

Wojo didn't know who Billy Bate was. He took a long look at every calendar page and whistled long and low each time he turned to the next month. When he was done, he picked up the phone and called Lew Desmond.

Lew had cut his public relations teeth working for Wojo

back when the senator was a county executive, but he was the polar opposite of his former mentor. Forever in control and impeccably dressed in a style befitting a 1940s male movie star, he became a legendary flack on his own, although he was often blamed for creating the media monster Wojo had become. Lew demurred, claiming the opposite was true, that he learned everything he knew about public relations from the senator. However it came about, Lew knew everybody worth knowing. Wojciehowicz figured there was a good chance Lew knew Bate.

"Desmond!" the senator barked. "Wojo here. I didn't interrupt you jerking off, did I?"

"Always a pleasure hearing from you, Senator," Lew responded dryly, successfully disguising his disdain for such language while ignoring the question. "What can I do for you?"

"I was looking at this calendar I got from some guy named Bate," the senator said. "You know him?"

"I know *of* him, Senator. He was recently added to the board at Gibbons College. But then..."

"Gibbons College?" the senator cut in. "Where the hell is Gibbons College?"

"It's on Long Island, in Suffolk County," Lew explained. "You spoke at the commencement there two years ago."

"Now I remember," the Senator said. "Raised fifty grand from the people I met there."

"As I was saying," Lew continued. "Bate was named to the Gibbons board, and he showed up for his first directors' meeting dressed up as Tortu from *Black Maria*.

"Like a what?" the senator barked.

"Not like anything," Lew said. "The meeting just happened to fall on Halloween, so he dressed up as 'Tortu,' the lead character from *Black Maria*, the Broadway musical."

"Why the hell would he do that?" Wojo asked.

"I have no idea," Lew said. "But my guess is the thought process behind that decision was the same as the one behind the decision to send a calendar filled with pictures of his girlfriend."

"Did you get one?" the senator asked.

"Everyone got one," Lew said. "The guy's crazy."

"Does he have a checkbook?" the senator asked.

"I understand he does well for himself," Lew replied. "Runs something called Carpe Diem Construction Camps in Mockingbird Heights."

"Get him to host a book-signing party for me," the senator said, then hung up.

Lew sighed. He no longer worked for the senator, but his career and client base benefited greatly from Lew's access to him. Wojciehowicz knew this and exploited it at every possible turn. Lew picked up the phone and called Carpe Diem's offices. He asked to speak to Billy, but still being new to the game, Billy did not recognize the name and passed the call to Grace.

Grace knew the name and understood right away the call's significance. She stood up in her office while speaking to Lew, a subconscious reflection of her Catholic-school upbringing, where she was taught to rise before speaking to someone of authority.

"Good morning, Mr. Desmond," Grace said. "To what do I owe the honor?"

"I'm not sure talking to me is an honor, and for God's sake, call me Lew," he said. "I was hoping to talk to Billy Bate about this calendar thing."

"What about it?" Grace asked, sitting down almost out of embarrassment.

"What would drive a grown man to send a calendar filled

with half-naked pictures of his girlfriend to the power elite around Long Island?"

"Trust me, it wasn't my idea," Grace said.

"No doubt. But where are you going with it?"

Grace exhaled. "You have to understand, Lew," she replied. "Billy's not like most people. He needs to be liked and to be talked about. His ego must be massaged on a regular basis. I'm probably speaking a little too frankly here, but knowing where Billy's coming from helps you understand why he does what he does."

"My entire industry is based on men—and women, but mostly men—needing to draw attention to themselves, rational or otherwise," Lew said. "That's not necessarily a bad thing, either. Nobody ever went broke appealing to the male ego."

"So you get it," Grace said.

"To a certain extent, yes," Lew said. "You know who also gets it? Senator Wojciehowicz. He wants Billy to host a book signing for him."

"A book signing? Wow!" Grace thought for a moment. "How does it work?"

"Simple. You get a box of the senator's new book, *Senate Stew and Other Recipes for Success in Public Office*. You invite people to come down to pick up the book and have it signed for them by the senator. For a fee."

"Sounds like something Billy would want to do. Does he split the money with the senator?"

Lew laughed. "Oh my, no. The senator keeps the proceeds."

Grace chafed at her sounding so politically naïve. "I don't suppose the senator provides the books for free, does he?"

"You're catching on," Lew said. "Here's how it works. Bate buys a hundred books, gets 100 people to come to the signing, and charges them $100 per person to attend. They come down, get the book signed and their picture taken with the senator, assuming Billy wants to spring for a photographer, which I recommend he do. When it's all said and done, Billy hands over ten grand to the senator. Not bad for an hour's work, huh?"

"Not to mention a hundred books sold," Grace said.

"I'll have the senator's office send you the date and time the senator will be available for you to do this. Good luck."

Grace hung up with Lew Desmond and walked down the hall to her boss's office. Billy was thrilled at the news, seeing it as an opportunity to hobnob with the big guns and giving Grace her first inkling that Billy did not realize he was being used.

Neither did the local business owners in Mockingbird Heights. The initial reaction when Grace reached out to them was excitement. She also told Grail about it, and much to Grace's surprise, she and her husband expressed an interest in attending.

Up until this point, both Grail and her husband, Ron, had no use for Billy Bate or anything relating to him. They enjoyed hearing about his exploits, but they thought his need for attention showed a lack of character. As far as Grail and Ron were concerned, no amount of money or prestige could make up for shortcomings in the character department. Grail considered Billy to be a phony, which was the lowest thing she could call somebody.

Nonetheless, Grail and Ron were among the first visitors to Carpe Diem the morning of the signing. Ron was wearing a sports jacket over a polo shirt. Grail had on a blouse and pants. Grace was thrilled they got there early because she was hoping to get them in and out with as little interaction with Billy as possible, since Grace knew Grail and Ron had no qualms about speaking their minds. Grace also had no intention of charging either one $100. She knew she could slide them in and out without Billy taking a full accounting.

When Grace saw her sister and brother-in-law, she walked over to them and brought them right up to the table where the senator was sitting.

"Senator Wojciehowicz, I'd like you to meet my sister, Grail, and her husband, Ron," Grace said, gesturing to the photographer to come over and take a picture.

"That's a nice sister you have there," the senator said to Grail, even though Grace had only met him a few minutes earlier. "I'd bring her down to Washington with me, but I get the sense she'd rather jerk around here in Mockingbird Heights."

"I don't know if Grace would do well in Washington," Ron said. "She likes to earn an honest living."

The senator laughed out loud, much to Grace's relief. Unfortunately, his laugh also got Billy's attention, and he scurried over to the group as Grace was trying to get the photographer to take the picture without Billy, who wedged himself in.

After the picture was snapped, Ron reached out to shake the Senator's hand, but Billy got in the way again.

"This must be quite a thrill for you, meeting an actual United States senator," Billy said.

"It is," Ron responded.

"Too bad you didn't see a need to wear a tie," Billy said." I would think meeting a senator would inspire you to dress appropriately."

Grace wondered if Billy realized how rude a comment this was. Ron took it in stride. "I don't judge a man by the clothes he wears," he said. "Nor do I worry about comments from a man who does." He brushed past Billy, picked up his signed book, and walked out the door with Grail in tow. Grace hid a grin and brought other attendees to the table. Billy pretended nothing had happened and positioned himself next to the senator so he could be in all the pictures.

The day was an unqualified success. Billy was now pals with a United States senator, one who was only too happy to attend Billy and Melinda's upcoming wedding.

Chapter 27

Wedding Bells

"Now hold on," Catherine interrupted Angelo. "This guy sends out calendars of his wife in bikini poses ..."

"Girlfriend. They weren't married yet. I'm just getting to that part," Angelo said.

"Okay, girlfriend. The mother of a pre-teen son, in her mid-to-late 30s, was okay with this?"

"Okay with it? She loved it!" Angelo said.

"How was this helping Billy build his business?" Catherine asked.

"It didn't. At this point, the two Petes were running things, with occasional input from Billy. And Shadler was still around, keeping an eye on the cash flow and everyone else. For the most part, though, the company was on autopilot."

"Is that a good thing?" Catherine asked. "I thought in the business world the mantra is, 'if you're not growing, you're dying.'"

"It is and it's true," Angelo said. "You can look at the demise of any business enterprise, and more often than not, it starts when the owner takes his or her eye off the ball, strays from the main mission."

"Why didn't somebody say anything or do something?" Catherine asked. "It seems to me the same ego that drove Billy to succeed, to prove his father and just about everyone else wrong, was now driving him down a path of self-destruction."

"In retrospect, yes," Angelo said. "But at that point, business was good. Pete and RePete were doing their thing with Billy, mostly preoccupied with his 'Billy Projects,' as Snodgrass liked to call them. Grace was exhausted keeping up with Billy while trying her best to raise a toddler. Shadler was on the Back Nine of his CFO career, and everybody else was just happy to collect a paycheck."

"All right," Catherine said. "Let's get back to the wedding you just mentioned. What made it so special?"

"It wasn't just a 'wedding,' per se," Angelo said. "It was more of an 'event,' an official 'coming out party' if you will. It kicked off a series of events that parlayed Billy into a *major* player on Long Island, but also led to his ultimate demise less than four years later, again in retrospect. If you were charting the growth of his ego on a graph, the years 1993 through 1996 would represent the apex. It was also during that time when Billy started to explore other business options, one of which was at best nefarious and, at worst, borderline criminal, while seeds of unrest and instability were planted at Carpe Diem."

"Oh boy," Catherine said, shifting in her seat. "Do tell."

Chapter 28

Jack's Death: Crisis Averted

"Ah, yes. 'The Wedding,'" Angelo said, with a chuckle. "It took place back in December 1993. Long Island was in the midst of a terrible economic slump brought on by the demise of The Grumman Corp., a defense manufacturer that at one point employed 33,000 Long Islanders. It was a company town, Long Island was, in that you either worked for Grumman or you worked for a company that did things to support Grumman."

"What happened to Grumman?" Catherine asked.

Angelo snorted. "That's a long story that's still being written," he replied. "Talk about the highs and lows of a business operation. Leroy Grumman started it all in 1929 when he convinced four co-workers to join him in a new venture. No doubt his ego played a role in that. He even convinced one of them to get his mother-in-law to mortgage her house. For the next 40 years or so, it was a great company to work for, by all accounts, culminating with their role in landing a man on the moon in 1969."

"Then what happened?" Catherine asked.

"Peace broke out," Angelo said. "By the late 1980s, Grumman was just a shell of itself, and Long Island was at a crossroads. Fortunately, enough former Grummanites struck out on their own–again, ego in action–to start myriad small businesses, and by the year 2000, Long Island's economy was booming again."

"And Grumman?" Catherine asked.

"It was absorbed by another defense manufacturer and became Northrop-Grumman."

"Wait a minute," Catherine said, sitting up. "That's the company responsible for polluting Long Island's water supply and is dragging its feet in the remediation process."

"Correct," Angelo said. "I wasn't there in the 1940s, 50s and 60s, so I don't know if the company's practices regarding the disposal of toxic waste materials was conceived out of ignorance or criminal incompetence, but either way it left behind a mess that will take decades–and billions of dollars–to clean up."

"Geez," Catherine said.

"Exactly," Angelo said. "Let's get back to the wedding."

"Was it in a church?" Catherine asked. "Was Father Cappuccino–the priest who ignored the pornography–involved?"

"Macchiato," Angelo replied.

"What?" Catherine asked.

"Macchiato. Father Macchiato." Angelo said. "But he didn't marry Melinda and Billy. Father Macchiato was a priest from the local parish. Billy had to have a famous priest at his reception."

"Don't you mean he had to have a famous priest perform the marriage ceremony?" Catherine interjected, thinking perhaps she caught a professional journalist in a lapse of accuracy.

"There's not a priest in the world who could have done that," Angelo said.

"Why not?" Catherine asked.

"Because technically, Billy was still married to Marietta," Angelo explained. "Billy and Melinda got married on a Sunday, but the divorce was not official until the prior Thursday."

"Cutting it close, no?" Catherine asked.

"As a business owner, Billy preached planning and preparation," Angelo said, "but he hated dealing with emotional buttons, and officially divorcing Marietta stirred up pain. I think he still loved Marietta, if for no other reason than she was his daughter's mother. He also appreciated the fact that she was the first woman to show him affection and had rescued him from such lonely misery."

"Do you think he ever considered going back to Marietta?" Catherine asked.

"No," Angelo said. "Marietta looked good in an evening gown, but not glamorous. Perhaps more telling was her having zero desire to play dress up to please others. Billy also put off the divorce because he realized his still being married to Marietta made Melinda uncomfortable, and he loved to keep people on edge."

"Geez," Catherine said again.

"His steering clear of pain almost cost him a boatload of money at one point," Angelo said, with a chuckle.

"How so?" Catherine asked.

"Grace told me this story," Angelo said.

"Billy's father, Jack, was dying. The doctors told Billy it was days, if not hours. Billy was working in the office, and Grace was in there with him when Martha, his assistant, put a call through. Billy listened and turned pale. Grace said she thought for sure this was it. Billy hung up and said, 'I gotta go' and flew out the office's back door to the parking lot. Grace said could hear his car peel out, which was unusual for him, because Billy was a careful driver. Grace left his office–remember, nobody was allowed in there if Billy wasn't around–and spoke to Martha."

"Martha?" Catherine asked.

"Yes, Martha," Angelo chuckled. "She might have an old lady's name, but if I remember correctly, she looked like Long Island's answer to Cindy Crawford. For some reason, her parents saddled her with the name Martha. She had smoldering eyes and a dark complexion."

"Let me guess. And a body to die for," Catherine opined with a tinge of sarcasm.

"She might have qualified for such a description, I don't rightly recall," Angelo said, with a bemused smile.

"Anyway, Grace said to Martha, 'Boy, Billy must be upset about his dad. He sped off like he was driving the Batmobile, and Commissioner Gordon flashed the Bat Signal. I guess his dad's in pretty bad shape.'"

"He is," Martha replied. "But Billy's upset because his insurance broker reminded him that a week or two after his mom died, Jack married the Ecuadorian nurse who had been caring for her."

"And that's why he's upset?" I asked Martha.

"Billy pretends he doesn't care what Jack does," Martha said. "But years ago, he took out an insurance policy on his father listing his mother, Mrs. Jack Bate, as the beneficiary, and he neglected to change it after his mom passed away. If Billy doesn't get to the insurance office to sign a new policy before Jack dies, all the benefits will go to the new Mrs. Jack Bate."

"How much?" Grace asked.

"Three hundred grand," Martha said.

"Wow. So she gets the money? I could see how that would tick Billy off," Grace said.

"Oh, it's worse than that," Martha said, suppressing a giggle. "Billy borrowed against that policy. If he doesn't get there in time, not only does he not get the money, but he'll have to pay off a quarter-million in loans."

"Did he get there in time?" Catherine asked.

"He did. His father died later that day," Angelo said.

"Gives new meaning to the expression 'the devil is in the details,'" Catherine said. "So what happened with the priest?"

"Like I was saying, a priest could not marry Billy and Melinda because of the divorce, so Billy arranged to have Father James Joseph Quinn give a blessing at the reception."

"Why does the name sound familiar?" Catherine asked.

"He was part of a priest and rabbi team that toured the country for years trying to promote better relations between Catholics and Jews," Angelo said. "Technically, he is a monsignor. But everybody calls him J.J., or Father J.J."

"Oh yeah," Catherine said. "I remember seeing them on TV when my mother was watching the morning news shows. The Peace Patrol, they called themselves."

"Right. So Father J.J. is giving the blessing at the reception, touching all the usual bases about loving each other, but ignoring the elephant in the room, as the marriage clearly was not sanctioned by the Church. Grace said she was standing behind Billy and Melinda when J.J. said, 'In the event this union should result in children ...' Melinda turned to Billy and whispered, "Don't even think about it."

"Thank God she felt that way," Catherine said. "I can only imagine what those two would have spawned."

"No need to worry," Angelo said. "The only thing Billy wanted less than another child was for anything to alter Melinda's body."

"So, how did the reception go?" Catherine asked. "What can you tell me about it?"

"By all accounts, it was a perfect example of over-the-top extravagance," Angelo said. "Grace said she loved every minute of it.

"'This was no ordinary wedding reception,' she told me. 'It was a statement.' Billy wanted to establish himself as a leader, a man who gets things done on Long Island. There's a more colorful way to describe it, but ..."

"He took his dick out and slapped it on the table, is that what you're saying?" Catherine said.

"In a manner of speaking, yes," Angelo said, shifting uncomfortably.

"So what made this event so special?" Catherine asked, suppressing a grin at having unsettled a grizzled journalism veteran.

"Well, I tell you what," Angelo said. "You may recall the morning after Billy's passing, Grace called Doc Ronkee but had to cut the conversation short to catch a train. Later that morning, Doc called the Carpe Diem office to tell Grace he'd be happy to help her try to get an obit in the *Times*, that she could handle *Newsday*. Grace had never dealt directly with the Metro Desk at the *Times* before, so she was happy for the assistance. I'll share with you what Grace told me she shared with Doc Ronkee."

Chapter 29

Don't Mention Lennon

"Tell me everything about the wedding so we can figure out what should go into the obituary," Doc said. "Start from the beginning."

"They met on December 8th," Grace said.

"How do you remember?" Doc asked.

"It's easy. Billy and Melinda announced their engagement on December 8th, five years to the day they met, and got married exactly one year later. I also remember because it was the anniversary of the night John Lennon was killed."

"That's right," Doc said.

"I mistakenly brought it up once," Grace said. "Billy got pissed and told me not to mention it again."

"Billy was a big Lennon fan?" Doc asked.

"He said he did not want any negativity associated with his big day."

"Okay, so he meets Melinda," Doc said. "They date and move in together when?"

"I'm not sure exactly," Grace replied. "It was right around the time I started at Carpe Diem in January 1991. They must have been living together then because later in the year, I got invited to their house to celebrate the holidays."

"How was that?" Doc asked.

"A disaster," Grace said. "Billy invited me to come over on the Sunday before Christmas, the day when everyone is trying to get everything together, and he told me to bring Slade. I was not happy about having to spend a Sunday afternoon so close to Christmas at the boss's house, but I was curious to see how splendid it was.

"I was told to be there by 1:00 p.m., and I pulled up to the house about 20 minutes after the hour. I saw the guy who maintained Carpe Diem's construction equipment standing on the front lawn next to a woman who looked like she had been smacked in the face with a cast-iron frying pan. She was a fright to look at."

"Why were they standing on the front lawn?" Doc asked.

"Apparently, Billy also told them to be there at 1:00 p.m.," Grace said. "So they got there exactly at one. Melinda answered the door wearing a robe and snapped out, 'What do you want?' They said Billy invited them to come over. She said, 'Hold on a minute' and closed the door. A few minutes later, she reopened the door and told them Billy hadn't told her he invited people over, and she was going to need some time to get ready. Then she closed the door again."

"She didn't invite them in?" Doc asked. "Wasn't it cold?"

"It was freezing with six inches of snow on the ground," Grace said. "When I showed up, the maintenance guy and his scary-looking wife were standing outside the house wondering what to do."

"They stood outside the whole time?" Doc asked.

"More or less," Grace said. "We hung outside for another 10 minutes before Melinda let us in. The house was ultra-modern, with a black and white design, immaculate, but with a cold and unwelcoming feeling. There were perfectly wrapped gifts in every room. Billy and Melinda loved to give each other gifts, and Billy had them all wrapped at the local mall, including the presents he bought from catalogs."

"How did the afternoon go?" Doc asked.

"Eventually, other co-workers and their families stopped by. Once Billy was done showing everybody the latest electronic gadgets he had installed around the house, he parked himself on the couch and started playing on his laptop. Melinda spent the time talking to Candee and ignored everyone else. There were five cans of soda on the kitchen table. No food. No snacks. Nothing. We were left to our own devices, and several parents were petrified that their little ones were going to break something. Slade and I got the hell out as soon as we could."

"So how could a guy who was so bad at providing hospitality host such a spectacular wedding reception?" Doc asked.

"It all started with a fundraiser for Hamilton General Hospital," Grace said. "He was asked to chair the event and raised a ton of money. More importantly, he tasted the Tuxedo Life, and once he attended other black-tie affairs in the following months, it blossomed into a full-blown appetite for excitement and glamor. He saw how those events were supposed to work, and he discovered what did not work for him."

"Like what?" Doc asked.

"Billy once said to me, 'Most people involved in fundraising repeat whatever worked the year before. There's no imagination, no effort to make these galas more interesting. Nobody wants to take any risks.'"

"Let me guess," Doc said. "Billy preferred to push the envelope?"

"Billy's entrepreneurial instincts took over," Grace said.

"Any time he committed to chairing a fundraiser, his goal was to host one that people would talk about for years. He wanted to pull out all the stops and, in doing so, prove his theory that adding interesting twists to parties raises more money than going the safe, secure route."

"How did he come up with the ideas for throwing a great party?" Doc asked.

"My background became useful to him," Grace said. "I had experience organizing special events. Billy told me to find black-tie affairs for us to attend so we could steal ideas. For almost a year, Billy, Melinda, and I attended various dinners and fundraisers and evaluated what we liked and didn't like during the limousine ride home," Grace said. "I took copious notes."

"Did any one event stand out in particular?" Doc asked.

"The Bartender's Ball," Grace said. "I had publicized it back when I was working with Bruce Wright."

"What's a Bartender's Ball?" Doc asked.

"Long Island's restaurant and bar owners wanted to throw an annual party for the industry, but the hospitality business being what it is made doing so impossible because nobody had the time to organize it," Grace said. "So several key industry players arranged to have a local charity's development director coordinate the event. Whatever money the event raised was contributed to the charity."

"In other words, the industry gets its party and does some good for the local community," Doc said. "Great idea."

"Right," Grace said. "The party was in March, a downtime in the year, so more restaurants and bars could participate. It took place at the Muttontown Hotel, the nicest on the Island. Hospitality industry vendors by the dozens bought tables. It was like New Year's Eve and everybody dressed to look their best."

"Sounds like a festive night," Doc said.

"It evolved into an orgy of great food and flowing booze," Grace said, "with young people determined to have a great time. Billy and Melinda took in all this energy and decided right there they wanted their wedding reception to be as extravagant and elaborate."

"Anything interesting happen?" Doc asked.

"There was one little oddity," Grace said. "Miracles in Motion, the charity selected to benefit from the Ball, is a home for wayward teenagers suffering from alcohol and drug abuse. It was founded by a Gannonite Missionary named Pete Ciccino. He attended the event reluctantly as he was not comfortable benefiting from an event encouraging excessive alcohol consumption. I arranged to have him sit at our table, right next to Billy and Melinda, because I thought he would enjoy getting to know Billy."

"Why would you think that?" Doc asked.

"Father Ciccino was looking for new blood for his board of directors, and I was hoping Billy might want to get involved. Ciccino does nice work benefiting the community."

"So what happened?" Doc asked.

"Money was collected throughout the night for a '50-50' raffle where half the proceeds would go to Miracles in Motion and the other half to the winner. The cash prize was $35,000, and before the emcee revealed the winner, Billy leaned over to Father Ciccino and whispered, 'Be prepared: If I win the prize, I'll announce I'm giving all the money to Miracles in Motion.'"

"Did he win?" Doc asked.

"No, but he scored some major points with the padre," Grace said.

"Did he ever get asked to be on the Board?" Doc asked.

"Eventually, but it didn't work out," Grace said. "Father

Pete was not one to kiss ass nor was Billy inclined to contribute to something unless he was lauded over for doing so."

"So the evening was a waste?" Doc asked.

"Not at all," Grace replied. "Billy and Melinda got a sense of what they wanted their party to be like: a blow-out affair with guests dressed to the nines, constant entertainment, and nary a quiet moment throughout the evening. Money was no object. The goal was to have people shaking their heads in amazement at how special and marvelous Billy and Melinda were. My job was to make it happen."

Chapter 30

On the Air!

Billy wanted to make sure the invitations impressed upon the recipient that this wedding should not be missed. The invitations themselves included the *Black Maria* logo made from Swiss chocolate and featured cards with a hand-drawn illustration of Cupid shooting an arrow with Billy & Melinda written in script. He instructed Grace to send them via overnight delivery on a Friday afternoon so they would be delivered to the recipients' homes Saturday morning. Three hundred fifty of the 400 invitations were delivered that way. The premium paid for such service almost gave Shadler a heart attack, but Billy dismissed his protests.

The Saturday deliveries presented an interesting challenge for Grace. Many of the invitees were business colleagues or community leaders who barely knew Billy and had no idea about Melinda. Grace and an assistant brought on to help handle the reception responsibilities had to call them to get their home addresses. While most supplied the addresses willingly, sometimes Grace and her assistant had to press hard to get what they needed, like when Grace had Gibbons College President Chuck Biscuit on the phone.

"Hello, my name is Grace Duffy, and I'm calling from Billy Bate's office."

"Who's Billy Bate?"

"He owns Carpe Diem Construction Camps and is president of the Mockingbird Heights Chamber of Commerce. He's..."

"The guy who's seen *Black Maria* more than 100 times?"

"That's him."

"Did he do that?"

"Do what?"

"See *Black Maria* so many times."

"Yes."

"Why?"

"He likes the play. He swears every time he watches it, he notices some new nuance."

"Like what?"

"Like how a violin plays softly in the background any time the main character, Tortu, is not being honest with himself or others."

"I'll take your word for it. What can I do for you?"

"I need to get your home address."

"Why?"

"Because Mr. Bate wants to send you an invitation to his wedding."

"He can send it to me at work. You have the address here."

"I am under strict orders to get your home address."

"Why should I give you my home address?"

"All I can tell you, sir, is this is going to be a spectacular wedding reception. You'll want to be there."

"What makes it so special?"

"Billy has hired a 35-piece orchestra, and he plans to pour

Dom Perignon throughout the entire reception. And the event will have a *Black Maria* theme, including a performance from one of the actors from the show."

"Where's the reception going to be?"

"The Muttontown Hotel."

"Geez. Oh, what the hell. You can send the invite to ..."

Not all the invites were delivered via FedEx. Billy took things to the next level for the invitees he considered most important. He hired an entertainer named Mo Irby, a songwriter who had a minor hit in the 1960s called "Apples, Peaches, Pumpkin Pie." In addition to writing songs, Mo could improvise poetry with musical accompaniment on the spot. Billy arranged to have 50 invitations delivered by Mo, accompanied by a guitar player. The entertainers dressed in tuxedos and were driven around in Billy's limousine. Their itinerary included both county executives, the president of the Island's biggest chamber of commerce, and Senator Wojciehowicz.

Mo started with an invite delivered to Danny Gerard, a local radio talk-show host, while he was on the air. Danny was chatting up the morning traffic report when the listeners heard a commotion in the background.

Danny said, "What the hell is going on?" In walked Mo, having finally convinced the show's producer he meant no harm. Mo explained to Danny that he was there on behalf of Billy Bate, and Danny recognized Billy's name. He welcomed Mo and said, "What brings you here?"

Mo handed Danny a box with the invitation and started singing:

"Billy and Melinda

Sitting in a tree

I-N-V-I-T-I-N-G..."

"Hey–there's chocolate in here!" Danny yelled out as he looked at the invitation. Mo lost his place. He tried again.

"Billy and Melinda

Sitting in a tree

I-N-V-I-T-I-N-G..."

"Wow! A wedding reception at the Muttontown Hotel! That's got to cost some major bucks," Danny said. "Look at this invitation, ladies and gentlemen," forgetting for a second he was on the radio.

"Such beautiful paper and calligraphy. Jesus Christ, this is going to be soooommmmeeee soiree!"

Mo gave up on the poetry.

"On behalf of Billy Bate and Melinda Strutt," he said, sans musical accompaniment, "I would like to invite you to a gala affair on December 8th of this year ..."

Danny interrupted again. "How big a gift am I gonna have to give?"

Mo said he had no idea and bid Danny a good morning. There were 49 people on his list he still had to see.

The presentations had the desired effect. In the days following the invitation deliveries, the Carpe Diem phone lines lit up like PBS on Pledge Night. Long Island's elite were RSVPing and, more importantly, talking about Billy and Melinda and the Wedding of the Decade. At this point, Grace's biggest concern was would the event live up to the hype. Could it?

Chapter 31

The Wedding Reception

The excitement that Billy and Melinda felt during the planning fed the extravagance. In addition to the 35-piece orchestra and Dom Perignon poured throughout the seven-hour reception, dance troupes were hired to perform while the various dinner courses were served. Mo Irby was hired to sing and improvise poetry whenever the band took a break. Throughout the evening, two magicians did card tricks and told jokes.

December 8th fell on a Sunday, so that's when they had the reception. If it fell on a Wednesday, they would have had it on a Wednesday. Billy and Melinda insisted on having the party on the anniversary of their first meeting, even if doing so meant having a party on a night where people would have to go to work the next day. They also believed that their guests having to go to work the next day would lead to more chatter about the event itself.

The day proved sunny but cold. Grace drove herself to the Muttontown Hotel with a bag of jelly beans beside her on the front seat to feast on for the sugar rush. She arrived at the hotel around noon. Even though Billy and Melinda insisted their wedding HAD to be perfect in every way, Grace knew there was no such thing as the perfect wedding. They also told Grace that "under no circumstances was there to be a conga line on the dance floor." She was ready to roll with whatever punches were thrown her way, but she wasn't sure how she would go about breaking up a conga line should somebody start one.

When she got to the hotel's ballroom, she discovered the first punch: The table cards for the 507 guests were not in alphabetical order. It was not the worst thing, but not something you want to be doing a few hours before the event is supposed to start. The guests were instructed to arrive by 3:00 p.m. for the wedding itself. The reception–with a two-hour cocktail hour–was supposed to start at 4:00. The guests started showing up by 2:00 p.m. The women especially wanted to see what Melinda was going to wear. Some guys wanted to see, too, but for different reasons. Melinda obliged both sexes. Her ivory satin dress clung to every curve before crashing to the ground in a train of silk and sparkle. Billy reminded Grace of Clark Gable in *Gone With The Wind* in his tux and tails.

Jack Bate was also on hand. When he wasn't putting a dent in the Muttontown Hotel's supply of Jack Daniels, he was introducing his new bride–the rotund nurse who cared for Billy's mother until she died– as his "trophy wife," like she was Anna Nicole Smith and he was the billionaire she married. One wag quipped to Grace, "She looks more like a bowling trophy wife." But Jack was happy. The wife was happy. The only one who was not happy about her being there was Billy. He did everything he could to discourage his father from bringing her. He also tried to discourage Betty from bringing her fiancé, Jeff Doomey, to no avail.

Billy asked Melinda's son, James, to be the Best Man, and Melinda asked Billy's Betty to be her Maid of Honor. It was not as if Betty and Melinda were close–it seemed like a cute thing to do. Billy did enjoy playing 'Dad' to James, but a nice guy dad, not the prick dad Billy grew up with. James could do no wrong in Billy's eyes, and there was nothing he wanted that he did not get.

The plan was to guide everybody upstairs to the smaller ballroom for the wedding ceremony and then downstairs for the reception in the main ballroom. The hotel was set up for about 150 people to witness the ceremony, yet close to 250 showed up. This did not concern Billy and Melinda as they felt standing room only and having people jockeying for position so they could see lent to the buzz. The smaller ballroom was more functional than magnificent, but it served the purpose of providing a subtle backdrop for the wedding ceremony itself. An aisle was created by setting up chairs with a gap in the middle.

The Nassau County Executive was at the aisle's end with Billy and James, waiting for Melinda's arrival. Billy wanted the biggest politician he could get to officiate, and a county executive is the closest thing Long Island has to a big-time mayor. At the time, county executives were not legally allowed to marry couples, but Billy made some phone calls and wrote a couple of checks so special legislation could be enacted in the State Legislature to give the county executive the authority he needed. There was also some question as to whether the legislation would be voted on in time. During the ceremony, when the county executive said, "By the power invested in me by the State of New York ... last Tuesday.' It got a big laugh.

The ceremony was over in a flash. Neither Billy nor Melinda had any desire to write their own vows as they wanted to get on with the reception. Around 4:00 p.m., 507 men and women dressed in black tie descended the wide, spiral staircase leading to the Muttontown Hotel's main reception area to greet the newly-minted Mr. & Mrs. Billy Bate. Seating was tight, as the room was designed to accommodate 350 people comfortably. Eventually, everyone was seated, and the lights dimmed. The orchestra leader stepped up to the microphone, welcomed everyone, and then asked them to rise and greet their hosts for the evening. A lone spotlight lit a circle on the center of the dance floor, and as the music cued up, Billy and Melinda magically appeared–seemingly out of nowhere–as if they were in a Broadway musical of their own.

Speaking over the soft intro, the orchestra leader said, "As you know, Billy and Melinda met five years ago tonight at a performance of *Black Maria* on Broadway. They knew then what we know now–this love was meant to be. They were meant to be. So join me in celebrating–for the first time as husband and wife–Billy and Melinda Bate." A raucous round of applause ensued, and once the guests calmed down, they started to realize just how special this reception was going to be. The orchestra started playing the opening notes to "Izzat Love," the show-stopping, tear-jerking song from *Black Maria*, when the show's lead actor himself, Mike Nobile, sauntered onto the dance floor without any introduction or warning. Billy and Melinda twirled slowly and gracefully around the dance floor like Rhett Butler and Scarlett O'Hara while Nobile serenaded them.

> *Izzat love*
> *What I feel when you're in my arms*
> *Make me die before I'd do you harm*
> *When you're lost, I will lead you home*
> *If you're cold, you know I'll keep you warm*
> *Am I wrong?*

Or izzat love?
When I dream, there is no one else
In the end, who's your friend? Just myself
Izzat love to forget my pride
To conceal how it feels deep inside
Am I wrong?

Or Izzat love?
Izzat love to forgive all those things you've done
If you go, still you know I'm the one
Only love, love alone, can survive
Deep inside, I believe it's alive
Am I wrong? Or Izzat love?

The orchestra played it to the hilt, and Nobile sang as if Billy and Melinda were the only two people listening. The room erupted into a standing ovation when Nobile was done. Grace smiled. She wondered if the guests, including Billy and Melinda, knew "Izzat" was more than a clever combination of the words "is that" but rather an Arabic word meaning "personal dignity or honor." The song spoke to loving yourself and honoring who you are and the Higher Power residing within us.

At one point, a New York state senator asked Grace why the reception had a *Black Maria* theme. Grace explained the story about Billy and Melinda meeting at a performance of the musical. The senator thought about it and said, "Wow, can you imagine what the reception would have been like if they met at *Oh! Calcutta!?*" Grace laughed. The next day, a *New York Times* reporter who attended the event asked Grace if Billy and Melinda were happy with how the reception turned out.

"Well, nobody started a conga line," Grace replied, laughing. "A what?" the reporter asked, confused. "A conga line ..."

Grace said, immediately realizing that it wasn't worth the effort to explain the reference.

"H'mmm," the reporter said. "Did anybody say anything funny?" Grace shared the senator's line, and the reporter said, "Oh, that's good. But you better run it by the senator to see if he wants to be quoted."

Grace said, "He said it to me. Why wouldn't he want to be quoted?"

"Ask him," the reporter said.

Grace considered for a moment pretending she called the state senator and got his approval so the reporter would run with it, but the little voice in her head told her to make the call. So she did.

"Good morning, Senator. I was telling a reporter from the *New York Times* about your *Oh! Calcutta!* comment," Grace said.

He replied, "Good God, Grace! I can't be quoted saying that!"

"Why not?" Grace asked. "It's a funny line."

"I represent a very conservative district, Grace," the senator explained. "My people will kill me. The play's got nudity in it."

The quote was not used. Grace told Billy about the conversation he had with the senator when Billy came back from honeymooning in London, where he had gone with Melinda to see the British version of *Black Maria*. Billy laughed and then let Grace know he and Melinda had already hatched plans for their next extravaganza.

Chapter 32

Tina Louise, Of Course

"Their next extravaganza?" Catherine interjected. "How much attention did these people need? Don't most people just want to get on with their lives after a wedding?"

"Having dealt with business owners and politicians over several decades, I have come to recognize narcissistic behavior better than most," Angelo said. "Billy and Melinda Bate were textbook narcissists. They checked off all the boxes, to use a cliché. Grandiosity with expectations of superior treatment from other people. Fixation on fantasies of power, success, intelligence, and attractiveness. Self-perception of being unique, superior, and associated with high-status people and institutions. Needing continual admiration from others. A sense of entitlement to special treatment and obedience from others. Check, check, check, check AND check."

"Is narcissism the same as ego?" Catherine wondered.

"Good question," Angelo said, smiling. Catherine squirmed a little, somewhat taken aback at how happy she was to hear him say that. "A lot of people mistake narcissism for ego. They'll attribute someone's narcissistic behavior to him or her, quote-unquote having a 'Big Ego,' when in reality narcissists are painfully–and sometimes dangerously–insecure."

"So, what's the difference?" Catherine pressed.

"Ego drives a man or a woman to succeed, to produce things, to leave a legacy," Angelo said. "A narcissist, on the other hand, just wants to be noticed. It almost doesn't matter why. Just look at the Kardashians. They have no shame as long as they get the fawning eyeballs they crave. The mother pimped out a sex tape involving her daughter, for Christ sakes. Who does that?"

"But they're rich and famous," Catherine said, half-kidding.

"If that's what it takes to be rich and famous, you can keep it," Angelo said.

"Don't you want to be rich and famous, or at least rich?" Catherine asked coyly because she knew the answer. She just wanted to see how far she could push Angelo's buttons.

Angelo snorffed. That is to say, he snorted, but in a scoffing kind of way. He looked long and hard at Catherine, trying to decide whether he should share what he wanted to share with her.

"Here's what I think," he said quietly while leaning forward. "I think we're spiritual beings having a human experience, and when you're born, God gives you an easel and a palette. What you do with those tools–gifts, if you will–while you're here on Earth, for whatever length of time that is–is your gift back to God. And for the life of me, I couldn't imagine handing God a DVD of my daughter doing unspeakable things."

Catherine shifted in her seat. She had never seen the so-called Kardashian sex tape nor had any plans to do so, but she was aware of what was on it, and it was not a topic she wanted to explore with a man old enough to be her father.

"So," Catherine offered after some thought, "Billy's ego

drove him to build Carpe Diem Camps, an endeavor that provided a much-appreciated product and service for thousands of customers while also creating careers for dozens of people across the country. His narcissism, on the other hand, caused him to expend much time, money, and energy on activities with very little benefit, save what it did for the Long Island catering industry."

"Excellent analysis," Angelo said.

"Thanks," she said. "Let's get back to this 'next extravaganza.' I get the feeling Billy wasn't big on so-called 'downtime.'"

"I asked Grace about that during one of our many chats. She said Billy was driven by the phrase 'Carpe Diem.'"

"Billy loved and lived the expression," Grace said. "He greeted the day differently from most folks. I remember telling him once that I never had a boring day on the job in the five-plus years I worked for him. It wasn't always fun, but it was never dull. I had to stay on my toes. One phone call from Billy and whatever I had planned for the day was out the window. "

"Can you give me an example?" I asked her.

"One morning, he called me down to his office," Grace said. "'What are you doing for lunch?' he asked, conveying that whatever I was doing, I wasn't doing it anymore."

"What did he have in mind?" I asked.

"When Billy got into the office, he realized there was a conference on 'Operating a Small Business in New York State' in Albany, so he decided to attend. We drove out to Republic Airport in Farmingdale, and the next thing I know, we were on his plane with Billy at the controls," Grace said. "He loved taking his plane out and looked for any excuse to do so. We flew up, attended the conference luncheon, and flew back. I was back at my desk by 4:00 p.m. I remember picking up Slade from Grail. She asked me how my day was. I told her I had lunch in Albany, but other than that, it was uneventful. She thought I was kidding."

"So truly there wasn't downtime for anyone in Billy's life," Catherine said again.

"Apparently not," Angelo said. "But in retrospect, everything done up until that point—every little project and event attended—simply served as a prelude to the event Billy and Melinda concocted to celebrate their second wedding anniversary."

"What happened to their first anniversary?" Catherine asked.

"They used the occasion for a 'Big Announcement' about their plans for the second anniversary," Angelo said.

"What big announcement?" Catherine asked.

"Billy and Melinda wanted an event bigger than the wedding," Angelo said. "They decided to purchase every ticket in the theater for the December 8th performance of *Black Maria.*

"Every ticket?" Catherine asked.

"Every ticket. Billy wanted to make sure everyone in the theater that night was there for them. He and Grace contacted the theater and convinced them to block out whatever tickets were still available and then to contact the hundred or so people who had already purchased tickets. The request was made more than a year in advance, so it was still possible to do this."

"How many total tickets are we talking about?" Catherine wondered.

"One thousand, six hundred and nine,' according to Grace. 'It's impossible to forget the number,' she told me."

"So what were they going to do with one thousand, six hundred and nine tickets?" Catherine asked.

"The idea was to make the tickets available to charities and not-for-profits in the Metropolitan Area," Angelo explained. "They could take as many as 100 tickets, and the only proviso was that they had to sell them to donors and benefactors for $250 each, and the ticket buyer had to agree to dress in black tie for the show. The organizations got to keep 100 percent of the proceeds, but Billy wanted only high rollers at his event. Eventually, 45 charities participated, and more than a million dollars was raised on their behalf."

"How exactly did this work?" Catherine wondered.

"Take Gibbons College, for instance," Angelo explained. "They took 100 tickets and sold them to 100 supporters and in doing so raised $25,000 for themselves, a pretty good haul for one night, especially when you consider Billy covered all the overhead."

"So the charity agrees to sell the tickets and keeps the proceeds, one hundred percent," Catherine said. "What was the catch?"

"There was no catch," Angelo said. "Billy and Melinda wanted to host a party where they were the center of attention. Ironically, Grace told me her biggest challenge coordinating this event was convincing the not-for-profits that there was no catch. Billy and Melinda wanted to host a swell party."

"Can you walk me through how it happened?" Catherine asked.

"Sure," Angelo said. "It was rather clever and well executed."

"Did you report on it for *Newsday*?" Catherine asked.

Angelo paused. "Come to think of it, no, we didn't."

"Why not?"

"I don't remember, exactly. There could have been a few factors at play. For one thing, it was based in New York City. It also seemed awfully self-centered. Or it could have been somebody held a grudge because Billy invited the *Times* to cover his wedding, but not *Newsday*. Most likely, our not covering the event was a combination of all those factors. It's a shame, though. In retrospect, it seems like an interesting way to raise money for dozens of charities."

"Did Grace organize everything?" Catherine asked.

"Pretty much," Angelo replied. I remember talking to her about it, and she walked me through the particulars."

"First, they had to get some publicity for what they wanted to do, so they held a press conference, which was a challenge in itself because Billy came across stiff and nervous in front of cameras and microphones. Plus, several media outlets were skeptical, according to Grace, *Newsday* being one of them, like I mentioned. Grace said they kept harping on it being obvious that Billy and Melinda were doing it for attention. 'So what if they were? Look at how much good we did,' Grace said to me."

"How much did it cost Billy?" Catherine asked Angelo.

"Grace told me she figured it set Billy back about $200,000, about a hundred thousand less than the wedding," Angelo said.

"How did they make it happen?" Catherine asked.

"According to Grace, it involved a lot of old-fashioned outreach," Angelo said. "Don't forget, this was well before the Internet and social media. Email even. Grace said she had to do mailings to get the information to the charities about the event and then make the follow-up phone calls. It was a painstaking process that required a great deal of patience."

"Who was the first group to sign up?" Catherine asked.

"Gibbons College. Grace was participating in the Gibbons' Accelerated MBA program, and of course, Billy was on the board, so there were no introductions necessary," Angelo said.

"Wait a minute," Catherine said. "In addition to planning this event, Grace was going for her MBA AND raising a kid? What made her sign up for that?"

"I asked her the same thing when she told me about it. She said she didn't sign up for it. Billy did," Angelo said.

"Billy did what?" Catherine asked, confused.

"Signed her up for the MBA."

"Why?"

"Grace told me Billy said it would be good for her to have her Master's."

"So he enrolled her in the program without asking?"

"Sort of. Turns out he was having lunch with the business school administrators at the school about a month before the start of the fall semester. He called Grace and told her to come to campus. She joined them at the restaurant. He introduced her to everyone at the table by saying, "Fellows, I want you to meet your newest MBA candidate. What could she do at that point?"

"Did he offer to help her pay for it?" Catherine asked?

"To be fair, he paid for everything," Angelo said, "but he did so in a way that was very 'Billy-like,' Grace said."

"How's that?" Catherine asked.

"All the tuition bills were in her name. Every time she got one, she'd bring it to his attention and he'd say, 'Don't worry about it.' Finally, the week she was to graduate, she entered his office with the final bill. 'They're not going to let me graduate unless this is paid,' she pointed out.

"I suppose not,' Billy said to her. Go see Mitch Schoop and have him cut you a check.'"

"Who was Mitch Schoop?" Catherine asked.

"The company controller," Angelo said. "He cut the check, and Grace had to bring it to the registrar's office: $19, 638. They had never seen anyone pay for a degree like that. It caused quite the commotion, Grace told me."

"Okay, so Grace is going for her MBA, raising a child,

AND coordinating this massive event? How did she pull that off?" Catherine wondered.

"Grace said Grail was an absolute Godsend during this stretch," Angelo said.

"Jesus, I'll bet," Catherine said. "So Gibbons College was the first to sign on, which makes sense since Billy was on its board and they were used to him. Then what?"

"Grace said she used Gibbons as an example for all the other charities," Angelo explained.

"Did she have to handle the funds? Sixteen hundred-plus tickets at $250 a pop add up," Catherine said.

"No, the charities handled their own funds. All they had to do was commit to the tickets and charge at least $250 per ducat."

"A what?" Catherine asked.

"A ducat. Christ, I forgot how young you are," Angelo said, "A ducat. It's another word for a ticket, from the olden days."

"Okay, so Grace gets 45 charities to commit to over sixteen hundred tickets, and for all the guests to wear formal attire. How did they raise more than a million dollars? Two hundred fifty times one thousand six hundred and nine comes up way short," Catherine said, pursing her lips.

"Many people paid more than the $250 asked for,' Angelo said. "They also created a journal for the evening, and the proceeds from the ads, congratulating Billy and Melinda, found their way to the organizations selling them, again, one hundred percent. Billy bore the journal's printing cost. Billy and Melinda also decided to host a cocktail party before the performance at the Marriott Marquis hotel. Grace figures they had about fifteen hundred people attend. She told me she remembers because the bill came to $60,000, and Billy put it on his American Express card."

"His American Express card?!?"

"His American Express card," Angelo said. "She said she'll never forget the look on the manager's face. Talk about priceless. Believe it or not, Grace said Billy originally wanted to host the cocktail party at Mama Leone's," Angelo said. "It was right next to the theater, but it had been closed for years."

"What's a Mama Leone's?" Catherine asked.

Angelo sighed. "I really do underestimate how young you are. Mama Leone's was a classic, New York City Italian restaurant right by the theater district. At one point, it had devolved into a tourist trap, but in its heyday, it was the place to be. In the mid-'90s, perhaps about a year before the event, it closed for good when the building was sold. Billy thought it would be fun to get the building's new owners to reopen the restaurant just for this occasion." Angelo said. "Talk about ego running amok. Billy told Grace it would be cool to find out who had the keys to the place and to get them to re-open it for the evening–simply to impress people with how powerful he was."

"How did Grace convince him to go with the Marriott Marquis?" Catherine asked.

"She stopped by the hotel and counted the steps from there to the theater–72," Angelo said. "Grace told me the steps she took involved walking through Shubert Alley, which is pretty cool for some reason. That helped her convince Billy that having his guests walk the one block between the hotel and the theater was not so bad. Plus, the Marriott carried enough cache to warrant hosting the event."

"How did Grace coordinate everything?" Catherine asked.

"The charities sent her their list of attendees. She set up a floor plan. Billy instructed her to arrange it so his daughter, Betty, sat in a different row from her fiancé, Jeff Doomey. In a defiant moment, however, she switched the seats at the last second, and the two got to sit next to each other. Can you imagine?"

"No, I can't," Catherine said. "What other challenges came up?"

"Well, for one thing, the event was the same week as Grace's last week of her Master's program, plus Billy was hosting the Mockingbird Heights Chamber of Commerce's annual holiday party two days after the anniversary gig. But the real fun took place the night before, according to Grace," Angelo said.

"What happened?" Catherine asked.

"There was a dinner honoring Sir William Lloyd Donnellen, the guy who created *Black Maria*, scheduled in Manhattan for Monday, December 7th," Angelo said. "Naturally, Billy had to take a table at this event. Unfortunately, he did not get around to doing so until the last minute. Grace told me about the conversation she had with the event organizer when she called to inquire about table reservations.

"My boss would like to take a table at the dinner honoring Sir William Lloyd Donnellen,' Grace said.

"Event organizer: 'There are only two tables left.'

"Grace: 'We only need one.'

"Event organizer: 'I understand. I mention the two tables left because we have arranged to have a celebrity sit at each table. Each celebrity invited has Sir William Lloyd Donnellen to thank for his or her career. Right now, the only celebrities left are Tina Louise and Rita Moreno. Which one would you like at your table?'"

"Um..." Catherine started.

"I know, I know," Angelo said. "Tina Louise starred in a TV show, *Gilligan's Island*, that only ran for three years but, for some reason, lived on in perpetuity in syndication. She was also what they used to refer to as a 'Hollywood starlet' back in the early 1960s. She co-starred in a movie with Elvis, Elvis Presley. He..."

"Don't worry, I know who Elvis is," Catherine interrupted.

"Thank God," Angelo said. "Anyway, Tina was Grace's choice, but she knew she had to run it past Billy. Rita Moreno, after all, was one of the first women to score an EGOT–an Emmy, Grammy, Oscar, and Tony award. So she walked down the hall to explain the situation and ask Billy what his preference is. He looks over his bifocals and raises an eyebrow."

"Tina Louise! Why would you even ask?' Billy said to Grace.

"Just checking," she told him.

"On the night of the event, according to Grace, everyone was decked out. Billy and Melinda went off somewhere, and Grace was standing by their table, looking out for Billy's other guests and Ms. Louise. After a few minutes, this older and attractive woman walked up to Grace and asked where table 54 was.

"Right here," Grace said, wondering why she would want to know. Then Grace realized she was looking for 'Ginger' from *Gilligan's Island,* but Tina Louise was in front of her. She figured Tina was about 60 at the time and looked terrific."

"All those years stuck on an island must have served her well," Catherine deadpanned.

"Grace shared something else about that night," Angelo said. "It was vintage Billy and one of the reasons she was grateful for what she experienced working for him."

"Do tell," Catherine said, leaning in and shifting in her seat a little.

"Once everyone was seated at the table, Grace noticed Henny Youngman standing in the entrance to the ballroom looking rather lost," Angelo said. "Henny was a legendary comic, but at this point had to be over 90 years old. Grace nudged Billy, pointed to Henny, and said, 'He looks lost.'

"Billy said, 'Why don't you go over there and help him?'

"Help Henny Youngman?" Grace said. "Who am I to help Henny Youngman? He doesn't know me from a hole in the wall.'

"Billy replied, 'He's an old man who needs help. Go.'

"So she walked to Henny Youngman, a living comedy legend, and said, 'Mr. Youngman, my name is Grace Duffy. According to the seating chart, you're at table 59. I can take you there if you like.'

"To her surprise, he said, 'That would be swell,' sounding exactly how you would expect a 90-year-old comedy legend to sound. He took hold of Grace's arm, and she started to lead him across the room.'

"After taking several strides across the floor, he tugged on Grace's arm. 'Young lady,' he said, 'let's enjoy this. Walk slow.'

"So he and Grace walked slowly, deliberately, like a father walking his daughter down the wedding aisle. The room started to buzz. Grace said she could feel everyone's eyes on them. She said she muttered a prayer under her breath that he wouldn't choose this moment to drop dead. She had no interest in being a big item in the news as the woman who 'drove comedy legend Henny Youngman to his death' by walking too fast. They got to his table without incident, and he thanked Grace for her assistance. Grace told me what a thrill it was, and it would never have occurred to her to do it if it weren't for Billy."

"What happened to Tina Louise?" Catherine wanted to know.

"Billy had her sit next to him. But later on, it was just Grace and Tina at the table, so Grace slid over and into the seat next to her. Billy and Melinda and the other guests were off dancing or doing something else. She asked Tina how her evening was going, and she said, 'Fine.'

"Then she asked Grace about Billy. 'Who is he? What does he do for a living?'

"Grace explained Billy as best she could, and they chatted some more. Then Tina rested her hand on Grace's and asked if it was possible for Grace to sit next to Tina. 'Your boss is boring the shit out of me,' Tina said. 'I have a feeling the night will end up a lot more fun with you next to me.' Then she squeezed Grace's hand."

"Wow," Catherine whistled, "Tina's a badass."

Angelo laughed.

"Grace told Tina it would be hard to explain to her boss why she should sit next to the guest of honor, especially since he was paying for the dinner. She also said she couldn't wait to get home and tell Grail that Tina Louise hit on her.

"Hell," she said to me, 'I couldn't wait to tell anyone who would listen. Imagine spending the night with a woman who starred in a movie with Elvis and dated him, too? Try topping that!'"

"That's not bad for a Monday night," Catherine said. "How did the next night go?"

Chapter 33

The Second Wedding Anniversary

"Well, nobody famous hit on Grace," Angelo said, with a chuckle.

"You know what I meant," Catherine said.

"Of course I do," Angelo said. "But that's what Grace said when I asked her about it. Actually, she got a little wistful talking about the end. She said everything went fine, but that she couldn't help but feel it marked the beginning of the end."

"The end of what?" Catherine asked.

"She had no way of knowing it at the time, but she said she could sense that her time working for Billy was coming to an end. The 'magic,' if you will, was no longer there."

"Did she cite anything specific?"

"Here's what I wrote down from my conversation with her about it," Angelo replied.

"Grace said, 'More than fifteen hundred people descended upon the Marriott on a chilly December night for a pre-performance cocktail party. One-thousand-six-hundred-nine showed up for the performance and not a hitch through the night, except for my forgetting the big check for the photo op after-

207

ward. We had to send a messenger to Mockingbird Heights to pick it up.'"

"Did you get to see the show?" I asked her.

"I hate musicals," she told me. "I can't sit through them. I don't understand why people pay big money to watch other people sing and dance."

"So what did you do?" I asked her.

"I walked around and talked to people inside and outside the theater," Grace said. "I had a chance meeting with Shaun Cassidy, who was appearing in a musical across the street and apparently was done for the night! Before the *Black Maria* performance was over, I walked back to the Marriott Marquis to make sure everything was set up for the photo op with the big check. I found Senator and Mrs. Wojo waiting for us in the room where the pictures were to be taken. Billy had wanted the senator there because he–the senator–attracted a crowd. The senator only attended an event if his bank account benefited. I figure his presence there set Billy back about another ten grand."

"What did the senator say when he saw you?" I asked.

"Where the hell is everyone?" he barked in his Long Island-by-way-of Brooklyn accent. 'What the fuck do you have me here for if there's nothing going on!'?"

"Seems pretty harsh, but typical," I told Grace.

"His voice had an effect similar to dropping battery acid on a snowball," Grace said. "I explained the performance was still going on and asked if I could get him or his wife something to drink.

'I gotta pee,' his wife said to no one in particular.

"'Take her to the ladies' room,' the senator told Grace. She turned to walk with the wife, having learned about escorting celebrities the night before, and the wife hissed, 'I know how to go to the bathroom. Get the hell away from me.'"

"Sounds like a lovely lady," I said.

"'Once she got back, I tried to keep them both entertained while we waited for the show to end,' Grace said. 'But they got impatient. I told them I was going to see where Billy and Melinda were. I was hoping I could get them back over to the hotel so we could take the pictures with the senator before he and his wife spontaneously combusted.'"

"Any luck?" I asked.

"Well, I found Billy and Melinda, and we were going up the escalator to where the photo room was. Unfortunately, we could see Senator and Mrs. Wojo going in the opposite direction on the other escalator. Billy yelled across the lobby to get his attention. The senator saw us, pointed to his watch, and shrugged his shoulders. It was 10:30 on a Tuesday night–where else could the prick have to be?" Grace said.

"Sounds like Grace wasn't a big fan of the senator," Catherine said, "but she has a point, especially if Billy paid him to be there."

"As I mentioned earlier, I got the sense the thrill had been snuffed out for Grace," Angelo said. "Maybe it was sheer exhaustion, but Grace no longer had the patience to placate egomaniacs, which was rather unfortunate because Billy's next 'Big Adventure' required a lot of patience and placating. Billy's decision to open a restaurant greased the skids for Grace's departure and, in retrospect, expedited Billy's demise."

Chapter 34

Billy Opens a Restaurant

"Billy opened a restaurant?" Catherine asked. "Did he know anything about the restaurant business? I heard that owning a restaurant never ends well unless you know the business inside and out."

"Well," Angelo said, "He didn't, and that's exactly what Grace tried to tell him. But here's a great example of where that ego thing can really bite you in the ass. Billy's ego–the same one that drove him to such success with Carpe Diem–wouldn't let him think he could fail running a restaurant. Plus, he wanted a place where he knew he would be treated like a big shot in front of his Long Island peers, not just in front of the people he met with in New York City at Clegg & Cleary's.

"So two months after the anniversary gala, Billy jumped at the opportunity when three partners whose restaurant in Mockingbird Heights had hit the skids pleaded with him to bail them out. Grace begged him not to do it. Grace knew that only people with the restaurant business in their blood can succeed. Billy did not have the restaurant business in his blood.

"If you think about it," Catherine offered, "the situation

was vintage Billy. Desperate people needing a handout, and Billy to the rescue. The restaurant was local, so he could be a big shot. It was deeply in debt, so he would look like the hero for stepping in and saving the day. And it would give him a chance to hire more single moms."

"Wow–you're really picking up on this," Angelo said.

"He called it 'Billy's American Dream,' Angelo continued. "He kept on one partner to manage the place–Lorenzo DeTorre. Lorenzo knew the restaurant business, all right. He graduated Magna Cum Laude from the "One for You, One for Me" Restaurant Management School. Billy knew about DeTorre's shenanigans, but the more people tried to point out Lorenzo was stealing from him, the more Billy dug in his heels, determined to show the world he was smarter than everybody else.

"At one point, DeTorre convinced Billy to air condition the kitchen. Hearing this convinced Grace that the manager was purposely concocting ways to piss through Billy's money. But firing DeTorre meant Billy would have to admit he made a mistake keeping him on in the first place. Not going to happen. Grace gave up after a while."

"So here's another example of the ego proving to be counter-productive," Catherine said. "Did Billy enjoy owning a restaurant?"

"He loved everything about it except for the losing money part," Angelo said. "He especially enjoyed hosting small lunches and dinners for Long Island VIPs, playing the big shot."

"Long Island has big shots?" Catherine asked.

"Good point," Angelo said, chuckling. "I suppose 'relatively speaking' is the operative phrase when talking about big shots and Long Island," Angelo said. "Grace told me one such gathering involved a member of Congress and two county legislators. A new waitress, with little going for her other than a sweet personality and a killer body, bungled everyone's order. Nobody seemed to care–or at least they demonstrated more patience than a not-so-pretty waitress might have been granted. After she tried–without much success–to straighten everything out, she walked away from the table, and they all watched her do so. Billy said to no one in particular, "And all this time I thought 'fucked her brains out' was just an expression."

"That's mean," Catherine said.

"Well, the fellas at the table found it uproariously funny, according to Grace."

"What did she do?" Catherine asked.

"She told me she kept her head down and made a mental note to get the hell out of there–there being Carpe Diem–as quickly as possible."

"Sounds ominous," Catherine said. "Was this the beginning of the end?"

"I suppose," Angelo mused. "I think of it more like the seed of an idea that, once planted, quickly blossomed into reality, with the events that took place over the ensuing weeks serving as so much water and fertilizer."

"That's one hell of a metaphor," Catherine chided.

"By the end of spring, the bloom was off the rose..."

"Hello, 9-1-1? I'd like to report a beating." Catherine wisecracked, pretending to hold a phone to her ear.

"All right, all right," Angelo said. "Seriously, though, in retrospect, you can see where Billy's ego contributed to him making decisions and taking actions that had dire consequences. The fallout was exacerbated by a devastating loss–the magnitude of which was not fully realized even by those relatively close to him."

Chapter 35

Shadler Dies & Melinda Cries

"Grace told me her concerns about the impact Billy's restaurant would have on his physical and financial well-being intensified when Stanley Shadler died," Angelo said.

"Why's that?" Catherine asked.

Here's what I have in my notes," Angelo said.

Stanley was a World War II vet and a father figure, especially to Billy. As a financial officer, he often played bad cop to Billy's good cop. If there was talk about getting a new refrigerator for the company kitchen, for instance, Billy would make like he was all for it, but then Stanley would say, "Well, we're going to have to have a great quarter to cover such an expense." Most likely, Billy had no desire to spring for a new appliance, but Billy hated being the bad guy. Stanley couldn't care less.

His co-workers respected Stanley because he spoke his mind. He could be blunt on occasion, but he always treated others with respect. He used the candy bars on his desk to get to know all the employees. Folks would come into his office to grab a quick snack, and he would conversationally ask about their department or co-workers. Stanley often said he did not know if it was the chocolate or just most people's inherent need to unburden themselves. Either way, he was able to keep tabs on the Carpe Diem staffers. What Stanley could do better than anybody, however, was get in Billy's face and tell him to knock off the stupid shit, like the time Billy agreed to sponsor a charity breakfast for $5,000 so he would have the opportunity to sit next to the reigning Miss America and get on television. Stanley got on him for that one.

Stanley was diagnosed with Parkinson's Disease in later years, diminishing his ability to serve Billy. He started to shake noticeably and then had a small stroke after the wedding. Once he recovered, he had to cut down on the time he spent in the office, although sitting at home did not do him much good, either. The man preferred to keep busy, and one day he decided the wood behind his home needed to be cut into smaller logs. He knew his wife would not be happy if she saw him doing what he wanted to do, so he waited until she left the house to run errands. She left, and Stanley escaped to the back-yard with a small chainsaw. He had already cut a few logs when the chainsaw got caught in a piece of wood. He yanked hard to free the saw when it sprang loose and nailed him in the neck, cutting a major vein. By the time his wife returned, he had bled to death in the backyard, with the chainsaw still buzzing.

Stanley's passing was the closest Billy ever came to crying in front of his employees. When he got word that Stanley had died, he called everybody into the company conference room. Before he said anything, he had Grace place boxes of tissues at various locations throughout the room, a not-too-subtle way to tell people they were about to hear something unsettling. He then said, "Stanley Shadler won't be coming to work anymore. He died." He then turned and left the room, leaving behind a staff stunned not only by the devastating news but also by how it was shared with them.

Fortunately for Billy, the holidays were right around the corner. One of his favorite "special projects" was bailing inmates out of jail, with Grace's assistance, so they could be home with their families for Thanksgiving. This helped him keep his mind off losing Stanley.

"Bailing people out of jail?" Catherine asked. "What was the point of doing that?"

"Grace said Billy provided those released with groceries and fifty bucks," Angelo said. "Billy figured–correctly–that springing some people down on their luck would be a media bonanza. Once the prisoners made their follow-up appearances in court, Billy got his money back, minus a small processing fee. In all the years he did it, the people he helped always returned. The Long Island, New York City, and national media portrayed him as a wealthy benefactor, shelling out thousands to benefit others. So, for less than a couple of hundred bucks, he gained worldwide fame as a kind-hearted, gentle soul."

"What was involved?" Catherine wondered, a little bewildered.

"The process took about a month," Angelo explained. "Around the middle of October, Grace would notify the sheriff at the Nassau County Correctional Center that Billy wanted to bail out inmates. The sheriff's staff determined who might be eligible, as no candidate could be serving time for violent crimes or DWI. Their families had to want them out, too, which wasn't always the case. The candidate pool quickly went from a few thousand to a dozen or so. Several prisoners turned down the offer, opting instead to spend the holidays "inside" where they knew they would be fed and be amongst friends."

"Billy and Grace met with the candidates who did want out and then arranged for the big release on the Wednesday before Thanksgiving. When the reporters came calling, Billy spun a yarn about how during World War II his mother received a telegram from the U.S. Army reporting his father was lost and presumed dead. He said that her listening to Bing Crosby sing 'I'll be Home for Christmas' gave her reason to hope."

"Was that the case?" Catherine asked.

"Who knows?" Angelo replied. "The reporters covering the story took it at face value. You almost had to, really. How could you check? Why would you check?"

"How did Grace feel about this project?" Catherine asked. "Did she have any interesting encounters? What kind of people were released? What were their crimes?"

"She said one prisoner was there because he held up a soup kitchen. Even he admitted it was a stupid thing to do. Another older, black fellow told Billy and Grace that he passed out drunk in the back seat of an elderly woman's car on a Saturday night. He did not wake up until she started driving the car to church on Sunday morning. He sat up suddenly in the back seat, wondering where he was. She freaked out, nearly had a heart attack, and insisted on pressing trespassing charges. It was not exactly a *Driving Miss Daisy* moment."

"After Billy's bail-out program generated heartwarming stories in the media, the Good Billy and the Bad Billy started to intersect more frequently, creating chaos for Grace," Angelo said. "He made even more commitments to good causes, hospitals, and schools, but then he stopped honoring those commitments, leaving Grace to handle the inevitable phone calls from the charitable organizations looking for their money."

"Grace said this was right around the time Billy started having problems with Melinda. His need to attend black tie affairs every night transitioned from being an exciting challenge to a pressing problem. Putting on a tuxedo, sitting on the dais, and being told how wonderful he was became an addiction. After a while, it got to be too much for Melinda. She tried to explain to him it was one thing for him to stand there in his tux, but she had to wear high heels and a fancy gown, hardly able to breathe some nights."

"Did she express that to Billy?" Catherine asked.

"Grace said it came to a head one night," Angelo replied.

"It would be nice if every once and a while we could spend a nice quiet evening in our beautiful home,' she said to Billy, telling Grace about it the next day, once she realized Billy was ignoring her pleas. Melinda understood her job was to stand next to him and look beautiful. She was good at it, too. She kept herself in phenomenal shape, but the nightly excursions started to take a toll. She developed an ulcer and eventually became so weak she had to check herself into a hospital. Billy did not accompany her because he did not believe she was sick."

"How could Billy know if somebody was really sick?" Catherine asked.

"He couldn't, of course. But empathy was never Billy's strong suit, according to Grace," Angelo said.

"If you want attention so badly, then go to the hospital yourself," he said to her, according to Grace, while she was curled up on the bathroom floor in their home. Melinda gathered the strength to get to Hamilton General on her own. Since Billy was on the board of directors there, Melinda got the royal treatment. Her blood pressure was extremely low due to the internal bleeding from the ulcer, and Melinda's doctor told her that if she hadn't been in such great shape, she would have been a goner. He said the same thing to Billy when he came by the hospital with her formal gown, insisting she attend a dinner with him in New York City. The doctor took him outside Melinda's hospital room and tried to explain to him how sick she was.

'She's fine,' he told the doctor. "As soon as you stop coddling her and she realizes she has responsibilities to honor, we'll all be better off.

"The doctor stood his ground despite Billy's status and made sure Melinda got the rest she needed. The damage to Billy and Melinda's relationship was irreparable, however. Shortly thereafter, Billy returned to his Power Puffs, and Melinda spent more and more time holed up in her in-house imprisonment.

"That's awful," Catherine said.

"One afternoon, Grace had to drive Melinda to her doctor for a follow-up visit once she got out of the hospital. After they were in the car for a few minutes, the tears started flowing like sweat on a boxer.

"Everybody thinks living with Billy is paradise," Melinda blurted between sobs. "I assure you, it is not. If it is not about HIM, or if it doesn't benefit HIM, he does not want to hear about it. He controls every aspect of my life. I have no freedom. And I know he's fucking around on me. I know it."

Grace shifted in her seat. She knew she was better off saying as little as possible. She assured Melinda that everyone knew living with Billy was not easy. She chose her words carefully because she did not want Melinda ratting her out once she and Billy kissed and made up, although the odds of that happening were not good. Melinda had no options unless she wanted to go back to being a single mom, working for a living, and sharing a one-bedroom apartment with her son in Rum Junction. She was trapped and she knew it, just the way Billy liked it.

Chapter 36

The Promissory Note

"Sounds like Grace had her hands full," Catherine said.

"The circus was no longer entertaining was how she put it," Angelo said. "While she considered herself fortunate to live under Grail's roof and have her help raising Slade, the young boy's impending need to attend nursery school served as a constant reminder that this living situation was clearly a short-term solution. Grace received her MBA shortly after Billy and Melinda's second anniversary event. She knew she needed to make a move to enhance and expand her capacity to raise a son and pay for his education. She was ready for more sophisticated challenges than coming up with different ways to satisfy Billy's ego, which was growing faster than a teenager going through puberty and was just as hard to feed."

"Why would Billy pay for an employee's education but still have them perform the same tasks as before?" Catherine asked.

"Grace said Billy wanted her to get the MBA because he believed better-educated employees were more valuable. My guess is, he paid for it because he thought the gesture would inspire greater loyalty, but that's not how it worked out with

Grace. She might have stayed if Billy had given her more responsibilities in line with her new degree. Instead, he kept pushing Grace to find new ways to draw attention to Billy. The phone calls from charities wondering when Billy was going to live up to his donation commitments became increasingly frequent, while at the same time, Grace had to dodge requests from other charities who wanted Billy as the honoree for their next fundraiser. Obviously, they weren't aware Billy was neglecting the part where he came across with the actual funds. All they knew was that they saw his name popping up everywhere."

"I thought charities 'honored' people because they did something on behalf of the organization worth honoring," Catherine asked, immediately aware of how naïve this made her sound.

Angelo chuckled. "I'd like to think that's the case more often than not. Most charities or not-for-profits have an annual gala to raise money and 'honor' one or two people. In a perfect world, the honor would be recognizing something specific the honoree did, like you said, on behalf of the organization. Regardless, the expectation is for the person being honored to increase attendance and boost the advertisements sold in the journal. The first few times Billy was 'honored,' the Carpe Diem vendors were happy to take seats and buy ads. By the fourth and fifth time, however, most told Pete and Re-Pete the Carpe Diem business wasn't worth the cost of 'honoring' Billy. Nonetheless. Billy still accepted offers from the charities.

"It didn't stop there, either," Angelo said. "Grace told me that Billy also pledged $250,000 to Hamilton General Hospital, where he was a board member, and then $500,000 to nearby Molloy Medical Center. When asked by the Ham Gen officers why he donated twice as much to Molloy, even though he was on their board, he replied, "Because they asked for it.

"That was Billy's way of teaching Ham Gen a lesson about being bold. He then joined the board at Molloy and arranged to have Melinda replace him at Ham Gen," Angelo said. Ham Gen decided to name its emergency room after the Bates in an effort to appease Billy and welcome Melinda. They also hoped the accompanying fanfare would inspire Billy to fork over his commitment, but it didn't. Despite his public statements indicating otherwise, by the time Billy died, he had given only $25,000 to Ham Gen and $50,000 to Molloy. He also committed to but never delivered $10,000 to nearby Mitchel College to cover the cost of a symposium on Long Island's aviation history.

"That's some legacy," Catherine said.

"Truly unfortunate," Angelo replied. "It all got to be too much for Grace. She worried her personal reputation was becoming tainted by Billy's lack of trustworthiness. She wanted to move on from Billy's grasp, but her options were limited. Long Island is the world's largest small town, and few people wanted to be on Billy's bad side by recruiting Grace to work for them."

"So, just like Melinda and the other single moms at Carpe Diem, to a certain extent, she was trapped," Catherine pointed out.

"Well, fortunately for Grace, Gibbons College President Charles Biscuit had an ego even bigger than Billy's. He relished opportunities to show his trustees how powerful he believed he was," Angelo replied.

"Biscuit approached Grace at a Board of Trustees reception at Gibbons and asked her if she ever considered a career at the college. Grace smiled because that's exactly what she was thinking when Biscuit approached.

"'It would be an honor to work at Gibbons,' Grace said to Biscuit."

"Later on," Angelo continued, "when Grace shared this story with her sister, Grail told her, 'What you should have said was, 'I would love to work here, but Gibbons can't afford me.'"

"But they can," Grace said she told her sister.

"I know and you know, but they don't know," Grail said. "As a result, they might offer you more money."

Sounds like a lot of ego-driven wheels were turning simultaneously," Catherine said.

"Oh, it gets better," Angelo said. "Weeks later, Gibbons' VP Murray Jules invited Grace to dinner. He told her the school wanted to bring Grace on board to replace him once he retired. Murray said he would need to handle the situation delicately. Grace understood. By this time, she wanted to get the hell out of Carpe Diem. Murray told Grace he would stop by Carpe Diem one night after business hours. Grace was not to let anyone know she knew he would be coming.

"A week or so passed when Grace was working late, around 6:00. She heard Billy greet Murray outside Billy's office and invite him in. They closed the doors, and after a while, Billy called Grace into his office. When Grace walked into Billy's office and saw Murray sitting there, she tried to look surprised.

"Billy told Grace, 'Murray says Gibbons would like to hire you away from me. But don't worry—I told him they can't afford you.'

"Grace blushed. It was the best thing Billy could have said, not only from a negotiation standpoint but also because Grace's utter shock at hearing those exact words registered on her face, which Billy took to mean that Grace was surprised to hear this. Grace pretended to laugh and said, 'It's an honor to be considered.'"

"When Grace got the offer letter from Gibbons," Angelo said, "she faced the daunting task of telling Billy. The right opportunity presented itself shortly thereafter.

"Billy had purchased a table for a Gibbons College fundraiser and told Grace to invite his latest Power Puff–Donna Devore–and her family.

"Donna Devore?" Catherine asked. "Whoa, boy. Sounds too much like devour."

"Donna had everything Billy wanted in a woman, according to Grace," Angelo said. "For one thing, her youthful exuberance and understated, natural beauty were such that when you saw them together, you would automatically assume the older man in the relationship is wealthy enough to attract such a woman. She had cheekbones like a goddess, strong and inviting, supporting bluish-green eyes that sparkled when she smiled, so much so that you had this immediate need to please her just so you could see them light up."

"You sure Grace wasn't into women?" Catherine asked sarcastically.

Angelo ignored the comment and continued. "Next came the 'single mother status' that he knew from experience would make her more open to his support and easier to control."

"Sounds like they had a real Norman Rockwell family night planned," Catherine said.

"'Twas indeed," Angelo said, "with Grace, Billy, his mistress, and her brother and parents. Grace said took it as a sign from God she was doing the right thing by leaving.

"The plan for the night was to have Donna and her brother meet Billy and Grace at a Park 'n' Ride along the Long Island Expressway in Suffolk County, and from there they would all go to the country club hosting the event. As Billy and Grace sat in the limo in the Park 'n' Ride parking lot, Grace figured it was now or never. She told Billy she accepted the offer from Gibbons and would be leaving Carpe Diem.

"Grace said all Billy would say is, 'If that's what you want to do, then fine.' He took a sip from the cup in his cup holder and looked away.

"The brother tapped on the window and got into the limousine. He had no idea why there was virtually no conversation in the car. A few minutes later, Donna arrived and got into the car, but her presence did nothing to lessen the tension. The fundraiser itself dragged on to the point where Grace contemplated walking home from the event rather than endure another moment under Billy's steely glare, especially during the ride back to Mockingbird Heights.

"So once again Grace finds herself in a situation where she has to keep working with–or for–someone who she's parting ways with. Yikes!" Catherine said.

"Oh, it was much more uncomfortable than what she went through with Bruce Wright," Angelo said. "The morning after the fundraiser wasn't so pleasant, either. Billy called Grace into his office and, once she sat down, Billy presented her with the Promissory Note she signed when she needed Billy's help to pay off the IRS from the public relations firm debacle. She borrowed $50,000 from Billy, but at this point, it was three years after the fact. With the meter running at 12 percent per annum, she now owed Billy close to $60,000."

"Wait a minute," Catherine said. "She borrowed money from Billy to pay the IRS? And she didn't bother paying it back for three years?"

"That's because when Billy gave her the money, he said she wouldn't have to pay it back, according to Grace. Of course, there were no witnesses, and he did have her sign the promissory note 'for accounting purposes, purely a technicality,' he said to her at the time."

"So he did something truly magnanimous while simultaneously trapping her," Catherine said.

"Exactly. Grace told me she looked at the document and said, 'Billy, you know I can't pay you this money.'

Billy said, 'You better start thinking of ways to pay it back. Twelve percent interest gets ugly pretty quickly.'

"He said it in such a cold, matter-of-fact way that Grace knew Good Billy was no longer at her disposal," Angelo said. "She was now dealing with Business Billy, and she was going to see firsthand why Billy had been so successful in that part of his life. Grace told Billy she would think of something and thanked him for lending her the money in the first place. Then she left Billy's office.

"Grace returned to her office and stared out the window. She didn't have sixty grand and had no idea where or how she could get it. Grace assured herself she could find a solution, and doing so strengthened her resolve to leave. The last thing she wanted to do was go back into Billy's office and beg for her job back, which is exactly what Billy expected her to do," Angelo said. "One benefit of losing your parents suddenly and tragically is that you develop a supernatural resolve to handle any situation, no matter how nasty."

"Why didn't she do something about paying the money back as soon as she received it?" Catherine asked.

"Grace told me she was in denial about paying back the money ever since she took it," Angelo said. "She said she knew she couldn't work at Carpe Diem for the rest of her life to work off a loan, but she also realized she should have taken a more proactive approach and dealt directly with the debt. But Billy liked to entrap people with his benevolence and then do everything in his power to keep them under his thumb."

"Poor Grace," Catherine said. "Talk about between a rock and a hard place."

"Fortunately for Grace, her sister Grail understood this, too. 'If it was about the money, he would have paid you more and made payment arrangements from the get-go,' Grail said when told about the conversation, 'but what he wanted was for you to be his indentured servant.'"

Angelo continued.

"Nothing more was discussed about the Promissory Note during her remaining days at Carpe Diem, and soon it was time for Grace to move on to Gibbons. Billy arranged for a "good-bye" party at Billy's restaurant. Grace was champing at the bit…

"Champing? Don't you mean chomping?" Catherine interjected.

Angelo stopped mid-sentence.

"Check your AP Stylebook," he said bluntly. "Champing at the bit is the original and better form."

"As I was saying," Angelo continued, "Grace was champing at the bit to put Mockingbird Heights in her rearview mirror. She also wanted to cap the night off with a gesture enabling her to express her gratitude for everything Billy had done for her in front of everybody without getting too sappy or, worse, insincere.

"As the party came to a close and it was Grace's time to say goodbye, she gave a little speech with Billy by her side. She told everyone she would miss them. Then she asked someone with a camera to take a picture of her and Billy. Grace told the photographer to shoot the picture at the count of three. When she shouted "three!" she turned to Billy and planted a big kiss on his cheek, like Sammy Davis Jr. in the famous episode of *All in the Family*. The camera clicked and flashed, and the room roared as Grace gave Billy a big hug, and Billy hugged back.

"Grace saw Billy on a few occasions at Gibbons' functions, and Billy was pleasant and didn't mention the money owed. Not his style. His business manager–the guy he hired to replace Shadler–would call Grace about once a month to discuss it.

He'd said, "Grace, we have to talk. We have to figure out a payment plan." But he didn't press the matter, and Grace could not help but think Billy told him not to.

"She wasn't sure if this was wishful thinking on her part, but she did know Billy was looking to buy a newspaper on Long Island because he had shared this news with her and, in a roundabout way, asked Grace if she would consider being its editor. Grace told him she would. Grace thought Billy might be trying to ascertain whether she would go back to Carpe Diem, and Grace's response let him know she would.

"Grace's last conversation with Billy took place after a Gibbons' Trustee meeting on the Thursday night before he died. Billy wanted to show Grace his new Cadillac, which had all the bells and whistles you'd expect from a car Billy owned. Grace said, 'That's so cool!' and 'Wow!' enough times to make Billy feel good. He did not look good. Billy's cheeks were ashen, and his hacking cough had a disturbing rattle to it. Grace told Billy he should take better care of himself, and Billy assured her he was "going to a chiropractor and drinking more water."

"'Are you eating anything green, besides the Froot Loops, I mean?' Grace said she asked him, knowing Billy wasn't.

"No, I haven't gotten that desperate yet,' Billy laughed.

"He got into his car and took off to spend time with someone other than his Melinda, most likely Donna. Billy didn't tell Grace where he was going, but he didn't have to because Grace did not care. That's the last time Grace spoke with or saw Billy.

The following Wednesday morning, she got the page from Grail.

Chapter 37

Fingering the Flame

"That sounds sad," Catherine said, "almost as if Grace knew it was the last time she would see Billy."

"Obviously, she would have no way of knowing it would be," Angelo replied, "but keep in mind two things. One, she knew Billy was burning the candle at both ends. He never took care of himself. Two, Grace lost her father suddenly and unexpectedly. I'm sure after that she never lost the sense that anytime she said goodbye to someone, it might be for the last time."

"That's a tough way to go through life," Catherine said. "Being on edge, the instability can wear on you."

"Indeed," Angelo said.

"Billy worked so hard over such a long period of time to build something of substance," Catherine said. "How could things fall apart so quickly?"

"That's a great question," Angelo said. "The answer lies within the context of your original question of 'what role does the ego play in determining one's success in business?' The same ego that drove him to such success ultimately expedited his demise. Billy needed to hear how wonderful he was. Marietta stopped telling him after the baby was born, and Melinda gave it up when she became sick. Like a junkie looking for his next high, Billy needed to find a new source of platitudes and excitement and now it was Donna Devore's turn.

"Billy didn't consider what he did cheating because he was 'providing for' Melinda just as he had–and continued to do so– for Marietta. He relished the rush resulting from the clandestine maneuverings mixed in with knowing Melinda wouldn't confront him because she did not want to get booted off his gravy train."

"Did he ever talk to Grace about this? Did he discuss his personal life or share his philosophy–assuming he had one– with her?" Catherine asked.

"Funny you should ask," Angelo said. "Grace told me that Billy tried to explain his behavior in his odd and awkward way when she was still working for Carpe Diem. Grace was going over a project late one night in the office when she heard a woman and Billy in the hallway. The woman giggled, telling Grace to stay put and not interrupt, like a child hearing strange noises coming from her parents' bedroom. Eventually, she heard someone leave and figured it was safe. She walked down the hall to Billy's office to see if everything was okay.

"Billy was sitting at his desk, Grace said. The music from *Black Maria* was playing on his office stereo system. Grace ducked her head into Billy's office and asked Billy if everything was all right.

'I heard a commotion,' Grace said.

"Billy laughed, assured Grace everything was fine, and then asked her to come in and sit down, which was the last thing Grace wanted to do. It was already well past midnight, but Grace sat down. Billy watched the flame of a lit candle on his desk. It was the only light in the room, other than from the knobs on the stereo. The office was a mess, like it sometimes was when Billy would come in late at night to get caught up. Sometimes he stayed there all night, and in the morning, there would be a pile of filing for Martha, his secretary.

"They stared at the candle's flickering flame while 'The Night The Carousel Burned Down,' one of the songs from *Black Maria,* played on the stereo":

> The children all cried when the carousel
> > burned down
> The old ladies sighed, and the carousel
> > burned down
> The rest of us lied as the carousel burned down
> And the flames did fly
> The pipes steamed and shrieked out a blazing
> > goodbye
> And we all left town the next day.

"Grace was not a big fan of Broadway musicals, but hearing this song intrigued her enough to wonder why Billy liked *Black Maria* enough to see it more than 100 times, at God knows what expense. So she asked.

"Billy explained that it's a powerful story about a man, Tortu, who realizes everything he was taught as a kid was bullshit."

'Look at how we educate young people. Go to a kinder-garten class, and everyone wants to participate, to try to answer the teacher's questions because they think they know the answer. By the time they're seniors in high school, though, they dread being called on because they're afraid they might be wrong, or they won't look cool in front of their friends. Educators do everything they can to discourage initiative, risk-taking, and creative license. We spew out information and demand it be regurgitated with precision and without looking at your classmates' work, as opposed to presenting a challenge to a group of students and showing them how to work together to meet the challenge. We force little kids to sit still for hours on end and then give them more work to do when they get home. So Tortu goes on a crusade to draw attention to the need to change all this, which is not well received by the Powers That Be. They do everything they can to brand the man a lunatic.'

'Okay, I get that,' Grace says. 'But why have you seen it so many times?'

'I get asked that a lot,' Billy says. The truth is, I feel like each time I see it, I pick up on some new nuance.'

'Like what?'

Billy thought for a moment. 'Okay–just recently I learned something about the title itself. *Black Maria.*'

'And that would be ...'

'Well, Black Maria is old-timey slang for a police van that's used to round up criminals, so I always thought that's what the title was referring to, since Tortu is rounded up like a common criminal. But I've since learned that Thomas Edison built a tiny movie studio in the 1890s in New Jersey. They called it a Black Maria because of its resemblance to the police vehicle. But here's the interesting part. It was built on a flat, circular piece of wood, like a Lazy Susan, so it could be spun around to maximize exposure to the light provided by the sun.'

'You're losing me,' Grace said.

'Life is like a Black Maria,' Billy said. 'We're constantly twisting and turning so we can maximize our exposure to light, but too many people think the light represents pleasure.'

'What does the light represent?' Grace asked.

'Purpose. Man needs a purpose, a goal worth striving for

and working for, one that benefits his fellow man. Yet too many of us chase the light of pleasure because that's what we're trained to do. We're told that true fulfillment comes from external sources, the newest products, the latest music, or the movies with the biggest stars. Nothing could be further from the truth, but we're also made to feel that our inability to find that fulfillment, that happiness must be our fault because "everybody else" seems happy. Then we're told we're unhappy because of something or some things that happened in our past, and we play the blame game. As a result, we're more stressed, more convinced of our failings and shortcomings than ever.'

'How does working toward a purpose change that?' Grace asked.

'Before you work toward a purpose, you have to realize that true happiness comes from within,' Billy said. 'You have to understand that one can be as happy as one wants to be simply by allowing yourself to be happy, that you don't have to rely on outside sources, and you absolutely have to let go of any hurts that happened in the past.'

'And then ...?'

'Then you realize you need a purpose, a reason to get out of bed in the morning so you can make the most of your time here on Earth. Hopefully that purpose benefits others in some way.'

'So *Black Maria* is about letting go of the past so we can be happy in the here and now and clearly see what our true purpose in life is?'

Grace sat there in silence, trying to process these ponderings, especially coming from a man known for his penchant for pornography and his pursuit of Power Puffs and other 'external forces.'

'I love to stare at a candle's flame,' Billy said after a few minutes, oblivious to the statement's non-sequitur nature. 'Everything seems so balanced. The curves. How it tapers off at the tip and burns so evenly and magically–it's so powerful yet so fragile. One puff and poof–it's out. Yet if I knock the candle over, the little flame could start a ruinous fire.'

Billy continued: 'Here's the cool part. When you pass your finger through the flame, real quick, nothing happens to your finger, but you feel a little sensation–enough to respect the heat. But if you're not careful and you linger too long near the flame, you get burned and end up with a nasty blister. I call it fingering the flame. Get close enough to feel the danger, but get out before you get burned. Do you know what I mean?'

Grace said she knew what he meant, although she wasn't quite sure.

'I first became fascinated with candles and their flames when I was an altar boy,' Billy said. 'I always volunteered to light them before Mass started, and insisted on being the one to blow them out afterward. But I would never just blow them out. I would always 'finger the flame' first. I swear it brought me closer to God.'

He pondered this for another moment and then wrote something on a piece of paper.

Grace considered what he was sharing with her and how she should react as he stuffed the paper in his pocket.

'I'm not a big fan of the term "fingering the flame," but I know where you're coming from,' Grace said, before sighing. 'After my father was murdered and seeing my mother go through the motions until she went to join him, I was deter-mined to live life to the fullest. If there was a hedonistic plea-sure, I wanted to feel it. If there was a sexual experience to be had, I wanted to have it. If there was a far-flung corner of the world worth traveling to, I wanted to see it.'

'But you never traveled anywhere,' Billy said.

'I know,' Grace sighed. 'You can thank Drex and his sperm.'

'Drex?' Billy asked.

'Yeah, Drex. I know, I know,' Grace said. 'The name alone should have been a red flag. He was tall, strong, and hot. I needed–wanted–all three."

'Oh, yeah. Drex. He was a military man, right?' Billy asked. 'Killed in the line of duty during the Iraq War.'

'No...' Grace said but then caught herself.

Fuck it, she thought.

'No, Billy, that's what I tell everyone,' Grace blurted. It felt so good to admit it she let her guard down and her secret out. 'He was, and is, a dirtbag. He led me to believe, or–more accurately–I allowed myself to believe–we had a future together. Then I got knocked up, and the day I gave birth to Slade, the bastard disappeared on me. He came back the next day all apologetic and I forgave him. Then nine months later–to the day!–he tells me he was busy partying with his friends when Slade was born. 'One thing led to another,' he said, and he ended up banging his friend–our friend–in the back seat of MY car while I'm in the hospital, giving birth to HIS son. Now his friend–my FORMER friend–has given birth to another son.'

'What happened to Drex?' Billy asked, amazed he didn't know this.

The office darkness brought to mind the confessional she knew as a girl and at the moment the burden of keeping such a secret seemed so overwhelming Grace let loose, sharing something only Grail, Bernie–and Drex–knew.

'My child's father is a heroin addict," Grace said. "He held up a bank to support his habit. He got caught, did some time. Got out, tried to get clean. Failed. Held up a gas station. Got caught again. Did some more time. Got out. Didn't even bother with rehab. Robbed another bank and now he's a lifer in a federal penitentiary. Three strikes and you're in. Forever.'

'Wow,' Billy said, trying to decide how to react. 'I had no idea.'

Grace immediately regretted confiding in Billy.

'I would appreciate your keeping that between us,' she said.

'Oh, you know you can trust me,' Billy said, and Grace heard herself snort.

'Seriously, Billy,' Grace pleaded. 'I don't want Slade growing up knowing his father is a loser, and God knows what people would think if they knew. The military story works much better.'

Billy assured her she had nothing to worry about, but she realized letting her guard down with Billy could cost her big time, somewhere along the line. Billy started to pretend to get back to the piles on his desk and Grace took the gesture as her clue to leave. As she did, she heard the *Black Maria* chorus singing:

> Weren't you there when the carousel
>> burned down
> The fire and confusion, the smoke and the
>> sound
> I swear you were there when the carousel
>> burned down

The song kept playing through her mind as Grace drove home. She pictured Billy passing his finger through the candle flame and found the gesture to be both profound and stupid at the same time. Profound in that he was right: to live our lives more fully, we need to inject a little excitement, a challenge, or anything that forces us to expand our boundaries. But stupid in the sense that, well, passing one's finger through a candle flame struck Grace as something 10-year-old boys did to amuse themselves. And fingering the flame! Ugh. Only Billy could come up with that.

Well, maybe Bernie, Grace thought, and laughed. She pulled into the driveway next to her apartment in Grail's house, but rather than go in, she decided to walk the three blocks into town to visit Bernie. Slade was sleeping with his cousins, and Grace needed to unravel the mystery of Billy and what had just transpired."

Chapter 38

My Heart is Off Limits

Bernie was alone and wiping down the sinks behind the bar. Grace could see from the upturned bar stools that he was getting ready to close.

"Well, hello, Grace Duffy! How are we doing this fine evening? Or is it morning?" Bernie asked.

"What time is it?" Grace asked.

"Just past two," Bernie said, not even looking at his watch. "Quiet night. Can I get you something?"

"Is it too late for a Dewars and water?" Grace asked, sliding into her customary seat by the corner of the bar. "I need to unwind a bit, but I don't want you breaking any laws."

"For God's sake, Grace. Breaking the law for a broad is what gets me out of bed in the morning," Bernie said.

"I'm not a broad," Grace replied.

"Of course not," Bernie said. He mixed a Dewars and water for Grace and then dropped a lemon peel into the drink after twisting it above the glass for two seconds. He freshened his mug of coffee and brought the beverages over to where Grace was sitting and leaned on the bar.

"So what's going on inside that pretty little head of yours?" Bernie asked.

She re-played what had happened in Billy's office earlier that night.

"So Billy bangs a babe in his office and she goes home. He decides to get some work done but then sits behind his desk staring at a flame, listening to the soundtrack from *Black Maria*. And you walk in. That's some work environment there, Grace. Is OSHA aware of this?"

"Be serious, Bernie," Grace said. "What do you think of his 'fingering the flame'? Are our lives incomplete if we don't push the envelope every now and then?"

"Oh, for God's sake, Grace. You're a single mom," Bernie said. "You push the envelope every day. Trying to build a career and still be a loving, caring mother takes more courage and determination than you give yourself credit for."

"Thank you, Bernie. The truth is I love my son more than anything and meeting the challenges of my job provides some satisfaction, but I have to believe there's more to life than merely grinding out a living while hoping your kid becomes a productive member of society. Where's the excitement? Fulfillment? Happiness?"

"Listen, Grace," Bernie said, tossing his bar rag into a nearby sink. "Years ago I made a promise to myself not to let nobody else have any sway on the way I live my life. I didn't see the need to compromise and now I've come to realize that living is more than just surviving."

Bernie paused. Grace looked at him, expectantly.

"Really?" Bernie said, half-amused, half-bewildered.

"Really, what?" Grace replied, confused.

"You don't recognize the lyrics from 'Sweet,' the song from *Black Maria*? I thought you saw that play a million times because of Billy."

"You know I hate musicals," Grace said. "Especially THAT one."

"I'm no fan, either," Bernie said. "But the songs in this one were written by Todd Rundgren, one of the great songwriters of our time."

"Never heard of him," Grace said.

"Sure you have. How can you see a play multiple times and not know he did the score?"

"I suppose I don't pay attention to things that don't matter to me, Bernie," Grace said, the tone in her voice hinting at annoyance mixed with frustration. "What DOES matter to me is enjoying life rather than merely grinding out a living. How do I go about making that happen?"

"The answer's right here," Bernie said.

"In a bar? I don't think so, Bernie," Grace said.

Bernie laughed.

"No, not in a bar. There's more misery here than anywhere else. People don't drink because they're happy, Grace. They drink so they can mask their misery with what appears to be happiness. I can't tell you how many times I've seen people here laughing and telling stories one minute and then–a few hours after they should have left well enough alone and gone home–they're crying into their beer. The tears follow the laughs like dark follows sunset."

"So where then? Where is the happiness?" Grace asked.

Bernie leaned in so his face was inches away from Grace's.

"It's right here," Bernie said, pointing to her heart. "No matter where you are or what you're doing, you're as happy as you decide you want to be. What was it Voltaire said? 'The most courageous decision that you can make each day is to be in a good mood.'"

"A bartender quoting Voltaire. That's rich," Grace said, somewhat dismissively.

"I read. I know things," Bernie said, trying to lighten the mood without sounding defensive.

"I'm sure you do, Bernie, but that's exactly what Billy was telling me, and it sounds like something Grail would say," Grace said.

"That's because Grail's smart," Bernie replied. "Billy I'm not so sure about."

"Grail says it because she doesn't have to worry." She's got a great husband, money in the bank, nice kids," Grace said, with a tinge of jealousy.

"You have it backwards, Grace," Bernie said. "Grail isn't happy because she has all that. She has all that BECAUSE she's happy. It's that simple. There is no 'way to happiness. Happiness is the way.'"

"Have you been reading fortune cookies again, Bernie?"

"Mock me all you want, my friend," Bernie said. "But that's the way it is."

"If it's so simple, how come more people don't realize it?" Grace asked.

"Because there's more money in misery," Bernie said. "Take this bar, for example. If everybody realized all they need to be happy is to decide they're happy, this place would shut down in a month. Look at your TV commercials. Everything is predicated on, 'Buy this product and you'll be happy.' And don't get me started on the pharmaceutical ads. 'Taking this pill will solve your problem.' And then the announcer rattles off a dozen different side effects that 'might' happen. And nobody says 'boo.' We just keep taking the pills, eating the crap passing as food, and drinking the drinks, like good sheep do."

"How do you explain what happened to my father and mother?" Grace asked. "My father was a happy man until he was gunned down in his prime. And how was my mother supposed to 'be happy' after that happened?"

"What happened to your parents was tragic, Grace, but perhaps your father wasn't all that happy. I don't mean to cast aspersions, but something was going on subconsciously that caused him to attract such a situation. Nothing happens by accident."

Grace sipped her Dewar's and water. "So, it's his fault a random stranger snapped and shot the first person he saw walking across a courthouse lobby?"

"Not his fault, no." Bernie said. "There is no fault, or blame, to be assigned. It was just your father's time to go, and that's how he went. Whatever was going on in his head made it okay, and it's not for you to know until you join him."

"What about my mother? Was she at fault for dying from the grief?" Grace asked.

"She made her choice, Grace," Bernie said.

"What do you mean?" Grace asked.

"She could have handled her grief any number of ways," Bernie said. "After my father dropped dead from a heart attack, my mother spent years doing all the things she wanted to do when he was alive but didn't want to do, like seeing Broadway musicals. Once she felt she had crossed everything off her bucket list, she accepted death as the next inevitable phase."

"So, regardless of my external circumstances, whether I want to be happy or not is up to me?" Grace asked.

"Exactly. Look at Princess Diana, may she rest in peace," Bernie said. "She had every material possession imaginable, no financial worries whatsoever, people waiting on her hand and foot and yet she was miserable."

"I find it hard to fathom that you kept up with the goings on at Buckingham Palace, Bernie," Grace said.

"When you listen to people for a living, it's imperative you keep abreast of current events," Bernie explained.

"So, okay. For me to be happy all I have to do is to decide to be happy. That's what you're saying?" Grace asked.

"You got it," Bernie said. Then he leaned so close to Grace she could dip her toes in the pools of blue that were his eyes. "Of course, if you want to be REALLY happy, you could take a ride on the Bernie Love Train Express."

"Dammit, Bernie," Grace said. "Just when I want to take you seriously, you hit on me like one of your last-call trollops."

"Trollops?" Bernie laughed. "Have you been nipping at the 19th Century literature again, Grace?"

"You know damn well what I mean, Bernie," Grace said. "You and I have always had something special. To besmirch it with a one-night stand would be tragic. Your friendship means that much to me."

"You're putting me in the friend zone?" Bernie said. "That's for eunuchs and numb nuts."

"I'm keeping you at arm's length for my sake as well as yours, Bernie," Grace said. "I'll let another man into my life when he convinces me he'll cup my soul in his hands and protect me 'til my dying day. Until that happens, my heart is off limits."

The silence of the empty bar enveloped them. They looked at each other for a few moments, each trying to decipher what the other one wanted to happen next. Bernie leaned forward and Grace involuntarily closed her eyes. Their lips met, and the spark went straight down to Grace's toes and then hit all the nerve centers on the way back up to her pounding heart. Grace knew only one of two things could happen at this point and, invoking every ounce of strength and discipline she could muster, pulled back.

"That was everything I ever imagined and hoped for, Bernie," she said. "But I need more. When you're ready, we'll talk."

With that, Grace collected her things at the bar, finished her drink and sauntered out the door.

243

Chapter 39

Melinda's Revenge

"Poor Grace," Catherine said. "It seems to me she really needed to be with someone, someone who could provide comfort and perhaps a little guidance, a little self-assurance."

"Poor Grace? How about poor Bernie?!?" Angelo countered. "Getting him all worked up like that and then just walking away."

"Screw Bernie," Catherine said. "Grace needed support, and he's making jokes."

"That's not how I see it," Angelo said, "He listened. He consoled and counseled. He even reminded her she was desirable."

"Whatever," Catherine said, dismissively. "Grace had just spent time in an office, late at night, with a male employer who may or may not have recently concluded carnal relations with a woman not his wife. Grace spills the beans on a situation that could cause her great harm, personally, and said male responds by spouting some nonsense about fingering the flame–a term only a male would find appropriate–as the only means to finding true happiness. I think Bernie could have been more obliging, more sympathetic."

"He didn't charge her for the drink," Angelo said. "Does that count?"

Clearly it didn't, based on the expression on Catherine's face.

"Let's look at it another way," Angelo countered. "Billy, for all his foibles, just wanted to be helpful. He must have seen something in Grace that told him she was living an unfulfilled life. I got the sense he was encouraging her to expand her horizons, to challenge herself."

"But the minute she did–when she accepted the position at Gibbons–he hit her with the promissory note," Catherine countered.

"Well, yeah," Angelo conceded. "That was Billy. He liked to see people succeed, but only to a certain extent, and never to a point where he was no longer in control of that person."

"So his ego pushed him to want to help people, but only to the point where it reflected well on him. Is that right?" Catherine asked.

"I think you've summed up the situation pretty well," Angelo said.

Catherine smiled and shifted in her seat.

"So now we know the circumstances under which Grace left, and where Billy was with Melinda and his side action. What was going on at Carpe Diem? Was anyone minding the store?"

"Ha!" Angelo said, "Believe it or not, things were just starting to get interesting. Obviously, Grace was unaware of anything going on internally because she was at Gibbons College. But with Shadler out of the picture and Billy seemingly distracted dealing with his personal travails, Pete and Re-Pete decided it was time to either assume a bigger role in the company or start their own, one that would compete with Carpe Diem."

"Really?" Catherine said. "You said Billy was very good to both of them."

"He was, to a certain extent," Angelo explained. "But despite their successes running the company, Billy was spending money faster than they could bring it in, and the Carpe Diem bills weren't being paid. So they were running a company that seemed successful–success that Billy got all the credit for, naturally–but was actually hemorrhaging money through no fault of their own, and they were catching all kinds of flak from their vendors. Their frustration was growing and showing. Something had to give."

"And where was Melinda during all this?" Catherine asked.

"Oh yes, Melinda. Are you familiar with the expression, 'hell hath no fury like a woman scorned'?"

"No," Catherine said, bluntly.

"Well, trust me, she was pissed and determined to do something about it," Angelo said.

"About what?" Catherine asked.

"About getting treated like shit, about being dismissed as she was, without being freed from the prison of being Mrs. Billy Bate," Angelo said.

"So what did she do? Take a lover?" Catherine asked, shifting in her seat somewhat.

"No, nothing quite so pedestrian," Angelo replied. "Turns out she got wind of Billy exploring the possibility of taking on a new business venture, and she conspired to sabotage his efforts."

"Holy crap," she said. "Who knew Melinda had it in her? Maybe we should be discussing her ego."

Angelo laughed. "It wasn't really Melinda's idea to sabotage the business. She had some help from some outside, nefarious forces."

"Good Lord, who?" Catherine asked, moving to the edge of her seat. "Was Grace in on it?"

Angelo laughed again. "No, not at all. She did not get wind of any of this until she stopped by the Carpe Diem headquarters the morning after Billy died. She went there thinking she had to ensure a scandal-free burial of a philandering former employer who was on the Board of Trustees of her current employer. She also needed to know if he shared her secret that could derail her career, squelching any chance of her advancing professionally, while also trying to ascertain if the grieving, angry widow was going to insist Grace pay back a $60,000 debt that was compounding at 12 percent interest. What ensued over the next 72 hours, however, was far crazier than anyone could have expected.

Part IV

The Storm Before the Calm

Chapter 40

Power Puff Pandemonium

"Hang on," Catherine said. "We're back at the Carpe Diem headquarters?"

"Yes," Angelo said. "Now that you know a little bit about the primary characters, what transpired next might make a little more sense, although I'm still trying to figure it out all these years later."

"Okay," Catherine said. "So Grace goes to see Melinda the morning she learns of Billy's passing. While Grace is there, Melinda dresses down Pete and Re-Pete, and then Betty shows up. Melinda asks Grace to step out of the office, and Grace seizes the opportunity to call Ronkee to bring him up to speed. What happens next?"

"Here's how I remember it," Angelo said. "Grace said while she was on the phone bringing Ronkee up to speed, three former Power Puffs left messages for her, and each message was more desperate than the next. They read, in essence, that Grace had to get to Billy's office before Melinda found 'the box' in his drawer. According to the Puffs, when Billy cheated, he liked to take lots of pictures. He had amassed an extensive collection, which he kept in his desk drawer, apparently not realizing there was a possibility he might drop dead. Or maybe he did realize it but wanted to inflict as much emotional pain as possible on those who tried to love him upon his demise."

"Could anyone be so devious as to purposely collect something or some things, knowing how painful it would be for loved ones–or at least family members–to come across them," Catherine asked, too bothered at the concept to be concerned at how naïve this sounded.

"Grace said she wondered the same thing," Angelo said. "She thought about Billy and his final moments. Based on how he neglected his health–Grace and her former co-workers all said they knew this day would come–but she was sure no one, not even Billy, expected it would come so soon. Billy's grandfather–Jack's father, whom Billy idolized–smoked cigars and drank whiskey his entire adult life, and he lived into his 80s. But he was a simple man who worked with his hands, came home to his wife, and put his head on his own pillow at a reasonable hour, knowing he had to get up early the next day. Billy, on the other hand, ran a multi-million-dollar corporation with franchises around the country. He slept reluctantly, flouted all theories about eating right, and often, his rare attempts to stop smoking resulted in him sneaking smokes while wearing a nicotine patch, all while bedding different women on a regular basis. While this fingering the flame, if you will, lifestyle provided excitement, it also took a toll on his ticker."

"Wow," Catherine said. "It's a wonder Billy lived as long as he did."

"From here on out, it gets a little crazy," Angelo said. "Grace said what transpired over the next couple of days was so mentally challenging, she needed to verbalize her version so she could process what happened and move on. She dictated what she remembered taking place, and after listening to it, doubted that making it public would do anyone any good. She allowed me to listen, as well, and I have to admit, I have my reservations, too. It's one of the factors I considered when deciding not to write a book about it.

"For the sake of expediency, though, I will walk you through Grace's version of what transpired, but again, I have to warn you, it gets personal, graphic, and a little racy. I hope you can handle it."

"Good Lord, Angelo, spend some time on TikTok," Catherine admonished. "I doubt very much you'll tell me anything that comes close to what people reveal about themselves on social media."

"All right, then. You've been warned. Here goes," Angelo said.

"So Grace was thinking about Billy's intentions regarding the stowed photographs when she was shaken from her train of thought by Billy's secretary, Martha, on the office intercom," Angelo said.

"Grace, can you take a call from Victoria Nook? She sounds pretty frantic," Martha said.

"Sure, put it through," Grace said.

Victoria was a local businesswoman who was the best-looking woman in Mockingbird Heights, tantamount to being the prettiest girl at a *Star Trek* convention. On several occasions, she needed to tap into Billy's reservoir of guidance and positive cash flow. Grace knew from talking with her that Billy had provided her with some financial assistance over the years. Grace had no idea, however, of the extent to which Victoria showed her gratitude.

"Grace, you HAVE to get into Billy's office and get the box out from his lower right-hand drawer!" Victoria said.

"Geez, Victoria, not you, too?" Grace said.

"No, oh God, no," she said. "I wouldn't do that with a married man, much less with my friend's husband," Victoria said. "But Billy loved to show me pictures he took of other women. There must have been a dozen different girls."

"Why would he show you?" Grace asked.

"I think he got off showing me how he could manipulate women," she said. "You know what a control freak he was. He derived sexual pleasure from getting these women to take off their clothes and from showing me he was powerful enough to convince them to do it. I think he wanted me to see that more than he wanted me to see their tits. Or mine, for that matter."

"I don't think you're too far off," Grace said. "But you're too late. Melinda has declared the office off-limits. She's in there now with Betty."

"Good Lord, Grace," Victoria said. "I hope she's not going through his desk. There's going to be a bloodbath. And with his daughter, no less. Oh my God. What a mess."

"They're talking now," Grace said. "Maybe Melinda won't even go through the drawers until later." They said goodbye and hung up.

Grace hoped there might be some chocolate stashed in the Carpe Diem company kitchen, so she sauntered over there and started opening and closing cabinet doors. No chocolate. Then the door to Billy's office opened slowly, and Melinda stepped out. She told Martha to get the Christopher Moore Funeral Home on the phone and inform them she wanted to come by within the hour to make the funeral arrangements. Betty stood in the doorway, shocked and pale. She did not speak, move, or acknowledge anyone's existence. She stood there, wondering how one turn of events could suck so much oxygen out of her life. Grace tried to make eye contact to gauge whether she should say or do something for her, but to no avail. She looked like a little girl who was backstage at a *Sesame Street* show and saw Big Bird without his costume head, smoking a cigarette, and drinking a beer.

Grace turned to Melinda instead. "You want me to go to the funeral home with you?" she asked.

"Yes, please," Melinda said. "We're leaving in a few minutes." There was no mention of what transpired between Melinda and Betty while they were in the office, but it was clear Melinda came across the dreaded box and shared them with Billy's daughter.

The Christopher Moore Funeral home was two blocks from the Carpe Diem building. Even though Billy lived in a different, wealthier community, they all knew he would want to have his wake in Mockingbird Heights. It was still his town.

The funeral director met Melinda, Betty, and Grace at the door. He bade Melinda and Betty his "deepest, deepest sympathies," and they headed into his office. They decided to wake Billy on Thursday and Friday afternoons and evenings and then have the funeral on Saturday morning. Then the discussion took a turn down a street never visited before by the funeral director.

Melinda wanted to hire pyrotechnicians to shoot off fireworks at the cemetery. "Billy loved fireworks," she explained to the director. "And he loved to be different."

"Well, fireworks would definitely be different," he replied, not missing a beat. "But I am fairly certain the cemetery would not allow it. Nonetheless, I will check into it for you," he said, even though he had no intention of doing so.

They discussed the casket. Melinda wanted it fully opened so she could dress Billy in the white tie and tails and mask made famous by Tortu, the lead character in *Black Maria*. The funeral director said, "No problem," but Grace noticed him trying to suppress a smirk. Then it was time to choose a casket.

The funeral director took a deep breath and said, "You

know, Melinda, Billy was a special man. His funeral should warrant a spectacular casket. I have one in mind, but we would have to order it special because nobody keeps it in stock."

He opened a casket catalog and flipped to the back, to a sterling silver casket that looked like a rectangular spaceship.

"Perfect," Melinda said. "How much?"

"Like I said, it's a special casket for a special man," the funeral director said.

"How much?" Melinda asked again, displaying a business toughness Billy would have found pleasing.

"$19,900," the director said.

"I'll pay fifteen," she said in a business-like tone. "Not a penny more."

"Well, Melinda, like I said, Billy was special and I would love to do everything I can to give him a proper send off," the funeral director said. "But I am afraid my hands are tied. I am already offering it to you at my cost."

Melinda stood up and leaned over the director's desk, either for emphasis or perhaps to use her cleavage to distract him. She looked him in the eyes and said, "This will be the biggest funeral you ever do. Your funeral home will either hit a home run or put out some crap and turn off important people. Now, why don't you do the right thing and work with me here so we can put on the show that Billy's friends and family expect this to be?"

The funeral director sat back in his chair, cleared his throat, and thought for a moment. "I suppose we could provide the Silver Star casket for the price you mentioned."

Melinda smiled and extended her hand. "I look forward to working with you," she said. "Now, if you do not mind, I have too many details to take care of. If you have any questions or need help with anything, you can contact Grace here," gesturing in Grace's direction.

Betty was still reeling from what had happened at Carpe Diem and did not say a word. You could almost hear the thrashing inside her head as she wrestled with knowing the man she idolized, her father, loved to take photographs of naked women, most of whom were about her age or a little older. She finally spoke as they left the funeral home.

"Carpe Diem is close by," she said. "If you don't mind, I am going to walk back there and try to clear my head. I will call you later."

She walked away, perhaps in search of a time machine to rewind the past 18 hours. Billy still wasn't even dead a full day yet.

Grace was glad Betty offered to walk back because it gave her a chance to ask Melinda about having Billy dressed like Tortu, including the mask, at his wake.

"Tortu could only communicate with others when he was wearing his mask, and as a result, lived in a special, isolated hell," Melinda said. "Billy had crawled into a similar shell to hide from his father's abuse, and the only way he could escape from it was to hide behind the mask of being a successful business owner. Wearing the mask empowered him to experience everything the world had to offer and was the closest he ever came to truly enjoying himself. The man wearing the mask was the one I thought I fell in love with."

"Is that why he showed up for his first board meeting as a Trustee for Gibbons College dressed up as Tortu?" Grace asked.

Melinda chuckled. "Oh yeah, I forgot about that," she said. "Billy's first board meeting fell on Halloween. He thought it would be fun to dress up as Tortu. I begged him not to. The people on the Gibbons' board did not know who he was or how smart he was, or how hard he worked to build up his business. All they saw was a grown man dressed up as a character from a

Broadway musical. A sad, sullen character. I'm not sure they ever took him seriously. They took his money, though. That part, the college took VERY seriously."

Melinda lit a cigarette. They stood there, silently, as she smoked it. Grace felt compelled to give her another hug, but held back as she had already hugged her once and did not want to push it. Besides, Melinda seemed oddly content and at ease. After a minute or two, she dropped the cigarette onto the sidewalk and stubbed it out with the toe of her Louis Vuitton high-heeled shoe. She turned on that heel and, wordlessly, started walking back to Carpe Diem headquarters with Grace in tow. It was a little after five, so Pete and Re-Pete and the other employees were already gone for the day. Martha was trying to coordinate all the messages, flowers, and fruit baskets coming in. Word of Billy's death had spread quickly, and seeing what had already been delivered reminded Grace and Melinda that tomorrow would be an even longer, tougher day as the reality of what had transpired over the past few hours began to sink in.

"I'm going home," Melinda announced. "I'm going to pour a big glass of Remy, fix a hot bubble bath, and soak until all the pain melts away."

Grace told her to feel free to call her any time she needed.

Melinda smiled. "You know, Grace, Billy was very upset when you left. After seeing you in action today, I now realize the reason why he was upset is different from what I assumed then. I can see you cared about him because you're here to take care of me. That means a lot, and I'm grateful. Perhaps next week we can have lunch and explore our future together. Billy's not coming back, and you know Slade's father's not coming back. We single moms need to stick together, and I have no doubt we can make doing so worthwhile on many levels."

"I'd like that," Grace said.

With that, they parted ways. Grace got into her car and

headed home. As she drove, her mind entertained the visual of Melinda soaking in the tub with nothing but bubbles and brandy to keep her company, but then she quickly caught himself. *She's not even widowed 24 hours yet, and I'm watching her take a bath*, Grace thought. *I really need a boyfriend.*

Then she considered what Melinda said about their future together and what might happen over the next few days. She did feel she owed a proper send-off to Billy. Well, that and $60,000. She also needed to ascertain what Melinda meant when she said Slade's father wasn't coming back. Was that Melinda's way of letting Grace know she knew?

Grail was waiting with Slade when Grace arrived home. The boy was already fed and taking a bath in Grail's bathroom. Grace stepped into the bathroom ostensibly to finish what Grail had started but also to spend time in Slade's world and escape hers. After his bath, she bundled him up in his feetsy pajamas and carted him off to his bed in their apartment inside Grail's home. She read him his favorite story, *Alexander and His Busy Day*, and he was soon fast asleep.

Grace tiptoed away from the bed and closed the door. As she did, she was startled to realize that Grail was standing there in the hall, waiting for her. They walked in silence the short distance to Grace's kitchen area. Two mugs of hot tea were waiting for them, with some cookies. Speaking softly, Grail waited for her younger sister to unload.

"Well?" Grail asked.

"Well, what?" Grace responded, sipping at the tea.

"Dish, girl. What happened?"

"Billy's dead," Grace said.

"Yeah, I know," Grail said. "I told you this morning, remember?"

"Christ, that seems like a lifetime ago," Grace said.

"It was. Billy's lifetime," Grail said.

"Oh, Grail," Grace moaned.

"Too soon?" Grail cracked.

"What a mess," Grace said. "The man was all over the place. Women. Photographs. Betrayal. Lord knows what tomorrow will bring."

"How's Melinda holding up?" Grail asked.

"Better than you might expect," Grace said. "She even hinted at the possibility of my returning to Carpe Diem to work with her."

"Why would you want to do that?" Grail said. "Didn't you have enough of her and Billy? Remember how happy you were when you left for Gibbons?"

"Gibbons is fine," Grace said. "But the chances of making serious money are greater at Carpe Diem."

"At what price?" Grail snapped. "Your dignity? Do you really want to go back to the backwards limo rides and have smoke blown in your face?"

"I'd only go back if it were different," Grace said. "I'd want to be a part of the actual business and make some real money for a change."

"What about Pete & Re-Pete?" Grail asked. "Do you think they want you injecting yourself into their sweet deal?"

"I get along with them," Grace said. "And I get along with Melinda. It's Melinda and the Petes who don't get along."

"Getting along with Melinda when she's the boss' wife is one thing," Grail said. "Melinda is going to turn into a completely different experience when she's running the show, especially with the Petes nipping at her heels. I bet she redefines the term *business bitch*."

"I'm not sure that's a term," Grace said.

"If it isn't, it should be," Grail said. "Regardless, Melinda might promise you the world, but don't be surprised if her 'world' differs from Billy's—and yours. In the history of business, no one ever got rich writing checks. They get rich taking advantage of people."

"Thank you, Karla Marx," Grace said.

"What you knew with Melinda as the Boss' Wife will be different from what you will experience with Melinda, the Business Owner. And if you two start making goo-goo eyes at each other, all bets are off."

Grace blushed. "It's not like that. She's a beautiful woman, for sure, but I have my hands full with Slade, and the last time I checked, I like men."

"You're telling me you never thought about Melinda's Hot Sauce?" Grail asked.

"Oh, please," Grace said.

"Well, remember this," Grail said. "Melinda's values are not your values. She looks for happiness in the pages of catalogs and is driven by her pathetic need to have everyone notice her when she walks into a room. You, on the other hand, know what truly matters in life. You will opt for a hug from your son over the fanciest fur coat any day of the week. There's not a salary in the world that makes losing that worthwhile."

"I don't know," Grace said. "It'd be nice to not have to worry about money, and maybe even buy a house for Slade."

"Slade's fine for now, and so are you," Grail said. "There's more to life than making big money."

"That's easy for you to say, Grail. You and your husband have done well. I'm tired of living from paycheck to paycheck, having to kiss somebody's ass just to stay employed."

"And working for Melinda will eliminate the need to kiss ass? Are you kidding?" Grail shot back.

After sitting quietly for a few minutes, looking at their tea mugs, Grail took a deep breath.

"Here's how I see it, Grace. We're all connected. All of us. One World. We're all created in God's image, and because we're a slice of God, there are no limits to what we can do and who we can be. The limits you're experiencing and the barriers you're bouncing into are of our own making. Embrace God and free yourself to become the woman you've always wanted to become."

"What about Dad?" Grace blurted. "Where was God's embrace when that madman shot Dad in cold blood? Was Mom in God's embrace as she cried herself to sleep at night?"

"Bad things happen to good people, Grace. You know that. There's no earthly explanation as to why, and I'm in no rush to find out if the only way to do so is by moving on to the afterlife. All I know is you must live your life in the moment, the now. Neither the past nor the future really exists. Live in the now. Embrace your relationship with God and let His Love inspire you!"

"Is that what you do? Is that why your life is so perfect?" Grace asked in a tone that wavered between jealousy and snarly.

"I'm far from perfect, Grace," Grail said. "You know that. I know that. Nobody's life is perfect."

"Jesus was perfect," Grace said, more to be argumentative than anything else.

"And where'd that get him?" Grail countered. "Crucified, that's where. They shot Lincoln. Shot Kennedy. Shot Martin Luther King."

"They left Mother Teresa alone. She died of natural causes," Grace said, again just to be argumentative.

"Even the Mossad and the CIA know not to mess with a nun, Grace. Didn't you learn anything dealing with the Good Sisters at St. Williams? Vincent, Cornelius, Paula–they were all bat shit crazy," Grail said.

Grace and Grail laughed.

"It sounds so simple. Too simple. I need money to pay the

bills," Grace said, getting back to the topic at hand. "I need stability for Slade. I need ... I need ..."

"You need to get laid," Grail said.

"So what else is new?" Grace sighed. "It's been so long, but I'm not sure a one-night stand is the answer. I don't want to be another Bernie the Bartender, or one of his conquests, for that matter."

"Oh, for God's sake, Grace, you're overthinking this, as always," Grail said. "If nothing else, you're too big to be a coxswain."

Grace was stunned.

"He told YOU about the coxswain?!?

"Of course not, Grace," Grail said. "When have you ever seen me in The Broken Oar? I've heard the story from other people. Ronnie heard it, too. We've all heard it."

Grace teetered between hurt and dumbfounded. On the one hand, she thought she was the only person Bernie trusted with the story. On the other hand, what kind of person would go around blabbing about such a thing?

"Why would he tell other people about what happened?" Grace asked aloud, more surprised than expecting an answer from Grail.

"Because he's Irish, and Irish men are storytellers at heart," Grail said. "Besides, it didn't happen to him. From what I've heard, somebody in the bar told Bernie it happened to a friend of his, and Bernie took it there. Apparently, there are multiple versions of it. I'm guessing the version you heard had Bernie in the starring role for some reason."

"But why would he share that story with me, as if it happened to him?" Grace asked, again equally dumbfounded and hurt.

"Ever see a dog in a house go ballistic when the mail carrier walks up the front path to put mail in the mailbox?" Grail asked. "The dog is doing everything he or she can to 'protect' the home front–to keep it from being entered or violated, if you will–by trying to sound as ferocious as possible. Meanwhile, if the homeowner took the time to introduce the dog to the mail carrier, most likely the mail carrier would become friends."

"So, on the surface Bernie's trying to keep me at arm's length, but in his twisted little way, he also wants to be my friend?" Grace asked.

"Something like that," Grail answered. "Plus, like I said. He's an Irishman, and most Irish storytellers will embrace any opportunity to tell a funny story, even at the risk of doing so having negative consequences. They can't help themselves. That's the real Irish curse."

Grail and Grace looked at each other and then down at their teacups.

"You've had a tough, crazy day," Grail said after a few moments, "and the rest of the week should prove even more daunting. I suggest you get a good night's sleep tonight, but before you turn in, give your challenges over to God. Let him deal with them. Just surrender to that Higher Power within all of us and say, 'My problems are all yours, Big Fella. Knock yourself out."

"I wish it were that easy," Grace said.

"It IS that easy," Grail said. "There are no problems. There are no challenges. You simply let go and let God. Have faith. Relax and allow God's goodness to steer your decisions."

"Do you think Melinda's contemplating the same course of action right now?" Grace said.

"The Billy and Melindas of the world will never be happy, no matter how many presents they buy for each other, or how much their bank accounts swell. Their lives are driven by their egos, and ego stands for 'edging God out.' Without God in your life, nothing you can say or do or experience will provide enough satisfaction. There's always the need for something bigger, better, faster, sleeker, which is ironic because there's nothing greater than God's love. With it, you have everything. Without it? Nothing."

"Thank you for caring, Grail," Grace said. "You're right. I'm exhausted. I'm going to bed. Let's see what magic tomorrow brings."

Chapter 41

I'm Going to Miss the Bastard

"Poor Grace," Catherine said. "Did she really cop to needing to get laid?"

"She was fairly forthcoming with the nature of the discussions and conversations that took place over this period," Angelo said. "I think it was cathartic for her. I think she found the episode as disturbing as I did, and I have no doubt it felt good for her to unburden herself."

"She said she woke up the following morning, and as she fed Slade, she considered taking a personal day to clear her head. She realized staying home wouldn't do much good. There was a lot she had to do at Gibbons, and she had a feeling there would be phone calls from Mockingbird Heights. She was right. She no sooner sat at her desk when the first one came from Pete Snodgrass.

"You were nice to stop by yesterday, Grace," he said. "I don't know how you can handle Melinda." The bitch slapped a padlock on Billy's door. Can you imagine? A padlock! The balls! She's in over her pretty little head. This is going to get ugly!"

"I don't know what to tell you, Pete," Grace said. "She's been through a lot. She's feeling vulnerable."

"Fuck that and fuck her," Snodgrass said." I've been carrying that prick for years now. He stopped paying attention to the business a long time ago, right around when you came on board."

Grace wasn't sure if Snodgrass was blaming her for this development or putting a timeline on it. Either way, she did not care. Snodgrass had it too good for too long as far as Grace was concerned, and had been so obnoxious about it that Grace did not feel any sympathy for him.

"Have you gotten any funeral information yet?" Snodgrass asked. "I'm getting phone calls, and Melinda's nowhere to be found. She's probably too busy moving her spic relatives into Billy's house."

"They decided to have a wake tonight, tomorrow afternoon, tomorrow night, and then have the funeral on Saturday morning," Grace told Snodgrass. "Check with Martha to see if it's final."

Grace no sooner hung up with Snodgrass when the phone rang again. This time it was Santini.

"Hey, Grace, Santini here. I was thinking about something Billy used to have me do, and I thought you might find it interesting."

"Go ahead," Grace said.

"Every Valentine's Day, I had to take a Carpe Diem van over to Von Lessens. You remember Von Lessens. They made their own chocolate and ice cream. Anyway, Billy would have me pick up chocolates in heart-shaped boxes. Some years, there'd be as many as two dozen. I'd bring them back to the shop here in Mockingbird Heights, and Billy and I would attach a numbered Post-It note on each box. Then Billy would give me a sheet with names and addresses. Each name and address would have a number assigned to it, and the number would correspond to the number on the Post-It note. Once we had a system, I had to drive all over Long Island, dropping off the damn gifts."

"How long did it take?" Grace asked.

"Three hours at least," Santini said.

"Why did the Post-It note have a number and not a name?" Grace asked.

"Billy was petrified that a box might be delivered to the wrong babe," Pete replied. "This way, the worst that would happen is the gal would get a box of chocolates with a number on it. The guy thought of everything."

"Pretty funny and sad at the same time, Pete," Grace said. "But why are you telling me?"

"I don't know, Grace. I'm sitting here, thinking about all the crazy shit he used to do. I'm going to ... I'm gonna ... I'm gonna miss the bastard," Santini said, breaking into a sob. "The guy was nuts, but he sure as hell did a lot for me. I never thanked him. Never told him how much I appreciated everything he did."

"I'm sure many people feel that way. I know I do," Grace said.

"Billy wouldn't let anyone in. He wouldn't, or couldn't, let you be his friend, even though he wanted to be friends with everyone," Santini said. "Jack fucked with his head so much Billy didn't know what it was to have a true friend you could trust implicitly or who liked you for you. Billy was probably the loneliest, saddest guy I ever knew. I tried, man. I tried."

The sobs started again. Grace waited on the other end of the phone, listening as Santini gained control. "I'm sorry, Grace. I had to talk to somebody," Santini said.

"It's all right," Grace said. "We can talk more at the wake. Meanwhile, Pete, you have to know Billy appreciated everything you did for him. He had a funny way of showing it, and you sure as hell knew he wasn't going to express it to you directly."

"That's true," Pete said. "I gotta go. Take care."

After they hung up, Grace called Martha. Grace liked talking to Martha.

"Martha, it's Grace. How are you holding up?" she asked, though she knew the answer.

"Grace, you have no idea," she replied. "Snodgrass is driving me crazy. Melinda is hiding at home. Betty wants to cry on my shoulder over the phone, and everybody else expects me to know all the funeral information AND tell them every gory detail about Billy's death. Just to keep things really interesting, the Power Puffs are coming out of the woodwork."

"Which ones?" Grace asked.

"Well, you know about Donna, so let's leave her for last," Martha said. "First up is Cher, the stripper. Can you believe it? A woman other than the actual Cher calling herself Cher. Only Billy could find one of those."

"What did Cher do?" Grace asked.

"She took off with the company car Billy gave her," Martha said. "Melinda told me to track down the company cars and instruct whoever was driving them to return them to Carpe Diem within the next 24 hours or they would be reported stolen. Three ladies have agreed to bring their cars back, but the only one I can't track down is Cher. Her phone has been disconnected. And if she doesn't turn it in, Melinda has to keep paying the car insurance because you can't cancel car insurance without handing in the license plate. Who knew!"

"Holy shit," Grace said

"Oh, it doesn't end there," Martha said. "American Express called. They wanted to alert us to the fact that somebody named Amber charged more than three thousand dollars worth of jewelry to her Carpe Diem credit card this morning. I guess she was so distraught at hearing the news about Billy, she had to treat herself to some new shiny stuff. But the best was Janeece. What kind of name is that? It's like her mother meant to call her Janice and couldn't spell the name correctly. Anyway, Janeece cashed a check this morning for $27,000! She must have hit Billy up for a loan and decided to seize the day and cash it once she heard he had died. Melinda told me to stop the check or tell Janeece to return the money, or she will have her arrested. I'm not sure you can do that, but I bet we'll have fun trying."

"Wow," Grace said. She knew Billy was spinning plates, but she had no idea it was this extensive. It turned out Martha was warming up.

"I saved the best for last," Martha said. "According to Donna, she and Billy were supposed to sign a lease on an apartment and then move in together."

"When were they supposed to move in?" she asked.

"Wednesday," Martha replied.

"Wednesday, as in yesterday? That Wednesday?" she asked.

"You got it," Martha said. "Billy knew a confrontation with Melinda was coming. It must have upset him because he hated confrontations. According to Donna, they were getting ready to move in together."

"I had no idea there was so much trouble in paradise," Grace said.

"Oh, I could see this one coming," Martha said. "Last December, Donna was giving him grief about spending New Year's Eve with her. So was Melinda."

"What did Billy do?" Grace asked.

"He decided he was having heart problems and checked himself into Molloy Medical Center."

"He faked a heart attack?" Grace asked.

"Pretty much. Billy being on the board meant every doctor there had to make an appearance at his bedside. It was unbelievable how many people were inconvenienced on New Year's Eve so he could dodge a bullet. They wouldn't let Donna in because she wasn't family, and Melinda blew him off and didn't even visit. He checked out the next morning."

"Does Melinda know about Donna? About the lease?" Grace wondered.

"She does now," Martha said. "Donna asked to speak with her, and Melinda took her call. I couldn't believe it. They spoke for about an hour."

"Maybe they discussed Billy's photo techniques," Grace joked.

"I don't think so," Martha said, either not amused or not realizing Grace was joking.

"Any word on the funeral arrangements?" Grace asked.

"Yeah. Hang on a minute. Let's see. Here it is, confirmed. We're going to start the wake tonight, then have something Friday afternoon, Friday night, and do the funeral Saturday morning. That should be enough, don't you think?" Martha asked.

"Plenty," Grace said.

"There's one more thing," Martha said. "Billy's will. Believe it or not, Billy left a third of the company to Melinda, a third to Betty, and a third to James."

"James gets a third?!?" Grace said, probably louder than she should have.

"A third goes to James," Martha said. "He's what—12? This is going to go over like a bloodstain on a motel mattress."

"Has that news been made public yet?" Grace quiered.

"Well, James knows. He was in here before and told the

other secretaries, 'When I take over, I'm going to fire you because I only want hot chicks working for me.'"

"Christ," Grace said. "What did he say to you?"

"Oh, not to worry. He told me I'm hot enough for him to keep," Martha said. "Lucky me."

"Does anyone else know?" Grace asked.

"What–that I'm hot? I hope so," Martha said.

"No," Grace said. "Does anyone outside of Carpe Diem know about the will?"

"Technically, no," Martha said. "But it's the worst-kept secret in Mockingbird Heights. If Betty hasn't freaked out about losing her father, then this will send her over the edge, along with her family and Pete and Re-Pete."

Years ago, Billy put Marietta and his sisters on the Carpe Diem payroll and has been paying them ever since. Not a lot, but enough that they didn't have to sweat the grocery bills. Now, not only was Melinda–someone the Bate Family had merely tolerated–in charge, she and her pre-teen son owned the majority of the company Billy had built. So, the answer to the will question was known. What wasn't known was whether the gravy train would end before the first shovel-full of dirt was tossed on Billy's coffin. And Grace was still in no man's land about her secret and the $60,000 she owed Billy.

"Grace, hold on a second, I have another call coming," Martha said, putting her on hold before Grace could suggest she just call her back. Grace wanted to get some things done for Gibbons College–her employer–and she wasn't going to be able to do anything while on hold. Just as she contemplated hanging up, Martha came back on the line.

"You're not going to believe who just called and wants to speak to Melinda," Martha said.

"Let me guess ... a Power Puff who refers to herself as Madonna ..." Grace said, chuckling at her own joke.

"Oh, no no no no," Martha said excitedly. This was unusual because Martha prided herself on her unflappability.

"Well, who then?" Grace said, sounding more impatient than she intended.

"Jackson Ouellette."

"Jackson Ouellette!?!? As in billionaire Jackson Ouellette? The Jackson Ouellette in the picture I took of the three of them that night in the hotel lobby? That Jackson Ouellette?"

"Yes, one and the same," Martha said.

"Wow! What the hell does he want?" Grace asked.

"I don't know, but I have a feeling I'm about to find out. I'll call you later," Martha said, and hung up.

Chapter 42

The Three-Ring Circus

"Jackson Ouellette?" Catherine asked, excited that she actually knew of this person.

"Yep, Jackson Ouellette," Angelo said.

"Talk about egos. Holy smokes!" Catherine interjected. "Did you ever get to meet or interview him?"

"No," Angelo with an air of wistful exasperation that made him sound like a fisherman would use when describing the "big one" that got away. "By the time I got wind of his involvement in this unsavory episode, he had long retreated to his semi-recluse status."

"So what did he want with the likes of Billy, Melinda, and Grace?" Catherine asked, ever more intrigued.

"Hang on, and I'll finish telling you what transpired, again based on what Grace shared with me. Like I said before, it gets downright racy at times," Angelo said.

"Oh, please–some day I'll let you see what some of my friends share online. I'll be fine," Catherine said, "Racy away."

"I'm not worried about you," Angelo said, half-kidding. "I'm not used to discussing such things in mixed company, especially when said mixed company is young enough to be my daughter."

"I'd be honored if you simply thought of me as a fellow journalist, impervious to details that some may find disturbing," Catherine suggested.

"Well, okay. Buckle up, though. It gets bumpy."

Catherine shifted in her seat with anticipation and instinctively looked at her phone to make sure it was still recording and had enough battery power. All clear.

Angelo resumed his narration:

Grace tried to concentrate on her day job but couldn't get anything done. She checked in with Murray Jules, her boss at Gibbons. She told him she wanted to leave early for Billy's wake that afternoon and would probably need to be there the following afternoon and evening, too. She left out the part about the Power Puffs and Jackson Ouellette, figuring there was a time and place to have that discussion, and this wasn't it. At least until she had more information.

Murray rubbed his Old Man Face with his long, large hands that were decades removed from their days loading beer trucks as a teenager, and then let out a long, exasperated sigh.

"I suppose you should," he said. "Billy was a board member. I am sure his widow would appreciate you being there. You make sure she feels good about the support she received from Gibbons during her time of grief."

"No problem, Murray," Grace said.

As Grace drove to the funeral home, she tried to anticipate what to expect. She tried to envision the different people who most likely would attend, the business owners from Mockingbird Heights, the local elected officials, and the vendors who worked with Carpe Diem. Billy's family members and Marietta would be there, too. Grace had met his family at different functions, but she would be hard pressed to remember their names or their relation to Billy. Betty's cousins all had similar physical characteristics, including rather prominent noses, making the fact that Betty's nose had been "fixed" a few years ago painfully obvious anytime Betty stood amongst her family.

Then she wondered about Ouellette. Why the hell would he be calling Melinda? It's doubtful he heard about Billy's demise and wanted to extend his condolences. Did he even remember meeting Billy and Melinda in the hotel lobby that night, or having his picture taken with them? Is that possible, given how many people this man must meet on a daily basis, people who can legitimately refer to themselves as globetrotters and captains of industry?

Grace arrived at the funeral home and was greeted at the door by Candee Coyne.

"Thank God you're here," Candee said. "It's awful in there."

Grace laughed nervously and questioned why Candee thought her presence would make the situation any better. She was right about it being awful, though. Grace walked into the room where Billy was being waked and found a few dozen people standing around like pre-teens at a sixth-grade dance, looking at their shoes and not knowing what to say. The folks from the Mockingbird Heights business community gathered in one corner of the room while the Bate family members clustered in the opposite corner.

Fasberg, a local jewelry store owner, said, "Hey, look, it's Grace."

The other Chamber of Commerce folks gathered around her to find out if there was indeed life after Carpe Diem. There was, but not for Billy. Grace's walking in the room broke the ice, although the business folks stayed amongst themselves, and the family members spoke to other family members. Grace sought out Melinda and saw her speaking with the funeral director. She did all the talking, and he did a lot of nodding. Grace guessed the director had learned his lesson from the earlier negotiation session. Grace waited beyond the imaginary circle one senses when waiting for the opportune moment to interrupt. Grace also decided not to ask about Ouellette until she learned more from Martha.

Melinda ended the conversation, and the funeral director scurried away. She turned to Grace and said, "I arranged for Donna to have some private time with the corpse tomorrow."

The corpse. Not Billy. Not her husband. Not even the dearly departed. The corpse. Grace chewed on that for a moment before she fully comprehended what Melinda had told her: She was going to let the woman who almost stole her husband spend private time with him. This concession was rather unusual, even though Melinda didn't have to worry about Billy cheating on her anymore.

"Really?" was the best Grace could muster.

"I know it sounds odd," Melinda said. "But she gets to spend some time alone with him in exchange for promising not to show up at the wake or funeral. I think that's more than fair."

It was more than fair. It was also smart. Even though Donna had done all the damage she was going to do to Melinda's relationship with Billy, the last thing Melinda wanted was for Donna to create a scene.

"Besides," Melinda volunteered, "I don't want Donna stealing my thunder."

There was almost no chance such a thing would happen. Melinda was wearing a short, black cocktail dress with a low-cut neckline revealing the kind of cleavage that made Elizabeth Taylor an international star. Was it appropriate for the widow at a wake? Not under normal circumstances, but it wouldn't be a Billy and Melinda production unless he stood there not having much to say and Melinda played the part of The Knock-out. Billy wasn't standing and had even less to say than usual while Melinda played her part to the hilt.

Melinda looked around the room. "I don't see those blood-sucking politicians around," she said. "They kissed his ass but saw him as nothing more than a walking checkbook. I guess since he's no use to them anymore, they can't be bothered."

"They'll be here tomorrow afternoon," Grace assured her. "Early, too, so they can hit the links afterward while it's still light out."

"How do you know?" she asked.

"When Jack died, they stopped by his wake to show their respect for Billy," she explained. "But they did it in the afternoon, on company time. Far be it for them to show respect while off the clock."

Melinda snorted. "I despise those bastards," she said, spitting out the words like poison pellets. "They kept showing up, one after the other, with their hands out looking for checks. For this 'cause' or that 'campaign'. Always important with an exclamation point. Get this guy elected! Keep that seat! I swear they made up some of the candidates and races. And Billy never saw through it. He wanted so badly for them to include him in their so-called inner circle. It was pathetic."

"You don't know the half of it, Melinda," Grace added. "He used to send little memos to me to see him about different fundraisers. 'Pizzims,' we called them, because he would write PSM on little Post It notes. Please See Me. I threw away at least half without discussing them with Billy. I knew they were garbage."

"Well, it's nice to know SOMEbody was looking out for Billy," she said, moving in a little closer to Grace. "I hope I can count on you to look after me for the next few days." She gently took Grace's arm and brought her in close. "Lord knows I am going to need all the support I can get."

Grace recalled Melinda's session with the funeral director yesterday and realized this woman needed Grace's support about as much as Mike Tyson needed a bodyguard. Pulling her in even closer, she whispered in her ear, "I especially need you to keep an eye on Snodgrass," she said. "It seems you and Snodgrass are the witnesses to Billy's will. As much as I hate that son of a bitch, I need his cooperation when it comes to verifying its validity."

Oh my, the will, Grace thought, making a mental note not to let on that Martha already shared the highlights of it with her. She also decided to keep her knowledge about the Ouellette call under her hat, although she was dying to ask.

"I'll do what I can," Grace said to Melinda, but Melinda was already looking over her shoulder, watching as funeral home employees brought in more floral displays.

"Excuse me, Grace. I have to go tell those people where to put those flowers," Melinda said.

Grace wasn't sure what Melinda meant by that. She watched as Melinda looked at the cards on the displays and then directed the employees as to where they should place the displays in relation to the location of the casket. Grace quickly surmised that Melinda was deciding whose floral displays should have greater prominence over others. This reminded Grace of how political leaders decide who gets to stand near the podium when a major elected official speaks at a press conference. It's all about positioning. Your position in the pecking order, your proximity to true power, is determined by how close you are to the podium when the most important person in the room speaks to the media. Well, the second most important person in the room, anyway. The most important person is the one deciding who stands where, but most likely is not at the press conference. At this moment, Melinda was the most important person in the funeral home because she was deciding whose flowers would be seen more readily, and whose displays would be buried in the back.

The only thing more amusing to Grace than the idea that Melinda saw the need to position the floral arrangements was the fact that many of the people who sent them would actually measure their self-worth and importance by how close the arrangements they sent were to the casket. She knew the few times she attended wakes with Billy, the first thing he had her do was locate the flowers he sent.

"I really don't miss this part of the Billy Experience," Grace thought, chuckling to herself.

With that, she saw Martha had entered the funeral home. She resisted the urge to make a beeline to her so she could get the scoop on the Ouellette call–and anything else that might have transpired over the last couple of hours. It was a good thing, too, because Martha walked right over to Melinda and whispered into her ear. Melinda nodded, mouthed the words "thank you," and went back to her picking and choosing. With that, Martha looked as if she was trying to decide which was the lesser of two evils: hanging out with the family or the business people. Grace saw this as her opportunity and scurried over before anyone else could get to her.

Sidling up to Martha, Grace tugged on her arm and asked, softly, "So ... what did Ouellette want?"

"Yes, hello, Grace. I'm fine, thank you for asking," Martha said, sarcastically.

"I'm sorry, Martha," Grace said. "How are you?"

"Oh, don't mind me. I've had a day, though," Martha said. "Goddamn people are exhausting."

"I can only imagine what you're going through, Martha," Grace said. "Can I help you with anything?"

"Oh, cut the crap," Martha said. "I know you're dying to know about Ouellette."

"I am," Grace admitted, somewhat taken aback at Martha's curtness. "But I meant what I said. Let me know if I can be of assistance."

Martha sighed. "I'm sorry, Grace. I didn't mean to snap. This has been brutal. Phonies galore. And every time I think I can exhale another shit storm lands in my lap."

"Like the Ouellette call?" Grace said, trying to sound sympathetic while simultaneously pumping Martha for information.

"Yeah, like the Ouellette call," Martha said. "But you might want to sit down for this one."

Grace looked around the room to ascertain where Melinda was and to determine where she and Martha could sit and not be interrupted–or noticed. She took Martha by the arm and said, "Let's go out in the hallway and see what our options are."

They left the room where Billy was being waked and walked down the hallway until they found a spot where they felt they could chat in private. They sat down and leaned forward.

"Do you remember taking that photo of Ouellette, Billy, and Melinda?" Martha asked.

"Of course! I set it up and took it."

"Well, so does Ouellette. And he wasn't happy about it," Martha said.

"Happy about what?" Grace asked.

"The photo."

"What about it?"

"Remember how Billy pulled back at the last minute, to make it look as if Ouellette was introducing himself to Billy?" Martha said.

"Yep. Billy was proud of that."

"Well, Ouellette saw it and took it to mean Billy was trying to make him look bad."

"Why the hell would a billionaire like Ouellette care about something like that? And how did he see it?" Grace wondered aloud.

"He does, that's all that matters. He was pissed. So he started digging around to find out who this 'Billy Bate' character was."

"Uh oh," Grace said.

"Exactly. God knows what he uncovered originally, but the kicker is he learned about something even I wasn't aware of."

"Something Billy was doing? How could you not be aware of it? You know everything about him," Grace said.

"That's what I thought," Martha said, sounding annoyed and a little hurt. She looked to her left and right and then leaned in a little more to get closer to Grace, even though there was nobody within earshot of either of them.

"Billy was planning to start a new business," Martha said. "A marketing business, but with a twist."

"Marketing?!?!? Billy knew as much about marketing as he did the restaurant business," Grace said.

"Well, like I said, there's a twist. It wasn't really a marketing company, per se. The company was going to focus strictly on conducting polls and surveys."

"That's not much of a twist," Grace said.

"Let me finish," Martha admonished. "Bate International was going to conduct polls and surveys, but 'customize' the results to reflect whatever it was that the customer paying for the survey or poll wanted them to be."

"Huh?" Grace said, confused.

Martha looked around again. Seeing no one nearby, she continued.

"You know how a news story will say, 'According to a recent poll...and then report on the poll's findings? No one really pays attention to who conducted the poll or questions its legitimacy. They simply focus on the results. Billy's idea was to create a company that would 'accommodate' the client to the extent that the Bate International would release results reflecting exactly what the client wanted the public to believe as the truth."

Grace sat there, mouth agape.

"Billy was going to fabricate phony press releases to push a client's agenda," Grace said.

"No, it's more sinister than that. The plan was to actually conduct the poll or survey as commissioned by the client," Martha said, almost breathless from the magnitude of what she was sharing with Grace. "If the results were what they expected or hoped for, then full steam ahead. If they weren't, or if they knew ahead of time they wouldn't be, Bates International would issue a press release as if they were. This way the client would know the truth for internal purposes while at the same time pointing to the made-up results and their so-called 'third party credibility' as validation of their message, whatever it is."

Grace and Martha sat in silence, looking at each other while digesting what Martha had just shared.

"That's ... that's ... unscrupulous," Grace said, finally.

"Ya think?!?!" Martha said.

"I mean, in a way it's brilliant," Grace said, after some consideration. "Who questions the legitimacy of the surveys cited by the media? No one really pays attention to who conducted the poll, or what the questions were, or in what order they were asked. Everybody just accepts the results as legit. Even the media."

"Especially the media, and especially if the results fit the narrative," Martha added, showing a surprising–albeit cynical–understanding of how some news outlets operate. "Billy figured he could charge a fortune to give political parties and major corporations the quote-unquote third-party credibility they need to push a candidate, an agenda, or a brand."

"But why would he actually conduct the polls?" Grace asked.

"I wondered about that, too," Martha said. "Billy figured if anyone did challenge the results of the poll and asked to see the data, he'd have to have something to show. And let's say a really determined legal authority or journalist was to call some of the people on the list to determine whether they were really surveyed. Unless you called everyone on the list and got the exact same answer, there'd be no way to verify the accuracy of the results. Bingo bango, you can make up the results to say whatever you want."

"So if you didn't know about this up until today, how come you know so much now?" Grace asked, with just a tinge of trepidation.

Martha laughed.

"That's what the Ouellette phone call was about."

"Huh?" Grace muttered.

Martha chuckled this time. "Remember, I said Ouellette was digging up whatever he could on Billy. Well, guess who his primary source of information was?"

"Madonna!" Grace said.

"Who?"

"Jesus, not Madonna. What was the Power Puff's name again? Cher. Was Cher the mole?"

"No," Martha said. "This was a lot closer to home."

"Pete? Re-Pete?"

"Too close. It was Doomey. Little Jeffy Doomey was ratting Billy out."

"Really? But how?" Grace asked. "Billy didn't like Jeff being with his daughter. He sure as hell wasn't going to share any business plans with him, much less top-secret, bordering on illegal business plans."

"Billy did NOT share them with Doomey," Martha said, indignantly.

"So, how did Jeff find out about all this?" Grace asked, confused.

"That's the funny part. You know Jeff resented how Billy treated him and wouldn't accept his being with Betty, right?"

"Of course," Grace said.

"After the local papers published the photo you took, Jeff made a point of sending a copy to Ouellette, accompanied by a note that said Billy was bragging about how he upstaged Ouellette."

"Oooohhhh. Well, that explains how Ouellette found out about the picture. But I still don't understand why he cared."

"He did. It bugged him so much he brought Doomey into the city to meet with him so he–Ouellette–could learn more about Billy. And Jeff was only too happy to oblige."

"Okay, but Jeff still couldn't possibly know about the marketing company plans. How could he be the one who brought this to Ouellette's attention?" Grace asked.

"You're right, Jeff didn't know," Martha said. "But Ouellette told Jeff to 'dig around' Billy's office to see if he could come up with anything incriminating. Ouellette promised Jeff if he did, he'd be rewarded handsomely."

"And did he? I guess he did," Grace said, answering her own question. "But how did Jeff get access to top secret information?"

"That stumped me, too. According to Ouellette, Jeff snuck into Billy's office one night to see what he could find, and when he did, he found the files delineating Billy's plans to launch this thing."

"Wait a minute," Grace said. "Jeff SNUCK into Billy's office? How was that possible?"

"It's not really 'sneaking in' if your fiancé has a key to her father's office, is it?" Martha said, with a tinge of disgust and frustration.

"Betty had a key? I was under the impression only you and Billy had keys to his office," Grace asked.

"As did I," Martha said. "That's what Billy gets for doing things behind my back," Martha said, sounding more like an aggrieved wife than an administrative assistant.

"So one night, in the middle of the night, Jeff let himself in and looked around for whatever he could find that might incriminate Billy or at least get him in good favor with Ouellette," Martha explained further. "Once Jeff realized he had absconded with something so valuable, he went running to Ouellette."

"Wouldn't you or Billy notice the files were missing?" Grace asked.

"How could I know something was missing if I didn't know it existed in the first place?" Martha stated defensively. "And Billy couldn't ask me about them without copping to doing something without my knowledge, which he knew would upset me."

"Wow!" Grace exclaimed, mostly at the stunning development but also at the amount of sway Martha had over Billy.

"I do remember several weeks ago, Billy commented that something seemed out of order in his office. You know how persnickety he could be about his files," Martha said.

Grace wasn't sure if persnickety was the right word to describe Billy's attitude about his office, but she let it slide.

"So, how did you come to learn all this about Ouellette? Did he tell you directly?" Grace asked.

"Oh no," Martha said. "That's the fun part. He was on the phone with Melinda for close to an hour."

Grace whistled, long and low, just like Murray Jules had done when he learned of Billy's death.

"According to Melinda, Ouellette wants to come out to Mockingbird Heights to meet everyone and check out the operation," Martha said.

"She hasn't even buried Billy yet, and she's courting a new suitor?" Grace asked, even though she knew the answer.

"Thinking your husband–your at-times-mentally-abusive husband–might be fooling around is one thing. Knowing he had a foot out the door–with various other body parts planted elsewhere–will shorten a mourning period," Martha said. "This Ouellette thing could be the best thing that ever happened to us!"

Us? Grace thought, genuinely taken aback. She pondered what was said for a moment.

"Well, that's certainly an unexpected development," Grace understated.

"Ouellette told Melinda he's a man who strikes quickly when he sees something he wants, and he's wanted Melinda ever since the first night he saw her. Getting Carpe Diem and Bate International is just icing on the cake. Knowing Melinda, she probably started rubbing herself as soon as he said it."

"Oh, Martha. Be nice."

"I'm done being nice. You know Melinda is a power-hungry whore who ..."

"That's a bit harsh, isn't it?" Grace interjected. "She genuinely loved Billy and the life they had, up to a point. And he loved her, again, up to a certain point."

"Okay, I'll give you that," Martha said. "But ever since Shadler died, Billy's been out of control. I'm done sweeping up after his messes like some circus stagehand following the elephants around."

"Well," he won't be leaving any more messes for you, that's for sure," Grace said, trying to lighten the mood.

"Don't be so sure of that," Martha said. "You know Donna Devore's coming here tomorrow, right?"

Now it was Grace's turn to look around. "Yes, I am aware. Let's go into this room over here so we can get some privacy.

Grace and Martha stood up and reflexively, simultaneously, straightened their black dresses. They then looked around to see if there was a room where they could speak in confidence. They walked a few steps down the carpeted hallway and saw an open door leading to a darkened room.

"Let's go in there," Grace suggested.

"Let's make sure there's no one in there already," Martha said.

"The lights aren't on. I don't see how anyone could be in there," Grace said.

"I'm not worried about the people who need lights," Martha cracked.

Grace quickly caught Martha's gist and reached for the light switch, hoping she was right about the room being empty. It was.

They sat down again in adjoining, hard wooden chairs.

"All right, Martha. Spill the tea. What's going on at Carpe Diem?"

"Well, for one thing, Billy died yesterday."

"Seriously, Martha," Grace said, a little exasperated. "What's going on? Can I help you with anything?"

Martha looked directly into Grace's eyes.

"Billy wasn't the only one with a foot out the door," Martha said. "I was actively looking to move on, but it's so hard to do on Long Island because Billy had his tentacles into everything."

"Tell me something I don't know," Grace said, immediately regretting that she had interrupted Martha.

"Plus," Martha said, ignoring the interruption, "I think Pete and Re-Pete were looking to leave, as well."

"Pete and Re-Pete? Who had it better than them? Where were they going?" Grace asked.

"I get the sense they were looking to start a company to compete with Carpe Diem," Martha said.

"Compete with Carpe Diem?" Grace repeated. "How could they? Billy had them sign rock-solid non-compete agreements, if nothing else."

"There is no such thing as a rock-solid non-compete agreement in New York State," Martha said. "And, to be fair, it had to be exhausting for them to work at keeping the core business going strong as Billy spent so much of the company's cash elsewhere. Sooner or later, that's going to wear you out, especially when the creditors start bugging you."

"Creditors?" Grace gasped.

"Yep. Billy was spending the money faster than they could generate it, especially without Shadler around to close the door and rein him in. And then Billy started hanging around some questionable characters and doing something else I never saw him do."

"What's that, Martha?"

"Blow."

"Blow?"

"Blow. Lines of coke. He'd come into the office, dragging, close the door, and then ten minutes later the door opens and out comes Mr. Bojangles."

"Who'd give him the stuff?" Grace asked, shifting in her seat and wondering if she wanted to know the answer.

"I'm not sure," Martha said. "I can certainly see the unsavory crowd hanging out at the restaurant being a source. And Pete and Re-Pete did anything and everything he told them to."

Grace could picture Pete Snodgrass giving Billy the drugs, but being too smart to buy them. She could also see Pete Santini having enough street savvy to know how to do the dirty deed of purchasing, but also having too much regard for Billy to enable his consuming them. In that regard, they were the perfect team.

"H'mmm, I don't know about that," Grace mused. "Who else?"

"Doomey."

"Jeff? Seriously?"

"Yes, either to curry favor with Billy–if you want to give him the benefit of the doubt–or to expedite his demise, if you choose to look at things more realistically," Martha said.

"You're talking about committing felonies, even murder, Martha," Grace said.

"I know I've felt like killing Billy plenty of times," Martha said.

"Oh, me too," Grace said, "but not literally."

"I know, I know," Martha said. "Listen, let's get back into the main room before you know who misses us and wants to know what we're up to."

"What ARE we up to?" Grace asked, almost involuntarily.

"Oh, you're a part of the plan, Gracie girl. A big part. But that's for Melinda to tell you. Let's go rescue her from the three-ring circus."

Chapter 43

Too Nice to Assholes

Grace thought perhaps she and Martha should re-enter the room where Billy was being waked individually and was about to suggest one of them hold back when Martha shared that she was heading to the ladies' room to freshen up.

Perfect, Grace thought.

"You go ahead," she told Martha. "I'll see you inside."

There she found Melinda about ten feet away from the casket, exchanging pleasantries with Fasberg, one of the local Mockingbird Heights business owners. It was an open casket, with Billy "decked out" in white tie and tails, looking debonair but not quite dashing.

Melinda's distance from the casket struck Grace as curious. *Was she so distraught that being too close was upsetting?* Grace wondered. Or was she so mad that she didn't want to get too close? Perhaps she was subconsciously concerned that Billy could hear what she was saying under her breath or—worse—reading her mind. Regardless, Grace saw this as an opportunity to take the temperature of the room, at least as far as Melinda was concerned, so she sidled over in her direction. As

Fasberg walked away, Melinda turned, saw Grace, and rolled her eyes. Grace smiled demurely as she positioned herself to Melinda's right as she had done so many times before with Billy.

Doing so reminded Grace of the myriad black-tie affairs she attended with Billy and Melinda. Billy was a brilliant businessman but miserable at working a room. Grace showed Billy where and how to position himself so people would look for him. As someone approached, she'd say something along the lines of, "Hey, Billy, you remember (person's name). He's (insert the reason why Billy should know him)." Grace would listen with one ear as she scanned the room for other people Billy should meet while at the event. She also kept an eye out for people Billy was better off not meeting or being associated with, for whatever reason. In addition, Grace had to keep track of who Billy met and what they spoke about because she knew there'd be a follow-up meeting the next day so Billy could assess the value of having attended. The value was determined by how important, at least in Billy's estimation, the people he met were.

It wasn't an exact science, but it mattered to Billy, and if it mattered to Bill,y it mattered to Grace. She didn't always succeed at keeping away people that Billy was better off not knowing. After one such encounter, with Billy agreeing to provide "seed money" for a venture Grace and Melinda knew was doomed to failure, Melinda expressed her frustration to Grace in a private moment. "You know what Billy's problem is? He's too nice to assholes."

Grace found this comment amusing at the time but kept her amusement to herself, lest it appear she was questioning Billy's judgment.

Melinda must have picked up Grace's vibe. Without provocation, she turned to Grace and said, "I always admired how you screened people for Billy at those endless events we went to."

Grace assured Melinda she would look after her like she looked after Billy, and Melinda nodded. Grace wanted to believe her motivation could be characterized as "that's what Billy would have wanted." But Grace wasn't sure how Billy would have wanted her to handle this. For one, she knew Billy wanted a kick-ass sendoff. But Grace wasn't sure how Billy would have felt about Melinda taking charge the way she did. As much as Snodgrass had lost respect for Billy, for instance, he never would have stepped into his office so soon. And based on the newfound knowledge regarding Billy's plans to move out, there's a distinct possibility Billy might have wanted Grace and the Petes to crush Melinda the way a smoker crumples a pack of smokes once it's empty. When Billy was done with you, it was as if you ceased to exist. Poof! Gone! Stricken from the record books like dissidents in a George Orwell novel.

Regardless of what Billy would have wanted, Grace realized she had about sixty thousand reasons to "take care" of Melinda. Plus, Grace needed to know if Billy had ever spilled the beans about her child's father to Melinda. Grace knew—and, more importantly, Grace knew Melinda knew–public knowledge of her secret could prevent her from getting the vice president's job at Gibbons.

"Listen," Melinda told Grace, "tomorrow's going to be a long day, and then Saturday's the funeral. Oh," she said, almost as an afterthought. "I spoke to Micheline and Mike. They're coming out tomorrow night and will be at the funeral. Mike has agreed to sing "Ave Maria and something from the play."

Wow, Grace thought. *This should be interesting.*

There was no need to ask, "What play?" Mike Nobile played the lead in *Black Maria* and provided one of the few touching moments from Billy and Melinda's wedding reception. So, at least there would be some non-Long Island star power at the funeral.

Micheline Mirabito, on the other hand, was another one of Billy's forays into supporting the "arts" that quickly turned into folly. Just as he was convinced he could help make Mo Irby a star, Billy bought into Micheline's idea that America was ready for classic Broadway show tunes to be redone to a Salsa beat. The previous summer, he brought Micheline and the "Micheline dancers" out to Mockingbird Heights for a test drive—opening for a Fourth of July fireworks show. The only thing Billy loved more than being the center of attention was seeing a good fireworks show, so Billy and Grace worked with the local municipal officials and business owners to underwrite the cost and make the Fourth of July fireworks show happen for the local residents.

It did not go well.

Suburban white bread Mockingbird Heights was not ready to see six, scantily-clad Hispanics gyrating to Salsa music, even though it was to songs like "I Could Have Danced All Night," from *My Fair Lady*. At one point, the local newspaper editor, a nice woman who saw through Billy like Columbo saw through the guest-star murderer, turned to Grace and said, "You said Billy was going to provide family entertainment?"

"We did," Grace replied. "These songs are Broadway classics."

"The girls are half-naked!" the editor replied, laughing at the spectacle happening right before her eyes.

"Well," Grace said. "Billy's family is entertained. Does that count?" she said, tongue in cheek.

If she runs that line, I'm dead, Grace thought, later during the drive home. She didn't. There were a few letters to the editor in next week's issue, however, protesting the great Salsa assault.

So, Micheline and Mike Nobile were coming out.

"I look forward to seeing them," Grace told Melinda.

"Great," she said. "I've also asked Senator Wojo and County Executive Patrick Foley to give eulogies. I would like you to give one, too."

Grace was caught off guard.

"Wow! I don't know what to say, Melinda. Of course I'll do it. I'd be honored."

"Public speaking isn't my thing," Melinda said. "I'm sure you'll do a nice job. You knew the man as well as anybody, and you're one of the few people I trust. Certainly, nobody in THIS room qualifies."

Grace and Melinda fell silent. Melinda scanned the room again and sighed.

"I'm done talking," Melinda said. I'm going to slide out a side door. I suggest you do the same. Tomorrow's going to be a long fucking day."

Chapter 44

Nothing Sacred

Grace replayed her conversation with Melinda in her mind while driving home after the wake and again when she woke up Friday morning. She had never written–nor presented–a eulogy before, much less at the same occasion as a United States senator and a county executive. She was glad Murray Jules had given her the day off to attend the afternoon and evening wake. She needed time to create something worthy of the man while properly reflecting the attributes and foibles comprising the yin and yang of Billy's personality.

The day dawned unusually chilly for September. The sky was overcast, like a November steely gray. It was strange weather but perfect for writing a eulogy. Grace remembered how a legendary author once described the writing process: "Writing is easy. I open a vein and bleed." She also remembered reading that creativity is a matter of letting God speak through you. The trick is to put your ego on hold and embrace the idea that man is but a conduit for God's message.

Grace stared at her computer screen, trying to envision what Billy would have wanted her to say. Then she recalled what Grail said Wednesday night about "embracing your relationship with God and letting His Love inspire you." She thought about Billy being the center of attention at the wake and funeral and chuckled at the irony of how much Billy loved any situation where that was the case. Then she compiled a list of the people in Billy's life he might have loved, or at least should have loved. The words began to flow as Grace touched on every aspect of Billy's life and the people in it. Grace finished the eulogy and read it several times to make sure she had included everyone she needed to mention. She also wanted to make sure the eulogy reflected how grateful Grace was for having known Billy, and for everything he had done for her and taught her, either intentionally or by setting an example, good and bad.

Now it was time to try it on someone else. Grail was in the kitchen having coffee with the next-door neighbor, so she asked her and the neighbor to read it. Grail disliked Billy, and the neighbor only knew of Billy from what Grail had told her about him, so if the eulogy worked with these two, it was sure to win over the people who went to his funeral. Grace asked them to read it and then left the room so she would not distract them. After a few minutes, she heard the neighbor sniffle, and then she heard Grail crying. *Terrific*, she thought. *I nailed it.*

The phone rang. It was Lew Desmond, the PR flack. "How are you coming with your eulogy?" Desmond asked in a staccato style reminiscent of a 1940s detective movie starring Humphrey Bogart. How did Lew know Grace was writing a eulogy? There was no need to ask. Lew's stock-in-trade was having important information before anyone else. He was involved because Senator Wojo asked him to get involved, once the grieving widow had reached out to him regarding the eulogy. Billy had been generous to Wojciehowicz, and, like Jules and Gibbons College, the good senator did not wish to see his revenue stream dry up with Billy's passing.

"I'm done," Grace said. "And it's good." Even my sister got upset when she read it."

"Well, bully for you," Lew said. "For your sake, I hope it's good, because there'll be important people in the congregation. They'll be there for the senator, but I am sure they'll listen when you speak. I'll call you back in a few."

Typical Lew. Build you up with one comment and then bring you back to reality with the next. Grace hung up and came down from her writing high. She revisited the words on paper and tightened up the prose as best she could. Minutes later, the phone rang again.

"Change of plans," Lew said. "Wojo's out. He's not going to do it."

"Why not?" Grace asked.

Lew sighed, realizing his writing efforts had been wasted due to the whims of an egomaniac. "For the record, he had a last-minute scheduling conflict and needed to stay in Washington. Not for publication? He told the Merry Widow he would need a small stipend–ten grand–to appear at the funeral. Standard operating procedure for Wojo. I guess the senator figured she was as gullible as Billy."

"What did she tell Wojciehowicz?" Grace asked.

"Are you ready for this?" Lew asked.

Grace was.

"She told him, and I quote, 'Too bad your prick isn't as big as your balls, because if you're going to fuck me I want to feel it.' A direct quote."

"Wow." Grace whistled. If she didn't know up until then, she knew it now–there was a new sheriff in charge at Carpe Diem.

"Wow is right," Lew said. He added that the senator told

him it was the funniest thing he had ever heard. "Again, I'm quoting here," Lew said, "The senator said, 'When I hung up, I was more turned on by her than ever before. But screw it–I'm not saying a Hail Mary unless somebody pays up.'"

"So no words of wisdom and consolation from Senator Wojo?" Grace said.

"None," Lew said. "Good luck with your eulogy. I am sure it will go well. See you tomorrow."

Grace showered and then struggled with what to wear. She only owned the one black dress she wore yesterday, and she knew she would need it again for Saturday's funeral. She flipped through what passed for a wardrobe in what passed for a closet and settled on a gray cowl-neck sweater and dark blue skirt. She slipped both on and then foraged around for her low-heel black shoes from the back of her closet. She checked herself in the mirror hanging on the back of the closet door. She knew her outfit wouldn't get her on the cover of Vogue anytime soon, but it would have to do.

She ran through the eulogy in her head as she drove to the funeral home and decided it was as good as it was going to get. Upon arrival, she saw Melinda off to the side, listening to one of Billy's relatives ramble. Grace caught Melinda's eye and then came over, interrupting the one-sided conversation by telling Melinda the funeral director needed her. He didn't, but the idea was to get Melinda away from someone she did not need to be speaking to.

Melinda thanked Grace for getting there early. She let her know Donna Devore was going to be there–at the funeral home–during the three-hour break between the afternoon and evening viewings. The arrangement was made with the funeral director to let Donna have some private time, but Melinda asked Grace to hang around and make sure Donna was gone before the evening session started.

Billy met Donna Devore at Gibbons College a short while after Melinda had checked herself into the hospital. Donna was a single mom working her way through school to make a better life for her and her infant son. Billy wanted to help, so he started paying her tuition, and the next thing you know, they were an "item," as the gossip columns of days gone by used to say. Grace spent some time with Donna when she was studying and Grace was working at Gibbons. Billy called Grace at her office one day and asked her to go over to the student cafeteria to keep Donna company while she waited for him. Billy had a meeting with the Gibbons president, and he did not want her sitting by herself. His insecurities were such that he could not realize Donna was crazy in love with him and even if she wasn't in love, she was not about to screw up the deal she had with him by wandering off with another college student. She was a beauty, too. Long, straight chestnut hair and eyes the color of licorice jelly beans. She had small breasts, but Billy had plans for them. "A woman with the initials DD should have big breasts," he joked more than once with her. She hated the joke but loved pleasing Billy.

Grace crossed the campus to the cafeteria and had coffee with Donna. They made small talk. Grace considered making a joke about Billy paying for her MBA from Gibbons, and she didn't even have to date him, but reconsidered and let it drop.

"How do you like Gibbons?" Grace asked, not so much because she cared to know the answer but more as a means to fill the silent void.

"It serves the purpose," Donna said. "I don't spend too much time here. I go to class and then head back home to my baby." She sighed. "I used to be fun. I used to HAVE fun. One night, I had too much fu,n and nine months later, all the fun in my life disappeared, as did my father's child. Then I met Billy.

He makes me feel special. He takes away all my worries. He gives me hope for the future."

The following month, during the Commencement ceremony for Donna's class, she came up to the podium to get her diploma from the president, like everybody else. As she strode across the stage, Billy leapt up from where he was sitting with the other trustees and gave her a big kiss. It was so dramatic that the conga line of graduates came to a clumsy halt. Everybody in the audience was wondering what was going on while the other trustees tried to ignore it.

President Biscuit turned to Grace and mouthed the words, "What the fuck was that?" Grace shrugged her shoulders. She wasn't surprised–just grateful Melinda wasn't around. She also tried to figure out how long it would take for word to get back to Melinda about what had happened.

Grace was thinking about this when he noticed the county executive enter the funeral home, flanked by other government officials. Right on time, too. Since it was a Friday afternoon, Grace could not help but think the plan was to head out to the wake, spend the appropriate amount of time with the widow, and then hit the links. Grace walked across the room to greet County Executive Foley and thank him for coming. He asked Grace what the plan was for tomorrow. Grace told him he and she were giving eulogies.

"I was told Wojo was giving one," Foley said.

"Lew Desmond called me earlier," Grace responded. "Wojo's not going to make it. He has a conflict with another event down in DC."

Foley involuntarily snorted. "Too bad," he said, recovering quickly. "Did Desmond say what he was going to do with the eulogy he wrote for Wojo?"

Grace told him she did not know.

"I'll call him myself," Foley said, annoyed that Grace had

not already arranged to have an eulogy written that he could use. God forbid he should write one himself. "I'll get it," Foley said. "No sense in letting it go to waste."

The conversation ended, and Grace headed into the funeral home lobby to get some water. As she drank, Foley's lieutenant came over.

"What's your read on the widow?" he asked out of the side of his mouth, like he was asking Grace if she knew what horse was going to win the Fifth at Belmont. "Is she going to keep the money coming like Billy?"

"I don't know," Grace replied, though she did. The venom Melinda spewed earlier in referring to the politicians told Grace the checks were not going to flow anytime soon. She didn't say anything to the suit.

"Well, see what you can find out," he said, turning on his heel and walking away.

The suits made the right comments to the widow and then left. The relatives and Chamber guys hung around until they realized they were not going to be fed. No doubt if Billy were there in life rather than death, he would have arranged for a hot dog cart and an ice cream truck to be parked outside the Funeral Home. But he wasn't.

Eventually, everybody left. Grace was about to leave when Melinda came and reminded Grace of her promise to stay.

"Donna's coming," she said. "I would appreciate it if you could be here with me.

"Why are you afraid of Donna?"

Melinda and Grace turned to look in the direction of the inquiry. They saw Marietta–the first Mrs. Billy Bate–standing there in a conservative black dress with a high-neck collar and simple black shoes, the outfit you would expect a grieving widow to wear. Ten years Melinda's senior, Marietta was still sexy but in a much different way than Melinda. Her body enjoyed a fullness suggesting a nurturing nature that Melinda could not offer.

"Why are you worried about Donna?" Marietta repeated, approaching Melinda. She looked at Grace and smiled.

Grace looked at Melinda. Melinda rolled her eyes and said, softly, under her breath, "The hits just keep coming." Turning to Marietta, she smiled insincerely and said, "I am sure we can find some privacy inside these rooms. Let's go over here," gesturing to a viewing room currently only occupied by a dead person at the other end. Turning to Grace, she said, "Please keep an eye on the front door."

The two Mrs. Billy Bates headed off. They found two chairs so close together that their knees touched when they sat down. Marietta reached out for Melinda's hands. Melinda initially pulled back but then relented and let her hands rest between Marietta's. They ignored the corpse.

Marietta leaned forward and said, "This can't be easy for you. I know what it is to lose Billy, too. But you and I lost him over time, not overnight like Donna has."

"How dare you!" Melinda said, recoiling her hands. "I'm the widow here. Billy was my husband. We were happy. We had a storybook romance and a perfect marriage. I loved Billy."

"I am sure you did, Melinda," Marietta said in a comforting whisper. "I still do, too. And I will miss him. But I can assure you there is life after Billy, and it's a life free from the masquerade of pretending to be happy, pretending to love every minute of being by his side, pretending to maintain a veneer of perfection no two humans could ever possibly sustain, no matter how much they loved each other. As you know, it's no fun trying to look the other way when it comes to the girlfriends and the lies and the empty bed at night."

Melinda sighed. "When did you know it was over?" she asked.

"When he stopped bringing me to orgasm," Marietta replied.

"What!?!" Melinda asked.

"Oh, you know what I mean," Marietta said, looking around to make sure there was nobody within earshot. There was, but Billy seemed uninterested. "Billy loved getting me off. With his hand, with his tongue, with his dick–whatever it took. For the first years of our marriage, this was terrific, naturally. All my girlfriends envied me. Their husbands stopped trying once the honeymoon was over. Not Billy. He made sure I was satisfied sexually."

"So what happened?" Melinda asked, more out of salacious curiosity than caring.

"The more time I spent with Billy, the more I came to see what a control freak he was," Marietta said.

"Tell me about it," Melinda said, almost snorting.

"Well, I got to thinking," Marietta said. "I started to realize Billy's determination to keep me sexually content was simply another means of control, like a pimp getting his hooker addicted to cocaine so she would have to stay with him. Billy's lovemaking wasn't about making me happy–it was about keeping me under his thumb. Once I came to that conclusion– pardon the pun–it became harder and harder for him to get me off. It was like I couldn't come. I wouldn't give him the satisfaction of satisfying me. I developed a mental block, as if having an orgasm was a form of surrender to his will. So I stopped having them–with him, anyway. Fortunately, I never lost the, eh, personal touch. Eventually, he gave up trying, and soon after, he moved out."

"And you think that's what happened with me and Billy?" Melinda asked, her voice both indignant and curious.

"Isn't it?" Marietta shot back. "Everything was perfect between you two at first, right?"

"Oh, God, yeah," Melinda said.

"He couldn't get enough of you, and you couldn't get enough of his getting you off, right?" Marietta said.

Melinda involuntarily squeezed her knees together. "We did everything. Ev-ree-thing," she said, almost giggling. "He even let me experiment with other girls. He passed on fucking them, though, choosing instead to watch us go down on each other. He said seeing me get off was good enough for him. Then we would have the most powerful sex ever."

"No doubt it was something special, but for all the wrong reasons," Marietta said. "The pleasure was not in the orgasm for Billy. It was in the control it gave him over you. Trust me, I know. Women fuck who they want, for the most part. Men fuck who they can. Most guys I've been with need to get off because they need the relief. Then they can go without sex until they need relief again, and once they do, they don't care how or where it happens. Their orgasm has the same intensity whether they're with the woman they love or whatever happens to be available at the time."

Marietta continued. "Billy was no different, but with one exception. He understood that women experience orgasms with different intensities and satisfaction. He realized that the means for achieving higher pleasure and satisfaction levels are more mental than mechanical. Most women need a certain comfort level with their partner before they can let go. He also knew that when a woman has a great orgasm, she will do everything she can to hold on to the person responsible for it."

"I don't know," Melinda said, leaning forward. "I've gotten off more than once when I didn't even know the guy's name. I just needed somebody to fuck."

Marietta laughed. "I hear you. I've been there, too. Lots of women have. But for the most part, we prefer a situation where somebody we know and trust cares about our sexual needs and can help us reach those great climaxes."

"So everything Billy did for me was about controlling me, not about giving me pleasure," Melinda mused.

"That's my theory," Marietta said. "Your marriage was going great for you both until you got sick. He told you he needed you with him every night, and for the first time in your relationship, you stood up to him, told him you weren't interested in being the trophy on the end of his arm anymore. Right?"

"Sort of," Melinda said. "I ... I told him I couldn't do it," Melinda said. "I told him there had to be more to life than showing up at these endless dinners and having stupid people kiss your ass because you write checks."

"And then..." Marietta said.

"He stepped out on his own, and soon after, he stopped trying," Melinda said. "... and ... and ..."

"He stopped bringing you to orgasm, didn't he?" Marietta said. "He probably figured he couldn't control you anymore, or it wasn't worth the effort. Either way, it was the beginning of the end."

Melinda felt like she was going to cry for the first time since Billy died. Then she stiffened and stood up from the chair.

"This has been an interesting conversation," she said to Marietta as she placed her hand on Marietta's back so she should gently guide her back into the hall where Grace was standing–something she had seen Grace do dozens of times on Billy's behalf, anytime Grace could sense Billy signaling to her that the conversation had outlived its usefulness. "I appreciate your concern. I'll be all right."

"I am sure you will," Marietta said, glancing at Grace. "All the more reason we should be friends. You know, it's ironic. When I first met Billy, he could hardly say two sentences in a row. By the time he left me, he was a cross between Machiavelli and Svengali. Take it from me, Melinda. Living in Billy's cage–no matter how nicely appointed–is not worth the price you pay."

"I don't know about that, Marietta. I was pretty happy ..."

"You THOUGHT you were happy, but the easiest person in the world to bullshit is yourself. To be fair, initially, you figured you SHOULD be happy because you had everything you thought you needed to BE happy. You certainly made everybody else THINK you were happy. But you can't find happiness in material possessions or get it from somebody else, Melinda. It's a choice we make, to be happy regardless of outside circumstances."

"So I can be happy all the time, even now, just by deciding to be happy?" Melinda asked, with a tinge of derision.

"Too many people mistake pleasure for happiness. Being happy does not necessarily equate to an absence of problems or negativity," Marietta said. "Nobody goes through life without facing challenges. It's how we approach these challenges that matters. Access to the energy and happiness we want and need is controlled by whether we act with purpose as our highest selves. From that core flows the grace and love we need to discover and fully appreciate true happiness and meaning."

The three women stood there in silence. Grace surreptitiously eyed Melinda and then Marietta, and back to Melinda, while Melinda and Marietta just looked at each other, all wondering just where this conversation was headed.

"Thank you for your concern," Melinda said, finally, not wanting to let her guard down. "It might interest you to know that not only did Billy take hundreds of pictures of dozens of naked girls, but he did it in the apartment you shared when you first were married. He bought the building soon after you moved out. I know because he couldn't wait to take me there, literally and figuratively."

Marietta sighed. "Nothing was sacred to that man," she said. "My offer stands. If I can be of assistance, please do not hesitate to call me."

They hugged, and then Melinda watched as Marietta headed toward the front door.

"You're still getting cut from the payroll, you cunt," Melinda muttered under her breath.

Chapter 45

Doing the Donna Dance

Grace watched Marietta go out the funeral home's front door. She did not ask Melinda about the conversation, nor did Melinda offer to bring her up to speed.

"Any sign of Donna?" Melinda asked.

"Nope," Grace replied. Part of her was dreading Donna's visit, but part wouldn't miss it for the world. All of her, however, had to hang out with Melinda. They stood outside the funeral home while Melinda smoked a cigarette. What do you say to a widow while waiting for her dead husband's mistress to show up for a private viewing? Do you wonder aloud about what she is going to wear? Do you express amazement at the irony that not too long ago, Melinda was a single mom with a young child and no hope for the future, much like this young woman? Do you hypothesize as to who was more screwed–the single mom with the young child and no boyfriend or the recently widowed mom with the pre-teen, facing the prospect of saving a company on shaky ground thanks to Billy's death?

A car pulled up, and Donna Devore emerged from the

passenger side. Before closing the door, she leaned in and instructed the driver–her dad–to wait for her outside.

She looked good. Demure. Subtle. Sleek black dress playing down the good parts but making sure you knew they were there. Her chestnut hair hung shy of her shoulders. She approached Melinda and Grace. She looked at Grace and smiled weakly.

She looked over to Melinda and whispered, "Thank you for allowing me this time with your husband. He meant the world to me, and I am truly grateful." Melinda said nothing. She turned and opened the front door for Donna. Donna headed in. Melinda gestured to Grace with her head to follow Donna. She did. She showed Donna to the viewing room, but she was not sure what to do next, so she stood in the hallway. Melinda stayed outside the funeral home, lighting another cigarette.

Grace closed the viewing room door so Donna could have some privacy. She heard nothing from inside. No crying. No murmuring. Nothing. Just as Grace imagined Donna absconding with the body, she heard a screech like a raccoon being dragged by the tail across a field of pine cones. Then she heard, "YOU FUCKING BASTARD! HOW COULD YOU DO THIS TO ME! YOU'RE DEAD?!?! DEAD?!? WHAT THE FUCK GOOD ARE YOU TO ME NOW!!!!! WHAT THE HELL AM I SUPPOSED TO DO!!!! WHO'S GONNA TAKE CARE OF ME???? GET OUT! GET OUT OF THAT COFFIN NOW, BILLY! FOR THE LOVE OF GOD, GET OUT OF THAT COFFIN!!!!

This was followed by uncontrollable sobs from the viewing room. Melinda heard the commotion from outside, as did the funeral director, and both came into the hallway. Grace quietly indicated everything was fine. Melinda stood there with the director, listening to Donna crying and wailing. A little smile crossed her lips. A chill raced through Grace.

Donna continued crying, but it seemed to be subsiding. The director went back into his office. Grace studied her shoe tops while Melinda looked at the different prayer cards she had ordered for Billy. Four different kinds, because why offer one like everyone else when you can order four? Finally, Donna emerged from the viewing room. She seemed relatively calm and collected, although her eyes were puffy and the color had drained from her face. She ignored Grace and muttered her thanks again to Melinda, almost on the run. Within seconds, she was out the door and into her father's car. Melinda watched the car take off, and then she walked down the block, as if she wanted to make sure Donna had left town for good. She turned to Grace and informed her she was heading home for a shower and a quick change. She suggested she come home with her—they could find something to eat in the fridge. Grace highly doubted that. She figured entertaining guests was the last thing Melinda needed to be doing, so Grace told her she would be all right walking into town for a bite to eat.

"Suit yourself," Melinda said as they walked to her car. She was driving Billy's cherry red Cadillac Allante. She refused to drive the slinky Indy Pace Car he bought for her after the faked heart problem episode. She knew it was a guilt purchase, and she also knew if she ever got behind the wheel, then Billy would consider himself forgiven. She couldn't give him that comfort.

Melinda got in the car, started the engine, and looked up at Grace.

"Thanks for staying here with me," she said.

"It was nice of you to make it happen," Grace replied.

"Let's hope she sticks to her end of the bargain and disappears," Melinda said.

She spun off and out of the funeral home parking lot on her way to the house she once shared with Billy. James would probably be there, waiting for her, wondering where his dinner was. Grace found herself thinking about the shower and the quick change and what a delightful sight that must be, but quickly pushed it from her mind. You couldn't look at Melinda and not wonder what it would be like.

Grace headed to the restaurant Billy owned. Now it was in Melinda's hands, and based on what Grace had seen so far, it would not be in her hands too long. The restaurant was losing seven grand a week. It still being open could only be attributed to Billy's ego. He would not admit to such a failure, no matter what the cost to his bank account. Melinda had no such reluctance, however. There was no doubt in Grace's mind that soon after Billy was buried, the restaurant would be shuttered. She had no desire to discuss this with anyone while she was there, however. She sidled up to the bar and ordered a cheeseburger and an iced tea. In a few minutes, the manager–Lorenzo DeTorre–was standing next to her.

"How's Melinda doing?" he asked.

"She's fine," Grace replied.

"I heard the mistress came by and shared some interesting comments with Billy," he added.

Grace was bemused but not surprised that DeTorre already knew what had happened, even though, as far as Grace kne,w there were only three witnesses in the funeral home. *Restaurant people always had the juiciest gossip*, Grace mused. *Somehow, word had gotten out about Donna's tirade.*

"Has Melinda said anything about the restaurant?" Lorenzo asked.

"No, she hasn't," Grace told him, touched by his concern for the dearly departed. "I'm sure she'll let you know her plans as soon as she knows what they are."

Grace ate her burger and nursed her drink. She looked up and realized Pete and Re-Pete had joined her.

"What are your plans with this bitch," Pete Snodgrass said.

"What do you mean, what are my plans?" Grace asked, looking at Pete Santini to see if he could explain.

"She listens to you," Snodgrass replied. "Based on what transpired this morning, she's going to need somebody who can talk to her, because I don't see this thing working out."

Grace sighed. "What happened?"

Pete Santini stepped in.

"She called a staff meeting in the kitchen," Santini said. "Told us the party was over. Pete and I had to prepare a report on our departments, to 'justify our existence.' She said she also wants to see a business plan from us explaining how we expect to grow the business 10 percent a year for the next five years. AND SHE WANTS IT READY FOR MONDAY MORNING! Can you believe it?"

Grace wondered if they knew about Ouellette, but decided to keep her powder dry for the time being. "Weren't you guys complaining that Billy wasn't paying enough attention to the business. Isn't this what you wanted?"

"From HIM, not from her," Pete Snodgrass spat out. "I'd cut my dick off before taking orders from a LA-TINA, and if you're not careful, you're going to find those tiny tits of yours caught in a wringer."

"I'm sure you can work it out," Grace said, ignoring–for now–Snodgrass' vitriol. "I'm sure if you ..."

"I see you're drinking the Kool-Aid already, Grace. I hadn't pegged you for a lesbo, but I'm sure you'll be banging her, too."

Too?

Grace felt her ire rise, but caught herself in time.

"Listen, I'll talk to her if you want. I'm sure I can get her to understand how committed you guys are to the operation and ..."

"She better learn–fast–that we ARE the organization,"

Snodgrass blurted, "Her fake tits don't sway me. She better leave us the fuck alone."

Santini said nothing. Snodgrass turned to leave, gesturing to Santini to join him. They left. Grace turned to her iced tea, finished it, and got the bartender's attention. Once she did, she half-heartedly and insincerely asked for a check and was relieved when she was told not to worry about it. Grace dropped a ten-dollar bill on the bar as a tip and headed back over to the funeral home for one more round of waking.

Chapter 46

We All Grieve Differently

There was already a crowd at the funeral home when Grace arrived. She noticed right away that Melinda was not there.

Probably still home changing outfits, Grace joked to herself. The folks were buzzing about Donna's diatribe–and by the time the story circulated around town, the versions varied between her jumping into the casket with Billy to Donna and Melinda having it out on the funeral home floor. Melinda's absence seemed to validate the latter version. But everybody who was anybody in Mockingbird Heights was making an appearance tonight. The hallways were crowded, with the smokers huddled outside but close to the front door because of the unseasonable chill in the air.

Suddenly, there was a hush. Melinda had arrived. The crowd parted to let her into the main viewing room, like a movie star making a grand entrance. She wore another short, tight black cocktail dress, highlighting her breasts and legs. The high heels were four inches and had straps around her ankles. If it were possible to "dress to kill" in a funeral home, she pulled it off. While the "grieving widow" is the center of attention by default, she played the part as if she were auditioning for her own reality show. Maybe she was. After all, she was the reason they were there: To see what she was going to wear and to see how she was going to react to the gossip mongers wagging their tongues about the shrieking mistress. She exceeded all expectations, as small-town and small-time as they were.

Wordlessly, Melinda stationed herself by Billy and began to receive the mourners. Without being asked, Grace stood to her right, as she had so many times on nights out with Billy. Almost on cue, the mourners lined up to pay their last respects to Billy and condolences to Melinda.

Marietta was the first one and thanked Melinda for providing "such a lovely send off for such a great man." They hugged.

"We have a lot in common, you know," Marietta whispered to Melinda. "Call me if you ever want to talk."

Grace hated herself for wondering if Marietta's kind words were sincere or simply an attempt to keep in Melinda's good graces and on the Carpe Diem payroll. Billy's sisters were next. They, too, had their concerns about staying on the payroll but kept them unexpressed. Then other family members–the cousins and such. Fasberg and the Chamber people. The lawyers and accountants. Micheline Mirabito and Mike Nobile. The restaurant people who weren't working that night. The Carpe Diem staffers. Pete and Re-Pete begrudgingly paid their last respects. Billy being dead and Melinda being a force to be reckoned with was sinking in. Betty and her fiancé, Jeff Doomey.

As the mourners straggled out, Grace figured it was her turn. She knelt at the coffin and said a "Hail Mary" and then an "Our Father," the prayers ingrained into her as a Catholic school girl. She looked at the full, open casket, the white-tie and tails Billy got married in, and the Tortu mask in his hands. Her initial gut feeling was that Billy deserved a more dignified presentation, but at some point, Grace realized this was exactly how it should be. She considered what Billy had meant to her–both good and bad–and she felt that so much of the bullshit was unnecessary.

Billy was a man whose brilliance was matched only by his flaws. He built one successful business but little else. He had no real friends, just acquaintances looking for help ("too nice to assholes"). His family relationships were predicated on his ability to keep those family members on the payroll. The people he had done the most for–Grace, Pete, and Re-Pete–left him or mocked him behind his back. His only daughter loved him dearly, yet aspired to be a psychologist so she could someday figure him out. Grace remembered all the lunches and dinners where Billy refused to eat anything healthy. How they would stop at the local bakery for bear claws when coming back from meetings away from Carpe Diem. How he would smoke while wearing a nicotine patch on his arm. How he lived to work around the clock, and how he once insisted the Carpe Diem staff come in to work despite the fact that Long Island had been hit with close to two feet of snow.

Grace tried to be sad. She reminded herself that Billy lent her his brand-new minivan so she could take Slade to Sesame Place in comfort. About the great presents at the annual company raffle during the Christmas holidays and how Billy paid for her MBA and bailed her out of the various messes made by the PR firm she launched with Bruce Wright, including the nasty Internal Revenue Service situation and the sixty grand it cost to settle that deal. Then she thought about how Billy told her she wouldn't have to pay it back, but produced a promissory note shortly after Grace told him she was leaving. That's a lot to pack into six years. Grace tried to kid Billy once, saying, "It wasn't always fun, but it was always interesting." Billy did not find her compliment amusing. To even suggest Billy Bate's world had flaws was verboten.

At this point, Grace realized her attempt to be mournful was not going anywhere, so she got up from the kneeler. Melinda was the only other person still in the room. Grace asked her if she wanted to be alone with Billy. She shook her head no.

"I have a few matters to discuss with the funeral director. Would you mind bringing the car around?" she asked. Grace said, "Of course not," and left the building to find it. She saw Micheline outside the funeral home and asked her what her plans were.

"As far as I know, I'm heading to Melinda's house," she said. Not Billy and Melinda's. Melinda's.

"Do you have wheels?" Grace asked. "I'm getting the car for Melinda. We can head over there together."

They walked over to the Allante. Melinda had parked it out front when she got there. Micheline climbed into the back, and Grace slid into the driver's seat. She drove the short distance to the front of the funeral home so Melinda would not have to walk when she came out. After a few minutes, Melinda exited the funeral home and got in on the passenger side of the front seat. She looked in the back and noticed Micheline. Then she looked over at Grace.

"Thanks for driving, Grace. I'm not sure I can focus on the road right now."

"I can drive you both home and then figure out a way to get home from there," she said, hoping Melinda would offer to let her use the Allante. Billy certainly wasn't going to need it.

"Great," she said. "But before you run off, I hope you won't mind coming in with us to make sure everything is okay."

"No problem," Grace said, and the three sat in silence as the car headed home.

As Grace turned into the driveway, she remembered the first day she had come to the house, and of the maintenance man and his family standing on the front lawn. She pulled into the garage, and they got out. She waited there with Micheline as Melinda worked the code on the security system. Grace glanced over at Micheline and recalled the Fourth of July show she gave in Mockingbird Heights.

Damn she looked good, Grace thought. Raven locks of curly hair cascading over her shoulders, dark eyes smoldering like stones in a sauna, skin the color of brown sugar, and a smile bright enough to light up Broadway. Her breasts were not as full and firm as Melinda's, but they were real and segued nicely into a taut dancer's body. Melinda opening the door brought an abrupt end to Grace's reminiscing, and they walked into the kitchen from the garage.

"I need a drink!" Melinda said, heading to the cabinet where she kept the liquor.

"I need a nice hot shower," Micheline said. "I'll catch you all later." She headed to the staircase and ascended the steps. Grace marveled at how gracefully she carried herself.

"Impressive, isn't it?" Melinda asked.

Grace blushed at being caught leering.

"Here," she said, handing her a glass. "Dewars and water, right? Isn't that what you drink?"

It was. She took the glass and thanked Melinda.

"Let's go inside to the living room," Melinda said. "I've been standing all night."

They entered the living room, which looked like a page from an interior design magazine. A big, black leather couch was flanked by black leather chairs, a glass coffee table, and several glass end tables. One small lamp was already lit and glowed more like a lit candle than an electric light.

Melinda parked herself on the couch's corner cushion and gestured to Grace, "Why don't you have a seat and relax?" she asked.

Grace walked over to one of the black leather chairs, put her drink on the end table, and sat down. She looked over at Melinda, who had taken her shoes off and curled her feet under her as she sipped from her big glass of red wine.

"So, how are you holding up?" Grace asked, trying to fill the air with something. While she could barely make out Melinda in her black dress on the black couch in the dark room, she could smell the Scotch to her right and hear the shower in the distance. Grace tried to gauge what was happening without becoming overwhelmed or clouding her thought process with alcohol. She so wanted to take a sip from that drink, to feel the soothing warmth down her throat and throughout her body. She entertained her friends' wild stories from their college days and wondered if this could be her "sorority" moment. Then she remembered that this woman had lost her husband–her former employer and benefactor–only a few days ago, and she also remembered the promissory note for $60,000 with the meter ticking at 12 percent annual interest. She did not want to make a wrong move.

"I'll be fine," Melinda said, taking another long drink and letting the words hang out there.

They sat there for a few more minutes, the silence broken only by the shower water cascading in the other room. Melinda played with her wine glass, swirling the wine around and holding the glass' stem in such a way that Grace had to shift in her seat. Then Melinda leaned forward and put the wine glass on the coffee table. She got up from the couch, smoothed her dress, and walked quietly to Grace. Their eyes met. Grace watched as Melinda came even closer, leaning forward.

"I want you to stay with us tonight," Melinda whispered, breathily. Then she climbed on the chair and straddled Grace, putting her hands on Grace's shoulders. Her beautiful face was inches away from Grace's, and the combined scents of the wine, the Scotch, and Melinda's perfume made Grace a little dizzy. Melinda unzipped Grace's dress a little and nuzzled the back of her neck.

"Micheline is wild in bed," she purred. "Billy couldn't keep up with us. I'll bet you can." With that, Melinda kissed Grace on her neck and then pressed her magnificent body against Grace.

"Wow, Melinda," Grace said. "I don't know."

"Oh, you know," she whispered in her ear. "You know you do because you've dreamed about this moment. I see how you look at me. I saw how you were looking at Micheline before. This is it, Gracie. Two hot, Hispanic women at once. We want you to watch as we fuck each other real good and then we want to bring you pleasure like you've never had it before. That's how it works. Or you can go home to your boring old life and wait another ten years for Mr. Right to maybe get you off every once in a while before he starts snoring."

"Might I remind you," Melinda said in a tone that teetered between seduction and recruitment. "I now own a successful company and need somebody to run it for me. You can be set for life, and everything will be taken care of. Do you like driving nice cars? Going on trips? We can create something special here, Gracie. But right now there's a fire burning inside me, and I want you to feed that flame."

Grace's head was spinning. Here was her moment to "finger the flame," and it was all she could do to resist the urge to slide her hands between Melinda's thighs. She knew if she looked down, she would see those magnificent breasts and all hope of doing the right thing would be lost. But what was the right thing? Was it honoring one's standards–like not sleeping with your former boss' widow the night before his funeral–even if it meant blowing a chance to experience a wild sexual fantasy, especially when you couldn't remember the last time fulfilling your sexual pleasure was not self-induced? Grace also had to consider that she still had no way of knowing if Melinda knew the truth about Drex. If Melinda did and wanted to exact revenge on Grace for rejecting her advances, she could ruin Grace's career at Gibbons.

"I don't know," she said again.

"You know what you want. And your pussy knows what it wants," she purred, stroking Grace's thigh and sliding her hands across Grace's panties. "Good Lord, you're ready to go. Billy would've been all over that! Or has he already? I'm not blind or an idiot. I found that note in his pants pocket, the one that read, 'Grace comes when you finger the flame.' Well, I'm ready to finger that flame, Grace. I want what Billy got."

Grace had no idea what Melinda was referring to, but hearing his name brought her back to reality. She pictured him sleeping in the bed where Melinda wanted to have her romp right now.

Then she realized how wrong it would be to bang his wife in it before Billy was even buried.

"I have to go," she blurted. She mustered all her strength to stand up and hold Melinda so as not to knock her to the floor. They both got to their feet and gathered themselves.

"Melinda ..." Grace started.

"Don't say anything," Melinda said.

"No ... no–I have to," Grace said. You're a beautiful woman. I want to be supportive, and Lord knows my love life could use some attention, but this isn't me. My heart and soul must be involved in everything I do, and it has to feel right. This just doesn't feel right. My heart's hurting. Pounding, but hurting. I can't imagine what you're going through."

At that point, Micheline bounded down the stairs, wrapped in a towel. She looked at Melinda. "It's bedtime, Melinda." Noticing Grace was still there, she asked, "Are you coming?"

"Oh no, I'm just breathing heavy," Grace quipped, but the joke was lost on them.

"Grace is taking her flame and going home to be by herself," Melinda said dryly. "C'mon, Micheline. Let's go."

She took Micheline by the hand, and they headed upstairs. Grace stood there, deflated, pondering what had just happened. *Did she blow it? Did she pass on the greatest opportunity of her life, not only sexually but financially? Was there any merit in 'doing the right thing'? And what the hell was the flame thing all about?*

She walked over to the kitchen counter and saw the keys to the Allante. She decided to help herself to Billy's car and headed home. She could smell Billy's cologne as she drove, which made her realize there was a good chance the same aroma would still be evident in Billy's bed and no doubt would have haunted her while she pleasured his widow and her girlfriend. Then she pondered what was happening in the house right now without her, and whether she would regret not jumping in.

Slade was staying with Grail for the duration of the wake and funeral, so when Grace got home, it was to an empty, quiet apartment. As she washed up, she noticed the drain to the bathroom sink was clogged, so she donned sweatpants and a t-shirt and took care of the problem, tired as she was. Grace loosened the pipe and removed the clog. She tried not to think about what she could have been doing. She tried even harder not to think about a future where she wouldn't have to unclog drains or pay a grieving widow money she didn't have. Once she unclogged the drain, she took a quick shower and got ready for bed. She quietly slid under the covers, exhaled, and replayed in her head what had transpired just prior and had her "a-ha" moment.

Grace comes when you finger the flame.

She instantly associated the phrase with that bizarre conversation she had with Billy in his office. She remembered him writing something on a piece of paper and putting it in his pocket.

Oh, Melinda, you weren't even close! Grace thought and then laughed, for the first time in days. It felt so good that she fell right off to sleep.

Part V

Shine, You Diamond, Shine!

Chapter 47

Losing a Tooth

Grace woke up Saturday morning and immediately mentally replayed the previous night's events. Doing so made her head hurt. She pondered how she would deal with Melinda at Billy's funeral, which was only a couple of hours away. She questioned how she was going to handle seeing her and whether there was an appropriate way for one to deal with a widow at her husband's funeral on the morning after you turned down her request for a girl-on-girl-on-girl threesome.

And, oh, what a threesome that would have been, she mused. *Two hot Latinas with, apparently, some experience in this arena. And me. Grace Duffy. Single mom. Exhausted professional. Grieving colleague. Lonely woman. Oh, so freaking lonely. I can't even REMEMBER the last time I....*

With that, her mind turned to Bernie. *My God, those eyes,* she thought. Instinctively, she felt her hands pull up on the oversized t-shirt she wore to bed and tug at the string holding up her sweatpants. She entertained what it would be like to gaze up at Bernie's coral-sea-blue eyes as...

Her bedroom door blew open!

"Mommy! Mommy! Mommy!" It was Slade, bursting with excitement and holding something minuscule in his left hand.

"It's my tooth! My first tooth!" he exclaimed, holding it up for her to marvel.

"So it is," Grace said, turning it over in her fingers as if it were the Hope Diamond. "We'll have to be sure to leave it under your pillow tonight."

"I hope I get a hundred dollars!" Slade exclaimed. "Aunt Grail helped loosen it last night, and this morning I just worked on it some more, and it popped off! Isn't that great! I should get at least a hundred dollars, shouldn't I?" he asked.

"We'll see what the Tooth Fairy has in mind, Slade," Grace replied, but with a tinge of resignation and exhaustion.

Where did he get the idea that a tooth was worth a hundred dollars? Grace wondered, with her immediate thought being that Bernie must have had something to do with it.

Oh, Bernie, she thought again. But this time thinking of Bernie made her think of last night, which reminded her she had a funeral to attend, which made her think she had a shower to take. She didn't even want to look at her watch to see how far behind schedule she already was.

She winced again when she realized her attire options for the funeral were either the dress she had on yesterday, which was in a pile in the corner and most likely still reeked of the cornucopia of aromas from last night's fiasco, or the same outfit she had on Thursday.

We can add 'the grieving process' to the list of things that are more challenging for single moms, Grace concluded, *especially those with a limited wardrobe.*

Almost as if on cue, Grail appeared, holding aloft an appropriate black dress on a hanger and wrapped in dry cleaner plastic.

"I took the liberty of assuming you don't have something to

wear this morning," Grail said, with just a tinge of the smugness that comes with anticipating correctly.

Grace sighed. "You're a saint, a savior, Grail! Thank you so much." She took the dress, hung it on the back of the bathroom door, and headed to the kitchen sink and counter to make coffee.

"I figured you'd be pressed for options, apparel-wise, so I got my black dress dry cleaned...How'd it go yesterday?"

Grace busied herself making the coffee. She knew if she started sharing anything about what happened yesterday–and especially last night–with Grail, she'd be at it for hours.

"Oh, nothing out of the ordinary," Grace said, trying to avoid eye contact with her sister.

"Bullshit!" Grail blurted. "You haven't experienced anything ordinary since you met that man," Grail said. "C'mon, sister. Pour the tea."

"I'm making coffee," Grace said, trying to defuse the situation.

"You're so funny!" Grail said, "C'mon, what happened?"

"Seriously, Grail," Grace said, walking past her on the way to the bathroom. I have to shower and get ready. I'll fill you in after all this is over. Trust me, it will be worth the wait. Oh, and thank you for helping Slade with his tooth. I can't believe I missed out on that milestone. And I can't thank you enough for being there for me and for Slade these past couple of days."

"Yeah, well, you better clear your whole day tomorrow. You have a lot of catching up to do with him. And me!"

"Oh, Grail, you have no idea. Hang tight. One more day of this nonsense!"

"And then what?"

The question caught Grace off guard. She stopped her shower preparations for a moment and looked in the mirror over the sink.

"Honestly, Grail, I have no idea what today has in store for me, much less tomorrow."

"None of us do, Grace," Grail said. "The best we can do is live in the moment, day to day."

"Now you're full of shit," Grace said. "Your life is perfect. Everything planned to the T, every outcome what you'd hoped it would be."

"That's not true and it's not fair, Grace," Grail said. "We all have our little battles to fight."

Grace turned the shower on, one because she was pressed for time and two because she did not want to have this discussion now.

"You're right, Grail, and I am truly grateful for all your support and understanding," Grace said. "I promise we'll have a heart-to-heart once I get past all this."

"We're good, Grace. Do what you have to do today. But keep in mind the words of Isaiah: 'Let the Holy Spirit guide you, step by step, protecting you from the unnecessary trials and equipping you to get through whatever must be endured.'"

Grace laughed. "I'll be sure to do that, Grail. You're a real pip, you know that?"

Grail smiled. "Mock me all you want, but my life is perfect, remember?"

The two hugged. Grail turned to leave. Grace took off the sweatpants and the T-shirt and stepped into the shower. She momentarily entertained the notion of picking up where she left off before the Tooth Fairy business started when she was startled by a familiar sound, but one she hadn't heard in a while.

"Look, I'm peeing like a big boy!"

It was Slade, and sure enough, he was peeing like a big boy into the toilet just a few feet away from the shower. Could she credit Bernie for teaching him that, too? Or was this a Grail project? Either way, the mood was killed and the time was short. Grace finished her shower, fixed her hair and what little makeup she wore, and finished her coffee. She was ready for whatever.

Chapter 48

What's She Doing Here? What's He Doing Here?

The weather was chillier than you might expect for September. At least it was not raining, which complicated matters. There was no need for Grace to go to the funeral home. She had her moment, such as it was, with Billy the night before, so she drove straight to the church. She wanted to see if any media were there and, if so, to make sure they spoke to the right people for the best quotes. There was already a crowd at the church when Grace arrived. The scene reminded her of the buzz before the wedding because the Mass was not set to start for about an hour. There were some actual mourners there, to be sure. But you got the sense the people were there because they wanted to see what might happen.

Grace saw Lew Desmond and, not surprisingly, he was talking to a reporter and a photographer covering the funeral. They were discussing photo angles and going over where the most dramatic shots would come from. Lew pointed out where Melinda's limo was going to pull up—how he knew was anyone's guess. He wasn't even Catholic. He rolled through the itinerary and explained to the reporter who Michael Nobile was and why he was there to sing at the Mass. Grace walked up to them as they were talking, and Lew introduced her to the reporter. Grace explained who she was and her relation to the family. She left out the part about how she was invited to console the grieving widow the night before.

As they spoke, the church started to fill up with family members, friends, business associates, and the merely curious, with Gibbons College President Chuck Biscuit noticeably absent. The county executive was not there, but he was famous for holding up events because of his tardiness, so why should Billy's funeral be any exception? The senator was nowhere to be seen as no checks were being written on this day, at least not by Melinda.

Grace noticed Donna Devore in the congregation. She entered the church with her mother, father, and brother and parked herself along the main aisle, albeit toward the back. If the others in the congregation did not know who she was, they would know soon enough as the whispers began as soon as she got there. Word of her presence and her role in this scenario buzzed through the crowd faster than an Olympic sprinter running barefoot across blacktop on a hot summer day.

Grace pulled Lew aside and made sure he was aware of the situation—out of earshot of the reporter. He placed a hand on each of Grace's shoulders and turned her so they were face-to-face. He looked her in the eye and said, "Under no circumstances is there to be a confrontation. You must get her out, and you must do it quietly."

Grace looked at Donna and her family and noticed how sad they were. Genuinely sad. Nonetheless, Donna had to go, and soon, because Melinda was due to arrive. She remembered something she once saw in a movie and walked to where Donna was sitting. Leaning over, Grace looked right at her and whispered, "Mrs. Bate has asked you not to be here. She gave you some private time with Billy yesterday. The deal was you were not to make an appearance at the funeral."

"I loved that man," she wailed. "I want to be here. I need to be here. I'm not going anywhere." She started crying.

"We all loved Billy," Grace said, stretching the truth somewhat. "But the family has made it clear your presence is not appreciated, and I have been told to ask you to leave."

"I'm not going anywhere," she said.

"Donna, I'm sorry to have to do this to you," Grace said, leaning even closer. "But there is a uniformed Nassau County police officer waiting in the back. He is prepared to escort you out. The funeral will not start until you are gone."

Grace felt like shit. For one thing, it wasn't true. For another, Grace knew Donna did love Billy. As Grace stared at Donna and waited to see what she was going to do next, her mother leaned forward.

"This is the tackiest thing I have ever seen," she said. "My daughter loved Billy, and she deserves to be here."

Grace was caught off guard. What was tacky? Her asking Donna to leave or Donna's showing up for her married lover's funeral with her family in tow? Grace recovered enough to say, "Like I said, we all loved Billy. I'm simply letting you know what the family wants."

The mother started to say something else when Donna raised her hand.

"That's enough, Ma. Let's go," she said.

She gathered her belongings, and they left without incident. Grace walked away in the opposite direction, wondering what might happen if they noticed there was no uniformed police officer in the vicinity. She did not care–they were out of sight, which is all she wanted.

Grace stepped out to the front of the church. Lew was still talking to the reporter on the steps when the hearse pulled up.

The funeral home crew got out and walked to the back of the vehicle. They stood there, waiting for the limousine containing the grieving widow, which pulled up shortly. The crowd initially surged forward a little bit in anticipation, but then backed off in respect for who was going to get out.

Grace stood on the steps behind Lew and the reporter when the limo driver came to Melinda's door and opened it for her. From their vantage point, they saw one great leg and then another step out onto the sidewalk. This was not going to be a widow dressed in black with a veil covering her face. Quite the contrary. She was wearing a short white skirt, a white jacket with black leather laces in the back, and a cream satin blouse with a plunging neckline that left little to the imagination.

"What's with the outfit?" the reporter asked.

Grace jumped into the conversation. She explained some Catholics wear white to a funeral to celebrate a loved one moving on to eternal salvation and being with God, which is the Ultimate Reward and what Catholics aspire to.

They both turned to look at Grace like she was speaking Chinese. "He's talking about the cleavage, you idiot," Lew said.

The cleavage rarely registered with Grace anymore because she had spent so much time over the past few years with Billy and Melinda and seen her decked out in so many different · eye-popping outfits, the previous night notwithstanding. Melinda stood silently on the sidewalk as the funeral home staffers worked to get the casket situated on the sidewalk in preparation for bringing it into the church. When they were ready, she got behind the casket, and behind her were James, Betty, and Jeff Doomey. Behind them were Billy's sisters. Marietta was already inside the church. Melinda scanned the crowd, looking for Grace, saw her, and mouthed, "Donna?" Grace mouthed back, "Taken care of." Melinda smiled. The casket was carried up the steps, and they all entered the building.

Everybody did what they were supposed to do during the Funeral Mass, and Father Macchiato kept his sermon short. If he had noticed the pornography behind Billy's desk during their most recent visit, he did not mention it. Then it was time for Communion, and it took a while for those in line to receive the sacrament. Grace sat off to the altar's side, watching the procession. Then she looked over at the altar and noticed the flame emanating from the Paschal candle. She watched it flicker and dance and was reminded of that night in Billy's office.

Billy was right, Grace thought. *The flame is perfect. It offers warmth and light and even Peace of Mind. And yet, all I have to do is knock over the candle, and it could burn down the church.* Then Grace thought about Billy's comments regarding those who "linger near the flame," running the risk of getting burned. Billy assumed he was "fingering the flame" quickly enough, yet the truth was the flame fingered him for a one-way ticket to eternity. Grace indeed.

Communion was over, and everyone settled back into their seats. Michael Nobile walked up to the microphone on the altar and, after a moment, started to sing a cappella.

> *Ave Maria*
> *Gratia plena*
> *Maria, gratia plena*
> *Maria, gratia plena*
> *Ave, ave dominus*
> *Dominus tecum*
> *Benedicta tu in mulieribus*
> *Et benedictus*
> *Et benedictus fructus ventris*

Ventris tuae, Jesus.
Ave Maria

Grace wasn't sure what the words meant or if they could be applied to Billy's life. She did know Mike Nobile sang so beautifully that his voice set the hairs on the back of her neck straight up. It happened at the wedding reception and was happening again at the funeral.

He also set the proper mood for the eulogies. The county executive spoke first. Grace was not sure if he was successful in securing the eulogy Lew wrote for the senator. The county executive read it with the same fervor and feeling one might use to read a proclamation at a supermarket grand opening. Now it was Grace's turn. She walked up to the altar, bowed slightly in front of the crucifix hanging behind the altar, and nodded to Father Macchiato. She stepped to the pulpit and looked at the congregation. She tried to keep her hands from shaking. There was Melinda in the front row, stunning in her grief. Pre-teen James was behaving, but not happy about having to wear a suit on a Saturday. Betty was still recovering from the box of photos. If Jeff Doomey felt anything, he wasn't sharing it with the outside world. Grace couldn't bear to look at Pete or Re-Pete. She cleared her throat and adjusted the microphone.

"Billy Bate was a lot of things ... father, husband, businessman, philanthropist, captain of industry, community leader. He was one of those rare people you remember meeting for the first time, and the one thing everyone in this congregation has in common is that they will never forget the impact he had on our respective lives. The irony here is that Billy would have loved seeing so many people gathering around him, wishing him well in such beautiful fashion. In fact, love was a word that came up a lot around Billy.

"He would have loved knowing so many members of the

Mockingbird Heights Chamber of Commerce and so many of his other business colleagues came here today to pay their respects.

"He loved going to work each day and building upon the success of the day before, knowing so many people were willing to work with him to make his dreams a reality.

"He loved having the opportunity to help so many men and women make careers for themselves working at Carpe Diem Construction Camps while raising their children in a healthy, nurturing environment.

"He loved the idea that two talented young men—Pete Snodgrass and Pete Santini—spent their entire professional careers working with him.

"He loved his sisters, 'the roses to his thorn,' as his mother used to call them.

"He loved watching young James transform from being a little boy to a young man right before his eyes.

"He loved watching his little girl transform into a brilliant and beautiful professional woman, on her way to becoming a doctor. Nothing made him happier than when she stopped by his office for a visit, no matter what the reason. As much as Billy enjoyed sharing his toys—and Billy had some expensive toys—when Betty came by, she brought with her a bag of jelly slices because she knew how much her father enjoyed them. And Billy refused to share them with anyone. They were his because she was his and nobody else's.

"He loved his Melinda, and he loved knowing someone so beautiful loved him. He loved that he looked so dashing and handsome when he stood beside her. He loved how happy she made him feel.

"Some say Billy loved too much, and too many. Sadly, ironically, as much as he would have loved all this, I'm not sure he ever fully realized how much we loved him. We can all find solace at this moment in knowing he knows now.

"At times like these, I am reminded of the words Monsignor J.J. Quinn of The Peace Patrol: 'Life is not measured by years, but by celebrations of the heart.' And such celebrations should be shared by family and friends who made them possible. We must learn to write our hurts in the sand, carve our blessings in stone, and look to each day to celebrate Life.

"Or, as Billy would say, 'Carpe Diem–seize the day.'

"Peace, my friend. God bless you."

Grace stepped down from the lectern and walked off the altar. Her heart was pounding. *I got through it*, she realized.

The priest remained silent and seated for a few moments. Just as he was about to rise, however, Mike Nobile called out from the side of the altar.

"One moment, Father, if you will."

Father Macchiato looked over at Grace, who was just as bewildered. She shrugged, and they both looked at Mike Nobile.

Mike waved at someone standing off to the side of the altar, and then two men pushed a riser on wheels to the front of the altar. It had a bench and a small, upright electronic keyboard and a microphone. As Mike Nobile got situated on the bench so he could play the piano and sing into the microphone, the workmen sauntered off the altar. They soon returned, this time pulling a slightly larger riser on wheels. On it was a choir of six women of color, all dressed in matching blue robes with gold fringe trim.

Mike was ready to play. He turned to his right so he was facing the audience and smiled, relishing the commingling of anticipation and confusion. *It looks like Billy had one more splashy event in him, but how?*

"I've been asked to close the service by singing a song that meant a great deal to Billy, and since you're here today to celebrate Billy, there's a good chance it's going to mean a great deal to you."

Grace saw Melinda looking at her, and then Betty, and then back to Grace. Grace shrugged. Everyone was bewildered and curious.

With that, Mike played the iconic opening notes to "Shine," the show-stopping tune from *Black Maria*. The whoop of recognition from the congregation was spontaneous and natural, everyone seemingly forgetting–for the moment, at least–that they were in a house of God, not a Broadway theater. Nobile delivered the opening verses with his signature style—ominous bordering on mourning—building to a dramatic pause. Then the chorus burst in with revival-style intensity, as Mike Nobile pounded the keyboard like a man possessed, channeling the spirit of Jerry Lee Lewis.

> *He will turn on*
> *All the light*
> *That they've been*
> *Hiding away*
> *(Turn on the light!)*
> *Come on and shine, you diamond,*
> *Shine!*

And just like that, the song was over. A moment of stunned silence was followed by thunderous applause. Mike Nobile bowed, blew kisses to the chorus, and returned to his seat.

For his part, Fr. Macchiato handled everything in stride, as if this sort of thing happened at every Funeral Mass he celebrated. He rose, and the congregation rose. He finished the Mass and said the final blessing.

As he did this, Grace snuck out a side exit and walked

quickly toward the front. She wanted to make sure Donna had not reappeared. She hadn't. Grace stood outside the church doors and tried to catch her breath. Then she heard Michael Nobile singing "Amazing Grace" as the congregation filed out behind the casket. *Such a beautiful song*, she thought, feeling herself choke up a little. The sky was gray and leaden, but no threat of rain. The doors opened, and the crowd filtered out. Lew came by to shake Grace's hand.

"An outstanding piece of work," he said. "You even managed to keep it relatively honest, alluding to his excesses. Beautiful."

Talk about praise from Allah. As Grace basked in the glory, Mitch Shoop–the Carpe Diem controller–strolled over. "That ought to be worth sixty grand, don't you think?" he asked, with a wink. Grace laughed nervously and pretended the debt hadn't even factored into the process.

As Grace chatted with Shoop, a silent hush fell over those who were on the steps outside the front of the church. The casket was wheeled to the top of the steps by the main church doors. Behind the casket stood the beautiful Melinda, clutching a silver crucifix in her folded hands above her belly button and below her magnificent cleavage. She stood there for a moment, like a debutante making her grand entrance, while a couple of photographers clicked away. As the cameras flashed and clicked, a rumble could be heard from above. Way above. Unbeknownst to everyone there, Lew Desmond had arranged for military planes to do the missing man formation over the church–no mean feat given the precision timing involved and the vagaries of knowing when a church service was supposed to end. Melinda looked up, watched the planes roar by, and then looked out at the crowd. She smiled a little. This was no grieving widow. This was a woman who was this close to losing her husband to another woman and being out on the street. But fate intervened, and now the husband was gone and she was in control. She'd be calling the shots from here on in. She was The Man.

Grace looked over Melinda's shoulder and noticed, for the first time, a familiar-looking man surrounded by people clearly unaware of who stood among them: Jackson Ouellette. There was nothing physically imposing about him, unlike his social and corporate standing. His bald head and wire-rimmed glasses gave him the appearance of a run-of-the-mill accountant, the kind who volunteers to serve as treasurer for the local chamber of commerce. Grace gulped. Was he here to praise Billy, or bury him?

Chapter 49

Um ... That's Billy's Spot

Grace sidled over to Melinda while keeping tabs on Jackson's whereabouts out of the corner of her eye.

"I'll see you over at the cemetery, Melinda," Grace said softly.

"Hold on," Melinda replied, gently tugging on Grace's dress to bring her closer. "I want you to ride to the cemetery in the limo with us."

Oh, crap, Grace thought. *Who's us? Is she going to hit on me again? Is she going to make me pay for not giving in to her seduction? Was she going to mention the promissory note? Would Grace have to stick around with the family at the cemetery so she could have a ride back to her car?*

The angst on Grace's face made Melinda chuckle.

"Oh, don't worry. We're not kidnapping you. I just want to run some things by you."

Run something BY ME? Grace thought. *Boss Lady wants to run something by me?*

"Sure, no problem," was all Grace could come up with as a response.

With that, the funeral director came over.

"Mrs. Bate, we're ready when you are to depart for the ceremony," he said, touching her gently on the elbow.

Melinda looked at her elbow and then at the funeral director. He immediately pulled back.

"I'll be right with you," she snapped.

The funeral director stepped back and made his way over to the limousine, motioning to the driver to be ready to open the car door for Melinda. Grace took her cue from Melinda and stood there, motionless, waiting to see what would happen next. Melinda looked around, as if to see if there was anybody she needed to speak to or invite to the cemetery. Seeing nobody, she took a step in the direction of the limo and, without looking at Grace, said, "Let's go."

The driver was standing on the curb by the car. When he saw Melinda striding in his direction, he walked around the front of the car and opened the passenger door on the street side. This struck Grace as odd. Why not get in the car from the sidewalk side?

Grace knew she had to get in first because she would be taking her customary seat facing backward, with her back to the driver. Given how easily Melinda slid behind Billy's desk the other day, Grace had no doubt Melinda would be taking Billy's customary spot in the limo—right passenger side.

Grace assumed wrongly. It wasn't until she got herself situated and placed her dress over her knees that she realized there was somebody else already in the car: Jackson Ouellette! Not only was he in the car, but he was also in Billy's spot!

Chapter 50

Under the Bus in a Limo

Grace was stunned. She looked at Jackson, and he looked at her, smiling but without saying anything. Grace wondered if she should wait to be introduced or introduce herself. She pondered whether she should pretend not to know who he was or, more importantly, not to know why he was there. Melinda was no help. She fumbled through the purse she had left on the seat in the limo and found what she was looking for–a pack of cigarettes. She pulled one out, lit it, took a long drag, and then tilted her head back to let the smoke out. If her smoking bothered Jackson, he didn't say anything. Grace knew better than to even bring it up.

Melinda took another long drag and let out another jet stream of smoke. This seemed to relax her.

"The Petes are driving me crazy," she said. "Making all kinds of demands, trying to take advantage. Like I'm going to crumble, or the business will come to a grinding halt if I don't acquiesce. Stupid pricks."

Acquiesce? Grace thought. *That's a fifty-cent word coming from a trophy wife.*

"Um ... Melinda," Grace said, nodding in Jackson's direction. "Aren't you going to introduce us?"

"Why would I introduce you?" Melinda asked. "You know who he is. You took that photo, remember?"

Grace blushed at being ratted out.

"But Mr. Ouellette doesn't know who I am," Grace gently noted.

"I suppose not," Melinda sighed. "Jackson, this is Grace Duffy, the woman I was telling you about. She was the one who took that photograph you hate so much. In fact, it was her idea to set it up."

What a way to throw me under the bus, Melinda, Grace thought.

Turning to Jackson, she awkwardly leaned forward in the moving vehicle to shake his hand. He stuck out his hand but did not move forward to make it easier for Grace to reach him. Grace thought maybe he was retaliating–"pulling a Billy," so to speak–and deliberately causing her to have to make that awkward stretch forward. They shook hands, and Grace plopped back down in her seat and smoothed her dress. It was at this point that she realized the funeral procession was getting a police escort to the cemetery, again courtesy of Lew Desmond. Grace made a mental note to learn how he could take care of so many complicated details so seamlessly.

"What kind of demands are Pete and Re-Pete making?" Grace asked.

"The bastards want raises and more vacation time," Melinda said. "Like they don't have it easy enough. They're going to work harder for me than they have for Billy in a long time."

"If we don't fire them outright," Jackson said.

We? Fire Pete and Re-Pete? Did I miss a memo? Grace wondered to herself.

Grace's confusion must have registered on her face, because now it was Jackson's turn to chuckle.

"A lot's gone down over the past couple of days, Grace," Jackson said. "I have a list of things to bring you up to speed on."

Gone down? You mean like Melinda on Micheline? Or was it Micheline on Melinda? It pained Grace not to share this *bon mot* with anyone else. She would have to be satisfied with just making herself laugh. Then she looked at Melinda and got the sense that Melinda was suppressing a giggle.

Wait a minute, Grace thought, her mind spinning. *I'm thinking Micheline. Has Melinda already seduced Jackson, too? Who knew the grieving process could be so sexually stimulating? Or maybe something's been going on since before Billy bit the Big One? God, this woman's exhausting. I need a Dewar's and water. Where's Bernie when I need him?*

"Do tell," she said to Jackson. She looked over at Melinda, who was now fixated on enjoying her cigarette.

"I believe in getting right to the point, Grace," Jackson said. "I don't have time nor interest in bullshit."

"Right there with you, Jackson," Grace said, instantly regretting the assumed informality and realizing that this would be a good time for her to shut up and focus on what he was saying.

"My life changed the day you took that photo," Jackson said. "The moment I laid my eyes on this woman sitting to my left, I knew I had to have her. Not meet her. Not be her friend. Have her. Make her mine."

With that, he reached out with his left hand and took Melinda's right hand.

"Quite frankly, I was caught off guard by my reaction, and that doesn't happen too often. Everything happened so quickly. All I could do was gaze at her while the guy she was with introduced himself and blathered something about Jackson and Benjamin. Not a word of what he said registered with me, which was unfortunate because knowing who he was would have helped me track her down. Overwhelmed, I got out of there in a blink because I was stumped as to what to do next, and THAT doesn't happen too often, either."

Grace looked at Jackson and blinked a few times. She was at a loss regarding what to say. *Was he mad at her for taking the photo and not sticking around? Was he grateful to her for making this happen? Did they violate some kind of rich people's protocol?*

"I really had no intention of causing a problem for you, Mr. Ouellette," Grace mustered, finally.

"Oh my God, no, Grace. You didn't create a problem," Jackson said. "I'm forever grateful. If nothing else, I see every so-called 'problem' as a challenge–a game, if you will–and I like to win. I almost always win. And by all means, call me Jackson."

"Well, that makes me feel better," Grace said. "So what DID you do?"

"Nothing, at least not initially," Jackson said. "I had no way of tracking down who you were, where you went, or even why you were in the hotel that night. So I simply asked The Universe to find Melinda for me."

"The who?" Grace asked, thinking perhaps she had misheard what he said.

"The Universe, Grace. God. The Higher Power within. Whatever you want to call that Magical Force that manifests for you whatever you want, as long as you ask for it and believe yourself worthy of having it."

"Just ask The Universe and you get what you want?" Grace asked, perhaps with more cynicism than she intended.

"I know, I know, it sounds crazy," Jackson said. "But I'm

living proof that it works. I ask and I receive because I ask and I believe I am worthy of receiving. That's the hard part for most people. They don't even think to ask, and even fewer believe themselves worthy. And it's not their fault, necessarily. We're constantly bombarded with negative messages. The media knows there's real money to be made in pushing stress and strife, and the government knows a frightened nation is a compliant nation. That's how they stay in power. It's no accident some of the people running Congress have been there for decades. They know all this and between them and the media, it's one quote-unquote crisis after another, either stoking racial division or causing financial peril."

Geez, Grace thought. *He gets his Kool-Aid at the same place Grail and Bernie buy theirs.*

"So anyway, I put it 'out there' to The Universe to find this woman, and then I let it go. Lo and behold, a few days later, out of the so-called blue, an envelope is dropped on my desk containing a copy of the newspaper that ran the photo you took, with Melinda standing there right next to Billy. Holy crap! Even I was surprised by this development, which most people would call a happy coincidence. I don't believe in coincidences, Grace. I took it as a sign this was meant to be."

This? Grace thought. *This what?*

Grace tried to piece together the timeline. She had taken the photo about 18 months ago, right before she left Billy to work at Gibbons College. That was also right around the time the Billy and Melinda thing started to unravel. All this time, she attributed the demise of the relationship to Melinda getting sick and not wanting to be out every night with Billy. At what point did Jackson connect with Melinda? Assuming that was the case, did her being sick and then feeling abandoned make her more receptive to advances from another man? Or did the interest of another man–especially one with much deeper pockets and more power than Billy–inspire certain machinations she knew would hasten the end of their marriage? Was she really sick? And did Jackson have any reservations about pursuing another man's wife? If he saw every challenge as a game, perhaps Melinda was nothing more than a prize to be won, a trophy if you will.

Oh, ironies of ironies, Grace mused. *All this time, I was concerned about Billy's philandering, and here Melinda was, dancing on the dark side of town. Possibly, anyway.*

The Johnnie Taylor song from the late 1960s came to mind. What were the lyrics again? Oh yeah.

> *Who's making love, to your Old Lady,*
> *while you're out there, making love?*

"People I know and respect also believe in the Law of Attraction ..." Grace started to say.

"What I'm talking about goes way beyond the so-called 'Law of Attraction' pedaled by those charlatans behind *The Secret*," Jackson interjected, almost angrily. "This isn't some Southern California woo-woo with bongos, incense, and affirmations. This is a solid knowing. An inner conviction that we are part and parcel of the cosmos, the Pearl of Great Price, as it says in the Bible, and as taught by Neville Goddard. It's knowing each and every one of us is connected to a Higher Power that can provide us with all the resources we need, just as long as we ask specifically for it and believe ourselves worthy of receiving."

There's that 'believe yourself worthy' line again, Grace thought. *I'll have to try it sometime.*

"So anyway," Jackson continued. When I got the envelope with the newspaper and photograph ..."

Grace considered whether she should pretend to know or

not know that Jeff Doomey had sent it. Instead, she reminded herself to keep quiet and let it all play out.

"... and the letter from someone named Jeff Doomey, telling me how this guy Billy was bragging about how he pulled one over on me. It was then that I decided to do a little investigating, and the first order of business was to meet with this Doomey fella."

Jackson turned to Melinda. "Does Grace know Doomey?"

"Grace knows Jeff, but she doesn't want to Doomey," Melinda quipped. The joke was lost on Jackson. Grace didn't find it all that amusing, for different reasons, but had to give props to Melinda for the quick quip and her timing. Usually, good-looking people aren't funny because they have no need to be.

Grace jumped in. "I know Jeff. I know he loves Betty, and he was frustrated by Billy's inability or unwillingness to accept him. I don't see why he would send you a letter."

"Doesn't really matter why, now does it, Grace?" Jackson said. "All that matters is, Doomey's actions were the opening I needed to connect with Melinda. Jeff and I met. He walked me through Billy's history and shared enough about Melinda to convince me to trust my instincts. This was a woman I needed in my life."

Grace wondered what Jeff might have said or done to accomplish this, and did he do so knowingly? Here's another crazy idea: Was he in on this with Melinda? Did she put him up to sending the letter with the newspaper? Grace's mind was reeling.

"The next thing I know, I'm in my private dining room, sharing a candlelit dinner with this gorgeous creature over here ..."

Melinda pretended to be looking out the window, watching the highway motorcycle police racing ahead to block off each exit to the parkway as part of the police escort to the cemetery.

"... and she's telling me she can help expand Billy's business empire if only he would listen to her."

Listen to her, Grace thought. *That's a first. Nothing she ever said to me suggested she had any interest in Billy's business affairs, other than spending the money they made.*

"Now don't get me wrong, Grace," Jackson said. "I think Carpe Diem Construction is a cute little enterprise."

Cute? Grace wondered.

"But I have much bigger plans for Melinda, and you, if you're interested," Jackson said.

"Me? Why me? You hardly know me," Grace said, almost reflexively.

"I know you had the moxie to set up that photograph," Jackson said. "And Melinda tells me you're good at seeing without saying."

"I'm not sure what that means," Grace said.

"What was that old Yogi Berra line? Oh yeah...'You can observe a lot by watching.' One of the keys to running a successful operation, Grace, is to remain quiet and calm while observing what's going on. To comprehend what's being said and, sometimes more importantly, what's not being said. Melinda says you were always watching what was going on and being said/not said, and then sharing with Billy important insights that helped him make the most of any situation. That sort of thing is important to me and would be invaluable to Melinda as we get Carpe Diem back on its feet so it can support the launch of Bate International.

"Bate International?"

"Bate International," Jackson said. "A marketing firm with a twist."

"What kind of twist?" Grace asked hesitantly.

Jackson leaned forward.

"We conduct polls for people, businesses, and politicians. We go to them with the results. If they like the results, then full steam ahead. If they don't like the results, we adjust the numbers until they reflect the desired outcome. Then we create a multi-faceted marketing campaign around the results as if they were exactly what the client wanted."

"Adjust the numbers?" Grace asked, not sure where this was going but fairly certain she didn't like it.

"Adjust the numbers. Have them reflect a public sentiment consistent with what the client wants. You want Americans to prefer chunky peanut butter over creamy? Bingo–Americans love chunky peanut butter. Then you issue the press releases, do the interviews, etc., all based on the survey results that show Americans prefer chunky over creamy."

"But what if they don't?" Grace asked.

"Oh, but they will!" Jackson said. "Once the media reports that Americans prefer chunky over creamy and a few well-compensated celebrities start waxing poetic about the Powers of the Chunk, sales of chunky will increase because who wants to be seen buying the less popular peanut butter? Elected officials will get behind it because the only way to stay in power is to pretend to go along with what the electorate wants, and the next thing you know, October 6th is National Chunky Peanut Butter Day and Mr. Peanut is the Grand Marshal at the Rose Bowl Parade."

"What if somebody questions the survey results?" Grace asked.

"That's the beauty of it, Grace! What if they do? How are they going to check? Are they going to call each person surveyed and ask, "Do you prefer chunky peanut butter? Even if they didn't, by now they've heard that Americans prefer chunky over creamy, so who's going to admit to liking the less popular of the two?"

"That's sinister," Grace said.

"Sinister, or genius? Think about it, Grace. The only thing more bullshit than surveys is the media's reliance on the results without doing any due diligence. 'According to the latest poll,' the media loves to report, and the results are always taken at face value. No one ever asks who was polled, where they live, or what kind of questions were asked?"

"Genius or not, I'm not sure I'd want to be a part of this," Grace said.

"Oh, c'mon, Grace. NOW you want to be a Girl Scout? Didn't you help create the image of Billy Bate as a captain of industry, at least on Long Island?"

"But he was!" Grace interjected, unintentionally sounding as if she were trying to convince herself more than the others.

Melinda spoke up.

"The world runs on fear and bullshit, Grace. You know it. I know it. Jackson has made a fortune knowing it. It's my turn—our turn—to get on the carousel that just keeps going 'round and 'round. Scare 'em. Convince 'em. Ca-fucking-ching. It's one big scam, Grace. You're either in on it or you're the sucker falling for it."

The song, "The Night The Carousel Burnt Down" from *Black Maria*, the one playing the night she sat with Billy in his office "fingering the flame," came to mind.

> Weren't you there when the carousel burnt
>   down?
> The fire and confusion, the smoke and the
>   sound
> I swear you were there when the carousel
>   burnt down

We were all around
The rings charred and tarnished all over the
    ground
And our heads hung down
And we all left town
The next day.

Grace wished she could leave the limousine.

"This is a lot to process," Grace said, looking out the window and realizing the procession was getting ready to enter the cemetery. "Perhaps we can discuss this later."

"There is no later," Jackson said. "I believe the expression is 'Seize the day.' Carpe diem!" Jackson laughed, but laughed alone.

"Have you shared any of this with anyone else, like Pete or Re-Pete?" Grace asked.

"No. We'll set them straight as to who's running Carpe Diem on Monday," Melinda said. "They will either accept their New World Order or disappear. And they will have absolutely nothing to do with Bate International."

Monday? So much for the grieving period, Grace mused, picturing Pete and Re-Pete wearing black armbands on their jacket sleeves, like they used to do in the old days after suffering a death in the family. She inexplicably giggled. If Melinda heard, she did not give any indication.

"Grace," Melinda said, leaning forward so she could make direct eye contact. "I want you to come work for me and Jackson. I know how loyal you were to Billy, and I need someone I can trust."

The words "loyal" and "trust" hung in the air like a piñata filled with bees, and Grace wanted nothing to do with it. *Did Melinda think I was in on Billy's philandering and held back info? Or maybe she did, but now sees that as a good thing in case she wants to keep whatever this is with Jackson under wraps. And what about the loan? Would that be forgiven? Would I earn enough to be able to get the house I always wanted for Slade? And would I have enough time for him? And I still need to know if Melinda knows the truth about Drex. If she did, would she hold it over my head? And if she didn't know, would I spend the rest of my career worrying that she MIGHT find out and THEN hold it over my head?*

Almost on cue, Melinda said, "We'll double whatever you're making at Gibbons. You'll be able to send Slade to your pick of schools, and after a year, we'll write off that loan, too." *So, Melinda knows about the money. What about Drex?*

Melinda drew Grace in ever closer.

"And sooner or later, Gibbons is going to find out the truth about Drex, and any chance of you getting that dream job as vice president will disappear faster than Pete Snodgrass at five o'clock." The final nail in the coffin had just been struck.

Chapter 51

Doomey's Been Busy

The limousine followed the policemen on motorcycles through the main entrance into St. Charles Cemetery in Farmingdale. The sky was still remarkably gray and chilly for September, but one did not get the sense that rain was imminent. Jackson watched Melinda as she lit another cigarette, knowing that this would be her last opportunity to smoke for at least an hour. Grace strenuously worked to avoid making eye contact with either Melinda or Jackson, lest she betray how her mind went off in a thousand different directions, like a New Year's Eve crowd at Times Square after somebody set off firecrackers.

Okay. Stay calm, she told herself. *Let's assess. She knows about the loan, she knows about Drex, and I've already rejected her romantic overture, yet she still wants to hire me and pay big money. Why? Does she truly value me for me, or am I just the prize in her game?*

The questions ran laps in Grace's head while silence engulfed the limousine. Melinda smoked. Jackson looked out the window.

"When did this cemetery first open for business?" Jackson asked.

"In the early 1950s," Grace replied. "My mother's mother was one of the first people buried here. She passed away in 1952." Grace knew nobody in the limo cared about her grandmother, but she welcomed the opportunity to discuss anything besides Drex and the money she owed Billy and now, apparently, Melinda.

She was about to explain how the cemetery was owned and operated when the limo door on Melinda's side was opened from the outside. It was the funeral director. He told Melinda everything was set for Billy's graveside rites.

Melinda pivoted in her seat so she could place her feet on the pavement outside the car, snuffing out cigarette butt with her black, Christian Louboutin stiletto heels as she did. Jackson got out on his side of the car, and once he was outside, Grace made her way over to his side of the car so she could avoid direct contact with Melinda.

The three of them walked over to the gravesite. The coffin was positioned atop the bier, and off to the side was the mound of dirt that would ensure Billy's days of Broadway shows and dinners at Clegg & Cleary's were truly over. Grace looked around and determined that just about everybody who attended the Funeral Mass also saw fit to go to the cemetery. "Were they genuinely sad to lose Billy, or were they hoping for one last crazy thing to happen that they could talk about now that Billy was gone? Grace didn't know and at this point didn't care. She had more important questions to answer.

Grace took attendance as she got closer. Jeff Doomey was there, with Betty holding his left arm for support. Just to his right, but about a foot away, was Marietta. Next to her were Pete Snodgrass and Pete Santini, both silently hoping Melinda would fall into the grave or perhaps to make sure this was not some elaborate practical joke on Billy's part. It wasn't. Billy was dead, and once they all left, he was going into the ground, even if Melinda did not get the fireworks show she believed Billy would have wanted.

Or would she? After the limo ride and the funeral-ending show tunes arranged by Lew Desmond, Grace wasn't sure what to expect next, or who was calling the shots.

Melinda positioned herself next to the gravesite, and James stood alongside her, remarkably still for a pre-teen. Jackson had somehow once again blended into the crowd without creating a stir, no mean feat considering his social standing.

Grace stood a respectful distance from the ceremonies. Close enough to appear concerned, far enough away to dispel any notion that she considered herself family or employed staff. She sensed a presence and turned to her left. Lew Desmond had sidled up to her.

Grace whispered, "That was some show you put on toward the end. How did you do that?"

"Billy arranged it all," Lew said.

"What?!?!?" Grace shot back, perhaps louder than she wanted, as a few of the bystanders turned to look in her direction.

"What?" Grace whispered softly this time.

"Billy arranged it all," Lew Desmond said. "He called me to his office months ago." He said Jackson Ouellette 'had it out for him' and he–Billy–said he knew Jackson always gets what he wants."

"By murdering people?" Grace whispered back.

"C'mon, Grace, grow up," Lew said. "This is real life in 1997, not a 1940s mobster movie." Jackson doesn't 'murder' people. He has been known to, shall we say, expedite the demise of his enemies."

"Ouellette's a self-made, globe-trotting billionaire with

penthouse apartments all over the world. Why would he consider a small-time businessman, no matter how successful, an enemy?"

"Because Billy had something Ouellette wanted," Lew said.

"Melinda," Grace replied.

"Exactly."

"Jesus," Grace muttered.

The priest was leading the group by the gravesite in prayers as he dipped the aspergillum into the aspersorium so he could sprinkle holy water on Billy's casket.

"How did Billy get wind of this?" Grace asked.

"Doomey told him."

That Doomey fella's been pretty busy, Grace thought.

"Doomey?" Grace interjected, again perhaps a little louder than she wanted, but nobody looked over at her this time.

"Yep," Lew said before adding hastily, "Could you quieten your reactions a little?"

Grace nodded.

Grace took Lew by the arm and walked him a little farther away from the gravesite ceremony. They both turned their bodies to ensure their voices wouldn't carry and their lips couldn't be read, just in case anyone in the crowd was so inclined to do so. Melinda was still relishing the part she played of the grieving widow, clutching rosaries in her hands as if saying novenas was her form of meditation.

"So Doomey tipped off Billy that Ouellette was after him," Grace said. "Did he mention that he was the one who brought Billy to Jackson's attention?"

"We'll assume for the moment that Jeff left that part out," Lew said. "This guy is a lot shrewder than he lets on. I just hope–for his sake–he doesn't out-shrew himself. Ouellette plays for keeps, as you can see."

"So Doomey goes to Ouellette and rats out Billy. Then he goes to Billy and says, 'You have a problem with this Ouellette guy.' Then what?" Grace asked.

Lew looked around and sighed.

"As far as I can tell, Doomey played them both against each other. Billy must have been spooked, though. He spelled out exactly how he wanted his funeral–his send-off, he called it– to be."

That Billy could be so thorough about such an awkward issue did not surprise Grace. *But what about the will,* she wondered.

"If Billy was so concerned about Ouellette and Melinda," Grace asked, "Why didn't he change the will so Melinda wouldn't have control of Carpe Diem?"

"Ah, yes, the infamous, off-the-shelf, do-it-yourself will," Lew said.

"Well, for one thing, Billy did not know that Ouellette and Melinda were an item."

"An item?" Grace interjected. "Like a Page Six canoodling item?"

"Not exactly. Ouellette had his sights on Melinda, of course, but knew enough to keep his powder dry, so to speak. But Billy didn't know that. He assumed Ouellette was after Carpe Diem."

"What the hell would Ouellette have to do with Carpe Diem?" Grace asked. "That's such small potatoes compared to the empire he runs."

"Small potatoes to you, maybe, and yes, to Mr. Ouellette. But to Billy, as you know better than anyone, Carpe Diem was HIS world and therefore worth something. It never occurred to Billy that someone would value his wife more than his business."

"So Billy's ego let him believe that a self-made billionaire was willing to go to great lengths to steal his company. His ego also let him believe that his wife, the woman he rescued from a one-bedroom apartment in Rum Junction, would never let another man into her life."

"Bingo!" Lew said.

With that, the gravesite ceremony was coming to an end. Grace and Lew Desmond headed to where Melinda was accepting final condolences.

"I'm surprised you couldn't arrange for a fireworks show at the cemetery," Grace chided Lew as they walked.

"Oh, I could have if I wanted to, Grace. You'd be amazed at how flexible religious institutions can be if enough zeroes are involved," Lew explained. "But there's a small airport across the street from the cemetery, and I told the grieving widow that federal law prohibits shooting fireworks within a mile of an airport."

"Is that true?" Grace asked, surprised.

"I have no idea. But after the fiasco with the senator, I knew Mrs. Bate wasn't going to cut the check necessary to get the bishop to look the other way. At the same time, I didn't get to where I am today by telling potential clients I can't get something done. So I made up an excuse that sounded not only feasible but logical."

"There you are!" Melinda called out in the direction of both Grace and Lew, but without specifying who she was referring to. "Are you coming back to the restaurant? James is going back with Micheline, so there's plenty of room in the limo."

Grace looked around to see if Jackson Ouellette was still there, but he was nowhere to be seen. No doubt he was back in the limo already, and based on what Billy had insinuated to Grace in the past about his limo rides with Melinda, she knew not to be a third wheel.

"I was going to hitch a ride with Lew Desmond," Grace

said, catching Lew off guard somewhat, as this was the first he had heard of her plans.

"Yes," he rebounded. "Grace and I have a lot of catching up to do."

"Suit yourself," she said, with an inexplicable wink. "I'll see you back at the restaurant. I hope you're both hungry."

Chapter 52

The Point of No Return

Once you've benefited from a police escort, driving on a parkway under normal conditions, especially on Long Island, is like flying coach after experiencing first class. Grace and Lew Desmond inched along in the bumper-to-bumper traffic, neither one relishing the time they would have to spend at Billy's "after party." Lew was a cautious driver, his eyes fixed on the road ahead and his hands affixed firmly in the "10 and 2" position on the steering wheel. There was no need to listen to the radio for traffic reports, since there were no alternative routes for where they needed to go. They both knew they would 'get there when they got there.'

"So where do you go from here, Grace?" Lew asked.

Grace let out a long sigh, perhaps the first time since her beeper went off that she truly and completely exhaled. She assumed Lew knew about the loan and even her "Drex" secret because, well, because he knew everything else. Even if he didn't, he would know soon enough. Everyone would know, especially if she crossed swords with Melinda.

"I have no idea," Grace said, finally. "I like just about everything about my position with Gibbons, but I also want to make sure I can take care of Slade and build a future. Melinda and Jackson said I should be part of their team, but other than the financial rewards–which would be substantial, I suppose–I don't really see myself going that route, especially if it means working for someone who 'expedites the demise' of those he wants out of the way."

Lew chuckled.

"What's so funny?" Grace asked.

"The phrase covers a lot of ground, Grace," Lew said.

"Which phrase?" Grace asked.

"Expedited his demise," Lew replied.

"What do you mean?" Grace asked, pursing her lips, intrigued by the possibility she might learn something from a man known for his mastery of manipulating people and opinions. She turned in her seat so she could face him as he drove.

"Well, it doesn't necessarily involve actions that are illegal, Grace. I mean, you work at a college. Haven't you seen college professors or deans just inexplicably not get rehired? Department chairs claiming they're stepping down because they want to 'return to the classroom,' or my personal favorite, 'to spend more time with their family.' Trust me, Grace, nobody wants to do either. But it's better than admitting you lost at the game of musical chairs."

"H'mmph," Grace said, feeling a little naïve. "So you don't think Ouellette did anything nefarious regarding Billy?"

Lew laughed again. "Jesus, Grace, I know you're from Long Island, but I didn't think you were from the Turnip Truck part."

Grace bristled at the suggestion that she was so naïve, but she had no defense.

"So what do you think happened?" she asked.

"Oh, I KNOW what happened. It was brilliant," Lew said.

"Do tell," Grace said, "there's nobody here but us chickens. That's an expression I learned on the Turnip Truck."

Lew looked at Grace, ignoring her comment.

"Are you sure you want to know?" he asked.

"Shouldn't I know? Don't I need to know what kind of people I'd be working for? "

"Well, if you're going to work for them, then yes. If you're not, then you're better off not knowing," Lew said.

"I'm sorry, Lew, but we're beyond the point of no return. If nothing else, my career going forward will always be entwined with Billy's legacy and whatever Melinda has up her sleeve, especially if she's teaming up with a billionaire such as Jackson Ouellette. And you just KNOW the Gibbons people are going to want me to reel both of them into the community."

Lew laughed. "I hate to break it to you, Grace, but Jackson Ouellette is not going to be a part of Gibbons College. He's way too big for that. You could channel your inner Frank Mundus all you want, but it ain't going to happen."

"Well, that's not what Biscuit is going to want to hear, so I have to at least pretend to go after him. Unless, of course, you know something I don't."

"There are lots of things I know that you don't know, Grace," Lew said, teasingly.

"You know what I mean, Lewis. Tell me how Ouellette got Billy out of the picture. I need to know what I'm dealing with here."

"Okay, but as always, this conversation never happened."

"Understood."

"After speaking several times with Jeff Doomey," Lew started, "Ouellette understood that Billy was burning the candle at both ends. So ... he suggested to Doomey that 'perhaps Billy could use a boost,' and handed Jeff several baggies filled with pills. He told Jeff that the baggies contained his 'special mix' of vitamins that he–Ouellette–consumed regularly. He told Jeff to tell Billy, without explaining where they came from, to take them daily. He also told Jeff that the pills–vitamins, if you will–only worked on men over 40."

"So Jeff wouldn't take them instead of doing what he was told."

"Exactly. Jeff never asked what was in the pills, and quite frankly and officially, I don't know, either. Ouellette, no doubt, assumed Jeff would give them to Billy and Billy would take them as directed based on Jeff's say-so, especially since Billy, according to Jeff, was starting to feel the effects of his lifestyle and the pressures he was under. But here's a perfect example of how sometimes, most times, it's better to be lucky than good. For reasons he would have to explain to you personally–and I'm not suggesting you ask–Jeff gave a baggie each to Melinda, Pete, and Re-Pete and kept one for himself, with the helpful instructions that they share the baggie with Billy to help him "cope with" his hectic lifestyle. Turns out the night Billy died, several baggies were found on his person, as the police reports like to say, and all were empty.

"So an argument could be made that Billy simply consumed a toxic amount of vitamins," Grace said.

"That's one possibility. Or one of the baggies could have had pills that would make Billy's already abused heart go ping! But since there was no autopsy, we'll never know," Lew said.

"That's right, there was no autopsy," Grace exclaimed. "Who made that happen, or not happen?" Grace asked. "Normally, a 49-year-old man keels over, there's an autopsy."

"I don't know, I don't want to know, and I suggest you bury any curiosity you might have on the subject, too, Grace. It's like black specks in peanut butter. If what you don't know won't kill you–or perhaps keep you alive–it's best you don't ask any questions."

Grace wrestled with what she had just learned.

"Doesn't it bother you, working for people capable of doing such nasty things?" Grace asked.

Lew laughed. "I work for captains of industry, Grace, not Eagle Scouts. It's all part of the game, and if you don't know that going in, you're not going to last very long. At best, you're told the bus is leaving and there's no seat for you. At worst, well, just ask Vince Foster's family about that."

Grace sat back in her seat and looked straight ahead.

"I don't know," Grace said after a few quiet moments.

"What don't you know?" Lew asked.

"You asked me before, 'what's next for me?' I'm telling you I don't know.

"Well, you better figure it out soon," Lew said as he turned the car into the restaurant parking lot. "Because Melinda's going to want your answer soon.

Sure enough, as Lew shut off the engine and they unbuckled their seat belts, Melinda stepped outside the entrance to the restaurant to greet them.

Chapter 53

One of Us! One of Us!

"I was wondering when you were going to get here," Melinda said as Grace walked up to the restaurant entrance. "Jackson and I are dying to speak with you."

"We hit a lot of traffic," Grace said, turning to Lew Desmond for confirmation. Somehow, however, Lew had sidled away and was nowhere to be seen.

Other than the cup of coffee Grail had prepared for her that morning, Grace hadn't eaten or consumed any beverage–not even a glass of water–all day. She was famished, bordering on dizzy, but got the sense that neither Melinda nor Jackson would care. They wanted to know what her plans were. So did Grace, for that matter. She followed Melinda into the restaurant and grabbed a glass filled with ice water that happened to be on a table. She didn't know who it belonged to, nor did she care. She took a generous sip and held on to it like she was Gunga Din. She followed Melinda over to a table in the corner where Jackson Ouellette was already situated, and as they navigated through the crowd, Grace made eye contact with Jeff Doomey, who was pretending to listen to a conversation between Betty and one of Billy's relatives.

Jeff smiled at Grace and gave her a thumbs up, but Grace wasn't sure why. She'd like to think it was for the eulogy she gave, what seemed like a lifetime ago, or maybe just for all the help and guidance and support she provided over the past few days. Or maybe he knew something she didn't know—there was a lot of that going around—and wanted to welcome her.

"One of us. One of us," Grace imagined him chanting.

Finally, she and Melinda reached the table where Jackson was situated. He made a half-hearted attempt to stand up to greet them, like gentlemen did back in the day, but then settled in. A waiter came over.

"I'll have another one of these," Jackson said, pointing to his Martini glass, and so will she," Jackson said, pointing to Melinda. "How about you, Grace? Dewar's and water with a twist, right?"

Grace was too emotionally spent to marvel at how—or even wonder why—Jackson knew this but declined. Even under the best of circumstances, a Dewar's and water would dull her senses. If she had one now, she'd be under the table before it was done, and not in a good way. She momentarily hoped Jackson would order some food, but knew she had to focus on what was to be discussed. She took another long sip of water, reminding her for an instant of Billy's reaction when she told him she was leaving to work for Gibbons College.

"Nothing for me, thanks," Grace said.

"Let's get right to it, Grace. I—we—want you to work with us. We can start you at a buck fifty a year with plenty of incentives, a generous expense account, and a company car so you can bring Slade to his various activities in style."

Grace took a beat, momentarily thrown off guard by the fact that Jackson knew her son's name and how important it was to her that he be taken care of. Then she took a deep breath.

"I'm really okay with where I am now," Grace said, "And I'm not saying that as a negotiating tool. The world of academia is quite different from working in the private sector, and I feel more at home there."

"The World of Academia—as you so eloquently put it—is for assholes and losers, Grace," Jackson said. "You know that. It's one big circle jerk followed by an annual donning of the robes so they can jerk each other off in front of an audience. Is that really how you see yourself? Don't you want to experience everything the world has to offer? Visit foreign countries and make a difference while doing so? Once we implement our business model, we'll be influencing how the world thinks and goes about its business, Grace. Wouldn't you want to be a part of that?"

Grace remembered what Martha had told her about Melinda's and Ouellette's plans. Would she like to be part of a project that changed the world? Yes! Would she want to do so based on lies, or at best, misrepresentations? Well, no. But then, how much of what we hear and consume as citizens is the truth? Doesn't the government lie to us habitually? Vietnam? The Pentagon Papers? The Kennedy killings? What about business? How many commercials do we see on television that skirt the truth? Christ—we all start our lives believing in the Big Lie that is Santa Claus. Is lying—or misrepresenting—necessarily a deal breaker?

"From what little I know about your plans," Grace said, "I'm not sure I want to be a part of something so dependent on misleading people."

Melinda snorted. "Grace, you've been bullshitting people about Drex ever since Slade was born. Do you really want to climb that high horse now?

Slade! Of course!! Slade is the answer.

"Funny you should mention Slade, Melinda, and you're right. At some point, I'm going to have to tell him–and everyone else–the Truth, and when I do, I want to do so as someone who can hold her head up high as a woman of integrity, who honors and respects her principles."

"Oh, please," Melinda spat out. "You worked for Billy for five years. You saw plenty and never said a word. In fact, you helped Billy bend the truth more than anyone I know, with the possible exception of Shadler. Besides, remember what Katherine Hepburn said: "If you obey all the rules, you'll miss all the fun.""

The reference to the beloved Stanley Shadler–not to mention Katherine Hepburn–threw Grace for a loop.

Yes, she thought. *Stanley was Old School and, on more than one occasion, used those Old School values to bring Billy back into line. But Stanley also bent the truth when it came time to file taxes, and such machinations helped fuel Billy's financial successes, at least initially. Maybe she WAS being naïve."*

"It's never too late to do the right thing," Grace said, grimacing at her employment of a cliché.

Melinda started to speak, but Jackson put his hand on hers.

"It's been a long day, a long couple of days," Jackson said. "Let's let Grace think about our offer and the wonderful worlds we can bring her into, debt-free. Does that sound fair, Grace?" Jackson asked rhetorically.

"That's more than fair, and I promise I will give it great consideration," she said. "But right now I have to get something to eat and then head back to South Huntington. My sister Grail has been doing double duty watching my son, and quite frankly, I could use one of his special hugs right now."

Grace got up from the table, shook Jackson's hand while looking him in the eyes to gauge his thinking, and ... nothing.

She made a mental note to never play poker against him. She turned to Melinda.

"Melinda, once again, I am sorry for your loss. Thank you for letting me be a part of Billy's send-off. It really was everything he would have wanted." Grace desperately wanted to add, "Especially the chaos and the show-stopping funeral," but she would once again have to be satisfied with simply amusing herself.

"I should be thanking you," Melissa said, half-heartedly trying to sound sincere while noticeably not actually thanking her. "I do hope you give our offer serious consideration. Quite frankly, I don't think you have the future you think you have at Gibbons, and I hate to think of you missing out on the wonderful opportunity we've put on the table."

Grace chose not to consider this a veiled threat by Melinda that she would share Grace's secret with the Gibbons Administration. All she knew at that point was that she needed two things: a ride home and something to eat.

Chapter 54

A Certain Flexibility

"So ... how did it go?" Grail asked as Grace slid into the passenger side of Grail's car, using a sing-songy, comical tone to convey her seemingly contradictory disdain for the situation and desire to hear the latest gossip regarding what transpired.

Grace turned to the back seat. "Where's Slade?"

"Ron's looking after him. He was home watching TV when I got your call, so I figured I'd leave Slade with him and my kids so we can get caught up," Grail said.

"Great. Thanks," Grace said, exhaling. "I don't suppose you have any snacks. I'm starving."

"You mean Melinda didn't channel her maternal instinct to nurture and feed you?" Grail asked, mastering the art of rhetorical sarcasm.

"Yes, in fact, she did ask if I wanted something to eat," Grace said, before realizing it was Jackson who made the offer. "They even tried to ply me with alcohol. But I didn't want to spend one moment there more than I needed to, so I declined."

"Okay. So, how was the funeral?" Grail asked. "Did Donna Devore show up?"

"Oh my God, did she ever!" Grace replied. "But I dealt with it. I'll be happy to dish all the details to you later, but for now, I need to talk to you about the job offer they made."

"Melinda offered you a job on the day she buried her husband?" Grail asked, surprised but not surprised. "I suppose periods of mourning aren't what they used to be."

Grace snorted involuntarily before thinking, *Wait until Grail finds out what she offered me the night before her husband's funeral. It was last night, right? Christ, that seems like ages ago.*

"Melinda doesn't believe in wasting time, I suppose," Grace said. "Besides, the actual offer came from Jackson."

"Jackson, who?" Grail asked, sitting up in her seat and turning the radio off.

"Jackson Ouellette," Grace answered, forgetting that Grail had not been brought up to speed on this development.

"Jackson Ouellette!?! The billionaire Jackson Ouellette? THAT Jackson Ouellette? And he wants you to work for him?" Grail said, almost losing her place in the lane she was driving.

"Well, he and Melinda?"

"What do you mean, he and Melinda?" Grail said. "Are they a couple? Did he buy Carpe Diem? What the hell's been happening these past few days, Grace? What else are you not telling me?"

Oh, if you only knew, Grace thought.

"I can't really get into all the details because I'm still sorting things out," Grace said. "But here's what I know and where I'm at."

She recounted what she had learned about Doomey and Ouellette, the limousine ride to the cemetery, and Melinda letting on that she knew the secret about Drex.

Grail let out a long, low whistle, the same long, low whistle Murray Jules had let out when Grace told him about Billy. What was it about long, low whistles after hearing unexpected news?

"Christ Almighty," Grail said. "What are you going to do?"

"I have no idea," Grace said, sighing and sliding deep into her seat. "I'm truly stumped in terms of what direction to go in."

"What did they offer you? What would you be doing for them?" Grail asked.

"They–Jackson, really–didn't get into specifics. Generally speaking, though, I'd be doing well salary-wise and be part of a 'groundbreaking' new business."

"Groundbreaking? I don't like the sound of that," Grail said.

"Of course you don't," Grace said. "You wouldn't like anything Melinda does. To be fair, though, I'm not too keen on what they have in mind, either."

"Why's that?" Grail asked.

"It just doesn't seem kosher," Grace said.

"What doesn't?" Grail asked.

"Their business model. They want to conduct marketing surveys on behalf of clients ..."

"That sounds perfectly fine," Grail interjected.

"... while offering a certain flexibility, if you will, regarding the outcome of the surveys."

"Flexibility?" Grail asked.

"Um, yeah. Flexibility. In other words, if the survey results match the hopes and expectations, great–full steam ahead. If they don't, however, the company will present the results as if they had."

"Oooohhhh," Grail said. "There's an element of diabolical genius here, as long as you possess a certain amount of–what was the word you used? Flexibility? Yes, as long as you have a certain amount of 'flexibility' when it comes to integrity, morals, and ethics. Seriously, though. It sounds right up Melinda's alley. Fake results made to look great, just like her tits."

"For God's sake, will you let up on the tits thing?," Grace said, exasperated. "They're fake. So what? She's a beautiful woman," Grace said, surprising herself by coming to Melinda's defense.

"That's what pisses me off, Grace. She IS a beautiful woman. Why'd she have to go the phony boobs route? She has luscious hair, wonderfully straight teeth, and cheekbones to kill for. Is cleavage all that important? Are we nothing unless we have that critical three inches of skin-meeting-skin between some fabric?"

"If I concede your point, can we get back to the matter at hand, Grail? I'm trying to decide my future here, not to mention Slade's."

"Yes. Yes, of course," Grail said. "Tell me again. What was the offer they made you?"

"Nothing specific. Jackson simply said I'd be earning enough to take care of myself and to make sure Slade enjoyed the best of everything, as well," Grace said.

Grail looked straight ahead through the windshield, guiding the car down the middle lane of the parkway. "And in exchange for all this wonderfulness, you'll be expected to do what, exactly?"

"That's the thing," Grace said. "I don't know what will be expected of me.

Grail and Grace drove in silence for a few moments. Grace looked out the window, noticing that the trees alongside the parkway were starting to change colors.

Grail broke the silence.

"What does your gut tell you?" Grail asked.

"My gut?"

"Your gut," Grail said again. "You don't have to answer me now. But I would encourage you to take a long, quiet walk, or just sit in silence for a spell, and the answer will come to you."

"How do you know?" Grace asked.

"Because your 'gut instinct,' if you will, is God talking to you."

"You talk to God?" Grace asked teasingly.

"Yes, in fact, I do," Grail said. "I ask him for guidance, watch and listen for a response, and then thank him for pointing me in the right direction."

"Do you think Dad was following his 'gut instincts' when that madman shot him dead? Or was the crazy bastard following his 'gut instinct' because he thought God wanted Dad dead?" Grace asked bitterly.

"I can't even begin to explain how or why that all went down," Grail said. "But I do know it's in the past, and all the bitter feelings and questions won't bring back Dad–or Mom, for that matter. Let the dead bury the dead, Grace. Stay in the moment and focus on what your next steps will be."

Grace sighed. "Okay. You're right. So Ouellette–and Melinda, I suppose–want me to join their team. They said they will make it worth my while and that I'll finally be able to take care of Slade in style, buy a house of my own, even. All I have to do is pretend what I'm doing is real and not a lie."

"How is that different from what you did for Billy all those years?" Grail asked.

"That's the exact same point Melinda made," Grace said, knowing it would torture Grail to know she was thinking just like Melinda.

"Yikes," Grail said. "Seriously, though, is financial security– whatever that entails–that important to you, that you'd be willing to sacrifice your integrity and professional pride?

"It's not that simple, Grail," Grace said. "You and Ron have it pretty good because you made all the right decisions along the way. I have a lot of catching up to do."

Grail guided her car into the left lane and then sped up some so she could pass a car doing the speed limit in the middle lane–a cardinal sin when it came to driving on Long Island. Once back in her rightful place at the head of the pack on the parkway, she turned to Grace.

"Ron and I have it 'pretty good,' as you put it, because we believed in ourselves," Grail replied. "And you shouldn't feel as if you have to quote-unquote catch up to anybody, particularly me. Everything unfolds in its own due time. That's the perfection and beauty of the Universe."

"That's all well and good," Grace countered. "But I'm afraid..."

Grail interrupted.

"That's the problem, Grace. You're afraid," Grail shot out.

"Who isn't these days?" Grace shot back.

"I'm not. Ron's not," Grail replied.

"Well, bully for you!"

"Seriously, Grace," Grail said. "Be not afraid. It says so right in the Bible. In fact, it says it 365 times, once for every day of the year. That can't be a coincidence."

"How do you know how many times 'Be Not Afraid' appears in the Bible?" Grace asked.

"I just know. I read things," Grail said.

"You read the Bible?" Grace asked.

"No, not exactly. I read the lessons that other people take from it. Wayne Dyer, Neville Goddard, Joseph Murphy, Mickey Singer. Let them do the heavy lifting," Grail said.

"And what's your take on their take?" Grace asked aloud and then again in her head to see if the question made sense.

"Well, remember that Nietzsche..."

"Yeah, yeah, yeah–what doesn't kill me makes me stronger. What else ya got?" Grace snapped.

"No need to get snippy, sis. Just trying to help," Grail said.

"I'm sorry, Grail. That was rude. Seriously, what is your take on all this?"

"Okay, here goes," Grail said.

"It constitutes perhaps the greatest irony of all time, but we're all on our own individual paths to become who we are supposed to be. Yet we're also part of one big Universe, one Universal mind, one spirit. God created it, and he wants us to benefit from it, even as humans. It's what God's love is all about, tapping into that tremendous resource. Remember that Beatles' song, 'All You Need Is Love'? Love is all you need. Or the Todd Rundgren song from *Black Maria,* 'Love Is The Answer?' They weren't referring to love in the sense that we talk about, between two people. They're referring to a Universal force available to each one of us as children of God."

"So if it's universal and available to everyone, how come we're not all tapping into it? Grace asked. "Why does everyone seem to be so miserable? Why would a man use a pistol to shoot a total stranger and then himself?"

Grail sighed. She knew that was coming.

"I never pretended to have all the answers, Grace," Grail said. "My guess is, the lunatic just snapped. Whatever mental illnesses he suffered from that went undiagnosed, whatever poisons he was consuming because, for some reason, our government lets its citizens eat outright garbage in the name of maximizing profits, they became all-consuming. In his mind, shooting Dad in cold blood–for no reason–must have made sense. And Dad–God bless him–was simply in the wrong place at the wrong time. Or maybe he had some sort of death wish buried deep in his subconscious. Maybe he secretly, without even realizing it himself, wanted out somehow, and the Universe was granting him his wish."

"And Mom—was her wish that her life be turned upside down by some crazed gunman so she could spend the last year of her life in a fog of grief and despair?"

"I wouldn't wish what happened to Mom on my worst enemy," Grail said. "But the choices she made after Dad died were all hers. There are myriad ways she could have handled things better."

"Like how?" Grace asked, somewhat bitterly.

Grail pondered for a moment.

"Remember that lady a couple of years ago whose husband and son were among dozens shot by the crazed gunman on the Long Island Railroad? The husband died instantly, and the son was permanently injured. Up until that point, she was a registered nurse living a quiet, unassuming life. She could have moped and moaned like Mom did, but instead, she channeled some newfound energy and ran for Congress so she could champion laws that would prevent such a thing from happening again. She's still there, I believe."

"Well, bully for her," Grace said. "So what's your point? And what does this have to do with my making a decision about my future?"

Grail flicked the car's turn signal so it would indicate she was getting off at the next exit. As she glanced over her shoulder so she could maneuver to the right, she bit her bottom lip and thought for a moment.

"What you decide is up to you, Grace," Grail said as she transitioned the automobile into the exit lane. "The best way I can help you is to make sure you're making your decision in the right frame of mind."

"Which is?" Grace asked.

"A mind that's open to receiving guidance from God."

"Oh Lord, here we go," Grace said.

"Seriously," Grail said. "Mom was afraid after Dad died, especially because of the financial predicament he left us in. So she crawled up into a ball and hoped everything would go back to the way it was before. That's not how it works. Sometimes life hits you on the side of the head with a shovel. You either get back up and carry on, or you spend every remaining day frozen in the fear that it will happen again.

"Can you blame her?" Grace asked.

"To a certain extent, yes, as cold as that may seem. Fear is the absence of faith in your life. When you have faith in God, when you believe there's a higher power within you, supporting you at all times, then any vestige of fear vanishes once you confront those fears. And on the other side of our fears is the joy and abundance God wants for all of us."

"But if God exists within each of us, why do bad things happen to people? Or do they only happen to people who don't believe?" Grace asked.

"Having faith in God doesn't mean bad things won't happen to you," Grail explained. "It just means that, good or bad, God is always with you, ready to offer support and solutions when asked. But you have to ask, and you have to ask with faith that your prayers will be answered. It's almost as if the fear that stems from experiencing–or even just the anticipation of experiencing–bad things exists so we know we're on the right path as we overcome these challenges. Think of bad things happening as a guide to knowing you're heading in the right direction. Your ability to overcome those challenges empowers you to be ever more resilient. That's the truest freedom there is: Knowing that whatever obstacles come your way, you'll be okay."

"Well, it's nice to know I have that going for me," Grace said. If Grail picked up on Grace's half-hearted attempt to invoke the spirit of Groundskeeper Carl in *Caddyshack,* she did not acknowledge it. As she steered the car through downtown South Huntington on the way home, Grace sat up suddenly.

"Pull over here, Grail!" Grace ordered, pointing to a parking space just ahead on the right. "Speaking of overcoming obstacles, I'm going to have a chat with my friend Bernie."

"Is he working NOW?" Grail questioned as she pulled into the spot. "It's Saturday afternoon. Why would he be working?"

"He is. I'm sure he is," Grace said. "Besides, even if he isn't, I need a drink, and quite frankly, the short walk home wouldn't hurt. Tell Slade I'll see him in a bit."

Chapter 55

Calm Yourself, Gracie

"Thanks for the ride," Grace said to Grail, getting ready to close the passenger side door.

"Grace! Wait!" Grail said. "I was going to surprise you back at the house. I have two plane tickets to St. Bart's, and I've made all the arrangements for us to stay at an oceanfront resort and spa for a couple of days. You and I are going to get let loose and let some strangers touch our bodies! Lord knows you've earned it."

Grace was stunned.

"Strangers touch our bodies?"

"Oh, for God's sake, Grace. Grow up! I'm talking about massages. It's just going to be the two of us, and I may just let myself go a little crazy!"

Grace leaned back into the car to hug Grail and whispered, "God bless you, Grail. I don't know what I'd do without you." As she pulled away from her sister, however, she added, "I tell you what. I want you to go to St. Bart's, but with Ron. I'll watch the kids for a change. You go have fun and play 'catch me catch me' in the sand."

"But I wanted this for you!" Grail protested. "You need to unwind, to let loose. You're working way too hard, and the last couple of days have been a grind."

"I'm fine," Grace assured her sister. "I'm going to have a chat with Bernie and maybe a quick drink. I'll be back home in an hour, and you can start making the arrangements with Ron."

She closed the car door and headed to the Broken Oar. She had no idea if Bernie was working now, but if nothing else, she could find out when he would be there while she nursed a badly needed Dewar's and water.

Dear God, please let Bernie be there now, she wished silently. *Maybe that's not quite the sort of prayer Grail had in mind, but you have to start somewhere.* Grace laughed at her little joke and opened the bar's front door.

Sure enough, there was Bernie, standing behind the multitude of beer taps in the center of the bar.

His eyes–those gorgeous blue eyes–lit up.

Calm yourself, Gracie, she thought.

"My, my, my, look who's here," Bernie beamed. "This must be my lucky week. What's the occasion?"

Grace looked at Bernie with an expression that was a twist between quizzical and disappointment. "Did he really have no idea what she had been through the last couple of days? Did he not realize what she had to deal with this morning?"

"We buried Billy Bate this morning, Bernie. Haven't you been keeping up?"

"Was that today?" Bernie asked, half-kidding. "Seriously, my condolences, Grace. I know he played a big part in your life."

"Save it, Bernie. I know you liked him about as much as Grail did. But I appreciate that you at least cared enough to try."

She ordered a Dewar's and water.

"I'm guessing you've had a long day, Grace," Bernie said. "This one's on me."

Grace laughed. "Thanks. That's a gesture of condolence that genuinely means something."

He placed a coaster in front of her and set the Dewar's and water with a twist in a tumbler on top of it.

She took a sip and as she did, she was reminded of the tumbler of scotch from the night before–just a little over 12 hours ago. She felt her heart skip and a tingle between her thighs.

Calm yourself, Gracie, she found herself thinking again.

"I'm surprised to find you working this afternoon," Grace said, trying to control her emotions and conversation.

"Why'd you come down if you didn't think I'd be working?" Bernie asked. "You're not secretly seeing one of the other bartenders behind my back, are you?"

"I'm not seeing anyone, much less a bartender," Grace said, perhaps with greater disdain than she intended.

"And whose fault is that?" Bernie asked rhetorically.

"Never mind me," Grace said, trying to steer the conversation back to safer ground. "Why are you working this afternoon?"

"Oh, you know the owner. He's a real prick. He wants to maximize revenue at all times, and nobody makes the register ring like I do," Bernie said.

"I hope he appreciates you, Bernie. I hope he's not taking advantage of your workaholic tendencies," Grace said.

"Oh, he loves me. There's no question there, Grace."

"Really? How can you be so sure?" Grace asked.

"Because it's me! I'm the owner," Bernie replied.

"What do you mean, you're the owner?" Grace asked, confused.

"I'm the owner. I bought the place back when you were diddling that 'war hero.'"

"How come you never told me?" Grace wondered, surprised by this development.

"You never asked."

"Seriously? It never occurred to you that I might appreciate knowing that you own this establishment?"

"Would it have mattered? Would you have treated me differently, Grace?" Bernie asked.

"Well, no. At least I like to think not," Grace said, somewhat defensively. "But if you're the owner, how come you're working on a Saturday afternoon?"

"Oh, that's the landlord's fault. Seems he likes to get his rent paid on time, and in full. So I have to generate the revenues necessary to keep him off my back," Bernie said.

"Greedy pricks!" Grace muttered as she took another sip of her Dewar's and water, twirling the lemon peel around the rim of the glass after she did so.

"Oh, he's the worst!" Bernie exclaimed, slapping his bar rag on the counter for emphasis. "An absolute pig. Heartless! Relentless."

"Seriously, why does it always have to be about the money?" Grace said, taking a third sip from her drink and relishing the warmth cascading down her throat.

Bernie laughed.

"What's so funny?" Grace asked, a little hurt that she wasn't in on the joke, whatever it was.

"It's me, Grace," Bernie said. "I'm the greedy landlord. I own this building and all the others on this block. I pay myself rent and collect rent from the others. It's not a bad gig if you can get it."

"I had no idea, Bernie," Grace said, still in shock but sitting up a little straighter. "Why are you just telling me this now?"

"A gentleman never kisses and tells, and a smart businessman keeps his cards close to his chest," Bernie said. "Besides, what difference does it make? I like to think I'm the same man whether I'm the bartender or the bar owner."

With that, he poured himself a mug of coffee and raised it in Grace's direction.

"A toast ... to the late, great Billy Bate. May he rest in peace. Or relish the mess he left behind. Whatever."

"Here, here," Grace said as they clinked glass and mug. She took another sip, placed it on the bar, and looked up to see Bernie propel himself over the bar like an Olympic gymnast on the pommel horse.

"Where did you learn how to do that?" she asked, impressed.

"When you run an establishment where the consumption of alcohol is involved, you learn to respond nimbly to situations that escalate quickly," Bernie replied as he walked over to the jukebox. "You also learn how to set the right mood to evoke a certain response."

With that, he pushed a few buttons on the jukebox, and the opening notes of a song Grace knew all too well filled the bar that until this moment included just the two of them.

Name your price,
a ticket to paradise...

"Oh, Bernie, you know I hate this song ..." Grace protested, albeit mildly.

He walked over to where she was perched on the bar stool and extended his hand in a gesture that suggested they dance. She took his hand and they sauntered over to the open floor space where customers normally stood waiting for drinks. He drew her in close, and she put her head on his shoulder.

I've been from shore to shore to shore
If there's a shortcut
I'd have found it
But there is no easy way
around it
Light of the world,
shine on me
Love is the answer
Shine on us all
Set us free
Love is the answer

"You don't hate the song, Grace," Bernie said. "You hate what it's associated with, what it reminds you of. It's like Monday mornings. People don't really hate Mondays. They just hate that it represents the choices they made in life that limit the freedom they have to do what they want. That becomes painfully obvious on Sunday night and Monday morning for most people."

"And you don't hate Mondays because ...?" Grace asked.

"I love my life," Bernie said. "Years ago, I committed to letting go and letting God, and I've been stress-free ever since."

He and Grace continued the slow dance, simply just moving back and forth with their bodies pressed together, his hands clasped gently on her back above her waist, and her arms around his neck. She sighed and relaxed just a little.

The song ended with a choral crescendo. Bernie and Grace remained on the ersatz dance floor, their foreheads touching and their arms around each other. Then they heard the unmistakable clicks and gyrations of the jukebox getting ready to play another song: "Izzat Love," the other big hit from *Black Maria* that was performed at Billy and Melinda's wedding, as well.

"All right ... that's enough from that stupid musical," Grace blurted.

Bernie obliged. He went behind the bar, reached under the counter, and pressed a button that turned off the jukebox.

"Happy?"

"Thank you," Grace said. "Do you really see yourself as stress-free? Really? You own a bar. Isn't that stressful?"

"Oh, there are hassles and challenges, but in the grand scheme of things, I know I have the Christ within me to rely on," Bernie said.

"Now I know you're full of shit Bernie," Grace said. "You haven't been inside a church since we were kids."

He walked to the "civilian" side of the bar and gestured for Grace to return to her barstool. Bernie sat on the stool immediately adjacent. He turned on the stool so their knees were touching.

"The 'Christ within me' has nothing to do with church, or religion, Grace," Bernie said, leaning forward and speaking in a near whisper. "It's a belief, a conviction that God, or a Higher Power if you will, resonates through each of us. I like to think of it as living life spiritually, with no "I" or ego, by serving others and understanding that God wants our actions to reflect His Love for Humanity. God expresses Himself uniquely through each of us, and He is forever present. We can tap into that presence any time we choose to, or any time we have a problem that needs solving, but only if we're willing to surrender all control to it."

"Surrender? As in give up?" Grace asked.

"No, just the opposite. When you surrender to a Higher Power–the Christ within–you feel empowered to meet any challenge, to never give up," Bernie said.

"Just how does one access this Christ within? Rub a lamp three times while chanting 'Abracadabra'?"

"Oh, poor, cynical Grace," Bernie said. "You access the Christ within by sitting in silence."

"So you meditate?"

"Call it what you will, what you want," Bernie said. "The trick is to be quiet. Allow the muddied waters of your mind to settle so the mud drifts to the bottom and the mind itself becomes clear. It helps to be outdoors, in nature. Too many people go to church and think about fishing, when they'd be much happier and fulfilled if they went fishing and thought about God."

"If this is so helpful, why don't more people practice it?" Grace asked.

"You can only talk to God and hear what he has to say when you welcome the silence," Bernie said. "And only those who love God, themselves, and each other are comfortable sitting silently for extended periods of time," Bernie responded.

"If that's the case, why is there so much chaos and confusion in the world? Why don't more people make more of an effort to experience long periods of silence so they can commune with God?" Grace asked.

"We've discussed this, Grace. You can only make money when you own the noise that creates the problems that keep people distracted. There's no money in the silence. You can't own the silence. Only lovers own the silence. The government, corporate media, and Big Pharma can't own it, as much as they want to, and it makes them crazy. They try everything in their power to keep us from understanding and embracing our connection to God, and how crucial the silence is to our being able to access all that is good and has meaning. They distract, demean, diminish, and deny. They want you in a constant state of fear, too afraid to explore the silence lest you realize it's all a dream, a dream with the Happy Ending being our realization that we don't need them! EVERYTHING we need, we already have because we have this wonderful connection to our Higher Power, our God. If this ever was universally understood and–God forbid–accepted, the world as we know it would collapse. Of course, a much better world would replace it almost instantaneously, but that would not serve the purpose of the Inner Circle running today's world. Therefore, it cannot be allowed to happen.

"This is nothing new. The Bible is replete with references to 'the Kingdom within,' but the patriarchy that perpetuated the original telling of these truths didn't want the masses to understand this. So instead, they came up with obfuscating metaphors, rules, and regulations designed to keep most men and women oppressed and overwhelmed. Pure genius, in a diabolical way."

"You really know how to woo a woman," Grace countered. "Is this how you normally go about your conquests?"

"You're not a conquest, Grace. You're my soulmate. You know it. I know it. It's time we acknowledge and embrace it together. A genuine relationship is two imperfect people refusing to give up on each other."

Grace said nothing but drew Bernie closer. They stood and hugged again. This time, he hugged her tighter but still gently. The music had long since stopped, but they stood there, hugging, basking in the silence, and relishing the moment. They kissed passionately and deeply, like two hungry souls enjoying a lavish buffet.

Once they came up for air, Grace, with a tinge of mischief in her voice, whispered. "You know what I really want you to do?"

"Name it," Bernie whispered in her ear.

"Tell me that story again about your one-night stand," Grace said, with a giggle.

"I have a better idea," Bernie whispered back. "Let's go upstairs to my office and create a story of our own.

Chapter 56

Happily Ever After

"I suppose with all the stuff about God and Christ and how we determine our own happiness, it's safe to assume Bernie and Grace lived happily ever after," Catherine said.

"Well, they married and Bernie adopted Slade as his son, but that's not the point," Angelo said. "What matters is that Grace walked away from the whole Carpe Diem mess. She saw it for what it was and decided she wanted no part of it, financially secure or otherwise. She opted instead to 'trust her gut' and follow God's guidance."

"And where did God take her?" Catherine asked, perhaps with a little more snark than she intended.

"Do you recognize the name Grace Scanlan?" Angelo asked.

Catherine paused.

"The President of Gibbons College?" she asked, astonished she hadn't made the connection.

"One and the same. The first woman to lead that school, I might add," Angelo said.

"So Melinda never let on about Drex being in prison?" Catherine asked.

"Oh, she let the cat out of the bag, all right," Angelo said. "Probably the moment after Grace told her she wasn't going to return to Carpe Diem. Turns out it didn't matter. Nobody on the Gibbons board or in the Gibbons administration held Drex's story against Grace. She got promoted, paid off the loan, and she and Bernie bought a lovely home. The fears she conjured up in her head were unfounded, like so many other things we dread that never come to fruition. They appreciated her for who she is, how diligently she worked for Gibbons, and the vision she had for the school's future."

"Wow!" Catherine said. "So what happened to Ouellette? And did they ever figure out who or what expedited Billy's demise?"

"They did not. Billy was buried without an autopsy, and the issue was never raised. Everyone just assumed his heart gave out. Meanwhile, Ouellette and Melinda launched their endeavor. It worked well for a while before the other survey companies figured it out. They let the media know that Ouellette's polls were tainted. Once exposed, the media people were so pissed Ouellette couldn't get coverage if he claimed he had proof Elvis was still alive. His survey results had about as much value as being included in *Who's Who in America*. Once the wheels came off that bus, Melinda took off. I think she joined a cult. So that's a good thing, I suppose. And Ouellette ... well ..."

"Didn't he just launch a new venture?" Catherine asked, impressing Angelo that she was paying attention to business news.

"He did, indeed, and this one might have some legs," Angelo said. "He's using the facial recognition software created for security companies to ascertain what kind of brands people wear or carry."

"How does that work?" Catherine asked.

"Picture a crowd coming to Madison Square Garden," Angelo said. "Originally, the cameras used facial recognition technology to see if there were people there who shouldn't be, like people on the FBI's most wanted list. Now, the cameras pick up logos and brand names on the clothing being worn and the bags being carried by the fan base. It's a great way to determine who's wearing what, what's trending among certain demographics, and/or who's willing to be associated with different clothing brands, or backpack brands, etc."

"That's a little Big Brother-ish, isn't it?" Catherine asked.

"So you've read *1984*?" Angelo replied. "I was under the impression the schools stopped teaching it because it hit too close to home."

"I didn't read it for school," Catherine said. "I read it because I saw so many references to it online. I wanted to learn more."

"Too bad more people your age don't think like that," Angelo said. "They're so easily manipulated by a system that wants them only smart enough to work for the big corporations, but not too smart so that they figure things out for themselves."

"Well, I don't know how smart I am," Catherine said. "But I've learned a great deal listening to this story. Thank you for sharing it with me. Do you ever see yourself writing that book?"

Angelo sighed.

"I don't know. I don't think so. It's just so sordid and weird, even more so now with the passage of time. I'm happy for Grace and Bernie. I'd just as soon never hear from Melinda or Ouellette, or anyone else."

"Not even Marietta?" Catherine asked, half-kidding.

"Especially Marietta!" Angelo said. "I'd watch back-to-back episodes of *The View* before I'd meet up with her again."

"So what can we conclude about the ego? Is it necessary to

have one if you want to lead people, to run an organization? If not, what does it take to be a successful leader?" Catherine asked.

Angelo gave the question some deliberate consideration.

"The ego is like cholesterol," Angelo said. "There's good cholesterol and there's bad cholesterol. We all have to make sure we keep the good and lose the bad. Some people are driven more by their 'bad' ego than others. Others accept less than what they deserve because they see the ego as bad. Half the battle is recognizing the ego for what it is: a thing in the universe that creates thoughts about itself, as Mickey Singer puts it. 'It's like a magnet. It brings everything back to me.'"

"So is it bad? Is it necessary?" Catherine asked.

"It's both and neither," Angelo said. He paused. Finally, he said, "Wait here. I remember reading something recently that might help. Give me a minute to find it."

With that, he went back into the house. Catherine took advantage of the opportunity to stretch and walk about the deck. She noticed a small stream on the east side of the home, and that it flowed directly into the bay. The water was clear and moving, although not all that quickly. She wondered whether it was fresh water and, if so, how clean it might be. She considered what would happen if she reached into the stream to find out when she heard the door open.

"I found it!" Angelo said, rather proudly. "I read this last summer. It's a passage from *Conversations with God*, by Neale Donald Walsch.

"Always put yourself first. Then, depending upon what you are trying to do or what you are seeking to experience, you will make your choice. When your life purpose is very high, so will your choices also be. Putting yourself first doesn't mean you're being selfish; it means you're being self-aware. It is only through the exercise of the greatest freedom that the greatest growth is achieved, or even possible. If all you do is follow somebody else's rules, then you have not grown. You have obeyed. Obedience is not growth."

Angelo looked up as he closed the book. "I forget who said it, or who pointed it out, but somebody once said, 'You'll never see a statue honoring a conformist.'"

"So you need an ego to run a business," Catherine concluded.

"I suppose, yes," Angelo said, "but it must be channeled appropriately. If the ego drives you to benefit only yourself and no one else, or you at the expense of someone else, then you are doomed to failure. If, on the other hand, your reason for being, your purpose, is to benefit others and/or help those around you be better people, then full steam ahead."

"But how do you know if your purpose is what it needs to be? If you're on the right track?" Catherine asked.

Angelo laughed. "Yes, that is the $64,000 question."

"Why $64,000?" Catherine asked, confused.

Angelo chuckled again.

"It's just an expression. Never mind," he said. "The truth is, you need to listen to your intuition, because that's God talking to you. That's why meditation–or prayer–can be so beneficial. When you meditate, you get to quiet the monkeys chattering away in your brain. Eventually, they get tired of yammering, and God's message comes through. That connection is the God within, the Christ, if you will. Remember, the ego is Edging God Out. So quieting the mind is just the opposite. It's letting things settle so you can hear what you have to hear."

Angelo looked over at the side of the deck where Catherine had been standing when he came out of the house.

"Take this stream, for instance," Angelo said. "When it's clear and free of debris, the water flows freely and reaches its final destination–the bay–with minimal effort, and the bay flows into the ocean. When somebody throws something in there–like a soda bottle or a plastic bag–or even if something natural, like a branch of a tree or a big rock, lands in it, there's a disturbance. The water goes slower because it literally has to work around the obstruction. If the obstruction is too big, the water backs up and wreaks all kinds of havoc. Surrendering your life to God is like clearing your stream of all obstacles."

Catherine was puzzled.

"I'm hearing a lot of references to God, and a Higher Power, and even the 'Christ within.' Is this part of some religion I'm not aware of?"

Angelo laughed.

"Why is that funny?" Catherine asked.

"Organized religion and I parted ways a long time ago," Angelo said. "I was raised Catholic and spent the better part of my youth hearing that I was trash because I sometimes broke seemingly arbitrary rules like, 'you can't eat meat on Fridays.' No one ever said why we couldn't do so–just that it was a rule. And then suddenly it wasn't–except during Lent. Does God really care if I have a hot dog on a Friday in March? I don't think so."

"But you believe in God, right?" Catherine asked.

"Absolutely!" Angelo replied. "A great line from *The Big Bang Theory* comes to mind: 'I don't object to the concept of a deity, but I'm baffled by the notion of one that takes attendance.' My God is a loving God. It's a life force, a level of energy contained within each of us. The closer we are to that God, the easier it is for us to access that energy."

"So you're not part of any religion," Catherine said.

Angelo sighed, as if finally admitting something to himself.

"No, I guess I'm not. If I have to 'be' anything, I guess I would say I'm an Imaginist."

Catherine fidgeted in her seat. She had never heard this

term before, and she was nervous as to whether or not being familiar would make her seem naïve or, worse, ignorant.

"I'm sorry, but I'm not familiar with that expression. What is an Imaginist?"

"It's someone who believes in Imaginism," Angelo replied with mock incredulity. "You're not familiar with it?"

"Um ... no," she admitted.

Angelo laughed again.

"I'm just breaking your chops," he said. "The Imaginism movement is still in its nascent stage. It was started by Karen Garvey and basically stems from this quote by Neville Goddard: 'The world in which we live is a world of imagination. Man, through his imaginal activities, creates the realities and circumstances of his life. This he does either knowingly or unknowingly.' Garvey defines it as, 'When heart, mind, and soul connect with the imagination to create an expanded, fulfilling life."

"So if I want an expanded, fulfilling life–whatever that means–I have to ..." Catherine asked, hoping Angelo would complete the sentence.

"Embrace the silence whenever possible," Angelo said, taking the bait. "Silence is the cornerstone of Imaginism. The fact that no material entity can 'own it,' like Bernie told Grace, makes it even more powerful. And that's why people comfortable with the silence frighten those in power. Mastering others is strength. Mastering yourself is true power, and such mastery only happens when you're comfortable with yourself and your connection to God. Like Lao Tzu said: 'because one believes in oneself, one doesn't try to convince others. Because one is content with oneself, one doesn't need others' approval. Because one accepts oneself, the whole world accepts him or her."

Catherine sat back in her chair, overwhelmed.

"It's a lot to take in," Angelo said, recognizing her distress. "It's not something you absorb–or embrace, for that matter–instantly. But it's definitely worth exploring."

"I appreciate you sharing all this with me," Catherine said, pulling herself together. "But I'm not sure how it applies–or if it even does apply–to what it takes to lead an organization."

Angelo looked over Catherine's left shoulder and marveled at how the afternoon sun reflected off the bay. He smiled.

"Believe it or not, there is a connection," he said. "You can't lead without a vision. You have to see something–a mission, a new product or service, whatever–that most others don't see, and then you have to convince others that converting that vision into a reality is worth pursuing. And the best way to receive that vision is by sitting in silence whenever possible."

"Okay–I get that. But how do you go about convincing others that your vision is worth pursuing?" Catherine asked.

"Ah, now you're getting to the heart of the matter," Angelo said. "I don't know exactly how you do it, but I do know it has to be done. For 30-plus years, I was in the business of listening to, interviewing, or simply just watching dozens–if not hundreds–of leaders. The one thing they all had in common–the ONLY thing they had in common–was their innate ability to make people desire their approval."

"Is it something that can be taught?" Catherine asked.

"No," Angelo said emphatically. "It's like a good singing voice: You either have it or you don't. That's why I laugh when I see all these business schools on the Island teaching 'entrepreneurialism.' If you don't have that natural ability to inspire people, all the marketing, accounting, and business know-how in the world ain't going to help."

"What's the relationship between the ego and this innate ability to inspire?" Catherine asked.

"Great question! I suppose you can make the argument that

the moment a leader recognizes his or her innate ability to inspire is the seed that causes a leader's ego to grow. Again, I'm not sure how that realization manifests itself, but it has to happen at some point."

"Wow. That's some heady stuff you're throwing at me here," Catherine said, looking at her phone on the table. "Thank God I was able to record it all."

Angelo laughed.

"What's so funny?" she asked.

"Oh, it has nothing to do with this conversation," Angelo replied. "I was just reminded of the first time I interviewed a Fortune 500 CEO. I was really nervous, and back in those days–God, I hate that expression–but back in those days we had to bring a tape recorder with us. Well, I remembered to bring the tape recorder, but I didn't think to make sure I had the microphone facing the person I was interviewing. When I went to transcribe the recording, I could hear my questions loud and clear, but the interviewee's answers? Not so much."

"Ouch!" Catherine said.

"Yeah ... took me a lot longer to transcribe than it should have," Angelo said, chuckling at the memory.

"So what other pearls of wisdom do you have for me?" Catherine asked, sensing she had what she needed and not wanting to wear out her welcome.

"Let's see ..." Angelo said. "I tell you what. These thoughts always worked for me, but were not necessarily mine."

"Like what?" Catherine asked.

"Well, I always liked the four basic rules Harry S. Truman said we all need to follow: 'Trust in God. Have no fear. Tell the truth. Work Hard.' And, on a related front, there is Don Miguel Ruiz's Four Agreements: Always do your best. Keep your word. Don't make assumptions, and–and this one's the most challenging–don't take anything personally."

"Yeah–that's all good, but the last one is one I have to work on, for sure," Catherine said.

"Listen," Angelo said, "I've thrown a lot at you. I greatly appreciate the opportunity to share all this. It's been something of a catharsis for me."

"I hope you reconsider writing that book," Catherine said, getting up to leave, "although I certainly understand and appreciate your hesitancy."

Angelo also stood up. "Well, I hope you can muddle through the madness in that phone of yours so you can get an A on your thesis."

The two stood on the deck, not sure what to do next. Finally, Angelo stuck out his hand.

"Best of luck to you, young lady. I'd love to see a copy of what you hand in."

Catherine looked at his hand and smiled.

"You were kind enough to share so much with me this afternoon," Catherine said. "I feel as if we've been to battle together. The least I can do is give you a hug in return."

"Well, okay," Angelo said, laughing. "A hug it is."

They embraced and parted. Catherine gathered her things off the table, turned toward the parking lot on the other side of the fence, and started walking. She looked back to wave. Angelo returned the wave and headed back into the house. As he did, he looked to the right and saw a beam of light radiating from the Fire Island Lighthouse a few miles away.

"That's odd," he thought. "Why would it be on now? The sun is still shining." He shrugged his shoulders and went inside the house.

Catherine walked to the gate, opened it, went through it, and closed it behind her. She fiddled through her purse to make sure she had her phone as she walked to her car. Once confirmed she had it, she opened her car door and slid into the driver's seat. She took the phone out of her pocket and stared at it for a few moments, trying to digest the stories she had just heard, the guidance that came with it, and how it would help her nail her thesis.

Realizing she had everything she needed to write a killer thesis–something that had seemed an impossibility less than a week ago–made her then think that perhaps there was something to this Divine Intervention business. Maybe all she needed to do was to have faith, to maintain a firm conviction in the power of her connection to the "Christ within." After all, last week she was teetering on the brink of not graduating with her class and possibly flunking the most important class in her college career, and now she was sitting on a pot of academic gold. She shuddered and trembled as she considered the caliber of the bullet she dodged, and then the tears came, fast and furious.

"Thank you, Baby Jesus," she said aloud once she caught her breath. "This is just what I was hoping for."

———

THE END

Acknowledgements &
Thank Yous

To my remarkable mother and late father: your love, patience, insights, resilience, work ethic and unrelenting faith in God inspires me in more ways that you can ever imagine.

To Alex & Gabrielle, Max & Miranda: I am constantly learning from you, and it is my fervent wish that you can say the same about me.

To my six sisters, four sisters-in-law and 16 nieces, for showing me how to love and laugh.

To my six brothers, five brothers-in-law and 21 nephews: Trying to keep up with you has made me a better man.

To Robbie Woliver, Doreen Polizzi & Carla Hostettler: Your contributions to – and faith in – this project made the difference.

To Ed Healey and Mark Parrott: You know what each of you did for me and for that I am forever grateful.

To the myriad friends kind enough to read and provide feedback on previous versions of this project: I am forever in your debt.

To the legion of women I have been fortunate enough to befriend, work with and learn from over the years: Thank you for putting up with me.

To Stephanie Larkin, Renee Alborelli and the Nice People at Red Penguin Books for having faith in me and this project

God bless you all!

The hope here is Lovers Own The Silence reflects the lessons I learned from all of you.

About the Author

Michael Watt fancies himself more of a storyteller than a novelist. His career can best be described as an ongoing series of adventures, some more successful than others. A lifelong Long Islander, he lives in Babylon, New York, with his wife of 40 years, Sharon Greaney-Watt. They have two sons, Alex and Max. "Lovers Own The Silence" is his first novel.

www.ingramcontent.com/pod-product-compliance
Lightning Source LLC
Chambersburg PA
CBHW020523110726
47899CB00004B/1217